OF HALF A MIND

Bruce M. Perrin

First Edition

This book is a work of fiction. Names, characters, places, and incidents either are products of the author's imagination or are used fictitiously. Any resemblance to actual persons, living or dead, events, or locales is entirely coincidental.

Cover art by Courtney M. Perrin

Please visit the Author at
BruceMPerrin.blogspot.com

Mind Sleuth Publications
ISBN-13: 978-1-7320835-0-9 (paperback)

For Michele, my Renaissance woman.

Table of Contents

PART 1. The Great Experiment 1

Monday, August 3, 2:13 AM 2

Monday, August 3, 9:14 AM 7

Thursday, August 6, 9:22 AM 16

Thursday, August 6, 9:46 AM 22

Thursday, August 6, 10:17 AM 26

Friday, August 7, 12:21 PM 33

Friday, August 7, 9:46 PM 37

Monday, August 10, 2:53 PM 44

Monday, August 10, 4:09 PM 57

Monday, August 10, 5:17 PM 63

Tuesday, August 11, 12:57 AM 69

Tuesday, August 11, 9:28 AM 73

Tuesday, August 11, 10:14 AM 77

Tuesday, August 11, 1:03 PM 84

Tuesday, August 11, 1:22 PM 88

Tuesday, August 11, 8:13 PM 97

Tuesday, August 11, 9:46 PM 101

Wednesday, August 12, 8:37 AM 105

PART 2. The Data Chase 107

Wednesday, August 12, 8:38 AM 108

Thursday, August 13, 8:17 PM 113

Saturday, August 15, 1:57 PM 119

Tuesday, August 18, 10:44 AM 123

Tuesday, August 18, 2:54 PM 126

Wednesday, August 19, 12:51 PM 129

Wednesday, August 19, 2:23 PM 138

Wednesday, August 19, 8:43 PM 142

Thursday, August 20, 8:58 AM 148

Thursday, August 20, 12:57 PM 154

Three Months Earlier, Wednesday, May 6, 11:27 AM 162

Thursday, August 20, 2:44 PM 167

Thursday, August 20, 8:36 PM 173

Friday, August 21, 10:36 AM 177

Friday, August 21, 2:31 PM 184

Saturday, August 22, 5:37 PM 189

Saturday, August 22, 8:47 PM 194

Monday, August 24, 9:32 AM 198

Monday, August 24, 10:13 AM 204

Monday, August 24, 1:06 PM 207

Monday, August 24, 3:37 PM 213

Monday, August 24, 5:56 PM 221

Monday, August 24, 6:17 PM 223

Monday, August 24, 6:26 PM 225

PART 3. Convergence 231

Tuesday, August 25, 9:37 AM... 232

Tuesday, August 25, 10:43 AM 234

Wednesday, August 26, 6:11 AM 237

Wednesday, August 26, 9:23 AM 243

Wednesday, August 26, 2:09 PM 249

Wednesday, August 26, 2:33 PM 258

Wednesday, August 26, 2:53 PM 262

Wednesday, August 26, 6:03 PM 272

Same Day, Same Time.. 283

Thursday, August 27, 12:53 PM..................................... 288

Thursday, August 27, 1:17 PM 295

Friday, August 28, 1:04 PM 298

Saturday, August 29, 5:14 AM 307

Thursday, December 17, 9:22 AM 315

Acknowledgments 324

About the Author 325

Even when we are quite alone, how often do we think with pleasure or pain of what others think of us — of their imagined approbation or disapprobation; and this all follows from sympathy, a fundamental element of the social instincts. A man who possessed no trace of such instincts would be an unnatural monster.

CHARLES DARWIN, *THE DESCENT OF MAN* (1871)

PART 1. THE GREAT EXPERIMENT

MONDAY, AUGUST 3, 2:13 AM

He slammed the soundproof door of the experimental chamber, leaving the incessant screaming and the reek of urine, vomit, and sweat behind. Dropping into the chair behind his desk, he released a long sigh and went through it again.

His final objective floated in the center of his mind's eye. He could see it. He could feel its unrelenting pull. Then, each of the steps appeared in exacting detail. Break down this barrier. Build this capability. Supplant this weakness. As they aligned in the mental space of his thoughts, he was transfixed by their perfect symmetry. Every step at the proper time, each with its intended effect, leading to the next, producing a new realm of existence.

True, he wasn't trained in this field, but his methods to achieve this goal were so elegant, so logical. And if there was anything he trusted, it was his logic. In fact, he was so certain his procedure would work that he thought of himself as 'the Experimenter' in the reality-altering research he now conducted.

"It has to work," he muttered to the walls. Of course, he knew why it wasn't. It was the unknown element, the black box sitting in the middle of his perfectly ordered universe. It was the man. Humans introduced an element of chance, of unpredictability, of emotion. To control that element required stronger measures than the Experimenter had anticipated. But he was learning.

His first approach to the research had been a disaster. He thought he could simply explain the nature of his work and the advances it promised, and his subjects would fall into line. But the individual he had 'recruited' first, technically known as Subject Number 1, had proved intractable. No amount of cajoling had moved him. So, when wheedling failed, the Experimenter tried threats. They proved no more effective. Subject 1 was simply paralyzed by fear and motivated only to express his hatred.

After enduring days of verbal abuse and outright treachery, the Experimenter began to wonder why he ever thought that reason might prevail. The human species was hopelessly embroiled in petty jealousies, groundless loyalties, and trivial dreams. They wasted so much potential with their emotional baggage.

But while in the thrall of this thought, the Experimenter had accidentally delivered a lethal electrical shock to Subject Number 1. At least, he thought it had been a slip...but perhaps not. He preferred not to inspect his motivations too closely. In any case, that misstep had given him the key to the procedure he now used. That key was pain, because in the instant the electricity ignited the man's nervous system, Subject 1 showed an understanding of his true place in his now-small world.

Rousting himself from the reverie, the Experimenter saw that 20 minutes had passed. It seemed mere moments. He peered through a one-way mirror into the experimental chamber, concentrating on the source of his current displeasure – Subject Number 2. He was securely strapped into a modified wheelchair. In front of him, there was a simple display of four lights and four buttons. But the man wasn't looking at the display; rather, his head was turned toward the mirror, the spittle flying from his lips as he continued his verbal invective without realizing that no one could hear.

The Experimenter reached over to a computer keyboard on his desk and with a few strokes, he started the software that ran the equipment. Inside the chamber, a green, session-running light came on, signifying that the equipment attached to the man's head was coming online. After about a minute, one of the lights on the panel lit up. Another trial had begun, but Subject Number 2 didn't watch. Rather, with this first warning, he strained against the bindings that held him in place, his face crimson, veins bulging in his neck.

"How many times are you going to do that before you give up?" the Experimenter hissed to himself through clenched teeth. His fingers massaged his temples, pushing against the pain produced by the man's hopeless struggle. The light sequence ended. An electric shock was delivered. The man convulsed in agony, his mouth wide in a scream of pain and anger that reached only his ears.

The Experimenter released a long sigh, leaned back in his chair, and ran his gaze along the calming, gray walls of his lab, letting the automation carry on without him. After a few moments, he rose from his desk and paced to his living area – a corner of the room separated by a pair of partitions around a bed, table, and chair. He retraced his steps to the desk. If there was a way to achieve his ambitions more quickly, dozens of repetitions of this route had failed to make it clear.

He glanced inside the chamber once more, assuring himself that everything was in place. Electrodes that delivered the shock were attached to one of Subject 2's legs with his foot placed in a shallow, metal pan with water. The water was unnecessary; any type of connection to ground would work. But somewhere, the Experimenter had read about the near primal fear elicited by mixing water and electricity, and so, a bare foot immersed in the pan had become part of his standard protocol.

The procedure itself was genius in its simplicity. Four lights on a panel were illuminated in a random order, each lit for two seconds. After the fourth light went out, the subject had ten seconds to press each of four buttons below the lights in the same sequence using his right hand. If he failed to do so, the equipment would deliver an intense, electric shock. Because this procedure was so simple – mere child's play – Subject 2 had gotten shocked only once during the first trials. But now he was in the second phase of the protocol. Things had changed; the head-mounted device was now active.

Inside the chamber, the first light of another trial appeared. Subject 2 tensed in the chair, staring at the bulb that signaled the next round of suffering. A drop of sweat rolled down one cheek. But unlike the previous times, he didn't struggle. Rather, he remained motionless, staring intently at the panel as the lights were lit, one by one.

Noticing the change, the Experimenter moved closer to the one-way mirror, staring intently. When the light sequence ended, the subject's gaze dropped to his left hand, which was bound to the arm of the wheelchair. His fingers formed a fist. His muscles tensed as he tried to pull his arm free, but it was no use. His eyes shifted to his other hand, which laid motionless in his lap, exactly where it had been for the last eight hours when this session began. He scowled. His lips moved.

The Experimenter flipped a switch to activate a microphone, but the man had stopped talking. Then, he thought he saw a finger on the man's right hand twitch. It was the slightest of movements, if it was anything at all. He moved still closer to the mirror, his nose touching the surface. Through the speakers came a weak, raspy croak. "Move, damn it." And the hand did. It wasn't much at first, then it began flopping on his lap, like a fish pulled from the water and tossed on the bank to die.

The Experimenter lunged for the keyboard, quickly entering the command to withhold the shock, followed by another to end the session. Both he and his subject slumped into their chairs, a smug look of self-satisfaction on the face of the former, complete exhaustion on the countenance of the latter.

For a moment, the Experimenter considered restarting the computer program to reinforce this first, faltering action, but decided this small success was a good place to end for the night...or what was left of it. It was late, and there was much to do before he could retire. Notes on the progress to date were needed, lest he retread the same ground tomorrow. The electronics had to be removed, cleaned, and stored. Both the man and the chair needed to be cleaned. The floor too. Subject 2 also needed to be fed; the Experimenter wouldn't want him to starve now that he was showing progress. After that, it would be time to clean himself up and get some rest before starting his 'day job.'

He settled back, smoothed the front of his white shirt, and crossed his arms over his chest. To anyone else, that first, fluttering movement of the right hand would be pathetic, meaningless. But to the Experimenter, that simple act was everything. Because in that moment, Subject 2 had commanded his right hand with a part of his brain that would normally control the left side of his body.

The Experimenter had taken that same, first step long ago. And now, his subject had to follow. These tiny victories were necessary before the man was ready for the new challenges posed by the Great Experiment – an experiment that would perfect a device to rewire the human brain. And when completed, the technology it produced would change the capabilities of man more than the last million years of evolution.

The Experimenter, of course, would be the first to reap that reward.

"It was like an Edgar Allen Poe story," I said. "A heavy object – something like a large floor safe – was hanging by a rope over a person. A candle was slowly burning the rope. I was desperate to get to the candle, put it out, but every time I tried, it would disappear into a fog. Or other times, it was like my legs had become lead weights, and I couldn't move. Then...I'd wake up."

Rick Johnson tented his fingers in front of his chin, his eyes going to the ceiling as if deep in thought. "You're right, Doc," he said, his gaze returning to my face. "That's one weird dream. But fortunately, I can help."

Why did I ever tell Rick this story?

"With my extensive education and vast clinical experience...." Rick paused, clearing his throat loudly to signify what we both knew – he had neither. "I can tell you without a doubt that you developed some type of Dudley Do-Right complex as a child. With your fascination with the stock market, you replaced the train racing down the track with a falling safe. Obviously, that safe was about to fall on Nicole."

I rolled my eyes, unable to hold my guffaw. "A Dudley Do-Right complex? And I told you this was a year ago in college, right? I hadn't even met Nicole then."

"Amazing." He held his hands out in front of him, eyes wide in feigned wonder. "You foresaw the future."

I could only shake my head. Rick Johnson and I worked in the same division of the St. Louis-based corporation, Ruger-Phillips, named after its founding fathers. Rick's good-natured irreverence, coupled with a keen eye for technical detail, made him a great colleague. I had only worked with him once, three months previously, but he had become a friend. Even my nickname, Doc, was his idea. Not that I was the only PhD in the division, but it had caught on. The first time our Vice President called me Doc, you could have knocked me over with a feather. I'm not sure he knew my actual name, Dr. Sam Price, but he knew the shorter handle.

In addition to Rick's generally phlegmatic approach to life, he had an unnatural ability to remember trivia about everyone. The reference to Nicole was the perfect example. Nicole Veles worked at another company, Biomedical Engineering Associates, and had consulted on my first project for two days. But those sixteen hours had been enough for me to know that I'd like to know her better. My mistake, however, had been mentioning that fact to Rick. Now, he kiddingly implied that every slip of my tongue, every time I was late to a meeting, it was because of a tryst with Nicole. If only that were true.

"Well, thanks for the psychological consult," I said. "I'd love to discuss my prognosis, which I'm sure is dire, but I gotta run. Ken is filling me in on my next assignment in 15 minutes. I'll drop by later so you can tell me what I should put in the final report. Save me a lot of work that way – you know, all those hours poring over messy data and contradictory statistics."

"Nice try, Doc, but I know you love that stuff."

Since I couldn't deny it, I shrugged and left for the office of Ken Waters, my immediate supervisor.

My department at Ruger-Phillips specialized in Independent Verification and Validation contracts. In other words, we were the 'disinterested, third party' that made sure the work of others met the government's specifications. But Rick's and my roles in those endeavors were different. Rick was a simulator expert. From month to month, his lab might hold anything from a simulator for training nuclear power plant operators to one for Mars rover drivers.

I, on the other hand, worked in a discipline that was a relatively recent addition to the division – the use of cognitive science to optimize training. Ken had told me that it was a US Air Force project that had convinced the company to expand. By delivering a mild electric current directly to a pilot's scalp during training, they found that the time they needed to learn how to interpret radar signals could be cut in half. They called it Transcranial Direct Current Stimulation and using it, they produced a result Rick's field hadn't seen in years, if ever. So, with that research, the demand for my skills had been born.

While the formal recognition of the company's new branch appeared overnight on organizational charts, establishing a niche with my peers took a bit more time. Soon after joining the company, Rick, quite seriously, had asked me if I could interpret one of his dreams. After stumbling around for a moment, I tried to explain that I knew next to nothing about Jungian dream interpretation – I even went home and did a search on Jung to make sure I had recalled the correct name. As I explained to him, I had studied cognitive psychology and had taken as many statistics and research courses as I could find. Dream interpretation had no place in my course of study.

When this helped little, I told him that having me interpret a dream would be like him advising on highway construction – Rick was an electrical engineer who knew virtually nothing about the civil engineering side of his field. This explanation had worked, so now, he interpreted my dreams since I was, by my own admission, 'clueless.' It had become something of a running joke between us.

While the camaraderie with Rick formed quickly, the same couldn't be said about several of the other engineers in the division. They called what I did 'soft science.' While that was common usage, it still rankled a bit. So, when they used the phrase, I always asked, what could be harder than my job? Other than perhaps astrophysics, what has more uncharted territory than the human brain? I rarely received more than a grumble in reply.

As I turned into the wing of our building that held Ken's office, I heard Sue Jordan's familiar voice. I had run into Sue on my first day on the job. She was standing in the hallway, surrounded by a small group of people as she did an impersonation of her across-the-back-fence neighbor. The neighbor was cooking hamburgers on a grill, trying to divide her attention among the food, the local happenings, and as Sue put it, "the five kids, all under the age of four who were clinging to her legs or grabbing at her arms." The burgers had drawn the short straw. Everyone watched the twinkle of amusement in Sue's brown eyes as she got to the finale. "I told her. If she wanted to be a better cook, she needed to take up knitting at night."

Half the assembled group groaned. The other half chuckled and shook their head. And more than one said, 'that's Sue for you' as they wandered away. During my short time on the job, I had come to agree. Sue could always find the bawdier side of things and the respite was welcome.

Two days later, Sue and I were teamed on my first project, and I came to appreciate her professional capabilities as well. She was so obviously bright and capable that two months into that first job, I asked her why she didn't get her doctorate and run her own projects. In true Sue-like fashion, she asked, "And why would I want a degree that stands for piled higher and deeper?" At that point in our association, she wasn't sure how I might react, so she had quickly added, "Not that it applies to your education, of course." Now with five months behind us, she wouldn't bother and I wouldn't expect her to qualify the comment.

Today, Sue was standing in the hall with her back to me, towering over a mere wisp of a woman who probably still qualified for children's rides at amusement parks. As Sue was nearly six-feet tall, the physical difference between them was arresting.

"...and two full pounds of barbeque ribs," Sue said as I came into earshot. Her friend – a woman I knew only in passing – was covering her mouth, her shoulders shaking with the laughter she was trying to hide.

"Telling Al stories again?" I asked, nodding at Sue's friend.

Sue turned, pushing a strand of her brown hair from her forehead as she did. "You heard ribs and thought of Al? You know my husband all too well," she replied, grinning.

"Well, we share that vice," I said, returning her smile.

"I'm sure you eat two pounds of ribs in one sitting all the time," she said smirking. I'd obviously missed some important parts of the story. "If you did, you'd look like the letter 'b' when you turned sideways."

I chuckled, partly because of the image – I'm lanky – and partly to avoid blurting something like 'at one sitting?' Finally, I managed, "There's a lot of bone in ribs." Sue raised an eyebrow, so I moved on. "You're coming to the meeting with Ken, aren't you?"

"Yep. 'Bout that time, isn't it? I'll grab my notebook and meet you there." Sue turned and left with her friend in tow.

When I arrived at Ken's office, he was seated behind his desk. As usual, he was dressed in a crisp, heavily starched, white shirt with an open collar, black pants, and neatly shined, black leather shoes. I wasn't sure I had ever seen him wear anything else. I tapped on his open office door.

"Doc, come in. Have a seat," he said, nodding at the two chairs across his desk.

"Thanks. I saw Sue in the hall. She'll be here any minute."

"Great." Ken glanced at something on his computer screen, then turned to me and folded his hands on his desktop. "Good work on your first project – that skills management system," he said. "The customer really liked your analysis and they're planning for full production." The kudos were welcome.

"It was a team effort," I replied. Ken nodded but said nothing more, making me realize that this was probably what any technical lead would say assuming that his or her team hadn't mutinied half way through the job. "No, really," I said. "Sue Jordan suggested several of the tests we used, ran some of the analyses, and wrote up several sections of the final report."

Ken nodded. "Yeah, I know she's good...but it's always nice to hear it from somebody else."

Like most supervisors, Ken was responsible for performance reviews, assignments, recruiting and hiring, and allocations of the yearly raise pool for our department. It was deadly dull work in my view, and often, much ado about little. Last year, the raise pool had been under three percent, but the allocation meetings among the managers had lasted for weeks. I estimated that they were making decisions at a rate of about four cents an hour. So, the fact that Ken was not only good at these tasks, but also enjoyed them, came as a relief. He wouldn't be trying to delegate them, as so many supervisors did.

On the other hand, Ken's skills didn't extend to learning and training technology or research. I'm not sure he knew or understood much of what I did, making the division of labor between us clean and unambiguous. I trusted him to look out for my interests on the personnel side of the business, while he trusted me to do a professional, technical job for our clients.

"Hi, Ken. Am I late?" asked Sue, as she came through the door and took the chair next to me.

"Nope. Right on time," said Ken. "I'll get to it, since the group managers are meeting at 10:00 to review raise policies for next year." I could have quipped, 'what, you have a whole four percent to hand out?' But in fact, I felt lucky to get paid for doing something I enjoyed.

"This next assignment is six months," Ken continued, "during which you'll be evaluating a device designed and developed by Dr. Worthington at WHT technologies. You know the company?"

I glanced at Sue, who shook her head, then turned back to Ken. "I've heard of them," I said. "They're based here, in St. Louis. Aren't they a spin-off from the Washington University School of Medicine, with some staff from the aerospace company, Boeing? But I don't really remember what the acronym, WHT, stands for."

"That's not surprising," said Ken. "W and H are the founders, who are Worthington, your point of contact for this job, and Huston. Both are PhDs and MDs. And you're right, they were at Wash U earlier in their careers. The T stands for Technology. Not exactly a catchy name, but descriptive I suppose. As far as the Boeing connection goes, they hired a couple of people from them with government contracting experience, because we all know how tricky government contracting can be."

Actually, I didn't know, but it was something the managers always said.

"Dr. Worthington.... Let's see, first name is Ned," Ken said, checking some notes on his desk. "He's developed a technology that increases memory span."

Seriously?

I am sure that all new college graduates hope their first jobs will be world-changing. My first assignment, the skills management system, was anything but. It provided notifications when an employee needed to take a class to refresh a skill. True, it was based on the latest, scientific model of human forgetting, but the study I ran indicated it improved work performance by about two percent. Although that improvement would return the customer's investment over the long-run – or maybe the long, long, long-run – it was not exactly what I had hoped for in a field with such vast, untapped potential.

Unfortunately, memory span improvement, the focus of this next assignment, held no more promise. Memory span is simply the number of unrelated items someone can hold in their thoughts at one time. And, as every psychology student knows, George Miller published a landmark paper in the mid-1950s on it, establishing memory span as seven, plus or minus two. I even had an undergraduate psychology professor tell us that phone numbers were seven digits long because of memory span limitations. I wasn't sure that was true, since the demand for lines would seem to play an important role in their length, but the professor's claim had the desired effect – I never forgot the length of memory span. Seven, plus or minus two.

Most of what Ken had to say about the project was textbook – don't vary from the statement of work – we don't get paid for extras. Keep to the schedule. Stay within the budget or, if possible, below. But in the course of his talk, I heard, "The complete team will be three. We'll be subcontracting the third person from Biomedical Engineering Associates to study the electronic design and the physiological effects of the equipment." That was Nicole Veles' company. My interest was piqued, even though it could be any one of their 15 to 20 employees.

"OK, that's about it," Ken said after about a half-hour. "All the materials for this new job are on the server under the company name. I thought Doc could finish the final edits on the skills management project, while Sue prepped for the kickoff on this one. Make sense?"

"Works for me," I said.

"Me too," said Sue. "I'll probably have everything ready to go by tomorrow afternoon."

With that, Ken hurried off to his raise meeting, and Sue and I left. As I walked back to my office, I was thinking that the project had possibilities, especially if Nicole was involved. But world-changing?

Not a chance.

THURSDAY, AUGUST 6, 9:22 AM

By the time I finish a run, breakfast, and a commute, my workday usually starts between 8:00 and 9:30. That I had arrived at 7:00 this morning says something about my state of mind. I was more than ready for the next chapter of my professional life.

In the three days since Ken had met with us, I had busied myself with tying up loose ends on the last project as he directed and checking with Sue to see how planning and preparations were coming on this one. The fact that her estimated start went from Tuesday afternoon to Thursday morning within hours of our meeting with Ken caught my attention. She explained that the project wasn't what she had expected and gave me a short paper by Worthington to read. It was my 'homework,' as she called it.

I read it Tuesday night after work. It didn't take long, because to describe it as 'succinct' would be like describing a nanosecond as 'brief.' The section on his procedure was almost nonexistent, and where the technology should have been described, it merely said he had used a 'company proprietary device' called a Neural Activity Blocker...whatever that was. Only the analysis had much detail but it was underwhelming. Over the course of the study, memory span had increased to about 21 items, or three times the average. But equivalent or better results had been achieved by any number of common, memory techniques.

But for me, the red flags went up when I read his conclusions. He claimed his technology had "...expanded the amount of working memory available for the task." Working memory is roughly the same as consciousness; that is, it is what a person is thinking about at any given moment. Although there are different ways to measure it, all the research indicates it's limited and fixed. Simply put, you can only hold so much in your head at one time.

That finding is confirmed for me every day when I try to remember something like a phone number and someone asks, 'what was that book I saw you reading?' Or I catch a few notes of a favorite song and start thinking about the lyrics. Or about anything else. As soon as I stop thinking about the phone number, it's gone. For Worthington to claim I could recall the name of a book and still find that number in the back of my mind somewhere – well, it seemed a ridiculous statement. I suspected he had chosen his words poorly and nothing more.

I returned to Sue's office on Wednesday and expressed my doubts about Worthington's text. She agreed and offered me some more homework, but I declined, knowing that she'd have his findings fully summarized by meeting time. After a few moments of small talk, she peered over her reading glasses, her brown eyes narrowing on my face. Then, she handed me a couple of pages, saying, "You have your team now." It was Nicole Veles' resume. I thanked her and left.

So, while 'the next chapter of my professional life' was what I told myself – or anyone who might ask – I knew that wasn't the only reason for my early arrival. I was also looking forward to seeing Nicole again.

Nicole is a female engineer, which of itself, is rare. But with a Master's degree in Biomedical Engineering, she is a member of a very select group. That fact alone would have made her an interesting dinner partner or a fascinating individual to join for drinks, but additionally, I found her extremely attractive.

Of course, attraction is personal. For me, the driving factor is 'cuteness,' and Nicole fits my definition perfectly. She's about 5-foot, 6-inches tall, with a trim, athletic build, fair skin, and shoulder-length, light brown hair. But what sets her apart is her large, hazel eyes – eyes that sometimes seem brown, other times green in the way hazel eyes can do. They give her a youthful look of innocence that I find mesmerizing.

Nicole's look of naivete, however, is in sharp contrast to the technical expertise she holds. She has written papers with titles I can hardly pronounce, much less understand. To me, she is an enigma that defies any quick and easy characterization, but one that I have interest in understanding better.

As I approached the conference room for our kickoff meeting, I knew the women were already there. The sound of conversation, an occasional laugh drifted to my ears.

"Hey, Doc. Where have you been the last day and a half?" Sue asked, the familiar, amused twinkle showing in her eyes. "You were visiting me about five times a day, and then, you disappeared?"

"Just busy closing out the last project," I said, now wondering if Sue had given me the resume so she could get some work done. Her eyebrows went up in a look of skepticism, which answered that question.

My eyes swept around the table to Nicole. She stood. Perhaps the women had coordinated on attire...or maybe dressing similarly was uncoordinated? I wasn't certain, but in any case, both sported brown loafers and khaki pants, with only the style and shade of blue in their shirts varying. I had wondered earlier if my memory had become exaggerated over time, but Nicole was even more alluring than I remembered. The soft, smooth curves of her body made business casual look sensual.

I walked over and she looked up at me. The perspective made her eyes seem even larger than usual. I could easily get lost in them. I swallowed, unsure I'd find my voice. But I did. "Nicole, it's good to see you again. Welcome to the team."

I took her hand. It was warm, her handshake firm. At the touch, my heart rate went up a notch, my breath catching in my throat. But if I had the same effect on her, it didn't show. As she pushed a strand of wayward hair off her forehead, my eyes were drawn to the back of her hand. When she had been here before, there had been no ring on her finger. That hadn't changed, and I released a breath I didn't realize I was holding.

"Hi, Sam. It's good to be here," she said, smiling warmly, her hazel eyes meeting mine in a steady gaze. For reasons I didn't understand, Nicole had used my given name during our first project, and it appeared she would be doing the same again. At least I had convinced her to stop calling me "Dr. Price."

"I see you're all set with a temporary badge. That'll get you into all the open areas. If we need to go into any secure spaces, Sue or I will need to accompany you. But you've been here before. You know the drill. Any questions, concerns?"

"No, other than the somewhat cryptic paper that Sue sent to me. But I guess that's why we're here – to figure out what we need to do."

I nodded. "It is. Sue, I think that's your cue."

Sue was sitting at one end of the conference table. A projection screen was on the wall directly in front of her, with the computer that drove it at her elbow. Nicole was on one side of the table, so I moved to the other and took a seat.

"This project's a little different from anything I've seen before," Sue said, rubbing her chin. "So, I'm going to start with the simple stuff. What the customer – that's the Veteran's Administration – what they want us to do." She pressed enter on the keyboard in front of her and the first chart with the date and job title, the Memory Span Enhancement Project, appeared on the screen.

"About 19 months ago, Dr. Worthington at Worthington-Huston Technology proposed a study to the VA. There was apparently some give and take, and about a year ago, the VA funded at least part of the work. I don't know the details of what was dropped and what was kept, but one thing Worthington completed was the memory span research you've read about.

"Then, about a month ago, he went back to the VA, asking for more money. Before agreeing, however, they wanted an independent assessment of the work he's completed so far. That, of course, is where we come in. In general terms, Doc and I will be examining the study he ran, making sure his claims make sense."

I wasn't sure how they could, but there would be time for that discussion later.

"Nicole, from you they want a general evaluation of whatever his proprietary device is. What it does and how it works." Nicole nodded.

As Sue continued, it was clear she was covering much of the official language from our contract – the standard spiel. Check the methods used. Verify the analysis. Determine if the conclusions follow. Examine the device's primary inputs and outputs, and so on. If there was anything unusual in this part of Sue's talk, it was that the contract didn't give many specifics. But even that wasn't too surprising.

After twenty minutes, during which neither Nicole nor I had said a word, Sue moved to a chart with the title, 'Background.' She paused, looking at it a moment, then at each of us. "I know. Talking about the contract before the background is a bit...unusual. But I thought this should come at the end, because we're going to need some time.

"There were two documents on background. One was the paper that I gave to both of you. Doc, research and statistics are your thing. What did you make of it?"

I scratched my chin, more to give myself a moment to compose my thoughts than because it itched. "Using a device Worthington only describes as proprietary, an individual tripled his digit memory span after...I believe it was 153 hours of training?" Sue nodded after glancing at her notes. "Then he makes what seems an exaggerated, if not completely inaccurate claim that he has increased the portion of the brain working on this task."

"So, it's not just us," said Nicole, glancing at Sue.

"To think that he exaggerated?"

"Right. Sue and I talked about the paper before you got here. We were stumped but thought maybe you could explain."

I extended two empty hands out in front of me. "Nope. You can only hold so much in your head at a time, as far as I know. And the improvement he claimed? Anyone would get better after 153 hours spent developing a strategy." I turned to Sue. "You said there were two documents on background. What's the other?"

Sue let out a long breath. "It's a research review from his original proposal to the VA, the one from 19 months ago. I'd guess you'd call it 'deep background' for our project, since it has nothing to do with memory span...or any type of learning or training for that matter." She shrugged, as if saying 'that's all there is.'

"If it's not about memory or learning, what's it about?" I asked, frowning.

"Phantom limb pain."

What the hell?

THURSDAY, AUGUST 6, 9:46 AM

The Experimenter opened the door to 'the residence,' flipping on a switch as he did. Two transparent cages appeared in a pool of light in the center of an otherwise dark room.

The enclosures were constructed of sheets of laminated glass and Lexan, a combination commonly known as bulletproof glass. The first cage was small at three feet on a side, eight feet tall, and enclosed at the top. It was bolted to a tiled floor that sloped to a drain in the center. A large shower head was installed in the ceiling.

An attached, second cage was larger, at 10 by 10 by 8 feet. A heavy-duty, stainless steel toilet was installed in one corner. The only other adornment was the commercial tumbling mats bolted to the floor. Two sliding doors provided access to the cages from outside, while a third permitted movement between them. All three doors were closed and secured by a one-inch steel pin that could only be reached from outside the enclosures.

Movement caught the Experimenter's eye. Subject Number 2 was stirring. He sat up on the floor of the larger pen, rubbing the sleep from his eyes. "No," he moaned, when his gaze fell on the Experimenter. "You gotta let me outta here."

"I think not. We have much left to explore."

It wasn't that the Experimenter believed he could convince the man they were sharing some great, scientific adventure; he had abandoned any hope of that with his first subject. But the soft, calming words came naturally, much like the master might say to his dog before putting him to sleep. Death would come to Subject 2, but hopefully, it was still weeks away.

"Please. I won't tell nobody," the man pleaded, his voice cracking, his chin quivering. "I'll get outta town. Never be back."

"Sorry, I haven't been around more," the Experimenter said, ignoring the man's hollow promise. "I've been busy. But the good news is, I have most of the morning open. Shall we make the most of it?"

Subject 2 began scooting backwards, forcing himself into the corner farthest from the Experimenter. "I got money. You can have it, if you let me out."

The Experimenter had been walking toward a small storage cabinet in the corner of the residence but drew up short. "Really. You have money?" He chuckled at the preposterous claim.

The man blinked several times, his lips trembling. "Not me. My cousin. Please, you gotta call him."

"I see." The Experimenter continued to the cabinet where he removed a Taser from one of the top drawers.

"No," the man moaned. "You're gonna kill me with that thing." He began sobbing.

For once, the Experimenter agreed. The Taser wasn't optimal. He risked stopping the man's heart or injuring him in a fall. The tumbling mats helped with the latter problem, and he knew where to shoot someone to minimize the former. But there was still the possibility of losing his Guinea pig, and he loathed that thought.

So, he had started to research drugs. He needed something that incapacitated quickly and dissipated just as fast. As distasteful as he found it, date rape appeared to be the demand that was driving the generous supply he had found. But until he discovered just the right concoction, the Taser would do.

He moved the reinforced wheelchair near the closed door of the larger cage. On its seat were restraints for the hands and feet. Then, he positioned himself at a slot cut into the walls near the corner with the toilet. Knowing the subject would flee to the opposite side, the Experimenter would have a clear shot. It was close to the maximum range for his weapon but missing once or twice would only try his patience. It wouldn't change the outcome.

"Wait," the man pleaded between sobs.

In the dim light, the Experimenter could see the sheen of sweat on the man's face as he hugged himself and rocked slowly in the corner. He squeezed the trigger, the barbs of his shot finding their mark on the upper thigh. Perfect.

He pushed the gun through the slot in the glass wall. It fell to the floor, as it completed the 5-second burst of electricity that would temporarily paralyze Subject 2. The Experimenter opened the door to the cage and pushed the wheelchair inside. Retrieving the Taser in case the man required another volley, he moved to the subject and quickly attached the restraints. He rolled the man to his side, then laid the chair behind him and attached the arm and leg straps to its structure. Finally, he pulled the man's head against the high back of the wheelchair, securing it with bands around the throat and forehead.

The Experimenter had found that the limp, 'dead' weight of a tased man was difficult to lift. But with the man lashed to a rigid frame, the chair was soon righted. He pushed his prize into the adjoining experimental chamber.

A long, adjustable arm, much like those used for examination lights in doctors' and dentists' offices, extended into the room from the far wall. A thick wire cable exited the end of the arm and was attached to a cloth cap covered with an array of metal disks. The Experimenter placed the wheelchair directly below the cap.

"Why are you doing this?" the man moaned when he had recovered his senses. "I haven't done nuthin' to you."

The Experimenter ignored him, pulling the arm down and extending the cable until the cap rested on the man's head. After checking the cap's alignment, he secured it with a chinstrap. In moments, the electrodes were attached to the man's leg, the pan filled with water, and the panel with the lights and buttons positioned within easy reach of the man's right hand. The Experimenter stood to his full height and stretched, pleased that the preparations for the session were complete.

Perhaps realizing the futility, Subject 2 had stopped pleading and sat trembling in the chair, a breath occasionally catching in his throat and coming out as a sob.

The Experimenter started for the sound-proof door when a tone from his phone stopped him short. He had a text. He scowled as he read the words. Although he knew this flurry of demands was typical, it was trying. He turned to Subject 2. "Sorry. I'll set the computer for a couple of hours of practice, but that's all for today. I'll be back late, after I've dealt with other matters."

The thought of two hours of shocks delivered mechanically with no hope of reprieve, no possibility of sympathy was too cruel, and Subject 2 broke down and began to sob uncontrollably.

But then, the Experimenter knew, it would have been worse for his subject if he could have stayed.

THURSDAY, AUGUST 6, 10:17 AM

After recovering from my surprise at the words 'phantom limb pain,' I suggested we take a short break. Earlier, I had thought this point in the meeting might be a good time to talk to Nicole, maybe see if she had plans for the weekend. But under the circumstances, any ideas about socializing were swept aside by confusion.

As a company, we studied the effect of technology on learning. My coursework in school had been broader, but I'd never studied phantom limb pain. Sure, I knew what it was. Pain that seemed to come from a limb that had been lost from surgery or an accident. But what did that have to do with my field?

While pondering that question – and finding no answer – I had gotten a cup of coffee. I returned to the conference room, cup in hand, to find Sue and Nicole already there.

"Yeah, this isn't going the way I thought it would either," said Sue. "But I didn't think you'd be drinking already."

"Nine-thirty's too early?" I asked, trying to sound surprised. "So, are you ready to talk about phantom limb pain?"

"Unless the company's going to send me back to school, as ready as I'll ever be. I spent two and a half of the three days trying to crack the code on this part, and I can tell you what I have. Nicole, this may be more down your alley than ours, so please jump in whenever you want."

"Sure," she replied. She turned to me. "I have to admit, I don't know a lot about this specific topic. I can ask around at work, if you want?"

I nodded, appreciating her candor and her offer. "Thanks. We'll see if it comes to that, but like Sue said, this is deep background and may not be that important." We turned back to Sue.

For the first ten minutes or so, the background charts held what you'd expect – a definition, a few examples, some statistics. Admittedly, the problem was more common than I realized, with up to 80% of all patients experiencing sensations from the missing limb and nearly all of these involving some degree of pain. And while a wide range of treatments had been attempted, from pain-killers to acupuncture to surgically removing the damaged tissue, nothing seemed to work. At least, not for long, which brought us to Worthington's approach.

"Some researchers, Dr. Worthington included, believe that current treatments don't work because they don't consider the underlying problem," Sue said. "And that problem comes from changes in the nervous system, particularly in the brain, after a limb is lost. Those changes are called brain plasticity or neuroplasticity."

Sue paused a moment, looking first at me, then Nicole. "I supposed defining plasticity wouldn't be necessary in a proposal that's going to experts at the VA." She released a single laugh. "It's probably not even necessary for you two either, but me? I had to do a little digging to get comfortable with the concept. Want to hear what I found?"

"I would," I said. "I have some background from school, but maybe not enough. And it's always good if we start on the same page."

Sue nodded. "Quite a bit of the research I read dealt with recovering functions, like speech, after some sort of trauma to the brain. And the analogy that really helped me was to think about the circuits in the brain like roads. You have a way you drive to work each day. But one day, a bridge along your route is destroyed."

"So, in the analogy, the destroyed bridge is the part of the brain that's injured?" I asked.

"Exactly," Sue replied. "So, at first, you can't get to work. The bridge is gone and your path is blocked. But you start wandering other roads – maybe ones you use to get to a restaurant or the movies. Pretty soon you find a way to get to your job. It's slow and inefficient, but it gets you there. You keep using it and it gets faster. You find new shortcuts. After a while, your new route is nearly as good as the old one. Brain plasticity is the equivalent of finding and claiming these other roads for a new purpose."

"I can see why you like it," I said, leaning back in my chair and thinking that Sue's talk wasn't as bad as she had implied. We were making progress on understanding Worthington's field. But this moment of satisfaction took longer to form in my head than it lasted.

"Ah, hold on a second," I said slowly. "So, plasticity works. I get to the office on time with my new route. Where's the problem? Where's the phantom limb pain in all this?"

"Worthington's proposal covers that," said Sue. She paged through a couple of slides until she found what she wanted – a chart called Negative Plasticity. Its text was so dense and the font so small that when it appeared on the screen, I could swear the room got darker. "I'll give you two a minute to look this over."

The slide started off easily enough with an example of a man who lost his ring finger. The cortical area used to sense and control it was reallocated to the little finger and the middle finger of the same hand. The brain area had function A, controlling the ring finger, but after injury, got function B, controlling two of the remaining fingers. And importantly, he experienced no phantom limb pain.

Unfortunately, that case was only the first line on the chart, and the rest of the dense text was research on negative adaptations. First was the example of an amputated arm, but the brain areas serving the arm weren't repurposed. They remained allocated to a limb that wasn't there, producing sensations ranging from minor itches to searing, burning sensations. The next study was similar, except there was evidence that the cortical mass serving the missing limb had become enlarged. The chart didn't say this, but it was as if the area was searching for a purpose and grew to increase its sensitivity, when all it did was increase the pain.

There were a series of studies about where the pain originated. One researcher placed the blame on the brain itself. Another emphasized the random signals coming from the damaged area that the brain interpreted as pain. A third blamed the conflict between the neural signals and visual data. Or between those signals and memories of the limb.

The chart was like a crowd of people, all pointing their fingers in different directions. Here's the problem. No, it's here. It was academic back-and-forth; it was scientific give-and-take. I glanced at Nicole. She was staring sightlessly at the tabletop, her elbow placed there, her head resting in her hand. I suspected she was trying to find order, a conclusion in the tangled story these studies told.

"I give," I said finally, looking at Sue. "What the heck is this research supposed to tell us?"

There was a smile tugging at the corners of Sue's mouth. "It's supposed to tell you what I did for three days getting ready for this meeting," she said. "Also, it's supposed to tell you this." She advanced to the next chart, called 'Bottom Line,' which included only three phrases:

Our understanding of the role of plasticity in phantom limb pain is incomplete;
But plasticity produces it; and

Plasticity can fix it.

"How ingenious." It was Nicole's voice. Her hands opened in front of her, as a smile captured her eyes. "He suppresses normal brain activity to give the maladapted area something to do...something besides feel pain, that is."

My eyes went back to the chart, then to Sue's face. Sue was nodding, telling me that Nicole was right, but I was missing a step in the reasoning. "Why would he want to block normal brain activity? Why not block the maladapted area and stop the pain?"

"That would work for a while," said Sue. "Sort of like a pain killer, it would deaden the sensation while the device was on. But once it's turned off, the pain would return, and it might even come back worse."

The pieces finally fit, my hand slapping my forehead as if I wanted to trap this elusive thought before it escaped. "Right. If the device blocks the area of the brain controlling a healthy limb, that creates a void. There is a limb that can feel and move, but has no area serving it. Plasticity steps in to rewire the circuits that had previously controlled the missing limb to fill that gap. Now, the area that was maladapted has a new, needed function and the pain disappears."

"Voila," said Sue. "The pain is gone...at least in theory. That brings me to the end of my charts, leaving this final question – what's the relationship between this phantom limb pain research and increasing memory span? What we received from Worthington's proposal is exactly three sentences." She read them.

"By using the Neural Activity Blocker to arrest normal processing of the stimulus materials, additional areas of the cortex will be recruited for the task. After practice, the subject will be able to draw upon those facilities normally associated with the memory span task, as well as those areas plastically adapted to it during brain activity suppression. The effect of the process will be an increase in the cortical capacity that's applied to encoding, storing, and retrieving the stimuli, resulting in a measured increase in memory span performance."

I shook my head as Sue finished. Again, Worthington was claiming that he had physically expanded the areas of the brain devoted to the memory span task. That assertion still appeared brash to me, but not quite as implausible as it had seemed an hour ago. That was both an exciting and a disquieting notion.

"Do we know the areas of the brain he'd have to block to affect someone's memory for numbers?" asked Nicole.

"I don't. Doc, you have any ideas?"

I grimaced, considering the complexity of the answer to this seemingly simple question. "Not really, although I'm pretty sure those areas might change. If someone tried to remember the list by picturing the numbers, part of the visual cortex would be involved. If the person tried to think about their sound, a different area would become active." I paused, rubbing my forehead a moment. "It seems almost impossible to determine in advance all of the areas that might be involved and suppress them. And these three sentences are all we have?"

"Unfortunately, yes," replied Sue. "For anything else, we'll need to ask. Toward that end, I've scheduled a meeting with Worthington for next Monday, and I've been told that a colleague, Dr. Sebastian Atwood, will be joining him." Sue looked at each of us in turn. "That's it for me. Now you know what I know...although, Doc, you need to go back and study that chart on negative plasticity some more. You finished it awfully fast."

"Yeah, I'll be sure and do that tonight," I said, smirking. "It'll be something to put me to sleep, if nothing else."

After a few moments of silence, Sue said, "Well, if that's it, I'm outta here. Doc, you still having lunch with my husband tomorrow?"

"Yep, as soon as I finish my status reports with Ken in the morning."

"What's your husband do?" asked Nicole.

"No one. I keep an eye on him," replied Sue. "Oh, you asked what, not who." She put a hand over her mouth as if embarrassed. "He's a financial analyst. He and Doc share some sort of fascination with the stock market that totally baffles me."

"Yeah, Al, her husband, gets to play it," I explained. "I just live the life of a trader vicariously through him."

We all got up from the table and I walked over to Nicole, hoping to strike up a conversation. "I'm glad you were available to help us out. I can tell already that we'll be making much better use of your expertise this time." On the last project, she had been seriously over-qualified.

"Thanks, Sam. I'm looking forward to it," she said, looking up into my face and smiling. She laid a hand on my arm lightly as she spoke. I'm sure it was part of her usual method of communicating, but I found it hard to think of anything but her touch. "Actually, I wasn't available to work this project. But I rearranged a few things and asked to be assigned here."

Maybe it was my surprise at her comment. Maybe I was distracted by her touch even more than I thought. But whatever the reason, by the time her words became meaning in my mind, she had turned and left.

FRIDAY, AUGUST 7, 12:21 PM

Al and I were about as different as two people could be. I had black hair and was dark complected to his blonde curls and pale skin. I was quiet and analytic to his gregariousness. I was the gangly runner to his...well, let's say, he liked food a bit too much. Nonetheless, we'd become close friends.

Part of the reason was his job. Al worked in a company that was one of the more dramatic success stories in St. Louis, Missouri, and much of the financial world – the A. Huntington Taylor & Associates hedge-fund company. In terms of total assets under management, its $2 billion paled compared to a company like J.P. Morgan Asset Management, which controlled trillions. But it had achieved this level in only its first nine months of operation.

As someone in his first year of work, investing at the level required to join the Huntington Taylor family was impossible. But I looked forward to the day when I could, secretly holding the belief that the behavior of the stock market had as much to do with the psychology of the masses as business factors. So, until I could test some of those ideas, and probably lose my shirt by chasing the market, I talked to Al.

I was meeting him in his office in the Huntington Taylor Building, a small structure in an unincorporated community called Earth City located along Interstate 70 near the Missouri River. With its diminutive size – it housed perhaps 25 employees – and well-tended, austere grounds, the building could have easily been a suite of dentists' offices rather than the home to the financial analysts of a multibillion-dollar company.

I parked and went in the front entrance. A receptionist sat at a desk centered in the lobby, double doors to her right and left. She was working on her nails when I entered, but quickly dropped the file into a drawer. "Good afternoon," she said, smiling in a way that conveyed routine rather than warmth.

"Al Jordan, please."

She must have had everyone's office number memorized because without pause, she replied, "Room 114, down the hall to your left." She pulled the file out and went back to work on her nails without giving me another glance.

I opened the door to Al's wing and was greeted by an empty hall. Taylor couldn't be accused of wasting any of the return on his investors' funds with ostentatious adornments...or even a plant or picture, for that matter. About the only indication that the residents were engaged in anything like 'big business' was a sign that read, Information Processing Services, Authorized Personnel Only at the start of a short hall to the right. It ended with a set of massive, elevator doors, surveilled by two cameras – one on each side wall – and secured by a keypad and retinal scanner. No disinterested receptionist would suffice for this domain.

When I reached room 114, I could see the top of Al's head through a sidelight next to his door. He was leaning over in his chair, rummaging through one of the lower drawers on his desk, a somewhat sunburnt, nearly bald spot on his skull peeking through his blonde hair. I knocked and entered. "Hey, Al. What's up?"

Al sat up behind his desk, his grinning face coming into view. "Good. You're here. I was about to break out a package of cookies I've got stashed here...somewhere. They must be a month old, but I'm starving."

"Yeah, sorry I'm late," I replied, unsure that any cookies lasted a month around Al. "It's all your wife's fault. I had to report on all this convoluted research she's been telling us about."

He snorted. "Yeah, right, Doc. You forget, I've seen you two talking. If she hit you with some strange data, you'd say, thank you, can I have some more, please?" He drew out the last word like it was four-syllables long. "Can you drive? My AC's acting up." Al stood and headed for the door without waiting for a reply.

I spun on a heel to follow. "Yeah, it's no day to be without. That Mexican place again?"

"Sure. As for what's up," Al replied as we walked down the hall, "the S&P's down nearly three and a half points on heavy trading. We had some soft employment data released this morning, and that, plus concerns about Europe's economic picture has produced a sell-off."

I secretly held the opinion that most analysts were far better at finding explanations for what the market had done than finding predictors for what it was about to do. I never confessed that to Al, however, since he would want to know if I thought that about him, which I did. But there were some who had insight into economic forces, or if I was right, into the psychology of the masses, as they were regularly ahead of the game. Taylor was apparently one of them.

"I suppose Taylor & Associates dumped all the big losers before the drop," I said.

Al chuckled, then leaned closer to whisper to me. "Beats me, buddy. The word 'associates' in the title of this company is a complete misnomer. What we do on a moment-to-moment basis is known by Mr. Taylor alone." We were passing the information processing sign, and Al gestured at the elevator doors with his thumb. "He spends nearly all his time in there with his computers."

"Yeah, probably a massive, global economic simulation," I said matching Al's volume, as if we were sharing world secrets rather than idle speculation. "Or a highly advanced artificial intelligence? Or maybe an ultra-fast system for high-frequency trading?"

"Maybe," Al replied. "Whatever it is, it fills up his day. And mine too, for that matter."

"No kidding, the way you're in here at the crack of dawn every day. What am I saying? You're in here even before it's light."

"Sun's up by 5:30...most of the time. Besides, the early bird gets the worm."

"Worm's aren't awake by 5:30," I replied.

Al chuckled. "Yeah, you're probably right."

We had reached the door to the lobby and Al pushed through, saying more loudly than necessary, "Of course, we have some great, diversified products for the medium or long-term investor."

I looked at him out of the corner of my eye, barely suppressing a snicker. Did he really think the receptionist would report him if he wasn't in full sales mode?

I glanced in her direction and she had her smartphone out, stabbing at it. She did seem anxious to get something punched into it, but I couldn't decide. Was she shopping online or just playing solitaire?

FRIDAY, AUGUST 7, 9:46 PM

The Experimenter opened the door to the residence, allowing his nose to investigate. It signaled an all clear. When he had entered a couple of hours earlier, he had found Subject 2 covered in his own excrement. It was a curious defense mechanism, but not particularly effective. Using the Taser to herd his subject into the shower enclosure, the Experimenter had started a cycle of five minutes of hot, soapy water, five minutes to rinse, and an hour of air dry. With the room temperature set at 82 degrees and the quick-dry clothes, Subject 2 was now ready.

"You're dead," the man hissed through clenched teeth when he saw the Experimenter. "If it's the last thing I do."

Defiance? The Experimenter was surprised, believing that the first sessions would have crushed all rebelliousness. He tugged on an ear, pondering the meaning. Did this spell trouble for the coming sessions? He felt not, slowly shaking his head. His protocol left little room for disruptive passions. "Unlikely," was his only response.

The Experimenter drove the man from the shower cage with the threat of the Taser, then began the familiar process – paralyze him, put on the restraints, position the chair. At that point, the man started to recover; the Experimenter could feel an increase in resistance. He considered delivering another bolt of electricity, but the process was almost complete. He quickly secured Subject 2's head to the chair, then lifted him upright.

Perhaps realizing the futility of resistance, the man sat quietly as the Experimenter rolled him into the adjoining chamber. Even so, it was easy to see the muscles working in the man's arms, his hands clenching into fists. He positioned the chair, then pulled the cap down to the man's head. "Just a few final adjustments," he muttered. Proper alignment was crucial, so he crouched down until they were eye-to-eye, then leaned close. He gripped the cap's chinstrap while placing a hand on the top of the man's head to hold it perfectly still.

Subject 2 lunged forward.

When the Experimenter had attached the straps, the partially recovered man had arched his back, producing a small gap between his head and the chair's backrest. Now he used every millimeter of that slack, his mouth wide as it rushed toward the Experimenter's nose. If he could reach it, the wound would cause confusion, perhaps giving him a chance to escape. He had nothing to lose.

The Experimenter reacted, but too late.

The man reached the end of the slack and his mouth snapped shut, his teeth clamping down on...air. He screamed in agony, partially from the searing pain that shot through his jaw, but mostly from failure.

The Experimenter fell backward onto the floor of the chamber, his eyes blinking rapidly as the reality of what had happened became clear. Had he been closer, had the slack been greater, he would have lost the tip of his nose, perhaps all of it. His heart pounded. His breath came in gasps.

But the time to fight or flee had passed even before he realized the threat and he calmed himself. He considered the man's gambit with cold detachment. What did he hope to accomplish? A missing nose wouldn't free the man's feet and hands. It wouldn't get him out of the locked chamber. Even if the Experimenter had succumbed to shock, a possibility given the pain and loss of blood the attack would have caused, the action would only condemn the man to a slow and painful death. In the end, his ploy merely affirmed what the Experimenter already knew – humans were irrational.

"You can still let me go," the man pleaded, as terror returned in place of bravado. "I don't know you. Just let me go. I'll disappear. I won't give you no trouble."

The Experiment took the head straps in both hands, pulling them tight. In moments, the shock electrodes were attached, the water was added to the pan, and the console with the lights and buttons was moved into position.

"Shall we continue?" the Experimenter asked.

"No. Please." The man drew the words out in a slow, painful moan. Tremors overtook his body, as if he was freezing in a room now overheated by fear. The sounds of his plaintive whimper died as the Experimenter entered his work area and closed the soundproof door behind him.

He sat at his desk, knowing that Subject 2's rewiring wasn't as far along as he had hoped after the breakthrough on Monday. With other demands on his time, they had managed only two sessions. But even with this limited practice, Subject 2 had gained more control. The motion of his right hand wasn't perfect; it was never smooth. It looked like a small bird, flittering this way and that, until it finally landed on the right button. But the Experimenter deemed it good enough. It was time to make the task harder, to compel more of the brain to re-organize itself.

Taking the computer keyboard in hand, he entered the command to increase the number of lights to be remembered from four to nine. This new requirement would be difficult for most people, but it would be extremely taxing when only some, recently rewired parts of the brain were available for the task. He blew out a long breath and looked through the mirror, making sure everything was in place. Then, he checked his notes. Only when satisfied did he enter the start command. The green, session-running light appeared. The subject's body tensed, but then, he settled into the chair, his eyes peering forward as the cap on his head came online.

Everything looked good. Perhaps the man was ready for the next wall in his consciousness to come down. The Experimenter rolled his chair to the one-way mirror.

After a minute, the first of nine lights lit up, followed by eight more, each at two second intervals. Throughout the sequence, the man remained still, facing the panel. Now that it was complete, he should respond. But he didn't. There was no movement, not so much as a twitch.

The Experimenter moved his chair to the far edge of the mirror, trying to get a better angle to see Number 2's face. His eyes were open, but something about them wasn't right. They seemed distant, unfocused. His stillness was absolute. He wasn't breathing.

The Experimenter jumped from his chair and ran to his desk. The command to terminate the trial came too late, as the shock was delivered. He looked back into the chamber, seeing only a slight tremor in the leg. There was no scream of pain. There was no writhing against the bindings. There was no spit-laden stream of profanity.

He returned to the keyboard, intending to shut down the session, but stopped. He ran a hand across his chin and stared back into the chamber. Subject 2 was dead, or if not, his brain was now so oxygen-deprived that continuing research with him would be pointless. Anything he learned might not apply to the healthy, much less, someone like himself who was already partially awakened by the technology. He needed to diagnose the equipment, see what had gone wrong. And the first steps of that task would be easier if everything was running.

Cracking the door to the chamber, he was assaulted by the stench of death and defecation. He stepped inside and closed the door, not wanting the odor to reach his work area and beyond.

His first thought was that his subject had been electrocuted. He retrieved a multimeter from one of the six, gray cabinets lining the walls. He carefully attached it to the electrode and the ground. When the light sequence finished and no response was entered, the shock came. The reading on the meter was perfect. He turned off the equipment controlling the shock and removed the electrode from the leg. He placed it and the meter into their cabinets.

The Experimenter moved closer to Subject 2, looking carefully at his face. His lips were blue. A vein stood out on his neck. The Experimenter placed his ear near the man's nose, but he heard nothing. He felt for a pulse, finding at most something like the flutter of butterfly wings – something fast and very faint. If the man was alive, he was slowly suffocating.

The shock might have caused him to stop breathing, but the Experimenter thought not. First trial of the day? A shock precisely controlled and delivered to a leg? It didn't make sense. But looking at the headgear, another thought came to mind.

He reached up to remove it, but then saw one of the subject's fingers twitch. Was he still alive? Death from asphyxiation took time, and if the gear was causing him to suffocate, removing it might allow him to revive. That would never do. Of course, he could put a hand over the man's nose and mouth, finish the job. But he had time and somehow, the act was beneath him. Only a common criminal would strangle someone, and he was anything but common. Better to let the scrambled messages in the man's brain do their work, if that was what was happening.

So, the Experimenter started cleaning up. He first grabbed a sheet of paper and made careful notes. He mopped the floor. He removed, cleaned, and carefully stored everything but the equipment on the man's head. Twenty minutes passed quickly. The Experimenter was certain no one could be alive that long without breathing.

Carefully, he removed the headgear. The problem was immediately apparent. Even though Subject 2 had been able to jerk his head less than an inch, the desperate lunge against his steadying hand had been enough to dislodge some of the metal disks in the cap. He started to push them back into place, then stopped. He scratched his chin and let his eyes play across the unbroken, gray walls of the chamber. Then, he laid the piece of equipment down on a workbench and took a micrometer from a cabinet.

Working patiently, he recorded the precise location and orientation of each part. He was captivated by how the device had been transformed, by what it had become. Breathing is not a voluntary muscle action; people do not need to think about it to do it. True, people can hold their breath, but if held long enough, unconsciousness will follow and it will start again. But the Neural Activity Blocker had seized the voluntary part of the response, the muscles that controlled the lungs, and had refused to let go even in unconsciousness. It had caused Subject 2 to hold his breath until he was dead. In the Experimenter's mind, the transformation was astonishing. Only when the position of each of the disks had been recorded did he complete his clean up.

With order restored, the Experimenter exited the chamber and sat at his desk. With the premature loss of Subject Number 2, he must revise his plans. In his mind's eye, he dropped the activities that were now moot and added others in their stead. There was the matter of disposing of Subject 2's body, but the Experimenter wasn't concerned about that. The headgear needed to be reinforced, but that was a matter of a few hours work. Obtaining his next subject, on the other hand, was a labor of at least one night, perhaps more. He needed to start that chore immediately.

It wasn't that the supply of potential participants for the Great Experiment was limited. The pool was ample, because Subject 3, like numbers 1 and 2 before him, would come from the ranks of the anonymous homeless that could be found in and around St. Louis. But care had to be exercised in their capture. They were wary. They were well-schooled in self-protection and life on the street. In fact, if his aim had been to steal their pocket change, tattered clothes, or a half-empty bottle, the Experimenter might well fail. But their defenses against abduction were not as well honed. After all, who would want to take one of their number...other than the Experimenter?

MONDAY, AUGUST 10, 2:53 PM

The Worthington-Huston Technology (WHT) offices were in the Central West End of St. Louis. As part of the city built around the time of the 1904 Louisiana Purchase Exposition, better known as the St. Louis World's Fair, the area was dotted with impressive, three-story houses and mini-mansions. The building that housed their offices had been one of those residences, but fuel costs and real estate taxes had made its use as a single-family home impractical for any but the extremely wealthy. So, like many buildings in the area, it had been converted to commercial use.

Sue and I had ridden to the area together and when we parked, I saw Nicole emerge from her car a couple of spaces away. After a moment of small talk, we entered the building and climbed to the third floor. The center-hall landing had been turned into a reception area, with a large desk in the middle and six closed doors circling it. Two of the doors had nameplates – Dr. Ned Worthington and Dr. Jon Huston. The other four were sealed, most likely providing each of the founders with a sizable, attached laboratory space.

Behind the desk was an older, gray-haired woman, presumably Ms. Laverne Wells according to the nameplate. When she saw us, she jumped up and hurried around her desk, her brows knitted as she glanced at Worthington's office door.

"You're the folks from Ruger-Phillips?" she asked somewhat breathlessly, even though she had only gone a few feet.

"We are," I replied. "Sue Jordan, Nicole Veles, and I'm Sam Price. And you're Ms. Wells?"

"Laverne, please."

I'm no authority on what constitutes 'business casual' for women, but somehow, Laverne's attire appeared a bit formal, reminding me vaguely of June Cleaver from the 1950s television series, *Leave It to Beaver*. It was not so much the pale, tan dress or the light gray sweater that she wore, but the single strand of pearls around her neck. Wasn't that June Cleaver's trademark, one she wore even when she was doing the dishes or vacuuming the house?

Laverne's eyes flitted back to Worthington's door. "I expect Dr. Worthington shortly, as he has another pressing meeting at 4:00. Please have a seat," she said and gestured to the chairs along the wall.

We sat. Laverne started back to her desk, then turned around, so I stood. "Can I get you something? Coffee? I guess it might be a little late for coffee. I don't like to drink coffee after lunch. Makes it tough to get to sleep."

She paused, twisting a ring on one of her fingers. I glanced at the women, who both shook their heads. I was about to decline when Laverne added, "Of course, people are different. Maybe you like coffee in the afternoon? We have water too...of course."

"Thanks, but we're fine."

Laverne nodded slowly, then returned to her desk. I sat back down. The women were already huddled, talking quietly, so I drifted into thoughts of what had happened since we had last met.

I had spent Thursday afternoon going over everything we had discussed about brain plasticity and its possible roles in both causing and curing phantom limb pain. I was not sure if it was making more sense, or if it only seemed that way because I had reviewed it so many times. And if I was seeking full disclosure about my daydreaming, I had to admit that a few thoughts involved Nicole's final words – that she rearranged a few things to join the project.

Friday was marginally more productive. I pored through a physiological psychology textbook to find the brain areas involved in working memory. The list was long, including the parietal cortex, the anterior cingulate, and parts of the basal ganglia. The names meant little to me, but I read about the functions they served and the connections they had. I came away thinking that my earlier conclusion – that suppressing the areas involved in working memory would be "almost impossible" – might be an understatement. These areas were relatively large, highly interconnected, and served a variety of important functions ranging from action selection to emotion.

Movement in the corner of my eye caught my attention. Laverne was coming over again, so I stood to meet her. "Are you sure I can't get you folks something?" she asked, as she ran a hand across her pearls.

I looked at the women again. This time, Sue answered. "Thanks, Laverne, but we're OK."

I turned back. Laverne's eyes were returning to my face from a clock on the wall. Curiosity got the best of me and I glanced at it; it was nine minutes after the hour. But as absent-minded professors seemed one of the more accurate stereotypes in my line of work, I wasn't too concerned. The waiting, however, was weighing heavily on Laverne, as she had started fiddling with her ring again.

Perhaps some small talk would put her mind at ease. "I saw a real estate company and an insurance agency on the first floor. Does WHT lease the rest of the building?"

"We have all of this floor and share the second with an investor and a tax accountant. The businesses you mentioned have the first and everyone shares the basement...for storage."

I nodded. "You know who the investor represents?" I asked, not seeing much time-killing potential in the real estate, insurance, or taxes-in-August topics.

"No, maybe himself? I don't follow the market."

It hadn't taken long to dispatch that topic. I was about to excuse myself to read an imaginary text on my phone when another line of idle chatter came to mind. "Follow the Cardinals?"

"Who in St. Louis doesn't?" she replied.

I'd hit pay dirt. I wasn't from St. Louis, having grown up across the state in Kansas City, but I was learning what it meant to live in a 'baseball town.' Laverne was a typical fan, knowing the Card's standing in their division and in the wild card race. And since I had attended Saturday's game on an extra ticket from Rick, I gave her my first-hand account.

When we exhausted that topic, my eyes went back to the clock when Laverne peeked. It was 19 minutes after the hour, a delay not easily explained by being a bit absent-minded. Laverne must have agreed, because she was scowling at the door as she slowly made her way back to her desk. But near the midpoint of her journey, the door opened and a man appeared.

He was short and stocky, dressed in a black suit, white shirt, and black tie. If he traded his wire-rims for sunglasses, he could've stepped right onto the set for the movie, *The Blues Brothers*. Great. Now I have June Cleaver working for 'Joliet' Jake. I really needed to expand my taste in entertainment.

"Dr. Worthington will see you now," said Laverne without missing a beat, but looking none too pleased either.

Worthington said nothing. He forced a smile, nodded once curtly, and retreated into his office. He took a seat behind his desk and gestured at three wooden chairs placed against the wall across from him, perhaps five feet from the leading edge of his desk. We sat. In a chair to his right was a bearded, bespectacled individual. A heavy, metal door and one-way mirror on the wall immediately behind the desk confirmed my earlier suspicion about an attached laboratory.

"I'm Dr. Ned Worthington, principle founder and lead scientist at Worthington-Huston Technology. And this is my colleague, Dr. Sebastian Atwood."

Atwood nodded. He had curly brown hair that transitioned to a full beard of the same color and consistency. The facial hair made it difficult to guess, but I estimated he was several years older than me. His piercing brown eyes followed our movements closely from behind gold, wire-rim glasses.

"Nice to meet you, Dr. Worthington, Dr. Atwood," I replied. "We're from Ruger-Phillips, under contract to the Veteran's Administration. My colleagues are Ms. Sue Jordan and Ms. Nicole Veles. I'm Dr. Sam Price. Please, call me Sam." Worthington nodded but didn't reciprocate on the informality. Atwood sat motionless, saying nothing.

"Thanks for meeting with us on such short notice," I said. "I'm sure you're quite busy, so we'll keep this as brief as possible."

"Yes, that's accurate to say. I am busy, so brevity would be appreciated."

I glanced sideways at Sue and Nicole. Both appeared puzzled; I knew I was. People in Worthington's position generally wanted to convey some degree of amiability toward their evaluators. He, on the other hand, wanted to maintain his professional distance – his physical distance too. And every other researcher wanted to appear fully occupied, but all said they were happy to take time to answer your questions. 'I'm busy, get on with it' was a new approach.

"OK," I replied, trying to keep the surprise from my voice. "As I understand the situation, you originally proposed a treatment for phantom limb pain. That research transitioned into a learning technology – a means to increase memory span. But before approving more funding, the VA asked us to review the research."

I paused, believing Worthington or Atwood might wish to elaborate, but they didn't. The only response was Worthington making that circular gesture with one hand that could be interpreted as 'please continue' or 'spit it out.' It felt like the latter to me.

"Can you start by telling us more about the memory span study, and particularly, about the methods you used." Having identified a reasonable starting point, I leaned back in my chair for what I expected to be a sales pitch – why he was about to revolutionize training, perhaps even all of education as we knew it.

"You've been given my papers. They speak for themselves," he replied. "I suggest you read them and if you have any questions, call Laverne and she can schedule another meeting. Now, I have pressing matters. Sebastian?" Both men stood to leave.

I felt Sue and Nicole shift in their chairs, but I didn't turn to look. There wasn't time; the men were moving quickly. "Dr. Worthington," I called. "Please, wait a moment."

Worthington stopped and turned part of the way around, facing the corner of the room rather than directly at us.

"We've reviewed both your paper and your proposal. There isn't enough information in them to start our work." I didn't say that with insufficient information, we never be able to recommend more funding, but it was waiting on the tip of my tongue, if he needed to hear it.

Worthington's eyes returned to my face and he stood staring at me, the muscles working in his jaw. After a moment, he re-seated himself at the desk. Atwood did likewise, fueling a growing impression that he was a puppet in their association.

"Just what is it that you require?" Worthington asked, his tone sharp.

Believing that some flattery might reduce the tension and allow the meeting to continue along more typical lines I said, "We've reviewed your proposal to the VA, as I mentioned. We found your approach innovative and well grounded in theory and research." Worthington simply nodded, his glare unchanging.

"We've also read your paper on increasing memory span, but this is all we have received. One thing that isn't clear to us is how the neural activity blocking technique works to increase working memory. Perhaps you could start there?"

Worthington waved a hand in the air, as if chasing away some unseen insect. "I would have thought it obvious, but if we must....

"Based on research I conducted prior to the VA project, I was supremely confident that by blocking the portion of the somatosensory cortex that serves the contralateral, intact appendage, the maladaptive response that remains for a phantom limb could be supplanted via the brain's plasticity. To do so, I designed and prototyped an electronic device that suppresses neural activity, which we have named, appropriately, the Neural Activity Blocker. I also learned during this period that localizing the blocking signal to the area serving a single limb would be problematic. It would require a degree of precision in the triangulation of the signal that funding to date has been insufficient to provide."

I frowned, wondering if this was how he talks or if he was trying to scare us off with technical jargon? But cutting through his verbiage, he'd admitted he couldn't aim the device well enough to suppress the activity for a single limb. If that was true, then how could he possibly block something as complexly interconnected as working memory?

"So, what I proposed to the VA was a proof of concept demonstration," continued Worthington. "I recruited a single subject from a local university, identified only as A.T. He was paid for his time. Digit memory span was the task I selected."

Worthington leaned back in his chair, crossing his arms over his chest as if he was about to make 'the big reveal,' the key that would make all my misgivings disappear. I glanced at Atwood, who appeared bored. He was surreptitiously checking his phone.

"The demonstration I proposed," said Worthington, "involved blocking activity in one hemisphere of the brain, leaving the second to encode, hold, and reproduce the digits."

It was a big reveal, just not the one I had expected.

The human brain is composed of two separate and in many ways, independent halves or hemispheres. Signals from and to the right side of the body – the right hand, the right leg, or the right part of the visual field – are processed in the left hemisphere of the brain, and vice versa. So, with his deceptively simple statement, Worthington had shifted the conversation from the realm of medicine to an area where most cognitive psychologists would feel quite at home. Worthington was talking about a procedure that, if it worked, would parallel the so-called 'split-brain' studies.

Those studies had involved a very small group of individuals whose hemispheres were separate, usually as the result of surgery, but occasionally from injury, illness, or developmental problems. And what that research had found were significant and systematic differences between the right and left sides of the brain. In very general terms, the left hemisphere had been characterized as analytic or logical, while the right hemisphere was seen to be more holistic and intuitive.

While Worthington's reference to blocking one of the two hemispheres triggered thoughts of the split-brain studies in me, his procedure evidently meant something different to Nicole. "Are you saying that you conducted something like the Wada Test, but did so electronically?" she asked.

In the first reaction from Worthington that was not laced with boredom or disdain, he gave a single nod and said, "Precisely."

I had no idea what the Wada test was, but didn't want to sidetrack the conversation by asking Nicole for an explanation now. And frankly, I didn't want to give Worthington any more ammunition for his condescension either. I made a mental note to ask her later.

"With a choice of hemispheres to electronically suppress, which did you select?" I asked.

"You're the psychologist," Worthington replied. "Which would you choose?"

I could have turned the question back to Worthington – he was the one seeking funding, not us. But I might learn more about his thoughts if I gave him something to consider.

"Interesting question," I said, rubbing my chin as I gazed off to the corner of the room for a moment, although I knew exactly what I was going to say. "The digit memory span task is generally considered to involve working memory. Working memory, however, doesn't reside in only one of the hemispheres. But given that the left hemisphere is usually more involved in language and a common tactic to remember a list of numbers is silent rehearsal, I'd choose the left."

Perhaps we were making some small degree of progress with Worthington, as for a second time he seemed accepting of, if not impressed by the conversation.

"As did I," Worthington replied.

"So, your method was to block activity in the left hemisphere, letting the right adapt to the task?" asked Sue.

"Correct."

"And then you turn off the blocker and see how many items A.T. recalls when both hemispheres can contribute?"

I looked up from my note-taking to see Worthington nod, his expression conveying something like the satisfaction he might get if a particularly slow student had finally grasped a totally obvious concept. I was finding him quite easy to dislike, but reminded myself, 'it's only business.'

I glanced again at Atwood. He had abandoned any show of subtlety, as he stared at his phone's screen, lost to the conversation.

"According to the graph on page seven, A.T.'s digit span first grew to around 14 items, or nearly twice that observed in the general population," said Sue. "That was after about...68 hours of training and testing, if I'm reading it right. So, it's your belief that after this time, each hemisphere was contributing about seven items to the total when the Blocker was turned off?"

The same glare I had seen before returned to Worthington's countenance, except it was now directed at Sue. I didn't expect her to be fazed by his demeanor, and a glance indicated I was right. She sat calmly waiting for a reply, wearing that formal smile that doesn't reach the eyes.

"Yes, that's correct," he said after a moment. "The two hemispheres are each contributing to the performance."

The certainty in his statement seemed misplaced. Most people would get better after this much practice using means that had nothing to do with recruiting new areas of the brain. It was time to peel back a layer of the onion.

"Did you record the number of digits A.T. was recalling when the Neural Activity Blocker was turned on?" I asked. If that number was around seven, it would be additional proof that the right hemisphere had adapted and could handle the task by itself.

"You're making this too hard," replied Worthington, shaking his head and scowling. "Before any work with the Blocker, A.T. recalled about seven items. Now, he was recalling 14. That's two hemispheres working on one problem."

I waited, hoping he would answer my question, but he only glared. "So, you didn't record how many he recalled with the Blocker turned on?"

"No," he said, spitting out the word. "Budget was tight. We didn't waste the money when the result is obvious."

Nicole shifted in her chair and I looked over. She had her head tilted slightly toward Worthington, an eyebrow raised. Was she asking permission to speak? I gave her a slight nod, thinking that we needed to talk later.

"On the same chart Sue mentioned, it looks like A.T. reached a memory span of 21 items after another 71 hours of work or so. That can't be two hemispheres each adding their separate, 7-item capacity. Any idea what's going on?"

I knew this question was coming, although I didn't expect Nicole to ask it. Given the way he had been acting, Worthington might explode when such a basic inconsistency was mentioned. Nicole had to know that too.

But he didn't explode. He simply said, "An emergent capability."

Nicole, Sue, and I traded confused looks, so I asked, "What does that mean?"

"No one else has been trained as extensively as A.T. using the Neural Activity Blocker," Worthington said, implying that perhaps others had been trained for shorter periods of time. I needed to ask that question later.

"So, without that background, we weren't prepared to test more...let's say, complex possibilities. But one thing we did notice was that A.T. had an exceptional ability to manipulate numbers in his head. He could look at a list and not only remember it, but also see patterns in it. Or use it in calculations. This mental math ability seemed separate from just recalling the numbers, and if so, these two capabilities might combine to increase his performance."

Worthington glanced at his watch, causing me to do the same. It was nearly 4:00 and Laverne had told us that he had another appointment at that hour. We would have to schedule a second meeting if we couldn't wrap this up in the next few minutes. And frankly, I hoped we could avoid that.

"You know, there are other ways A.T. could be remembering these lists," I said, jumping to the central issue in my mind. "I'm sure you're familiar with various mnemonics that he could have used – things like some type of rhyme, story, or picture."

Worthington nodded. "You mean like what S.F. did?" he asked.

"Yes, like him," I replied, recognizing the participant's initials from a landmark, psychological study. "How do you know he's not doing something like that?"

For once, Worthington did not look irritated by one of my questions. In fact, he looked pleased, judging from the Cheshire-cat grin on his face. Atwood, on the other hand, looked like he'd taken refuge in daydreaming, his look faraway.

"You must know the limitation on the mnemonic that S.F. used?" Worthington said.

"Maybe," I said, unsure where he was going with this question. "If you mean that his mnemonic only works for numbers, then yes, I know that. Most mnemonics work for only certain types of information."

"Correct. A.T. was called away by personal issues shortly after we started our last tests, so the sample is insufficient for formal publication. But in the last few days of the experiment, in place of the standard lists of one-digit numbers, we used lists of letters and lists of nonsense syllables."

He pulled two graphs from a desk drawer and held them up. "Simply put, A.T.'s capacity for the letters and the nonsense syllables was only slightly lower than his span for digits. No mnemonic will fit all those types of data. In short, his memory span is approximately three times that of anyone else, because he could use more of his brain than anyone else."

Seeing the stunned look on our faces, he smiled smugly and said, "You would do well to accept my conclusions so we can expedite this process. Now, Sebastian and I must depart, as we're late for the next meeting."

We stood, and the women and I managed our surprise enough to say thank you, as Worthington showed us out.

I sat down in the reception area and jotted a note to myself. I wanted to know how we could contact A.T. Even the strictest protocols covering the use of humans in research allowed participants to be contacted in case of emergencies. Somehow, given the unparalleled results we had been shown, I thought we might eventually reach that point.

MONDAY, AUGUST 10, 4:09 PM

We stopped at Laverne's desk and she gave us an appointment with Worthington for 10:00 the next morning. As we left the building, a wave of heat and humidity hit us – summer in St. Louis.

"Rather than driving back to the office, do you two have a minute if we go to that Starbucks over there?" I asked, as I nodded down the street. Both women agreed.

When we got there, Sue and Nicole took seats at a table toward the back, while I ordered a scone. I didn't want it to look like we were there just for a meeting, which we were.

"Worthington's intense, isn't he?" I said, as I joined them and opened my notebook on the table in front of me.

Sue let her head droop in an exaggerated manner, then looked up. "That's not the word I'd use. And what's with the corpse he brought along? Atwood gives new meaning to the word, wallflower."

"Do all your meetings go that way?" asked Nicole.

"Pretty much sets new standards for me," I admitted. "And I mean, standards at the low end of pleasant and forthcoming."

I glanced at my notes, reviewing what we needed to discuss in the aftermath. I looked up at Nicole. "When Worthington said something about blocking one hemisphere, I thought of the split-brain studies. But you came up with something else. The Wada test? What's that?"

I knew I could have searched online, but as quickly as she had made the connection during the meeting, she would know more than enough to satisfy my curiosity. But rather than launching into an explanation, she winced and looked down at the tabletop. Even her shoulders slumped. I was thrown by the body language.

When she looked up a moment later, she was frowning. "I have to apologize. I shouldn't have changed the topic. It was just such an unexpected twist, when he described what he was doing."

These were the moments when I remembered that the gulf between business and education was vast. In graduate school, teams were rare. Teamwork was so unusual that when it was a requirement, that fact was highlighted in the course description, covered on the syllabus, mentioned during class orientation, and recounted frequently in the meetings leading up to the event. Additionally, it was always accompanied with the statement, 'we're teaching you a skill you'll need on the job'.

Of course, when the date of the team assignment came, the students didn't work together. Collaboration started and ended with dividing the work among the members. Maybe they listened to each other's presentations the day before the professor heard them, but maybe not. It wasn't that graduate students disliked each other. Rather, they survived by individual accomplishment and so, grew to trust their capabilities above all else. What could you expect?

For us to be successful, however, Sue, Nicole, and I needed to work together. Nicole couldn't be sending me glances when she wanted to speak, an issue that was second on my list.

"I can assure you," said Sue, "Doc doesn't want or expect an apology."

"Sue's right," I said, glad she had given Nicole a reason to believe me even before I spoke. "We represent two distinct bodies of knowledge – Sue and I cover one and you have the other. By yourself.

So, you have to get your questions answered when they come up, not later when we've all forgotten what we were talking about."

It was a dicey policy if there were team members who liked to digress. But Nicole was so far on the other side of this tendency, I had no concerns opening the floor to her.

"So, go where your concerns lead you. We'll consolidate later. I should have said this at our kick-off and I didn't. For that, I'm the one that needs to apologize. I'm sorry."

Nicole looked at me, a slight smile coming to her lips. "OK, thanks. I'll do my best to hold up my end of the bargain."

Nicole took a long breath and released it slowly, her eyes gazing out the Starbucks' window. Turning back to us, she said, "The Wada test involves delivering an anesthetic – usually sodium amobarbital – to one of the hemispheres of the brain via one of two carotid arteries. The result is that the functions of the anesthetized side are temporarily suppressed, and you can study what's left in the other. So, you can see why I thought of it when Worthington said he was blocking a hemisphere."

"No kidding," said Sue. "Like you said, Worthington has the equivalent of the Wada, but with electricity instead of drugs. That would mean he doesn't have to worry about side effects."

"True," said Nicole. "It's just that we don't know what risks he's accepting in place of the ones he's avoiding."

"And we'll need that answer before we're done," I said.

Nicole nodded, then slid forward on her chair and folded her hands on the table. "These explanations – they're a two-way street?"

"Sure. What's the question?" I asked.

"Nonsense syllables?" she said, unfolding her hands as if welcoming an explanation.

"They're consonant, vowel, consonant combinations, like B-I-V or T-O-R."

"Or S-E-X," said Sue. "No, wait, that's a word. It's just that it's been so long." She looked off, as if trying to recapture a distant memory.

I rolled my eyes, then turned back to Nicole. "To study memory, you need something that lacks meaning. Random lists of single digit numbers are an example. Most people don't see a pattern in 3-7-5-2-4-8. Nonsense syllables are another. Letters get used too, but it's easier to form them into a word or story. And the meaning from words will help you recall the letters."

"You mean like Roy G. Biv," Nicole said, leaning back in her chair. I'd heard that mnemonic, but from the expression on Sue's face, she hadn't. "It's the first letter of the colors of the visible spectrum," Nicole explained. "Red, orange, yellow, green, and so on."

"Guess you've heard of that trick," I said.

"Who hasn't, if you've ever had a professor who likes to have you memorize lists," said Nicole. "Now what about...who was it, S.F., and why that made Worthington's graphs so surprising to you two. I didn't quite get that."

Sue looked at me, shaking her head. "You probably remember the exact findings, don't you?"

"Some, maybe," I admitted, certain I could recall a few details from the landmark study. I turned to Nicole. "You know that most people can remember a list of about 7 items, right?" Nicole nodded.

"S.F. could remember lists as long as 79," I said.

"Seriously? You could read off 79 random numbers and he could repeat them back? Was he born with this ability?"

"Nope. He started off recalling about seven numbers, like anyone else. But he developed his own mnemonic to help as the lists got longer. He was an avid runner. So, he took strings of numbers and formed them into stories, mostly about people's ages, dates, and running times."

I paused for a moment, because doing this off the top of my head was tricky. "So, S.F. would take some numbers like 3-2-3-5-9-4-1-2-2-5 and turn them into a story about a 32-year-old running a sub four-minute mile on Christmas Day. Then if he recalled the story, he would recall all 10 numbers."

"Well, that pretty much blows the whole you-can-remember-seven-things rule out of the water," said Nicole.

"Yes and no," Sue replied. "People still remember about seven things, but that could be seven single digits, or seven nonsense syllables..."

"Or seven running stories," said Nicole, finishing the thought. She tapped her forehead, as if she should have guess this implication. "If those stories all contained 10 numbers, you're up to 70 digits. But it must have been a lot of work for S.F. to be able to do that consistently."

"Yeah, harder than learning Roy G. Biv. I don't remember the exact number, but he spent weeks working on it."

"So, what was that number again?" Nicole asked, raising an eyebrow.

"3-2-3-5-9-4-1-2-2-5"

"Not bad," she said, smiling at me.

"Well, I cheated a little. Three minutes, 59.4 seconds isn't just any sub-four-minute mile. It was the time of the first one ever run, which I happen to know. But yeah, the technique's good, if you practice it...a lot."

Nicole raised a hand to her chin, her fingers tapping her lips. "Now I see why you and Sue were so surprised by the results on those other two graphs. If A.T. had learned to use something like ages, running times, and dates, it wouldn't work on letters or nonsense syllables. He'd be back to recalling seven items...but he wasn't."

"Which means there's something else going on," Sue said, "like increasing the brain areas that contribute."

"Yeah, maybe," I said. It was an admission I wouldn't have made so readily a few days ago, but the evidence was mounting.

"Well, guys," said Sue, "I gotta get home or Al will be burning water for dinner. You think it'd be worthwhile meeting here around 9:30 tomorrow? Give us a chance to talk about how to approach Worthington. Other than carefully, that is."

After Nicole and I agreed to her idea, Sue said her goodbyes and left. With the phrase, 'no time like the present' running through my head, I turned to Nicole. "Care to grab a beer somewhere and we can talk about what we heard today?"

There was some hesitation, and my mind raced through the possibilities – she prefers wine, or maybe, she's a teetotaler. Or worse yet, she's involved with someone. I really knew nothing about her other than she wore no ring, and under the circumstances, I was generating negative possibilities rapid fire.

"You know, I'm pretty tired," she said. "That session with Worthington was a bit draining."

I was busy formulating something to say to cover my retreat when she said, "I have a six-pack at my apartment. Would you like to come over to my place for a drink?"

In my usual glib way of accepting an unexpected offer from a fascinating and very attractive woman, I replied, "Sure." She gave me the address, and after I promised to give her a five-minute head start, she left.

MONDAY, AUGUST 10, 5:17 PM

When I knocked on Nicole's door, she called from somewhere inside, "Come in; door's open."

I entered and walked down a short hallway that led to a living room. I wasn't sure what to expect, but I liked what I saw. The area wasn't the picture of geometric perfection, with every item aligned precisely on tabletops and books arranged alphabetically on shelves. Neither were there dead goldfish floating in a bowl nor discarded pizza boxes hiding under the sofa.

The room was simple, with a comfortable, lived-in feel. There were a few pieces of unopened mail and a set of keys on an end table. A light blanket laid across the arm of a loveseat – presumably used more frequently in the winter. The loveseat faced two chairs, with a small, flat screen TV mounted on the wall between them. Behind the chairs was a brick fireplace with an oak mantel. On the mantel and at various spots on the wall were works of art, mostly watercolors. Unless there was another artist named N. Veles, the pictures were hers. I have little artistic talent, but I know what I like. And I liked them.

The room also reflected an interest in antiques, with an emphasis on old scientific equipment. A microscope from a bygone era, a set of scales under glass, and a set of antique calipers covered tabletops around the room. Other than the loveseat, which was upholstered, the furniture was mission-style oak, reflecting the general age and style of the apartment building, and presumably, her tastes as well.

The warm, comfortable feel that was building in my mind was put on hold for a moment, however, when I noticed the two books on her coffee table. The first must have been four-inches thick and had the title of *Digital Circuit Analysis and Design*. The second was a paperback romance novel with a couple embracing on the cover. With interests and tastes so diverse, Nicole was truly a Renaissance woman.

Am I out of my league?

Nicole entered, a beer in each hand, just as I stood up from reading the titles of her books. She had changed since work and looked more relaxed in a pair of cutoff jean shorts and t-shirt. Her legs were lightly tanned and well-toned, most likely the result of miles on the bicycle parked in a corner of the room. "I see you do a little light reading," I said.

She glanced at the two volumes. "Yeah, I was really surprised by the depth of character development and the plot twists – they were mind-blowing. You usually don't expect to find that in a book on digital circuits."

I chuckled. "I wouldn't."

She walked over and handed me a beer, a light floral scent reaching my nose. Had she fit a shower into my five-minute delay, or was this the first time we had not been surrounded by the smells of coffee, the street, or industrial cleaner? She looked up at me, her hazel eyes appearing more green than brown.

"I hope you like dark beer."

"I do. And a porter at that," I said after reading the label. "Pretty much my favorite."

She sat in one of the chairs. I took the loveseat across from her, bemoaning the fact that I didn't know her well enough to pat the space beside me. "Besides reading, what do you like to do?" I asked, expecting the question to lead to a discussion of her art. But she went elsewhere.

"I suppose that, plus music and movies are my main indoor pastimes. But outside, I like biking and hiking, in that order."

"Me too," I replied, "except I'd have to reverse them. Biking's great, if you get out on some of the trails in or around St. Louis. I've always wanted to ride the entire length...."

"Of the Katy trail," said Nicole, finishing my thought before I could, then grinning at me.

"You too?"

She nodded. "Definitely. It goes, what, maybe three quarters of the way across the state? I hope they finish it someday, so I can ride all the way to where I grew up – Independence."

My eyes went wide. "Seriously? Independence, Missouri? Home to Harry S. Truman?"

"Yeah, you know it?"

"I grew up on a farm...well, technically, about a mile from the city limits, although it's probably ten miles from anything commercial."

"So, we grew up within 10 or 15 miles of each other." She tilted her head, her gaze going far off for a moment. "I wonder if we ever met?"

"No," I said, bringing her eyes back to mine. "I would have remembered you."

Nicole smirked, giving my trite line all the respect it deserved. "I like your antiques," I said, moving on. "I have a few, including a reproduction phrenology head. The kind that was used by psychologists in the mid-1800s."

She paused, the beer bottle only inches from her lips. "Sure. Those heads with areas labeled for different traits like truthfulness or friendliness."

I sat up a bit straighter, looking at her closely.

"Don't be surprised," she replied to my reaction. "The idea that different types of thoughts or emotions are in specific areas of the brain parallels current findings, right?"

"Yeah, I guess. But I always thought that reading bumps on the head paralleled reading tea leaves." Her comment, however, triggered thoughts I had while driving over. "Do you think.... Oh, sorry, I was going to launch into shop talk."

"Isn't that what I already did?" asked Nicole, holding out a hand. "I'm guessing you're as surprised as I am about where Dr. Worthington's technology might be going."

"Assuming you're totally astonished, then yes. What I was going to ask was, do you think there were other capabilities affected – other than those used for memory span?"

She frowned. "Why do you ask?"

"Well, when Worthington asked which hemisphere I'd block, I said the left because language is usually located there. But maybe A.T. did something different when he was trying to remember the numbers. Something that didn't involve language."

"And if he did," Nicole continued, "it might become the deficit that plasticity tries to fix."

"Right. There's a lot of other functions on the left side besides language. I believe the split-brain studies put logic, science, and math skills there."

"Those studies? They're the ones where the hemispheres were surgically separated as some sort of medical treatment, right?"

"Yeah, they cut the corpus callosum as a last-ditch effort to control epilepsy. The treatment went out of favor around the end of the 1900s."

Nicole looked at me closely, her brow wrinkling. I wondered if I should say, 'random factoid, not sure why I remember that.' But she'd find out that I'm a research nerd eventually anyway...if she didn't know already. I took a breath.

"Yeah, one semester, I became fascinated by that research. Once the corpus callosum is cut, nearly all the communication between the hemispheres is gone. Because you can get information to one side at a time, scientists can study the hemispheres separately. And the patients? They can end up with one side not knowing what the other is doing."

"Seriously?" asked Nicole.

"Sure. I remember one case study where a patient was trying to button his shirt with his right hand, while the left hand was busy unbuttoning it. As one scientist put it, we really can be of two minds."

"Interesting," Nicole said. "But I can't picture it – having two different consciousnesses." Her open hands were in front of her, her gaze shifting back and forth between them as if looking for the two worlds sitting there.

"You know," continued Nicole after a moment. "Besides the things A.T. might have done to remember those numbers, it seems like a lot of other things could have popped into his head. What if he was planning a trip? Or thinking about a movie?"

My reaction didn't quite reach the level of a gasp, but I was struck by the thought. "The procedure probably kept him pretty busy...but yeah, a lot of other thoughts could have slipped in. And if they involved a function that was suppressed.... Wow, we could get plastic changes that weren't expected.

"If nothing else," I said after a moment, "we should compile a list of capabilities located in the left hemisphere. If we find evidence that the capability changed anytime during the study, it'll help us flesh out the effects of the device. But as a guide to what we should look for.... Well, it won't be perfect."

"Is that because there can be variation in where a function is located?" she asked, narrowing her eyes.

"Exactly. People are different, and averages tend to hide all that variation. Saying that math is in the left hemisphere is like saying that the average person is right-handed. Or saying that the average biomedical engineer is an asocial male with a pocket protector, while you're...."

What am I thinking?

My common sense engaged, because the phrase running through my head to finish that sentence was 'sexy as hell.' I managed to mumble, "not one."

If Nicole read my mind, she took it in stride and laughed. "A pocket protector? Yes, I seem to have misplaced mine, but I have slide rules that match all of my outfits."

I laughed. Stealing a glance at the clock on her mantel explained my near *faux pas*. It had been nearly an hour since I had arrived. My beer was gone, and I was hungry and mentally fatigued. It was time for me to go.

I thanked Nicole as she walked me to the door. Given that this was a date only under the broadest of all possible interpretations of that word and that we had found common ground in an extremely esoteric topic, I decided not to try for a kiss and merely said 'good night' at the door.

After I did, she said, "Good night to you too. And by the way, thanks for noticing that I'm not male, asocial or otherwise." There was a slightly mischievous smile on her face as she closed the door.

I stood in the hall, staring at the wall. I hadn't seen that coming.

TUESDAY, AUGUST 11, 12:57 AM

The Experimenter skulked in the shadows born of the hour and the concrete structure above his head. "What an idiot," he mumbled under his breath, as he scanned the eerie blackness of massive support columns and immense footings. It was part of a bridge over the Mississippi River, but its designer was a fool. There were a dozen ways to simplify it, make it the elegant engineering marvel it could be.

Or maybe its design was an intentional miscarriage of logic and reason, spawned by human greed or politics. A tidy sum had gone into making it as unwieldy as it was.

His musings were broken by a soft sound – breathing. It emanated from deeper in the shadows to his right. The Experimenter changed course. After walking about halfway there, he stopped and donned a set of night-vision goggles. He disliked them. The glowing, wavering images they produced were chaotic, unpleasant. The sensation, he knew, was a byproduct of using the Neural Activity Blocker; he perceived too much.

Numbers were troubling enough. He had difficulty stopping the process of combining and re-combining them in constantly evolving patterns, producing an ever-expanding array of results – sums, averages, correlations. But complex patterns of bright colors were worse, much worse. It was almost as if his mind was trying to decompose them into wavelengths, intensities, and saturations. Art was not a pleasing and soothing experience; it was disturbing, nearly debilitating.

The gray-green ghosts from the night-vision goggles were not as bad simply because of the limited color in this shimmering world, and after a few moments he adapted. He looked around. Sometime during the day, sunlight had warmed the concrete where he stood, making it glow under his feet. A few yards to the right, the surface plunged into darkness and it was from this void that the sound emanated. He looked closer, but saw nothing. He stepped to one side. There, behind a pile of discarded clothing, bags, and boxes laid a figure.

Could this be Subject 3?

The Experimenter crept forward, as the stench of an unwashed body, urine, and spoiled food reached his nose. He removed his Taser from a pocket and raised it to his eyes. The gun's sights were a mere dot of green, the human figure beyond them the size of his fist. He lowered the weapon, not wanting to chance a miss from this distance.

He inched forward, testing each footfall before shifting his weight. The stench worsened. That problem was correctable, but there was something else. He bent closer, listening carefully. There it was – a slight wheeze with each breath, a rattle in the lungs. The man would not long endure the rigors of Blocker training with a respiratory problem. The Experimenter removed the goggles, pocketed the Taser, and moved on.

After a few moments walking, the Experimenter heard voices off to the left. The authorities? Some of his prey? These were fertile hunting grounds and he didn't wish to leave, but neither did he care to stumble upon anyone alert at this hour. He veered to the right.

After rounding a second set of footings, he saw two shopping carts against an embankment. They were placed on their sides, end-to-end, forming a crude wall. Inside the makeshift compound slept a figure. The Experimenter crept forward and donned the night-vision gear.

Despite the warmth of the evening, the figure was heavily clothed, producing only a faint, spectral glow in his glasses. The barbs from the Taser might not penetrate that much cloth and paper, so he shifted to the right, deeper into the shadows. Here, part of the figure – perhaps a leg – was more exposed, its glow in the night like a welcome sign to the Experimenter. He listened closely. The breathing was deep and slow, with no sound of illness. The scent that reached his nose was putrid, but perhaps less than most. He could find no fault.

He raised the Taser, steadied the weapon, and squeezed the trigger. The barbs flew true. The glowing shape jerked with their impact, then started quivering as the burst of electricity continued.

The Experimenter pulled a light-weight tarpaulin from his backpack and spread it over the ground. He rolled the figure into the middle. He removed the restraints from his bag and secured the person's hands and feet. Then, he pulled on two handles that were attached to ropes laced through the edges of the canvas. The tarp drew up around his prey like a cocoon.

His van was about 50 yards away, parked next to the river. It was too far to chance leaving his prize, so he pulled it across the concrete in its canvas bag. This mode of transport made more noise than he would have liked, but between the sounds of the nearby river and the sporadic traffic overhead, it was acceptable. About halfway there, the Experimenter tired. As he rested, the figure started moving. He depressed the stun gun's trigger a second time and stillness again prevailed.

Reaching the van, the Experimenter opened the side door. He had installed a small, electric winch for heavier loads, but this individual weighed little. He hefted the figure inside, then shoved it toward the door on the far side of the van. He climbed in, closed the door behind him, and started attaching the leg and arm restraints to the tie-downs in the back. Even in the relative emptiness of the back of the van, the bindings were necessary – a lesson he had learned with Subject 1.

His prey started moving, so again the Experimenter hit the Taser's trigger. A yelp of pain reached his ears as the burst of electricity disrupted the normal messages between the brain and the body. But something was wrong with his prey's voice. He put on a pair of disposable, latex gloves to examine his acquisition. After a moment, he recoiled, turning away in disgust. When he turned back, he hissed, "You're a...woman."

Even though he knew of no differences between the brains of men and women – and even if none had ever been found – he wasn't going to chance it. The mere thought of a woman's thoughts contaminating his own? It made him ill. He removed the restraints from her hands and feet, then opened the door on the far side of the van. He placed his feet against the woman's back and shoved with all his strength. A moment later, he heard a splash, only then remembering how close he had parked to the river.

"Good riddance," he muttered, reasoning that it made little difference if she pulled herself from the river's muddy grasp or not. He had left no fingerprints. There was none of his DNA. There was no way he could be traced to this time and place.

He repacked the tarp in his backpack, checked his goggles, and closed the van's door as he exited. He still needed Subject Number 3, and although it was getting late, this was fertile hunting ground.

TUESDAY, AUGUST 11, 9:28 AM

By the time I reached Starbucks, I'd already hit my self-imposed coffee limit, with a cup before my jog and another after. So, I opted for another scone, more to disguise our meeting than because I was hungry. I took a seat toward the back. The place was busy, as one might expect for that hour of the morning, but most of the people were absorbed in their morning paper or surfing the Internet on phones or tablets. Soon, I saw Sue and Nicole enter and head for the counter. My scone cover was apparently unnecessary.

"Morning, Sue," I said as she approached the table, coffee in hand.

"Hi ya, Doc." She took the chair across from me, then pulled a small notebook and her reading glasses from a bag. Nicole was only a few moments behind and took the seat beside Sue.

"Morning, Nicole."

"Hi, Sam. Oh, I forgot to ask. Did you like the beer?"

Sue peered at me over her glasses as if to say, 'exactly what happened after I left you two yesterday?' Of course, the answer would have had her rolling on the floor, so I'm glad she didn't ask.

"Yeah, I did. I even jotted the name down for future reference."

Nicole smiled. The dim lighting of the restaurant was accentuating the brown in her hazel eyes, and I found it impossible to look away. Sue cleared her throat, which brought me back to the present.

"OK, for the 10 AM with Worthington," I said.   "Given the chilliness of the reception yesterday...."

Sue snorted quietly. "Chilliness? And yesterday, you said he was 'intense.'   Did I miss a class at work on mastering the understatement?"

I gave her a what-can-I-say shrug, then continued.   "I was thinking we could focus on the research files mentioned in the contract and limit our questions. He's not going to volunteer much anyway. And once we've studied the data, we can come back with specifics."

"Yeah, pick your battles, as the saying goes," said Nicole as Sue nodded her concurrence.

"OK, toward that end, I went by the office earlier and copied the section of the contract that describes those files."

As I dug through my papers, Sue said, "Right with you, Doc." She was waving a couple of pages at me. Another copy of the section appeared in Nicole's hand.

"I should have known I didn't need to make a special trip." I glanced at my copy, reading the entries. "We should get the data from each trial. That'll be at least the numbers he was trying to remember, his answer, and his response time. We also get the completed Beck Anxiety Inventories, the observation reports for each post-treatment period, and the specifications on the Neural Activity Blocker. Sue, did you run across what's in those reports?"

"I did, and it was just the standard. A.T. filled out the Beck, then answered a few questions. After that, he sat in a waiting area for 30 minutes while someone took notes on what he did. Then, they let him go, reminding him he shouldn't do things like write a will that left all his worldly possessions to the experimenter." Sue struck her most thoughtful pose. "I never really understood the need for that when I was running studies."

"So you wouldn't inherit a pile of dirty laundry and a few, lightly used textbooks," I said. "That's all that most graduate students have. Now, is there anything we need to ask Worthington before we go off and study those files? And don't let his intensity and chilliness stop you from asking." The emphasis I put on the two adjectives brought a smirk to Sue's face.

Sue started tapping her pen on the tabletop, staring at her notebook. Nicole looked at me, a slight frown on her features.

"I should ask how the Blocker stimulates the brain," Nicole said after a moment.

"Think there's some surprises there?" asked Sue.

"Possibly. There's some cutting-edge work in the field – things like nanobots or neural lace that positions itself around or on the cortex. If Dr. Worthington used something like that...well, a word or two from him on who to talk to could save us hours looking for the right lab."

I nodded, appreciative of her foresight. "OK, that's on the agenda. Other ideas?"

"I think we should ask for more information on A.T.'s behavior after each session," said Sue. "We'll have the observation reports, but I'd like to know if Worthington thought there were other changes? Places where the Blocker's effects bled over into other behaviors?"

"Is there some reason why you think there might be?" I asked, thinking her question sounded a lot like what Nicole and I had discussed.

"Yeah. The technology's new, its use for training was unplanned, and frankly, the approach is a bit brute force. He's blocking half the brain. What besides memory span might have been affected?"

I glanced at Nicole, smiling and shaking my head.

"Sam and I were wondering the same thing last night," said Nicole. This time Sue didn't peer over her glasses, as she probably got a better grasp on our evening.

"We thought we'd compile a list of left side functions and then watch for anything related in the reports," I said. "But your idea's a great addition – see what Worthington recalls that's not in the written stuff. How about we put it first on the agenda, then follow up with Nicole's question? Anything else we need to ask?"

"Not that I can think of," said Sue.

"Nothing from me."

We left to meet with Worthington.

The wait with Laverne was nearing 15 minutes, and it was taking a toll on her. When she got up from her desk for the third time, she nodded with her head toward a corner of the room. I followed her over.

"Dr. Worthington's really not so bad," she said barely above a whisper. "He's actually quite brilliant, and underneath it all, he's a caring person."

I had leaned close to hear, but with those words, I drew back and looked at her closely. Did she really believe this, or was she trying to convince herself? The sadness in her eyes implied the former.

"It's just that he's been under so much pressure with all the late nights and research set-backs. And his wife hasn't helped things either, with all her eleventh-hour demands," Laverne said.

I smiled and nodded, impressed by her loyalty. "Don't worry. Dr. Worthington's conduct in these meetings has nothing to do with our job. We're only interested in...." I got that far in my disclaimer when the door opened and Worthington appeared. I gave Laverne a parting nod and smile, hopefully lessening some of her concerns.

As before, Worthington walked ahead of us, sat behind his desk, and then gestured to the chairs aligned against the far wall. Unlike before, Atwood wasn't in attendance. "Well, did you figure out my study?"

In the end, our work would be unaffected by his attitude, as I had told Laverne. But that didn't mean I liked dealing with him. I felt my muscles tense and my blood pressure increase with his conceit. "I believe we've derived all the information it contains."

Perhaps he didn't recognize all the possible meanings of the statement, as he replied, "Good. So, you have other concerns?"

I was glad our agenda was short. "We have only two questions, and then, we'd like to get the files mentioned in our contract and we'll be on our way."

Worthington scowled, but said nothing.

"We'll be receiving the observation reports and the results from the Beck Inventory," I said. "But we were wondering if you had any comments on A.T.'s behavior beyond what's in those documents?"

Worthington leaned back in his chair, folding his hands in his lap. "If there's one issue you need have no concern about, it's any negative effect of the technology on A.T.'s state of mind or his actions." He waved a hand, as if swatting away a pest. "There was nothing troubling in his behavior during the study."

"So, no new behaviors emerged?" Sue asked. "Nothing seemed to become more prominent?"

Worthington's face reddened, but the emotion passed quickly. He leaned back and stared at the wall over our heads. "He was more intense, more driven than I first expected, but nothing more. Certainly, there's been nothing of concern in his actions since he left."

"But A.T. withdrawing from the project prior to completing the final tests – could that have been the result of some negative side-effect?" Nicole asked.

Worthington's expression darkened again, the color lingering this time. He grasped the arms of his chair, sat up, and glared at her. "His leaving was a setback. His explanation for withdrawing seemed weak at the time, although technically, he didn't need any reason at all. Mostly, it was just a surprise."

Worthington leaned back and looked at the wall again, as if his own words had calmed him. "It's only that he was making such good progress using the Blocker. And he had taken an interest in it. He'd even made some suggestions about adjustments. But in the end, the call to go on to bigger and better things was probably too much for him to ignore."

The word that caught my attention was 'adjustments.' Worthington's paper had said that A.T. was a student at a local university and was being paid for participation. I had thought 'starving, psychology graduate student.' Having been one, I knew that paid studies were valued – easy money for little work. But if he was suggesting changes to the hardware or software? Well, a psychology curriculum wouldn't have given him the necessary background.

"What kind of adjustments?" I asked.

The words had hardly passed my lips when Worthington snapped, "Out of scope for this discussion...and your job."

That was possible. Any talk of future development would be beyond our contract; we only had a requirement to understand the current system. "OK," I replied. "Anything else you noticed about his behavior?"

Worthington blew out a breath, shaking his head in disgust. "No, you're wasting my time. We developed a post-treatment protocol and followed it precisely. If A.T. had been affected negatively, we'd have seen it."

"Did you review the post-treatment observation reports?" asked Sue.

Another flicker of anger crossed Worthington's features. "None was required. I recorded those observations – every last one of them," he said, emphasizing each of the last five words.

I knew Sue wouldn't be intimidated by Worthington's blustering, so when she gave me a slight shake of the head indicating she had no more questions, I was certain she was satisfied with the information we had, or perhaps, only satisfied that we were unlikely to get more. But I knew Nicole less well. At a glance, she didn't appear bothered as she shook her head too, but maybe she had a good poker face.

There were a few issues that still bothered me – mostly A.T.'s 'intense interest' followed by an abrupt, poorly explained departure. But I had done enough research to know that on occasion, participants just decide to leave. Or they get a better offer. For all I knew, A.T. had won the lottery. We had pressed Worthington on this issue as much as we could.

That left the final question. While I would introduce it, it would be up to Nicole to ferret out any details that were unclear. I didn't know if she had done this kind of interview before, and if not, I couldn't imagine a worse situation or person on which to learn.

"We'd like to learn more about the electronics involved in the Neural Activity Blocker. And specifically, we'd like to know how the Blocker stimulates the brain. We suspect you didn't drill holes in A.T.'s head for electrodes."

I knew the statement wasn't that funny, but on the off chance it might reduce the tension, I threw it out. But Worthington's reaction couldn't have been worse if I had called him a liar and fraud. His faced turned red, a vein popping out on his forehead. His whole body tensed, as he leaned forward in his chair.

"You think I'm an idiot," he spat between clenched teeth. "How the Blocker works is irrelevant to you."

Knowing we had at least three copies, I pulled out my list of the information we were due. I looked at it a moment, less to refresh my memory than to consider my approach. I stood, walked to the desk, and extended the paper. He didn't move, so I pulled it back and read from it.

"Under contract, we should receive, and I quote, 'descriptions and functional diagrams of the Neural Activity Blocker sufficient to determine its impact on the activity in the brain.' Unquote. That's directly from the VA."

"Lies," he screamed, as spittle flew from his lips. "The VA is fully aware of the device's capabilities. They'd never request such a thing."

He paused, glaring at me. The silence of the room was unnerving.

"I believe you'll find...," I started, but he held up a hand.

A bitter laugh escaped his lips, as his eyes moved from my face, to Sue's, then Nicole's. "Until now, I had no idea what you were up to." He spoke slowly, softly, continuing to shift his glower among us. The change in volume and tone felt even more threatening than the previous shouting. "You're nothing but common criminals. The only question remaining in my mind is, who's behind this?"

He looked at Sue and me, his lip curling in disgust. "You, Dr. Price, Ms. Jordan. You probably have no clue as to what my discovery represents, as there are no rats in a maze in my work."

He shifted his eyes to Nicole. "Ms. Veles, on the other hand, at least works at an organization that might, with enough time, be able to make some sense of my creation. But she never heard of me before two days ago."

How does he know all that?

Of course, Ruger-Phillips was identified on numerous documents Worthington had, but Nicole's company wouldn't be mentioned by name. He had been checking up on us and his familiarity with the members of my team was troubling.

Worthington turned in profile, staring at a blank wall. His hands were clenched on the arms of his chair, his knuckles turning white. "No, you three have no concept, no idea, meaning that Jerome Caufield is behind this." He snorted in derision. "I stopped the doctor from stealing the Blocker once. But now, it seems he's enlisted some simple-minded dupes who plan to hide the deed under the guise of a forged, government contract. I never should have revealed anything to that quack."

I considered denying any connection with Caufield, but for all I knew, he was a VA bureaucrat somewhere on the signature cycle for our contract. It was best to ignore Worthington's accusation for now.

Faced with the question of 'what next,' I did what came naturally, what I was known for. I persisted. In the face of near certain defeat, I tried one final appeal in hopes it would expose this tirade as nothing more than a misunderstanding.

"We're here only to fulfill the requirements of our contract to the VA. That contract requires an accounting of the physiological effects of the electronics, and we can only get that from the specifications. We require that information if we're ever to understand A.T.'s experience."

Beads of sweat popped out on Worthington's forehead. He stood, walked around the desk, and stood mere inches from my face. His labored breathing brought the smell of stale coffee to my nose.

"You're a fool," he snarled, stabbing the air with a finger. "Do you really believe I'm going to hand over documents that would allow the doctor to duplicate my triumphs? You say you want to know what the experience is like? It's like white noise, but one that opens your mind rather than fills your ears. It provides a clarity, a precision, and a breadth of thought like nothing you'll ever experience."

I stumbled back, my eyes searching his face. "You used.... Tell me I'm wrong, but that sounds like...you used the Blocker on yourself?"

Worthington's face distorted with rage, his eyes bulging. He bared his teeth as if to snarl something, then clamped his mouth in a tight line. He looked down. My eyes followed his, finding the page of our contract still in my hand. He grabbed it, ripped it up, and threw it in my face. Then, he spun and stormed from the room into his lab.

I made my way back to my chair and the three of us sat there dazed. Perhaps I should have tried harder to find something to break the tension, but being glib or dismissing the incident as trivial or meaningless was more than inappropriate; it was dangerous. Finally, I found my voice.

"Can we meet back at the Ruger-Phillips offices at 1:30? We need a new approach for this project. One that puts a lot of distance between us and that man."

I received their quiet concurrences and we left.

TUESDAY, AUGUST 11, 1:03 PM

"You can't do this," Subject 3 rasped when the Experimenter entered the chamber. "I got rights. Lemme go." Then, he started coughing.

It had taken until almost 3:00 AM for the Experimenter to find his latest test case. He had rejected one candidate who was twitching wildly in his sleep. Another was so skinny, the Experimenter wasn't sure he would survive the drive back to the lab, much less the research. And then, there was the woman. He shuddered at the thought. But for all his care, all his hunting, the wheezing man who now sat before him was the best he could find.

The Experimenter walked over and faced him. "Time for you to go, get something to eat, and get some rest."

"Don't need nuthin' from you."

"Perhaps not, but I need the device on your head."

Subject 3 stared at the Experimenter, his throat so dry he gagged when he tried to swallow. The cough returned, worse this time.

"That's right," said the Experimenter when the hacking stopped. "I use it. You'll come to appreciate it too, trust me."

"I'll die first." The Experimenter nodded, thinking the man's statement might be more of a prophecy than a rebellion.

He went to his work area and entered a command on the keyboard. Returning to the chamber, he pulled a heavy, cloth cap from a drawer. It roughly resembled a driving cap, with that flip of material resting on the bill. "Shall we try this on for size?"

There was no response. The Experimenter would have been surprised had there been one, because the command he had entered caused the Blocker to paralyze the man's voluntary muscles. The involuntary muscles would continue to function. His heart would beat. His lungs would breathe. His eyes would blink. But much of the rest of his body was useless.

Subject 3 had been using his right hand during the earlier session, so the Experimenter now secured it to the chair. He checked the bindings on the man's feet and head. Then, he carefully removed the Blocker from his head.

Subject 3 came to life – or at least as much life as possible when lashed to a wheelchair. The room was filled with a tormented howl. The Experimenter made out the words 'gonna kill,' but wasn't sure who was killing and who was dying. He placed the 'driving cap' on the man's head, flipped a tiny switch on the back, and the room was again plunged into silence. It worked.

Crammed under the crown and inside the extra fold of material on the driving cap were a high-capacity battery and a microprocessor. Wires from the tiny computer led to a series of metal disks embedded in the material. It was a portable Blocker. And it was set to paralyze the man, using the same configuration as the full, laboratory version, just in a much more compact form. With the battery, it could immobilize the wearer for about 20 minutes on a charge. The Experimenter smiled. He'd eliminated the risk of tasing his subjects during the return to their prison.

He wheeled Subject 3 to the residence and into the larger cage. There, he tipped the chair to the floor and removed the bindings. He dragged the man to one of the walls, leaning him against it. After removing the wheelchair and securing the cage, the Experimenter reached through a slot, removed the paralyzing cap, and quickly pulled it out of the enclosure. There was little chance the subject would recover his wits in time to grab the Experimenter's arm, but he held the Taser in his other hand, just in case.

Subject 3's face screwed up, preparing to release another howl of protest until he noticed the food setting in front of him. It could be poisoned, but he was hungry. What had it been since his last, good meal? A day? Two? Whatever, it had been long enough, and he started eating greedily.

The Experimenter left the residence and returned to his work area via the chamber. To allow his research to go more quickly, he had automated much of the rewiring protocol, allowing the computer that drove the equipment to adjust the mental tasks. He had also refined his methods. There was, for example, no longer an abrupt shift from a sequence of four lights to one involving nine. The challenge was introduced slowly, automatically by the computer.

He consulted the log from the software. The session had begun just after 6:00 AM. During the seven hours of treatment, all under the direction of the computer, the man's suffering had been considerable, but that was the nature of these first trials. He retrieved his notebook from a desk drawer and updated it.

He rose from his desk and entered the experimental chamber, taking the notebook with him. First, he cleaned the Blocker cap, then removed a large, plastic cover from his personal, treatment chair. He rolled it into place under the cap, his heart starting to beat faster in anticipation of the coming mental voyage.

He checked his notebook to refresh his memory, although the act was unnecessary. He was all too familiar with the problems he would soon address under the Blocker's electronic guidance. First, there were the people hired by the VA – Price, Jordan, and Veles. The sight of their names in black and white on the page made his blood boil. It was an instinctive response, an animalistic drive born from the threat they posed to his biological need. They couldn't be allowed to come between him and the electronics that gave him true life.

And then there was the good doctor. He knew too much and had ambitions far too great for his poor station in life. At first, he had seemed brilliant, capable of understanding how completely the Blocker could crystalize one's world and expand one's vision. But the Experimenter no longer believed that. Any time spent trying to enlighten him would be wasted; he was intellectually inferior and hamstrung by his emotional attachments. No, the doctor must die, lest the information in his head become known and the Great Experiment terminated before fruition.

He checked the configuration of the device once more, assuring himself that it was set for his own, personal needs. Then, he adjusted the timer.

"Tell me what I need to do," he said aloud as he flipped the switch. Soon he would know, because in the cold, hard calculus of the Blocker-created world, there was never error.

TUESDAY, AUGUST 11, 1:22 PM

I like action-adventure novels. In some of the books of that genre, there is a hero who has a tiny voice in the back of his head that lets him know when something bad is about to happen. I had nothing like that, as I sat picking at the chef salad I had bought for lunch. No, I had something akin to the blast of a fire-engine siren two inches from my ears and the flashing lights of a slot machine that had made the $100,000 payoff directly in front of my wide-open eyes. Worthington was dangerous. Of that, I was certain.

That thought drove the plan that was forming in my mind. It consisted of equal parts of reporting everything we had learned to my management and then enlisting the help of the VA to obtain the data we needed. I wanted to avoid rolling the dice in further direct contact with Worthington. Having made up my mind, I disposed of my half-eaten salad, and went to meet Sue and Nicole in one of our conference rooms.

I had just seated myself across the table from the women when Sue said, "I know who Dr. Jerome Caufield is. I should have said something last week, but I never thought his name would come up."

"A professional rival?" I asked, voicing a suspicion that had come to mind.

"No, a marriage counselor."

"Really," I said slowly. "How does he fit in?"

"When I was prepping for our first meeting, I did a little checking on Worthington. I found the standard credentials and a few press releases, but I got a few other hits too. About three months ago, in May, he and his wife of six years, Elizabeth Scott-Worthington, filed for divorce. It got nasty enough that she moved out and dropped Worthington from her last name. According to the papers, Dr. Worthington claimed that his wife had conspired to steal his research...which is weird, because her family has money. Anyway, her co-conspirator and partner in crime was their marriage counselor...."

"Dr. Jerome Caufield," Nicole and I said in unison.

"Yeah," said Sue. "They must have reached some type of agreement, because the story disappeared soon after. But with the display in his office this morning? Well, he hasn't forgotten."

"Thanks, Sue. At least that's one mystery solved," I said.

I had made up my mind about what needed to be done over lunch, but as someone who thought of himself as persistent and who very much wanted to make this project an early career success, I was having trouble finding the words. I made a fist and tapped it against my chin. Finally, I said, "I think we should bring in reinforcements."

"The VA?" asked Nicole.

"Yeah. Worthington must have seen the contract, but it's like he doesn't remember, or doesn't believe it. But whatever, we can't get caught in the crossfire. Either the VA explains it to him and we get the information we need or...."

"Or they realize he's batshit crazy and end the project," said Sue.

I nodded. Her term wouldn't be found in the *Diagnostic and Statistical Manual of Mental Disorders*, but she had finished my thought perfectly.

"I think that's the right call, Doc."

"I agree," said Nicole.

"Thanks," I said, feeling a wave of relief now that it was out in the open. "OK, let's focus on the scenario where the VA doesn't terminate the project. Even under the best possible circumstances, there'll be a delay between our request for the VA's help and getting the data back. So, Sue, you want to get an early start on the final report? You dug up a lot of background material that needs to be turned into eloquent prose."

"I feel the force of my inner muse already," she replied. "I could also knock out that section you two came up with during your drinking game last night."

"Sue! We had one beer," protested Nicole. She shook her head slowly, a show of mock irritation mixed with amusement on her face.

"I assume you're talking about the same section you mentioned?" I said, looking at Sue. "Document the functions that the Blocker might strengthen in the left hemisphere."

"That would be the one," she said. "Personally, I think we should all work on developing the list. Then, we'll all know what to look for in A.T.'s behavior. I can write it up for the report...unless you want to, Nicole?"

"Sure, I'll do it," said Nicole. "I'll probably have the time before you do." Then, she smiled. "That one chart on negative plasticity alone will probably take a week to turn into text."

"It's a plan," I said. "And it's still early. Shall we hit the list of left hemisphere functions now?"

Sue and Nicole gave each other a knowing look.

"What is it, ladies?"

Sue laughed. "I guess we can't pass this off as a spontaneous remark. We were wondering if you were overlooking the elephant in the room?"

"You mean Worthington's behavior?" I asked.

"And the possibility that he used the device on himself," added Nicole.

I took a moment to massage my forehead – preventative, I thought for the headache that was trying to form there. "Yeah, I know. If we don't mention his behavior and the analysis and conclusions from the study check out, Worthington could end up with more money from the VA. Then, if he goes off the rails...well, technically, we're not liable, but that wouldn't help my conscience."

"Or the other side," said Nicole. "We bring these allegations to the VA, casting doubt on his character when it's only a temporary break by an otherwise brilliant and caring person. Yeah, we could hear Laverne whispering to you," she said, answering my questioning look.

I rubbed the back of my neck with a hand. "I've been replaying that last few minutes in my mind. Did it seem to you that Worthington was talking about using the Blocker on himself?"

Nicole glanced at Sue, then turned to me. "At the time, we had the same thought – it was a firsthand account. But thinking back, it isn't clear. He could have been repeating something A.T. said. Even his anger can be interpreted two ways. Maybe he was angry because he got caught. Or maybe he was upset because we had accused him when he was innocent."

I put an elbow on the arm of my chair, scratching my chin with a hand. Their concerns were well reasoned; I was obviously not the only one letting this project ruin their lunch.

"I was planning to draft something on our meetings," I said after a moment. "Something more than a typical summary. More detail on who said what and when, but without speculating about causes. Seem reasonable?"

"Yeah," said Sue, shrugging. "Probably the best we can do. Nicole and I could also write up our own notes, give you something to check against...if you want."

"Definitely," I replied. "Then, I'll give the consolidated report to Ken, who can send it up the management chain and to the VA. Everything that's got our alarms going off will be spelled out in detail, so hopefully, they won't ignore it. Agreed?"

"Yeah," Sue said, as Nicole nodded. "How about we take a short break, then hit the left side functions?"

We all agreed and the women left to see something at Sue's desk.

*   *   *

When I returned, Sue was sitting at the computer, a blank page with the title 'Left Hemisphere Dominant Functions' projected at the front of the conference room. She was completing the first entry, 'Processing stimuli in the right visual field.' Nicole was at the table with several of Sue's textbooks open in front of her. The word, 'Candidates' was written on a whiteboard behind her. I had brought a few more texts and dumped them on the table across from Nicole.

"Looks like you two have a process going already," I said.

"We do," said Nicole. "You and I will jot the possible left side functions on the board. Since different researchers may call the same thing by different names, we'll decide on one term. Then, if it's a consistent finding, rather than something one lab claimed that no one else could duplicate, Sue will record it on her list."

"And so far," said Sue, "I'm just recording the fact that the left side of the brain serves the right side of the body. No controversy there."

I nodded. "Great plan."

Over the next 45 minutes, the list grew. When we stepped back and looked at our work, it was clear why the left hemisphere was usually called the 'analytic and logical' one.

Left Hemisphere Dominant Functions
Processing stimuli in the right visual field
Controlling muscle responses on the right side of the body
Perceiving stimuli on the right side of the body, e.g., touch

Language (reading, speaking, writing)
Math
Science
Analytic and logical reasoning
Mental manipulation
Semantic priming
Image generation
Processing pleasurable experiences
Decision-making
Routine or well-rehearsed processes

"That's some useful mental abilities," I muttered, mostly to myself.

"You'd say that," replied Sue, "because they're all yours."

I chuckled, readily seeing my love of all things scientific and data-driven. "There's no one in this room low on this set."

"Yeah, I'm all over the 'processing pleasurable experiences' one," replied Sue.

"If this technology is perfected someday," said Nicole, "do you think people will be dropping by the local brain rewiring shop and saying, I'd like to be a little higher in math ability? Sign me up for a week of training."

"Possibly, if we're right about how the Blocker works."

I ran a hand through my hair. If our findings continued in the current direction, then identifying the faculties bolstered by the Blocker would be pivotal. Nicole would be drafting that section of our report. But even with our short association, I was comfortable with the assignment. She had good instincts and explained complex issues in a way that was easy to understand. I could undoubtedly take a lesson, as much of my writing involved statements that were so highly qualified, the gist was 'maybe, maybe not'.

"I'm good with this," I said. "Anything to add before we move on?"

Everyone was quiet, so I turned to the last issue on my mind. "We need to take self-protective measures," I said more bluntly than I intended.

Nicole frowned. Sue looked startled, then asked, "Are you serious?"

I released a long breath. "I am. The look of hatred in Worthington's eyes, his clenched fists convinced me. I'm not saying he's planning something, but under the right conditions? Yeah, I think he would lash out at any of us."

"To protect his research?" asked Nicole, her forehead wrinkled. Her eyes went from mine to Sue's and back.

I held my open hands out in front of me. "Yeah, you heard him. Right now, he thinks we're the middlemen. But even if he finds out that Dr. Caufield isn't involved, he'll just find another villain. Or we'll become the bad guys."

Both women were quiet for a moment, frowns on their faces as they looked off at the wall or down at the tabletop. "OK," Sue finally said. "I don't want to second guess when being wrong means I get hurt. Al will be home by the time I get there, and besides, I'm armed."

Missouri had legalized concealed weapons, so anyone you met on the street could be armed, but I never would have guessed that Sue was. Perhaps seeing some surprise in my expression, she added, "Al got it for me. He wanted me to have some protection when he was out of town. At first, I objected, but he also paid for safety training and practice. I have a gun and I know how to use it."

"OK, but don't shoot Al when he comes home tonight," I said.

"How long do you think we need to keep our defenses up?" asked Nicole.

I rubbed the back of my neck, believing the answer to that was measured in months, not days. "Worthington was obviously furious this morning. If our request for the study files is pursued by the VA – and I think it will be – then it'll get worse. His anger will be focused on us. How long does that last? I don't know, but he can obviously hold a grudge. What's it been since the Caufield incident – three months?"

"Yeah, May. You really think this could go on for three months?" Sue asked. She straightened her shirt like she was trying to smooth wrinkles that weren't there.

I hung my head in thought for a moment, then looked up at the women. "Unfortunately, we might be talking about six months or more of watching our backs, although the next couple of weeks are probably the worst. In six months, our work is done and the VA will be closing the loop with Worthington, for better or for worse. If any threats become public before then, we can probably get some additional police presence."

I gave them a moment to think about the situation, see if they had other questions or comments. When they didn't, I said, "We're obviously well outside standard operating procedure here. I'd like for both of you to seriously consider leaving the project for your own safety. If you do, we'll make that fact known, hopefully insulating you from Worthington."

Before I had even finished, both women were shaking their heads. "He's not running me off," said Nicole.

"Please sleep on it," I said. "You can let me or Ken know anytime if you change your mind."

The thought of offering Nicole refuge at my apartment flitted into my mind – you know, do the chivalrous thing. But immediately I felt my face warm at the connotations, as well as the absurdity. I knew how to handle a gun, having grown up on a farm where squirrel, duck, and quail hunting were among some of my favorite past-times.

But I had not owned or touched one in years. Chivalrous becomes foolhardy, when the only protection I could offer was the Louisville slugger in my closet.

Fortunately, Nicole already had an option in mind. "I've been meaning to visit my aunt, who lives across the river in St. Charles. I can spend a couple of nights there and work out something more permanent."

"OK," I said. "I have a meeting with Ken tomorrow at 9:00. We should have general guidance from him by afternoon. Can we meet at 1:00? I'll let you know how Ken reacted and we can review progress on our writing."

Sue and Nicole concurred and we adjourned. Perhaps it was ridiculous, but I walked them out to their cars, then returned to my office. I wanted the report about Worthington's behavior drafted before my meeting with Ken, so I had some writing to do. And because one of Ruger-Phillips' primary lines of business was with the government, there was hardly any place in St. Louis that was safer. Worthington would have to be insane to try to pass our armed guards.

Unfortunately, perhaps he was.

TUESDAY, AUGUST 11, 8:13 PM

I was getting tired, glad that my report on our meetings with Worthington was nearly complete. Even without checking, I knew everyone else had left for the day; the motion-controlled lighting in my wing of the building had gone dark, leaving only the aisles and my office in pools of illumination. My only companion was the soft whisper of automation – the slight whir of my computer, the quiet hum of the building's air conditioning.

The still of the building made the ring of my phone seem louder than normal, and my head jerked up when it sounded. My heart started pounding. Was Sue in trouble? Did Nicole get hurt? I couldn't live with myself if either of them came to harm because of this project.

"Hello," I said, deviating from the standard office welcome due to the hour.

"Dr. Price?" The voice on the other end of the line was male, thick, and sluggish. I didn't recognize him.

"Yes," I said slowly. "This is Sam Price."

"This is Dr. Worthington."

I pulled the receiver from my face and stared at it. That couldn't be right. I put it back to my ear. "I'm sorry. Can you repeat your name?"

"Dr. Ned Worthington...from WHT."

Now prepared, I had listened closely. Stripped of the adrenaline-fueled fury of this afternoon, the voice on the line was indeed Worthington's. I sat staring out my office window, seeing nothing.

Would he call me if he had harmed Sue or Nicole?

My hand ached. I looked at it, realizing I had been gripping the phone so tightly my knuckles were turning white. I took a deep breath, trying to relax.

"What can I do for you, Dr. Worthington?"

"I'm sorry to bother you at the office in the evening, but this is the only number I had. We need to talk."

Something in his tone said this wasn't a ransom negotiation or a threat. It sounded like...regret. But for what? Were his next words going to be, 'I only meant to scare her?' The wave of anxiety that had flooded my body changed to anger at the thought.

I found it impossible to sit. I got up and paced the two steps it took to reach the end of the phone cord. I took another breath to steady myself, to try to lessen the pounding in my chest. "OK," I said slowly. "What's the problem."

"Things have gotten out of hand," Worthington said. "I don't know how I could have become so...," he hesitated several seconds, perhaps searching for a word. "So dominated by my work."

My emotions morphed again, settling on confusion this time. I walked the two paces back to my desk. "What is it you want from me?"

"There's no one else I can turn to," he said. His speech was still slow, cautious, as if he was picking his way through a minefield of thoughts. "People don't understand and it takes so long to explain. Some never see it, but I can tell. You're starting to. My world is about to collapse and I fear for my life. But even more, I fear for the lives of those around me. You've got to help me."

Could this really be a cry for help? I wasn't sure, and I now regretted not taking at least one class in abnormal or counseling psychology during all my years of education. But then, that might not have helped either. There was a good chance – better than 50-50 in my mind – that Worthington suffered from a self-inflicted, electronic manipulation of his nervous system, the likes of which no one had ever seen. If so, there would be no standard diagnoses or prescribed treatment plans in any text.

But what line should I take? I didn't want to ignore him, if there was even a remote possibility he was seeking help. I also wanted to avoid anything that might nudge him back into a blind rage. I started hesitantly, "I'm not a clinical psychologist, as I believe you know. But you're right – my background and work on this project have given me some insight into what you're doing. Maybe, you and I, working with someone with an appropriate professional background, could get things under control."

The thought of a team of people to treat him, several standing by with syringes loaded with powerful sedatives, if necessary, was a comforting image right now.

Worthington hesitated. Finally, he said, "Yes, I suppose that would work. I want to avoid making this a circus. I've hurt enough people already. Is it possible that you could come by my home this evening, and we can discuss where this might occur? And who might be involved?"

Had this been a slasher film, I would have agreed and gone to his house, either to be gruesomely murdered or to have thwarted him, only to see him slip away into the night so there could be a sequel. I wanted to avoid either of those possibilities.

"I'm really sorry, but I have plans for this evening. However, my company has a building close to your office. It has a small conference room immediately off the reception area. I could be there at 1:00 PM tomorrow. Would that work for you?"

Worthington hesitated again. Finally, he said, "I believe that time's acceptable. I'll have Laverne call to confirm in the morning."

"Good," I replied and gave him the address. Government work was conducted in that building, so a guard would be posted in the reception area – an armed guard. I also expected that Ken would come along or have someone else join me. I would have plenty of help, if Worthington needed to be subdued.

"Again, sorry to bother you so late. Good evening." Worthington hung up.

I slumped back in my chair and stared at the phone again, knowing I had never had such a bizarre couple of days.

The Experimenter had heard that Thomas Edison failed 1,000 times before inventing the lightbulb. But when asked, Edison said he hadn't failed; rather, he had discovered 1,000 different ways not to make one.

The Experimenter wasn't sure the story was true, but he took a lesson from it anyway. When the misaligned Blocker had forced Subject 2 to hold his breath until dead, he hadn't failed. What he had done was discover the perfect way to kill the doctor.

Yes, the man would be wary. He had to feel some of the threat posed by the Experimenter, even though there was no objective proof of any malice. But even if he sensed peril, the doctor would be too curious, too enthralled in the pursuit of a quantum leap in the evolution of human thought to resist the opportunity to try this latest, portable version of the device.

Now standing on the doctor's front steps, the Experimenter rang the doorbell and waited. No response. He rang again. The man must be home; he had no life. Several more moments passed, then the door cracked open, a chain coming tight over the gap. Even though the Experimenter could see less than half of the doctor's face, the way he jerked back, his eye blinking rapidly confirmed his expectations.

"You? Here?" stammered the doctor.

The Experimenter said nothing. He merely smiled, then held the offering in front of him – a Blocker, configured in the 'driving cap' style.

"Is that...?" The eye that the Experimenter could see through the door got wider.

"It is," the Experimenter said. "And it's more than you could have ever imagined. Much, much more."

The doctor's breath was coming faster, as he stared through the gap between the door and its frame. His brow wrinkled. "You'll let me...?"

"Of course. You'll be amazed to see where it's gone. Or more correctly, where it's taken me."

The doctor hesitated a moment more, then removed the chain and opened the door.

The Experimenter stepped inside. The lights were bright. The scene swirled, as the colors assaulted his vision. He hadn't anticipated that the man would have restored this much of his decor, but he was prepared. He reached into a pocket and pulled out a pair of glasses.

"Sunglasses?" asked the doctor.

"Just a bit of headache," lied the Experimenter. In fact, he had found the glasses online. Sold as an aid to help people understand colorblindness, his was set to approximate protanopia. With a bit of extra tint, they transformed the colorful surroundings into a world of muted blues, yellows, and grays. Not quite the soothing consistency of his lab, but close.

"I see," said the doctor, and then his gaze turned back to the Blocker. He held his hand out. It was shaking; he pulled it back. He bit his lower lip, then said, "I shouldn't." His gaze moved to the face of the Experimenter before dropping back down to the cap. "But perhaps a little. It couldn't hurt."

"Of course not. Look where it's taken me."

The doctor looked up again at the Experimenter, then nodded. "Indeed. This way." He turned and led the way into his home.

When they arrived at his study, the doctor turned and reached for the cap, his hand stopping partway to its goal. He clenched his fist and closed his eyes. When he opened them, he took the cap and donned it. He sat down on a recliner. "How do you turn it on?"

"Let me," said the Experimenter. He reached down and flipped the switch on the back of the cap.

The doctor slumped in the chair, his mouth dropping open. Drool ran down his chin.

"Oh, that's right," said the Experimenter in mock surprise. "I forgot it's in the same bent and twisted shape that Subject 2 left it. And as I recall, that configuration killed him."

The Experimenter pulled on a pair of latex gloves, walked back to the front door, and opened it. Outside, he wiped the doorknob and the button for the doorbell, then returned. "Not that this will ever be investigated as a murder, but you can't be too careful. Now, if you'll excuse me, your demise will take a while and I have much to do."

The Experimenter located the doctor's home office, took a digital camera from his pocket, and took pictures of the room. He wanted to leave everything exactly as he found it.

A search turned up the safe the Experimenter knew would be there. When it was installed, the doctor would have enjoyed some of the Blocker's benefits, including the ability to manipulate numbers rapidly, almost without effort. But he would also have trouble with new memories. So, the combination to the safe wouldn't be based on a birthday or an anniversary, like so many people did. The doctor would know his own birthday, because he had known it before using the device. But he wouldn't remember that the combination was based on it. Rather, the combination would be derived from numbers in plain sight. In the sparsely decorated and neutrally painted office, the framed black and white diploma with a single date, May 4, 1994, was the only possibility.

The Experimenter formed combinations, trying them on the safe. His fourth iteration was the product of adjacent numbers, that is, 20 - 9 - 36. The safe yielded.

All the documents the Experimenter expected were there. First, he found the *Advanced Design Document* that described the next generation of the technology – everything to take the current device and evolve it. These plans were much too valuable to be relegated to the building housing the WHT offices.

The safe also contained the specifications for the original Blocker. The Experimenter decided to leave them. He had no need for them and there were probably other copies. And besides, they could be derived by reverse engineering the current device anyway. Better to leave something to disguise his theft.

Finally, the safe contained the sole sheet of paper that clearly linked him to the doctor. He held the salmon-color page in front of him, a cold smile coming to his face. With it gone, anything else that might have been observed or recorded could be explained as chance. He loaded everything into a backpack and returned to the study.

The task was complete; the doctor was dead. He removed the cap and surveyed the room one last time, making sure nothing had been disturbed. The man looked as if he had settled down to enjoy a good book, but it was a respite that would never end.

The Experimenter left the residence feeling more powerful than ever, certain of his ability to tap the farthest reaches of his mind. With the good doctor gone, no one could stand in his way.

WEDNESDAY, AUGUST 12, 8:37 AM

I passed the office door for the third time, and for the third time, the woman inside glanced up from her work as I went by. She was about my age, maybe a little older, and attractive. On my first pass, she had smiled. On the second, she had looked at me more closely, her eyebrows furrowing. The third lap had produced a scowl. I suspected she was dialing Security to report a stalker, but at least I had a good story. 'My boss sits three doors down and I need to talk to him. See, I have a meeting this afternoon...with a crazy man.'

Ken's door opened. He had been on a call. I had heard him each time I had passed. Even though it was still 20 minutes until our meeting, there wasn't any harm seeing if he was available now. I stuck my head around the door frame. He was sitting behind his desk, his elbows resting on the top, his fingers steepled in front of his face. His white shirt looked crisp enough to hold that pose without him.

"Morning," I said, planning to follow up with, 'I know it isn't time for our meeting yet,' but I never got the chance.

"Doc. Where have you been?" Ken asked, the pitch of his voice a notch higher than normal. He motioned toward a chair and I sat. "I've been trying to call you."

Out of reflex, I looked at my watch. Was our appointment at 8:00 rather than 9:00? But before I could ask, Ken continued.

"There's been a death. It'll be awhile before we know how this affects your project, but I thought you should know about it as soon as possible."

My mind was racing. It was job-related, but it couldn't be Sue. He wouldn't be talking about the effect on the project if it was someone that close. And for the same reason, I also felt it wasn't Nicole. Besides, I had gotten a text from her only fifteen minutes ago. That left Worthington's nemesis.

"Is Dr. Caufield dead?" I asked.

Ken dropped his hands and stared at me. "What? Who's Caufield?" He shook his head and didn't wait for an answer. "No, it's Dr. Worthington. He was found dead in his home this morning."

Worthington?

PART 2. THE DATA CHASE

"Worthington's dead?" I could hardly believe the words and squeezed my eyes closed. He had been right; his life had been in danger. While I never considered going to his house, I could have suggested a more public setting. If I had, he might still be alive. I placed my forehead in a hand, my elbow propped up on the desktop, and slowly shook my head.

"Are you OK?"

I sighed. "Yeah. I mean, no. It's just that I talked to him last night. Only hours...maybe minutes before he died."

"I know," said Ken. I looked up at him, my eyes narrowing.

"Apparently, Dr. Worthington's an early riser," said Ken. "So, when he failed to show up at his office, his admin, Ms. Wells, called his house. When he didn't answer, she called the police. His body was discovered a little after 8:00. She called here to confirm a meeting with you. Is that right? You called him last night to set up a meeting?"

I shook my head, my frown deepening. "No, he called me. He wanted to talk, so I suggested a meeting later today."

"OK," replied Ken. "Anyway, we were on the phone when Ms. Wells learned about her boss. She took it very hard." Ken paused and looked at me closely. "Want to tell me what's going on?"

I nodded, releasing a long breath. "Yeah, I do. Maybe we can start with this." I gave him a copy of my draft report on the meetings. He read it, asking only a few clarifying questions. Then, I recounted the phone call. When I finished, I admired Ken for the first question out of his mouth.

"Is your team OK?"

"Physically, yes. Mentally? It's already been a stressing couple of days, but I think they'll be fine."

"Good."

Ken resumed much the same pose I had seen when I arrived – elbows resting on the desktop, his fingers steepled in front of his face. After a few moments, he said, "I can't even guess how this will affect the project. It probably depends on the cause of death. Best case, we'll be shut down a few days. Worst, the project will be terminated."

I gritted my teeth, then nodded slowly. That was unwelcome news, but only what could be expected. Ken got up from his desk, walked to the window, and looked out. After a moment, he turned back to me.

"What you've done so far is good, but you need to finish it. Incorporate Sue's and Ms. Veles' notes on the meetings. Then, document the phone call, including the time and as much of the discussion as you can remember. We should have all of this written up."

"Why? Is there something going on I should know about?" It came out in a rush.

Ken held up his hands. "No, I don't know of any problems. It's just a precaution."

I nodded. He was right, but the mixture of some guilt, a touch of lingering anxiety from the threat to my team, and a large measure of frustration about the job were whirling in my head. I needed to focus. "Yes, of course. I'll get on it."

"We know we're in for a delay, but not the length," continued Ken. "So, let your team know. I have plenty of work for you and Sue, until we get word from the VA. If a break causes Nicole's management any problems, have them call me. How much time do you think you need to get everything down on paper before we close up shop?"

"Are we starting the project close-out forms or just documenting our work to date?"

"The latter."

"I'd say a day or two should do it. We've already discussed some short-term writing assignments, and Sue and Nicole have started." I didn't say they had started because we had expected a battle between the VA and Worthington for data and these reports were a way to keep busy until the smoke cleared. That stratagem was already outdated.

"Good, have them wrap up their current work and then we'll see what happens." I left to spread the bad news.

Even though Sue's desk was in the next wing, I decided to call Nicole first and went to my office. What I had expected to be a six-month window to get to know her had shrunk to as little as a day. Maybe there would be an opportunity to see if she wanted to go to a movie or have dinner.

But then the reality of that possible conversation hit me – 'Worthington's dead and the project may be too. How about seafood on Saturday night?'

I placed the call, still looking forward to talking to her, but she wasn't at her desk. I left a long message with all the details. After hanging up, I realized I should have asked her to phone me. Now, I had no excuse to call. For someone who was skilled in planning a technical effort, why were my insights on the personal side all hindsight?

I walked over to Sue's desk. She looked up when I was still ten feet away. "If you lived with someone, I'd say you were in need of some make-up sex."

Normally, that would have elicited a groan, but today, I just dropped into the chair across from her and rubbed my forehead with a hand.

"What's wrong?" she asked.

"Worthington's dead."

A hand flew to Sue's mouth.

"He didn't come into work this morning and Laverne called the police. They found him at home. That's all we know at this point."

Sue slowly shook her head, her gaze far away. "Wow," she said under her breath.

"Yeah, hard to believe. Anyway, we can finish our current writing assignments, but then, we're shutting down until this gets worked out."

The faraway look didn't leave her face. After a few moments, I said, "Sue?"

"Yeah, sorry. Finish our current assignments. Got it." She paused, then looked at me. "Do you think he was killed?"

The word that came out of my mouth was "No," but the idea had already flashed through my thoughts. I had wondered that because of what Worthington said about being in danger, but Sue had never heard those words.

"Why do you ask? You think Worthington's stories about Dr. Caufield are true?"

"Maybe," she replied. "But isn't the field of suspects a lot bigger than Caufield? I mean, if the Blocker works, it's a goldmine. The kind of power and wealth it promises could tempt anyone."

A few seconds passed as I watched her face. Finally, she said, "It was a stressful couple of days, and my imagination is running wild. Forget I said anything."

But hearing Sue give voice to the possibility got my mental gears cranking again. If Worthington was killed, whoever did it was still out there and it was possible that we might be considered threats.

Threats to what, I wasn't sure, but ignoring the risk didn't seem a good idea.

I slid forward in my chair, then leaned closer to Sue. "I guess there's a chance that Worthington was killed," I said slowly, quietly. "So, maybe it's not the best time to let your guard down. Keep Al close and your eyes open." I didn't add, 'and your gun handy,' because I was still getting used to the idea that she even had one.

She nodded. "Yeah, no need to take chances." The way she agreed so quickly made me think she had already come to the same conclusion.

"I left Nicole a phone message earlier, but I think I'll call back. Give her a heads-up too."

"I can tell her, if you want. We're talking at 9:30, so we can coordinate on some of the text."

"Thanks, but I should call."

Sue nodded and smiled, a twinkle coming to her eyes. "Of course you should call. We can always count on you men for that."

I got up from the desk and left. Only when I was halfway down the hall did I stop to wonder – did Sue mean men could be counted on for protection? I chuckled to myself. No, of course not. After all, this was Sue talking.

THURSDAY, AUGUST 13, 8:17 PM

The Experimenter flew from his bed in the corner of his work room, his t-shirt and underwear drenched in sweat. He pulled in deep, ragged breaths, not sure if he was suffocating or hyperventilating, but he couldn't stop. His gaze swept around the partitions and the walls beyond, panic keeping his eyes moving faster than his thoughts.

"Where the hell is it?" he whimpered. Or was it just a dream?

Then, he saw it. It was real, and it was sitting exactly where he had left it – his bedside table. He reached a trembling hand forward and lovingly caressed the cover. These pages, so inauspiciously named the *Neural Activity Blocker Advanced Design Document*, were nothing less than his destiny.

When he had returned from Worthington's home late Tuesday, the Experimenter had been euphoric. His whole body vibrated with the prospect of shattering new mental barriers. But after a few moments of near visceral ecstasy, his ever-present logic returned. Did Worthington really have plans worthy of the Blocker's evolution? He had claimed so, but academics could assert world-changing breakthroughs when all they had done was coin a new term for a twenty-year-old concept.

Then, he had skimmed a few pages, soon realizing that it wasn't an evolution of the device. It was a revolution. It was more than he had ever imagined, more than he had ever dreamed even under its liberating forces. His imaginings paled in comparison to what he found in black and white on its pages.

So enthralled did he become that 15 minutes to skim a few pages turned into 27 hours of continuous study. He had poured through the text and diagrams, the lists and tables, the figures and graphs so many times that much of it was now indelibly etched on his brain. When exhaustion finally overtook him, the Experimenter had eaten rapidly, then slept four fitful, dreamless hours until waking moments ago.

He took up the pages again, but this time to start planning for development. It was a matter of only an hour, but the answer it gave him was distressing. Using every waking minute, every shred of his mental and physical ability, it would be Monday before he could have the upgrades fabricated. It would be over 74 hours. It would be 266,476 seconds before he could take his first steps into this new reality. And every one of those seconds would be a stab to the heart of his mental being.

He steeled himself and took the first step in this long journey, but before the first hour had elapsed, a shortcut appeared on the periphery of his consciousness. He stopped and examined the option more closely. It wasn't a replacement. No, eventually, the upgrades had to be built to specifications. But while the final components were being constructed to the highest standards, the current device could be modified quickly. Those changes would be enough for the Experimenter to send Subject 3 on the first forays into this new, uncharted territory.

He began working feverishly, as he modified the metal disks that drove the signal into the brain. Additional disks required new wiring, so he designed the modified cables in his thoughts. But as that mental blueprint came into focus, his body had finished only the second of 30 new disks.

"Faster, damn it," he said, glowering at his work. But it was no use. Each time he pushed his hands to match the speed in his head, they faltered, then failed him.

He trapped his hands under his arms, forcing the shaking to subside. He went back to construction, directing his mind to circle back. There was no shortcut for the disks, but their connections didn't have to be part of a redesigned cable. He could wire them individually. It would be messy, but it would work.

The hours continued, the Experimenter berating his body, while his mind created workarounds for its shortcomings. In the end, he completed his new configuration in less than six hours, exactly as he had forecast.

He entered the residence, flipping on the overhead light that illuminated the cages. Subject 3 sat up, then collapsed back on the mat.

"Water," he pleaded so softly the Experimenter had to strain to hear.

He grabbed a couple of water bottles and tossed them inside. Then, he retrieved two sandwiches from a refrigerator and tossed them in as well. Subject 3 attacked the sustenance, greedy gulps of fluid interspersed with gagging bites of sandwich.

The Experimenter went back to his work area and retrieved his notebook. His last visit to the residence had been just before he went to see Worthington. That was almost 49 hours ago. Unless the man was weakened by other health issues, he wouldn't be that close to death. But if the Experimenter hadn't identified a shortcut and had continued to work on the 74-hour, full-scale rebuild....

Earlier, he had decided to add water and feeding tubes to the experimental setup. Then, during programmed pauses with the Blocker, subjects could feed themselves. And since he was letting the software control the equipment, soon he'd be able to hook up a subject and leave him there for hours, maybe days. The automation could handle everything, until they reached a point where they were breaking new ground. The Experimenter wanted to be present when that happened. He made a note in his book, completion of the task now assured.

He returned to the residence. Subject 3 was on his knees, hugging the toilet as he retched.

"Eat more slowly."

The man turned and glowered at him, but said nothing.

When the gagging stopped and the man sat back on the mat, the Experimenter placed a cookie and a small container of orange juice inside the cage. The subject seized the drink, then carefully opened it as if it held liquid gold. He drank it in two long gulps, not spilling a drop. He reached for the cookie, but before his hand got there, he redirected it to the floor to steady himself. Then, he collapsed slowly onto its surface.

"I should have warned you to eat the cookie first," the Experimenter said to himself, smiling.

* * *

Subject 3 woke to find himself bound to the wheelchair in the experimental chamber, a weight on his head, one foot slightly cooler from the water surrounding it. "No," he sobbed. "You gonna kill me."

"Not today," said the Experimenter. He retreated to his work area, closing the soundproof door that was again about to earn its keep.

Concerned that the drug-laced juice had not completely left his system, the Experimenter used the keyboard to queue a familiar task – a simple mental manipulation that the man had already mastered. The Experimenter drummed his fingers on the desktop, watching as Subject 3 responded to each example perfectly. He stood, walked to his sleeping area, returned, and sat again. "I'm wasting time," he grumbled.

He grabbed the keyboard and terminated the exercise. He looked through the mirror, smiling as his eyes gazed upon the temporary masterpiece crowning the man's head. "Time to put the new design to work."

He checked his notebook, then selected the first of the three activities that used the Blocker's advanced features. The green, session-running light came on. New electronic messages, unlike anything delivered by the original device were now being driven deep into Subject 3's cortex.

The Experimenter got up from his desk and walked over to the one-way mirror. He placed his hands on the surface, a habit he had tried to break but couldn't. At the moment, he didn't care. "Oh, to be inside his head."

But that desire was short-lived, as Subject 3 cringed. The man had little freedom of movement, but the tremor in his legs as he drove against the footrest, the ripple of muscles in his arms and neck as he strained were unmistakable.

"What the...," the Experimenter started, only to be interrupted by a spasm that racked Subject 3's entire body. Veins popped out on his neck and forehead. His face was distorted by...what was this, rage? Fear? The Experimenter wasn't sure.

He rushed back to the desk and flicked the switch for the sound system. He flinched, as an animalistic shriek emanated from the speakers. He turned the volume down and grabbed a microphone. "Talk to me, damn it. What do you see?" The only reply was the sound of gagging, as if the man was swallowing his tongue.

The Experimenter reached for the keyboard. But before his hand arrived, he heard a sickening crack. He stared at the mirror, spellbound. Subject 3 had struggled so savagely against the restraints that he had broken an arm. A shattered bone was sticking through the skin, blood dripping onto the chamber's floor.

There was no need to stop the session now; Subject 3 was damaged beyond any use the Experimenter had for him. So, he turned the volume up, hoping to catch a word that might shed some light on the man's mental anguish. He could make nothing of the choking gasps he heard. He returned to the mirror, pressing his face against its cool surface. It was a matter of only a few more moments before every muscle in the man's body seized in a final convulsion. Subject 3 was gone.

"Damn him. Not a clue," snarled the Experimenter.

He opened the sound-proof door and started to clean up, then stopped and smiled. "I guess you were right," he said to the lifeless figure strapped to the chair. "I did kill you today."

SATURDAY, AUGUST 15, 1:57 PM

The sound of a slamming car door caught my attention and I walked to the window of my apartment. Rick Johnson was just coming up the front steps of the building, so I buzzed him in before he reached the top.

I left my door ajar, taking a seat on the couch in front of the muted TV. The baseball game didn't start for another ten minutes, and I didn't need to hear how the Cardinals were making a late season charge toward the playoffs. That was a story everyone in the city already knew...by heart.

"Hey, Doc," Rick said, pushing my door open. Other than the bedroom and bathroom, you could see my entire apartment from the doorway, with a galley kitchen to the left and my living and dining area to the right.

"Thanks for letting me watch the game here. I can't see anything on our 24-inch, antique of a TV." Rick's wife was having a neighborhood gardening group over and she had banned him to the basement.

"No problem. Seems the least I could do, after you game me the free tickets last weekend. Want a beer?"

"Thought you'd never ask."

I returned with a couple of bottles, then sat on the other end of the couch.

"I can lock up, if you need to leave early," Rick said, as the statistics we didn't need to hear continued to scroll by on the screen.

I frowned. "What are you talking about?"

"To go on your date with Nicole, of course." I took the TV off mute, even though the game hadn't started.

"I'm just saying, what's it been? Two weeks?" asked Rick.

"Nine days."

"But who's counting, right?" replied Rick, grinning. "What's the holdup?"

I let out an exasperated snort, then shook my head. "There's no holdup. You've heard what's been happening on my project, right?"

Rick laughed. "I'm in the next wing of our building, not the next county. Your technical contact bites off your head, then shows up dead. What's that got to do with Nicole?"

Since Rick wasn't going to give up, I turned the volume down. "I tried."

"Oh, sorry," Rick replied, shaking his head and looking down into his beer. He took a sip.

"No, she didn't turn me down. I called Wednesday to ask, but she was busy. And besides, it's not really a good time to be asking her out."

I could feel Rick's head jerk around to stare at me from the other end of the couch, but I didn't turn. I didn't want the lecture. Fortunately, the game started and we drifted into talk of standings and streaks and possible opponents if the Cards made the playoffs.

Six innings and two beers into the game, Rick asked, "So, why isn't it a good time?"

"Huh?"

"Why isn't it a good time to ask Nicole out?" I shrugged. Rick nodded at the TV with his head. "We're in a commercial break and I'm curious."

I held out my hands. "It's like that old saying. Relationships formed under extreme circumstances seldom last."

"Never heard it. And besides, since when do you follow old wives' tales?"

"There's research supporting it," I said without thinking. Unfortunately, I couldn't renege on an explanation by saying it was the alcohol talking. I'd had this thought earlier in the day before any beer.

Rick said nothing, but held out a hand as if giving me the floor. "In the studies I'm thinking about, researchers would give people something to get their heart rate and blood pressure up – you know, like a dose of caffeine. Then, these people would do different things, like watch a scary movie. Or one about bullying to make them angry. What the studies found was, even though the changes in the body were the same – the same pounding heart, the same sweaty palms – people thought the reason they were worked up was different. Basically, when the body reacts, the brain looks for a reason, and it'll take whatever's handy."

Rick stared at me blankly for several moments, scratching his chin. Finally, he said, "So, you're concerned that Nicole got rattled, her blood pressure went up, and now she thinks she's attracted to you rather than afraid of a mad man?" Rick started laughing.

My blood pressure shot up and I was certain my brain had found the real reason – annoyance with Rick. But unfortunately, there was also an element of truth in his words. "Look, I just think we need some routine. We need a few days when we don't need an armed guard to go to work and no one turns up dead."

Rick slowly shook his head, grinning at me. "For a smart guy, sometimes you think too much. The time is never right." He paused a moment, then added, "But you know, this could still work out for you. By the time Nicole realizes she was confused by everything that's been happening, maybe she'll find something in you to like? Who knows?" He held out both hands, his eyes wide as if this was the most improbable outcome imaginable.

I sighed. "Yeah, who knows."

The pitcher's duel we had been watching morphed into a home-run fest in the seventh inning, ending this topic of conversation. It was just as well, as I conceded to myself that Rick was more right than wrong. I just had to make watching my back and checking all the doors and windows my new norm.

And hopefully, it wouldn't get worse.

TUESDAY, AUGUST 18, 10:44 AM

It had been a week since Worthington had died. It felt like a month to me, because so far, we had heard nothing from the VA.

Sue and Nicole had completed their sections of our work-to-date summary by Thursday morning of last week. I reviewed what Nicole had written about the functions that would be enhanced if the Blocker worked. It was well done – concise, clear, and well-qualified. Even my compulsion to cite every 'unless-this' or 'except-for-that' got little exercise. She knew where we were on thin ice and said as much.

The latest report on Worthington's behavior, which now incorporated the women's notes, was the last piece of our summary, and I delivered the whole to Ken after lunch. He reviewed it immediately, which was fortunate, because at 2:00, the VA requested our input.

Then, we heard nothing from them on Friday. Monday was the same. So was Tuesday, until Ken called, asking me to step into his office.

"Morning," I said as I entered.

Ken was typing on his computer keyboard. He glanced away from the monitor long enough to gesture to the chair across from him.

"Morning, Doc. Getting the right words for this email is proving impossible." He shook his head, scowled, then spoke as he hit a few more keys. "Sometime, I'm going to have to re-read that document you wrote for the VA. Well, that doesn't work."

I narrowed my eyes, trying to separate his reactions into email *vs.* VA-report relevant. What didn't work? Was that frown for me or his note?

Finally, he raised his hands in a show of surrender. "Your description of our status must have had some magic words. The VA added three weeks of labor to the contract with an immediate re-start."

"That's great," I said and meant it.

"I haven't had time to study the additional work," Ken said, "but it looks like they're requesting two things. They want a more detailed breakdown of the electronics, once you have the necessary papers. And second, they reviewed the data on the safety of the technology a second time, but they'd like your team's opinion too – a second, independent psychological assessment. Great job on the interim report."

"Thanks, Ken. Most of the credit goes to Nicole – Ms. Veles. She wrote the description of the likely results from using the device, including the possibility it could have some unintended side effects. I think that's what got the VA interested in more analysis and a quick restart."

"Yeah, I remember that section," Ken said slowly, tapping a couple of fingers on his chin. "With the writeup on Dr. Worthington's behavior, you painted a picture that's...well, nothing concrete but a bit disquieting. You think you'll want some help on the safety analysis?"

Is that code for get someone with experience?

I didn't want that, but I didn't want to mismanage the effort either. "Can we leave that option open? Once we see what they have, I'll know better."

"Sure. And I'll pass along your compliment about Ms. Veles' work to her management."

"Thanks."

"OK, review the VA's new requirements and let me know if there are any issues," said Ken. "Otherwise, we'll accept the extensions. Dr. Jon Huston, the other half of the WHT partnership, will be stepping in for the rest of the job. You'll be meeting him tomorrow at 1:00 PM at his office. I haven't been able to contact Ms. Veles' manager yet, so I'm not sure of her availability, but I've left a message. Any questions?"

"None that I can think of," I replied. I would have been happier if I knew Nicole was available, but since Ken had just found out, the lack of news meant little.

Ken gave me a copy of the revised requirements, and I left to find Sue so we could start reviewing them. I wanted to be familiar with the new work before we met with Huston. I only hoped that he would prove easier to work with than his partner. But on the positive side, I was virtually certain he couldn't be worse.

TUESDAY, AUGUST 18, 2:54 PM

"Damn," the Experimenter muttered to himself, emerging from his session with the Blocker. There were just too many unknowns in the emotional black box that was Subject 3 to deduce why he had died.

His first thought was that in his haste to test the features in the *Advanced Design Document*, he had crossed a wire, misplaced a coil, misdirected a signal. He'd even gotten paper to record his mistake, thinking there might be a future application for it. If it could be stopped short of killing, the effect of his error was clearly more motivating than an electric shock. But as he examined each connection and traced each circuit, he found no errors. It was perfect. Yes, it looked a bit like a bird's nest of wires and disks, but everything started and ended exactly where it should.

So, he had stripped the modifications from the Blocker and checked that it was back to its original configuration...three times. Only then did he don it, seeking solace and insight in the far reaches of his mind.

Initially, the device had chastised him. It had castigated him for cutting corners, for his haste, even though it had produced no faults. There was no room for half-measures or anything less than full commitment in the pursuit of his calling.

Emerging now from the Blocker's grip, the Experimenter rose and left the chamber. Closing the soundproof door behind him, he dropped into his chair and ran a hand through his hair. The Blocker's rebuke was still echoing in his mind.

"I can spare no pain in the quest for perfection," he said. Again, he said, "Spare no pain." And again. He took up his notebook and wrote the Blocker's dictum. He filled 20 sheets with his smallest print, 'spare no pain.' But when he looked away, he feared the maxim would flee his thoughts. He needed something. He needed a reminder in his everyday world of the preciousness of each step on his consciousness-shattering journey.

His eyes tracked around the room, soon falling on the perfect solution. He rose from his chair and walked to a set of gray counters along the laboratory's wall. He carefully positioned his left hand, little finger extended, and then slammed the paper cutter home with his right.

A shriek of agony escaped his lips as pain filled his mind. His awareness receded from the vastness of his being to less than a square inch of his hand. He started toward a drawer at the far end of the counter, but stumbled, nearly losing his footing in the blood pooling on the floor. He paused and took several deep breaths, restoring some of the immediate surroundings to his vision. When he reached the drawer, he removed a tape dispenser and crudely bandaged his finger. It would do...for now.

He returned to his desk and his prized notebook, carefully holding his left hand over a wastebasket. He couldn't chance losing anything he was about to record, because after berating him, the Blocker had made clear what needed to happen next.

The problem was the health of the homeless. Even the heartiest often had chronic illnesses that would not let them endure the rigors of his research. So, when in the grasp of the device, he had seen the solution, as clearly as he now saw the blood pooling in the bottom of the trashcan. He needed to tap into a new pool of potential subjects. He needed young, healthy males. They too would die, but they would endure longer and that was the crux. He needed more time, if he was to work out the details of his brain rewiring protocols.

The change in plans came with a cost. His new prey was in the mainstream. Their disappearance would be noticed. But since they should endure for weeks, rather than days, he would require fewer. And without bodies for the police to examine, no pattern would emerge. Each would be merely another lost soul, succumbing to the pressures of modern life, disappearing from society.

The choice was clear. Subject 4 would be from their number.

With that decision chronicled, the Experimenter put his notebook away and checked the nub that had been his little finger. The bleeding had stopped, but the pain now came in searing waves with his heartbeat. "Spare no pain," he muttered through clenched teeth as he leaned back in his chair.

The *Advanced Design Document* sat on his desk and he caressed it with his right hand. When the modifications from its pages were complete, the Blocker would not suppress brain activity. It would not let a three-pound lump of gray matter decide how to overcome a deficit, but rather, it would direct a rebuild. It would induce a precise image, or a specific smell, or a given feeling, or a certain touch. It would implant exact thoughts and specific memories.

The pain returned in a rush, but the Experimenter didn't cry out. Rather, he laughed. With the advanced capabilities of the Blocker, he would implant his thoughts, his aspirations, his memories in others. He would make copies of himself. He would be immortal. And today, he had bestowed on all those future generations a memory of a throbbing, searing pain from a severed finger. It was his special gift for his future selves.

The Experimenter laughed again at the thought.

WEDNESDAY, AUGUST 19, 12:51 PM

Sue and I reached the third-floor landing of the WHT building about ten minutes before our meeting with Dr. Jon Huston. Laverne was seated at her desk. She looked up and ran a hand over her string of pearls, a smile coming to her face. "Sam, Sue. Welcome back." She paused, then frowned. "Will Nicole be joining you?"

We walked to her desk. "We're not sure, but we hope so." Looking down at my hands, I said, "We were sorry to hear about Dr. Worthington."

When I looked up, she smiled sadly, then nodded. "You're very kind to say that. He'd become so unpredictable. He lost or pushed away about every friend he had. It's terrible the pressure he put on himself." She took a deep breath and tried to brighten her smile. "But life goes on."

"You did some redecorating," said Sue, looking around the landing. "The place looks great." There were three new pictures on the walls and a couple of plants stood in the corners of the room, a third beside her desk.

"Dr. Worthington didn't care for them," Laverne said, then chuckled. "I'm sure Dr. Huston was glad to move them back out here. His office was looking a bit like a home-decorating showroom. Would either of you care for a cup of coffee? A bottle of water?"

"I think we're fine," replied Sue, after we exchanged looks. "We'll let you get back to work."

"Thanks," Laverne said, then added with a tilt of her head toward Sue, "I guess." Sue returned Laverne's smile.

We took seats across from Huston's door. Sue pulled out her phone. I sat watching the stairs. I had been expecting a call from Nicole all morning, and when none came, my concern that she wouldn't be rejoining us had grown. After a minute or two, I heard footsteps and I listened carefully. But as the person came closer, I knew it wasn't Nicole...unless she had gained about 150 pounds. After a moment, an individual appeared – an electrician by the look of the tools and supplies he carried.

Laverne got up from her desk, saying, "I'd like to put the coffee maker over there," she said, pointing to an outlet on the wall to my left. They walked over, and soon the man was busy taking measurements and grumbling about 'turn of the century wiring.'

"Are you trying to finish this project without me?"

I nearly jumped out of the chair when I heard Nicole's voice. She was standing a few feet away, smiling at us.

"My boss was off yesterday and she just got caught up on her voicemail. When I learned we were meeting with Dr. Huston, I called Ken and came right over."

"You're right on time," I said, as a man appeared at Huston's door.

I glanced at Laverne, who nodded, indicating that this was indeed Dr. Jon Huston. He was tall and thin – a Stan Laurel to Worthington's Oliver Hardy. But the differences didn't stop there, as he apparently favored color in his wardrobe. He sported a tweed blazer, tan pants, a blue, oxford shirt, and brown loafers. It was all set off by a flowery tie in various shades of blue, brown, red, and green.

He walked across the landing as we stood to meet him. "I'm Jon Huston. Jon, if you please. You must be Dr. Sam Price," he said, shaking my hand.

"I am, and please call me Sam," I replied.

"Oh, I had heard it was Doc."

I started in surprise. "Sam or Doc. Whichever you prefer," I said, still wondering how he knew this detail.

"Doc it is," he said grinning. He stepped over to Sue to continue the introductions, taking each of our hands in both of his as he did. By the end of two minutes, we were all on a first name basis.

"Shall we step into my office, get down to business?" he asked. We agreed and he led the way. Inside, it was as Laverne had implied – somewhat overcrowded with pictures, plants, and knickknacks, but not overwhelmingly so. I did wonder, however, how the pictures and plants that now graced the reception area had ever fit.

He had a large desk, a chair, two wooden file cabinets, and a wooden bookcase at one end of his office. The other end held four, overstuffed chairs arranged in a circle around a dark, Persian-style rug. Interspersed among the chairs were two, small reading tables, each holding a lamp with a green, glass shade.

He gestured toward the chairs, saying, "Please have a seat." He removed his jacket, hung it on the back of his desk chair, and joined us. He looked at each of us in turn, then said, "WHT won't ever recover from the loss of someone as talented as Ned Worthington. It's not possible. But trust me when I say, I'll do everything in my power to make this project a success. I only ask for a little patience because frankly, Ned was the expert on the technology you will be studying."

"I speak for all of us in saying how sorry we were to hear about the death of your partner." I felt some relief too, as working with Worthington would have been difficult, perhaps dangerous. But that belief didn't diminish the tragedy of his death.

Huston nodded. "Thanks, Doc," he said softly. He glanced down at his hands a moment. When he looked up, he said, "I reviewed the material that Ned gave you and frankly, I can't explain it. He got so protective of the Blocker in the last few months. Didn't trust anyone." He sighed, then added, "Including me, apparently."

"Any idea why?" asked Sue.

"Lots of them," said Huston. "Long hours. Mentally challenging work. Intense competition. We're very much in the position of produce or find a new job. Losing control of a technology like the Blocker would be career ending."

I noticed that he hadn't listed Blocker use as one of the possible reasons for Worthington's paranoia. It must have crossed his mind, but the lack of evidence probably stopped him. Self-experimentation wasn't the kind of accusation a professional would make about a colleague without proof.

"I checked the contract," said Huston, "and pulled the list of materials you're to receive from us. Laverne...." Huston stopped and chuckled. "She wasn't looking forward to it, because Ned was a bit of a pack rat. But she was going to start pulling those files as soon as this meeting got started. She's probably doing it now."

"That's great," I said, sinking back in the chair. Tension that I hadn't noticed until now drained from my body.

"So, you're about to be inundated with data," said Huston. "But I've always found that a few key pieces of information at the start can really help. So, is there anything specific you'd like to discuss?"

The question we had planned for Worthington sprang to my mind. Nicole apparently had the same thought. "Can you tell us what technology the Blocker uses to stimulate the cortex?" she asked.

Huston drew back, his brows knitting. "How it stimulates the brain? Does that mean you haven't seen it?"

"No, we didn't get to that point in the discussion with Dr. Worthington," replied Nicole. She clearly knew how to be diplomatic.

"Well, we'll fix that. Perhaps tomorrow? I'm not sure about the state of his lab."

"That would be great," said Nicole.

"But to answer your question," continued Huston, "it uses TMS. That's, transcranial magnetic stimulation."

Huston could have said that it used a technology left by an advanced race of aliens for all this phrase meant to me. I glanced at Nicole, who gave me an almost imperceptible nod. That was good enough for me; my question could wait.

"In simple terms," said Huston, "the Neural Activity Blocker uses TMS to suppress on-going thought processes. So, if an individual was trying to remember numbers, as in the digit span task, beta and gamma waves would generally be produced. If the Blocker, however, was inducing something else, say an alpha wave, then the brain wouldn't be able to process the information."

I'd signed up for a biofeedback class once, which was designed to help people produce alpha waves. I remembered that these waves are associated with relaxed awareness, because people kept falling asleep. But the other brain waves and the types of thought that produced them? I'd need to find out later. But the basic idea of the Blocker – push task-relevant thoughts out of the mind in favor of daydreaming? That sounded familiar.

"Doc, you look like there's something on your mind," said Huston.

His comment made me realize I was frowning. "Just curious, really. You're saying that you're producing a drowsiness or a relaxed state in place of what the person was trying to do?"

"In the case of the Blocker inducing alpha waves, yes, that would be right."

"So, aren't you, in effect, producing something like an altered state of consciousness? The person is trying to remember a list of numbers, but ends up thinking about...I don't know, how peaceful the blue wall looks."

"Something like a drug interfering with a person's thoughts?" Huston asked, raising an eyebrow.

"Exactly." If I had pushed Worthington this hard, he would have thrown me out his third-floor, office window. Huston, on the other hand, was not only taking it in stride, but appeared to be enjoying a bit of a philosophical debate.

"Ned tended to see it the same way – like the Blocker was an electronic drug, and hopefully, one with none of the side effects of chemicals. In fact, he used the same protocols as pharmaceutical studies. Participants were informed that the device could produce altered states of consciousness, and that they might find the tasks we gave them difficult when under its influence."

I nodded, considering the approach. "Seems appropriate," I admitted.

"I noticed the VA asked you to review the safety analyses on the Blocker," said Huston. He stood, walked over to the bookcase, and removed a document that must have been three inches thick. As he turned back towards us, he said, "Ned and I always crosschecked each other's safety analyses, so I'm familiar with this part of the work. Later, I got busy with other projects, and Ned carried on alone. From a business perspective, being too busy is a good problem to have, but now I wish it had been different."

There was an undercurrent of melancholy in his voice, and Huston paused a moment looking away. Turning back to us, he said, "This should answer most of your questions. TMS has been under development since the 1980s, and it has an excellent safety record. The Food and Drug Administration has recognized it for the treatment of migraines and severe depression. That fact, of course, didn't relieve us of our responsibility. We conducted an analysis for our own specific use, and that's what's contained in this document."

"Thanks. We'll get this back to you when we're done," I said.

"It's yours. I had a copy made."

"Thanks," I said again. "We're to focus on the psychological side of the safety analyses. Did you witness any unusual behavioral effects?"

Huston chuckled. "Nothing more unusual than you'd see any time you isolate the hemispheres. I can describe a typical study, if you wish."

"I'd be interested," Nicole said.

"Sure. Let's see, what would be a good example?" He paused a moment, his chin resting on a hand. "OK, in one session we blocked the left hemisphere and showed our participants a picture of a common object – either an egg, a pencil, or a cup. Then, we asked them what they saw. What do you think we got?"

"Well, if the Blocker works, then probably nothing from most people," said Sue. "Or some word that's similar, but not quite right. Language tends to be processed in the left hemisphere and you're making it unavailable."

"And that's what we found," said Huston. "Then, suppose we let them try to find the object inside a bag without looking using their left hand?"

Suddenly, I was back in graduate school with a professor who preferred the Socratic method. Even the encouraging nods and smiles from Huston felt right. The shift in mood from our dealings with Worthington was so extreme as to be disorienting.

"Since they had processed the image on the right side of the brain," continued Sue, "the left hand should be able to find it by feel. But not the right hand."

Huston chuckled. "You're obviously familiar with the split-brain studies."

Sue nodded. "The research is pretty well known in psychology...well, in education and the popular press too, for that matter. Although it seems like it's been overextended in some fads."

"I would tend to agree," said Huston. "We ran other tests, of course, and you can read about those in the volume I gave you."

"During the safety analyses when you were blocking the left hemisphere, did you see any evidence of the participant's gaining any language ability?" I asked.

"No, these trials were only 60 minutes. Since silent rehearsal is a common strategy for remembering lists, we looked closely at language. We also looked at the ability to control the right hand, but we found nothing in either area."

"The right hand?" I asked, not sure why there would be change there.

"Yes, A.T. had to type his response with the right hand, and with the left hemisphere blocked.... Well, as you know, he'd have little control at first." He paused, scratched his chin. "In fact, that part of the task might have been harder for A.T. to develop than language. Didn't Ned mention that?"

"Not that I remember. Thanks." Clearly, Huston didn't realize how little, beyond disdain, Worthington had communicated to us.

Huston looked from face to face, then said, "I know we haven't covered much today, but if it's acceptable to you, I'd like to suggest we break until tomorrow. I have some phone calls I need to make. And tomorrow from 8:00 AM on, my calendar's open."

Seeing no hesitancy in the faces of my companions, I said, "Sure. How about we start at 9:00 AM."

"Excellent," said Huston. "I'll give you some history on the Neural Activity Blocker." He paused, as if considering his words carefully. "Frankly, not all of it is pleasant, but you should have the background. And in the meantime, you can do some light reading," he said, tipping his head toward the safety analysis.

He received the chuckles mixed with groans he expected. "Seriously, thanks for being flexible," Huston said.

We left his office, but didn't find Laverne at her desk. Perhaps she was on a break, or maybe she was digging up the files we had requested. I hoped the latter; I was anxious to get them.

When we reached the first floor, I said, "Rather than all of us driving back to Ruger-Phillips, what about a short recap now?" I had noticed a St. Louis Bread Company restaurant on our first visit. "How about the Bread Co just down the block?"

Nicole said "Sure," as Sue nodded her agreement.

WEDNESDAY, AUGUST 19, 2:23 PM

"Can you believe we're even in the same lab?" asked Sue, as she and Nicole approached the booth I had claimed at the Bread Co. "It's like night and day, the way things have changed."

I picked up my bagel and coffee and slid over when Sue stood next to me with an iced tea. Nicole took the other side.

"True," I said. "But it's almost too good to be true."

Both women stopped what they were doing and stared at me. But after a moment's reflection, I had no specifics. "It's probably nothing. Just the sudden change, like Sue said."

"Yeah, we may get what we need without the National Guard," said Sue.

I glanced at her out of the corner of my eye, taking a bite of a bagel. Noticing my look, Sue turned fully toward me and said, "Yeah, I sat by you so I could slip a hand on your knee when Nicole's not looking."

Fortunately, I got the napkin over my mouth before I choked.

"Or I figured we'd have the same questions for Nicole, and this way, we can both see her."

"OK, I can buy that," I said. "You first or me?"

Nicole put her drink down, as Sue raised a hand toward me.

"OK," I said. "Brain waves and how they're related to different mental states? I only remember Alpha waves for sure."

Nicole twirled a strand of her brown hair around a finger, then said, "This place has Wi-Fi, right?"

She pulled a laptop from her bag before either of us could answer. "In general, Delta waves are characteristic of a coma or deep sleep. Theta waves are produced during lighter sleep, during some types of emotions, and when dreaming. Alpha is relaxed thought, like daydreaming."

All the time she was talking, her hands were moving quickly over the laptop keyboard as she found the signal and logged in.

"Beta waves are dominant when someone is anxious or actively thinking about a problem. Finally, Gamma waves represent what you might call higher-level thinking – the integration of simpler thoughts, experiences, and actions. And here's the frequencies of those waves," she said, spinning the laptop toward us.

I glanced at the screen, not sure if I was more impressed with Nicole's ability to recall the detail or to find the website so quickly when she wasn't focusing. She probably noticed the look of disbelief on my face, as she said, "This is right off my company's home page, and I have that bookmarked, of course."

"It was still fast," I said. "And it's Delta, Theta, Alpha, Beta, Gamma from coma to complex thought, right?"

"In general terms, yes," she replied.

I glanced at Sue, who appeared happy to let me ask the questions. "TMS?"

Nicole spun the laptop back toward her, typing as she talked. "Transcranial magnetic stimulation. It creates a magnetic field outside the skull, which in turn creates electric currents inside. You stimulate the brain, but without putting electrodes on or through the skull.

"Yeah, I never liked the idea of having holes drilled in my head," said Sue. "And the point is to change the activity level in the brain using TMS?"

"When it's used for depression, yes, that's the idea. Long-term treatment increases brain activity in areas that were relatively quiet. But there's still a lot of research. People are looking at things like the frequency of the stimulation, its strength, its location. I'm not sure we've done more than scratch the surface. Here's a picture," she said, turning the laptop back to us again.

It showed something like two, thick metal disks – almost the size of tuna cans – attached side by side and held near a person's head.

"Some of the patents Worthington received were for TMS coil design," said Sue. "Guess that makes sense, if he's going to come up with something like the Blocker."

I took my last bite of bagel and washed it down with a sip of coffee. "That's it for me. Sue?"

"Nada," she replied. "You covered them."

We both looked at Nicole. "With Sam explaining what the split-brain studies were about and the list we put together of the left hemisphere functions...well, the discussion this morning seemed pretty clear." Nicole had mentioned our after-hours talk enough now that Sue had stopped giving me a knowing nod. But she did say to Nicole, "Show off."

Nicole faked a scowl in response. "But hearing about some of those safety studies," she said. "I mean, someone can see an object, can't name it, but can find it in a bag without looking. I understand why that happens, but it's so...."

"Weird?" suggested Sue.

"Or incredible," Nicole said. "It's incredible how these parts of the brain can be so well coordinated in everyday life, yet so independent when we give them the chance."

At her words, I recalled my amazement when I had first encountered this research. "With the constant communication between them," I said, "there aren't many clues about what they can do separately, except from some isolated case studies. But I guess Worthington's technology might change all of that."

Nicole picked up her tea. I leaned back and sipped my coffee. Sue sat looking out the window. I can't say what the women were thinking, but I was wondering – with a mixture of excitement and trepidation – about the prospects of all we were discovering.

WEDNESDAY, AUGUST 19, 8:43 PM

The white panel van sat in the darkness of a nearly deserted parking lot. Inside the vehicle, the Experimenter could just make out the sound of the trucks on Interstate-70, probably a quarter-mile away. In the dim rays from the dashboard light, he stared at the words in his notebook, 'Spare no pain.'

"It should be, share the pain," he muttered to himself. In the last 24 hours, he had found two good candidates for that fate.

The first was his office administrator. She had always been a bit emotional, but she had become hysterical when she saw the nub that had been his left, little finger. She had shrieked, knocking her desk chair over as she jumped up in horror. The Experimenter hadn't known that was possible with a chair on rollers.

She had finally calmed herself enough to call for transportation to the hospital, but not before she dropped the phone twice. When she hung up, she started fanning herself and bemoaning the cruelty of his accident. After a few moments, she stood and walked to the filing cabinets, as if she was going to straighten something there. But she touched nothing. Then, she returned to her desk to fan some more. And whimper some more. Soon, the pattern repeated.

His assistant's constant, pointless activity and her inane chatter battered his psyche. Finally, her emotional torrent became too much, and he went to his lab intent on returning with the Blocker to silence her, intent on sharing the pain.

But logic had prevailed. She was too close. Her disappearance would bring unwanted attention. He'd already resorted to electronic communications for most of their dealings. It just needed to be all of them, because she was and always would be so ordinarily human in her thinking.

As for the second candidate to share the pain, the Experimenter was about to meet with him. Not trusting his memory from the previous encounter, he read the man's name and physical description from his notebook. He exited the van and walked across the parking lot with his briefcase and a box of parts.

It was well past normal working hours for the small, local engineering firm, but with what he was paying them, they could meet him on his schedule. And the night was much less distressing. He pressed a doorbell and after a moment, a man fitting the description appeared.

"You must work long hours," said Nils Jurgensen.

"I do," said the Experimenter, looking at but not taking the hand Jurgensen offered.

"Well, I can respect that," said Jurgensen, the slight frown from the snub disappearing an instant after it formed. "I'm only too glad to come in when you have the time. Let's step back into the shop and take a look at those parts. I have some butts to kick, if they're out of spec."

The Experimenter donned his color-suppressing glasses. Jurgensen frowned, but said nothing. They walked past a reception desk, Jurgensen entering a code to give them access to a work area beyond.

"Ah, it's a crazy time for me. We just had our first child – a boy." Jurgensen paused, expecting the usual congratulations, but it never came. "Our current place is so small. I gotta find something bigger soon, or I'll never get any sleep. You have kids?"

"No, although occasionally I feel like I do."

They had reached a worktable and Jurgensen turned to look at the Experimenter, his forehead wrinkling.

"The people I work with require a lot of my time."

"Oh, sure," said Jurgensen. "Some of the kids we hire don't know a lathe from a lamppost."

The Experimenter handed over the box of parts and Jurgensen spilled a few metal disks onto the work surface. Retrieving a micrometer caliper, he measured several of them. By the second, he was already shaking his head.

"Well, you're right. They're off. No doubt about it."

"I don't make mistakes," the Experimenter said evenly.

Jurgensen's lips drew into a tight line and he nodded once. "Yeah, sorry. Any chance you can work with these? I can give you a great price."

The Experimenter glanced at the bandage on his left hand.

"Ouch," said Jurgensen. "What happened to your hand?"

"Sorry, but I have no use for your mistakes," said the Experimenter, ignoring the question. "I need them replaced."

Jurgensen took a breath. "Of course. Sure. Our work's guaranteed. Bring us some more stock and we'll machine the replacements for free."

Logically, it was a setback; the Experimenter had even expected it. But standing here now, the man's words felt like a physical assault. They were squeezing the life out of his body, as surely as fingers around his throat. Adrenaline poured into his blood stream. His heart pounded in his chest. His body trembled with pent up rage. He fought against the urge to lash out, knowing that the man was not actually threatening his life, but at the moment, logic held no sway with the ancient parts of his brain.

He set his briefcase on the work counter and opened the top. Reaching inside, he rubbed his hand across the fabric of the Blocker cap. His fingers tingled at the touch, a wave of relaxation spreading through his body. Even though this cap wasn't set for his use, wasn't even turned on, its mere presence reminded him of the electronic sanctuary awaiting him at his lab. Logic reasserted itself. Taking this man would get him nowhere.

"I don't have enough of the stock on hand," the Experimenter said, his voice reflecting the fatigue he felt from fighting his instincts.

"Sure, bring it in whenever you can. I'll make sure it's at the top of our queue." Jurgensen paused. "Look, I'm really sorry about our screwup. At least, as small as those parts are, it shouldn't cost that much."

"Three thousand, six hundred, seventeen dollars, plus shipping."

Jurgensen frowned. "That's just a guess, right?"

The Experimenter could have explained that given the exact dimensions of each disk, the loss from machining, and the cost of the stock, this price was exact. Instead, he said, "Ballpark."

Not trusting that his calm would hold, the Experimenter closed his briefcase, put the disks back into the box, and turned to leave. Jurgensen followed him to the front door.

When they arrived, Jurgensen said, "Sorry again. I should be able to get you the corrected parts the day after we receive the material." He paused a moment, looking at the Experimenter. "You know, I looked you up online."

The Experimenter's hand moved to the clasp on his briefcase, a finger nestled against it. He could have the Blocker cap out in seconds, but holding it on the head of a struggling man? That would be difficult. Unfortunately, the Taser was in the van.

"Really?" replied the Experimenter. "Find anything interesting?"

"Tons," said Jurgensen. "I have to say, we're honored to have someone like you, Dr. Atwood, coming to us. I mean, you've been involved with some real pioneering work. It's a real privilege."

The Experimenter stared at Jurgensen, his fingers continuing to caress the clasp. Finally, he dropped his hand and nodded. "Fix your mistake and we can both value the association." He turned and left the building.

The Experimenter walked across the parking lot, took a seat inside the van, and rolled down the window. Jurgensen was infuriating, but this was neither the time nor the place to remedy that situation. In a moment, the engineering building went dark. Jurgensen exited the front door, walked to a car parked alongside the building, and drove away.

The Experimenter reached for the ignition, his hand stopping just as it touched the key. In the pools of light from the street lamps, he noticed movement. He looked closer. A man was jogging along the shoulder of the road, his movements slow and jerky. He reached forward again to start the van, but again paused.

"Are you OK?" called the Experimenter, as the jogger passed within a few yards of his vehicle.

The jogger veered from his path, his hands coming up in defense. The Experimenter cracked the door of the van, filling the cabin with light.

"Sorry, I didn't mean to startle you."

The jogger dropped his hands and took a step forward. "Just cramping up a little. Spent half the day on a plane and probably didn't drink enough for this run."

"Yeah, you'll sweat it off here. Where you from?"

"Seattle," the jogger replied. "It's warm there too, but nothing like this humidity. I usually get in a four or five-mile run, no problem."

The Experimenter nodded. "Staying in shape. That's a good habit. You need a ride somewhere?"

"Oh, no, that's OK. I'm just going to the hotel up the street."

"Suit yourself," the Experimenter said, as he closed the door and reached forward as if to start the van. "Hey, would a bottle of water help? I have some in the back."

The jogger hesitated, then said, "That's OK. I'm almost back."

"It's no problem. I have a couple of cases in the back and I was going to get a bottle anyway."

The jogger hesitated again. "OK, thanks. I'd hate to strain a muscle, just for the lack of a drink."

The Experimenter got out and opened one of the side doors as the jogger hobbled over. "Looks like the water's on the other side. Have a seat and I'll go around and get it."

The jogger sat, turning halfway into the van to watch as the Experimenter opened the door on the other side and removed a bottle from the case. He tossed it across.

The jogger caught it and removed the top to take a sip.

The Experimenter slipped his hand into a bag hidden behind the cases of water. He withdrew the Taser, careful to keep it out of sight.

"You got a lot of hooks and rings in the back here," said the jogger, as he turned to look out into the night.

"Just tie-downs when I'm hauling cargo." The Experimenter raised the weapon, steadied his hand, and fired. The jogger slumped into the van, as the weapon delivered its paralyzing charge.

"You see, Subject Number 4, I don't like my cargo moving when I'm trying to drive," he said, as he retrieved the restraints from the bag. "Someone could get hurt."

THURSDAY, AUGUST 20, 8:58 AM

"**N**o really," said Sue, as we climbed the last flight of stairs to the third-floor landing of the WHT building. "I'd like a bumper sticker that says, children in the backseat cause accidents, but accidents in the backseat cause children."

Nicole groaned, saying, "That may be a bit long for a bumper sticker."

"No problem," she replied. "I'll get another that says, if you can read my bumper stickers, back off. You don't know me that well."

Nicole covered her mouth, shaking her head and laughing. It wasn't that Sue was that funny, but rather, she had been reeling off these one-liners since we ran into her in the parking lot. I had seen it before, so I stepped aside and let Nicole play straight man.

"Laverne's not here," I said, as we topped the last step. "But it looks like someone left us a note." I went over and read it, "Make yourself at home in my office."

I looked at Sue and Nicole, then my watch. "Almost 9:00." I tapped on Huston's door, in case he was already there, but heard nothing from inside. We entered. His jacket was draped over the back of his chair like the day before, but otherwise, there was no sign of him. We resumed our places in the conversation area. Despite the collegial atmosphere of the previous day, I felt somewhat tense. Even Sue had run out of quips, as we sat there quietly.

Huston burst through the door to his lab a bit breathless, almost as if he had been at a full run. "Good, you're here. You haven't had to wait long, have you?"

With this reminder of the vast difference between our original host and our new one, the tension drained away. "No, we just arrived."

"Excellent," Huston said. He was wearing a white lab coat, but removed it as he walked to his desk. He threw it over the arm of the chair with his jacket, making it look more like a coatrack than a place to sit. Then, he retrieved a few pages from one of the desk drawers and took a seat with us.

"Like I mentioned yesterday, I want to give you a little background on Ned's research. I guess some of what I'm going to say isn't strictly necessary, but it'll provide some perspective."

Huston checked the papers he had retrieved from his desk. "The proposal you read – Ned submitted it to the VA about 19 months ago. They were interested in his ideas, called several meetings with him, but they were slow to make a decision. So, he took the opportunity to get a jump start. That's not unusual for us. We often prototype a technology so we have something real to show a potential funding agency.

"Anyway, the early work was very successful, with one exception. Ned learned he couldn't control the Blocker precisely. So, he proposed a proof of concept – aim the Neural Activity Blocker at a hemisphere, rather than at the part of the cortex controlling a limb."

"There was a second proposal?" I asked.

Huston scratched his chin idly. "There would have been some paperwork, but at that point, Ned had been talking to them for a while. It may be only a page or two...plus a budget. I'll have Laverne find whatever we have."

"Thanks."

Huston glanced at his notes again. "It was in August, over a year ago, when the VA agreed to fund Ned, and within two months, the clinical trials with A.T. started. I was busy with other matters, but the reports I got from Ned were glowing. If anything, he felt that the effects of the Blocker were even more profound than he expected."

"More profound?" Sue asked, showing the same slight frown that covered each of our faces. "In what sense?"

"Facility with math." Huston rubbed the back of his neck with a hand. "One of the first times it came up, A.T. had just recalled a list, then added one more number at the end. When Ned asked what it was, A.T. said it was the sum. Of course, Ned thought he was joking, but he checked and sure enough, it was. When he asked A.T. why he had done that, he said the number just popped into his head."

I shifted in my chair, stealing glances at the women. Both were looking at Huston closely, their brows knitted.

"I know that sounds strange," said Huston, "but in the context of this research? Maybe not so much. The additional capacity A.T. would have from using the Blocker would have to go somewhere. Having it involved in mental math wasn't that surprising. And besides, Ned had always been enthusiastic about his research. I thought some of his claims might have been slightly exaggerated." Huston looked down at the floor and rubbed his forehead. "Not one of my better deductions, was it?" He sighed deeply.

He looked up and continued. "About six months ago, in November, things started changing. At first, A.T. seemed to get more invested in the research. He had figured out how to adjust the Blocker and argued vigorously to do so. But before you ask, I don't know exactly what he had in mind. Ned only told me after the fact, and he had already stopped him. Shortly after that, A.T. started regressing. He said he couldn't remember lists that previously had been easy."

"Are you saying A.T. held back because he wasn't allowed to change the Blocker?" asked Nicole.

"Maybe," said Huston. "We discussed the possibility, but had no way to know. Anyway, Ned was anxious to find something to reverse the losses, so he switched to recalling letters and nonsense syllables. At first, that seemed to work, but soon, A.T.'s ability disappeared again. At that point, Ned was sure he was feigning his loss, but he had no proof. Things continued to deteriorate. The morning I heard the study was over, I wasn't sure if Ned had canceled it or if A.T. had withdrawn. It was the latter. That was late December."

Someone knocked on Huston's door and we all turned as Laverne appeared. "Doctor H, can I see you a moment?"

"Please excuse me," Huston said, as he stepped outside into the reception area.

"What do you make of the tension at the end of the study?" asked Nicole after Huston had left.

"I'm not sure," I replied. "Huston's recalling this after several months of turmoil and his partner's death. It might be nothing, but we'll need to look at all of the other data around this same time."

"I'm surprised A.T. didn't go bonkers long before it was over," said Sue. "Four months, looking at numbers? And besides, this is all coming from Worthington's side. If he was anywhere near as volatile during the study as he was with us.... Well, faking the loss of his ability might have been the easiest way for A.T. to get out."

Sue paused, pulling on an ear as she gazed across the room. "But then, we're certainly getting indications – both from Laverne and Huston – that Worthington was different back then. You think that's possible?"

"It seems likely," Nicole said, "as consistent as they are. But the question is, why the change?"

"Hopefully, the rest of Huston's story will explain it," I said. "And personally, I can hardly wait to hear it."

✳ ✳ ✳

"Sorry, that took a lot longer than I expected," said Huston as he entered his office after about 25 minutes. He walked across the room and took a seat with us.

"No problem," I said. "Gave us all a chance to think about what you were saying."

Huston nodded, then grimaced in an exaggerated way. "Unfortunately, we have a problem." He took a deep breath. "Laverne has been through Ned's lab, and the files you need aren't there."

I flinched at his words and picked up the sound of Nicole and Sue shifting in their seats. I was searching for something to say when Huston continued.

"But it may not be as bad as it sounds. I think we've found them. The reason I was gone so long was because I called Beth – Ms. Elizabeth Scott, Ned's wife. She has several boxes of his notes and she's having his safe opened. Since the files you need aren't here, they must be somewhere in those boxes. She'll bring them by this afternoon at 1:30."

"OK," I said slowly, shooting glances at Sue and Nicole. "But wouldn't she rather go through them herself, then just give us what we need?"

"She did that and didn't find anything she thought was from the study, but she doesn't know what to look for. She's afraid she missed your files. I'd have Laverne check, but she'll be on vacation starting tomorrow." Huston scratched his cheek, then held out a hand. "I guess I could hire a graduate student to go through them, if you'd like that better?"

I paused, still wondering if there was an option that didn't involve going through a dead man's papers. But this was Sue's and my only job for the next five months, so to decline meant we would be sitting at our desks, waiting for Laverne to come back from vacation or some unknown grad student to pick through Worthington's notes...and probably miss what we needed.

I was about to agree to meet with Scott when Huston said, "Frankly, I was going to suggest you talk with Beth even before this came up. We're getting to a time when I didn't see Ned that often. Beth would know a lot more about what was going on."

I shifted in my chair, my gaze dropping to the floor. That didn't help resolve my quandary at all. If anything, it made it worse. I looked up at Huston. "That seems like a lot to ask," I said, frowning. "I mean, her husband just died."

Huston nodded slowly, looking at me. "I'll tell you what. I'll ask and let you know what she says. But she'll probably welcome the chance to have you hear about Ned from her perspective, rather than what you read in the papers."

I looked at the women, receiving a steady gaze and a slight nod in return. "OK," I said, turning to Huston. "We'll be back this afternoon to meet with Ms. Scott, if she's interested, and to get the papers."

"Excellent," he replied, returning to his upbeat, enthusiastic self. "What I propose is that you come by the office at 1:00 to see the Blocker. I checked, and it's ready and waiting. Then, you can meet Beth at 1:30. Work for you?"

"Yeah, sounds great." We said our good-byes and left.

THURSDAY, AUGUST 20, 12:57 PM

We hadn't even had time to ask Laverne about her vacation plans when Huston burst into the reception area. He must have heard us on the stairs.

"Excellent, you're here," he said. "The Blocker's this way."

He led Sue, Nicole, and I into Worthington's office. I could feel myself tense as we entered. Even when empty, the arrangement with the massive desk across from the chairs lined against the wall said arrogance. But Laverne had already started to work her redecorating magic, as a few pictures now graced the area.

Huston entered a number on a keypad and we entered Worthington's lab. Prominently displayed in the middle of the floor was a suite of equipment I could only assume was the Blocker. It consisted of two, gray metal boxes, stacked on each other. They were about 18 inches wide and about 4 or 5 inches tall. The front panels appeared to be brushed aluminum or something with a similar finish. The top box had a single switch, one knob, and a small, digital meter on the front.

The front of the lower box was considerably more cluttered, with a half dozen indicator lights, several push button switches, three toggle switches, and a second digital meter. Near the bottom, left corner, two cables exited the enclosure. The smaller one went to a computer that sat on a separate table; the other to a cloth cap with a chinstrap. Spaced across the surface of the cap were numerous disks, each about the diameter of a quarter, although considerably thicker. The cap rested on the arm of a reclining chair.

"Are those metal disks the TMS coils?" Sue asked as she pointed to them.

"They are."

"They're certainly a lot smaller than what we saw."

Huston looked confused until Nicole clarified. "I showed them a typical figure-8 configuration used for treating depression."

"Sure," replied Huston. "It was the design of these coils and the timing of their firing that were Ned's primary technical breakthroughs. Without those advances, we wouldn't have the Neural Activity Blocker." He paused a moment, then added, "I'd be remiss if I didn't also mention that Dr. Sebastian Atwood had a lot to do with the materials used in the coils."

"Yeah, we met Dr. Atwood at our first meeting," said Sue. "Although I don't remember him taking credit for the coils." She glanced at Nicole and I out of the corner of her eye, probably to make sure we recalled the man who hadn't even said 'Hello,' much less talked about his research.

Huston scratched his chin. "Really. I'm surprised about that. Sebastian Atwood is a material scientist – a very successful one in fact. But other than the metal used in the coils, he wouldn't know much about the technology." He paused a moment. "Maybe Ned thought you'd have questions in that area."

"Yeah, maybe," Sue said.

I couldn't see why Worthington would have anticipated questions about the metal when there were so many other things he had failed to disclose. But that unsettling thought disappeared, when Nicole asked, "Is this the only Blocker?"

"Probably," said Huston.

Perhaps seeing my frown, he elaborated. "Most of a Blocker is either commercially available components or uses cheap, raw materials, like the yards of wire in the coils. But their core is a somewhat expensive, proprietary metal, and we have less in inventory than I expected."

Then, Huston raised a hand and snapped his fingers. "Ned might have loaned some of the core material to Atwood's lab. I'll check on that."

Everyone became quiet, as we gazed at the boxes and knobs, meters and wires in the device before us.

Is that capable of all I think...and any of what I fear?

I glanced at Nicole. Her lips were slightly parted. Her eyes were wide. I could almost feel the awe and wonder radiating from her. She walked over to the device and ran a hand across each panel. I looked at Huston, who was smiling, as if he understood and perhaps shared her fascination.

"The top box is the power supply," said Huston. "The bottom is what you'd think of as the Blocker. The computer controls the settings for the equipment. Even though this layout is bulky, once perfected, Ned thought devices for specific uses, like relaxation or pain treatment, would be small enough to carry...well, maybe even in your pocket."

"Amazing," said Nicole, "given the size of TMS devices now."

Huston nodded, his look going far away, as if he too was in awe of his partner's accomplishments.

Knowing that Nicole would be digging much deeper into these electronics than I could ever fathom by asking about each knob and switch, I didn't. After a few moments, Huston asked, "Anyone want to give it a try? Just alpha waves to both hemispheres, so it should be relaxing."

I was about to volunteer when Nicole spoke up. "Does the Blocker produce the same sort of tapping sensation as most TMS devices? I've heard it can be a little...unpleasant, especially at first."

"No, it doesn't. By reducing and dispersing the stimulation, it's more like a humming...or maybe a white noise. Want to give it a try?"

There was that phrase again, 'white noise.' So, perhaps Worthington's earlier description was merely their standard. A flicker of recognition also showed in Nicole's eyes. Then, she rubbed her chin, her gaze moving off toward the corner of the room. "It's tempting, but no. I'll pass," she said, after a few moments.

Sue's head was shaking when I looked her direction. "I'll try it," I said.

"Great," said Huston. "Have a seat and I'll get you hooked up."

Huston produced a consent form from a cabinet along the wall. It was standard; I'd seen ones like it many times before. As I signed it and Huston readied the device, however, my excitement about experiencing the unknown became tempered by my concern about the same. Was this really a good idea? Logically, I knew there was little risk. My exposure was no different than dozens of others who had been in their safety analyses.

With this reasoning running in my head, which at least slowed the stream of adrenaline pumping into my bloodstream, I focused on my goal in volunteering. I wanted to see if the Blocker could really interrupt active thought. I decided I'd count backwards from 100 by 3's in my head, something I had tried several years earlier when I was being anesthetized for surgery for a broken ankle. I had only made it to the upper 80s on that occasion.

"OK," said Huston, when I was all hooked up. "Here goes."

100, 97, 94...91.

It wasn't that I couldn't continue counting, but it no longer seemed important. Not at all.

I remembered Nicole's mentioning a tapping sound. I listened. There was a slight background noise. Where was it? My gaze swept around the room, but it seemed to come from inside my head.

Perhaps there was a slight vibration in the chair too. Or were they the same? It felt soothing, almost like a tingling in my shoulders and back.

I looked up at the wall, noticing a clock hanging there. I watched as the second hand swept around the face. Four. Five. Six. My breaths were coming about every five seconds. No, I needed to stop timing them. I was starting to hold my breath.

Was Huston recording anything? Video? I wondered what it looked like. Maybe, not too bad. Oh, Laverne must have been in here. There's a plant in the corner.

"Doc?"

It was Huston's voice. I looked to my right. He was standing there. My thoughts returned to the here-and-now. "Wow," was all I could think to say. "How long was I...do you call it, being blocked?"

"As good a term as any," Huston said, smiling. "About three minutes. How was it?"

"Interesting," I replied. "It would definitely give biofeedback a run for its money. It wasn't that I felt disoriented so much as just...drifting from thought to thought. Like it was too much trouble to focus."

Huston nodded. "I've heard it described that way before." He glanced at his watch. "Unless someone has a question, we should head for my office. Beth is probably there already." We had none and left.

When we got to the reception area, Laverne's desk was empty. Huston turned to us. "Please give me a moment to talk to Beth. Then, we'll get started." He left us.

"I really should have been the one to try the Blocker," said Sue, as we waited for his return.

"Why's that?" I asked.

"Then, we could get an answer to the question, is the Blocker better than sex?"

I rolled my eyes. Claiming I could answer that question was not anywhere I wanted to go in front of Nicole, but I was struggling to find a different comeback.

"Beth's ready if you are," said Huston, as he appeared in his office doorway.

"We are," I said, thankful for the reprieve.

When we entered, a fifth chair had been added to Huston's conversation area. Seated in one of the chairs was a woman with dark blonde hair and brown eyes. Her face was lightly tanned. She was dressed simply in khaki pants, white blouse, and a light, navy blazer. She rose when we approached, confirming my impression that she was petite – perhaps five feet and an inch or two, if that. Huston did the introductions, which confirmed what I already suspected – this was Ms. Elizabeth Scott, wife of the late Dr. Ned Worthington.

She extended her hand to me. It was small, delicate, but her grip was firm. "Please, call me Beth," she said, her eyes locked on mine.

"I'm Sam Price, and this is Sue Jordan and Nicole Veles," I said, turning to my team. "Sam, Sue, and Nicole, if you please." Scott shook the hands of each of the women, then we all sat.

"Nice to meet all of you," Scott said. "I've brought all the papers from Ned's office and everything from his safe. The safe was empty, except for this."

She picked up a notebook from one of the side tables and handed it to Huston. Under the notebook was a box, about the dimensions of a sheet of paper and approximately four inches deep. On the floor, next to her feet was another box of the type used for copy or typing paper. If I remembered correctly, one could hold 5,000 pages.

Huston examined the notebook. "Excellent. It's the specifications for the Blocker," he said. He handed it to Nicole. "Our first delivery. Unfortunately, finding the rest of what you need is going to take some digging."

Sorting through five thousand pages, if the larger box was packed full, would take some time, but it was manageable. Then, Huston looked toward the corner of the room. My eyes followed his gaze where I found three more of the large containers.

I stepped over and removed a lid from one, nearly gasping at the contents. It was packed tight. It wasn't loose pages, but rather, sheets inside of hundreds of folders. I checked another. It was the same.

"I never expected there to be so much," Huston said. "The offer to hire a grad student still stands...or maybe a couple of them."

I'd been through the pros and cons of that offer in my mind and the magnitude of the task didn't change those factors. "Thanks, but no," I said, as I returned to my chair and sat. "We'll go through them."

"Do you happen to know what type of external drive Dr. Worthington would have used?" Sue asked.

Huston stood and walked over to his desk, where he pulled open a drawer. From it, he produced a thin, black external drive of about four by six inches and perhaps a quarter of an inch thick. "They would look like this."

Great. One of those could be slipped into a folder between pages. We'd never find them without opening each one. And the surveys? They might still be in their original, paper format. We would have to look at every page to be sure we missed nothing – all 20,000 or so of them.

My curiosity had grown, seeing the mountain of paper. Just how and where did it fit into Worthington's story? And why did he do it?

Huston returned the disk to his desk and rejoined us. Once seated, he nodded at Scott.

"I'm convinced that Ned's death was the result of some type of foul play," she said.

What an opening statement.

I would have been more shocked by her words, except Sue, Nicole and I had discussed the possibility at length. In fact, we were living our lives as if this was true. But it was still disturbing, hearing the statement come from her mouth.

"Ned had always been excited about his career, but his passion grew to new levels when he started on that damn Blocker," said Scott. She looked down at the floor, shaking her head before she continued. "And frankly, it was a bit contagious. I also began to think he was on the brink of a true revolution in the field – using the brain's natural plasticity to cure itself? Unbelievable. Truly unbelievable."

She was evidently not concerned about the rumors that she had conspired with Dr. Jerome Caufield, the marriage counselor, to steal the Blocker. Otherwise, this would have been an incriminating admission.

"But that was the mood last year, during the study. I understand you and Jon have already discussed that period, correct?"

"We have," I said.

Scott nodded. "OK. After the study, in January and February, Ned became frustrated. The disappearance of A.T.'s abilities bothered him. He couldn't explain it. And the money had been spent, so he couldn't investigate it. He spent February trying to get the VA to give him more funding, but they balked." Scott paused a moment, then shrugged. "I don't blame them. The reasons were obvious.

"In March or April – even though Ned never said so – I'm convinced he used the Blocker on himself in a last-ditch attempt to find a way out."

Again, her statement was troubling, but nothing we hadn't considered before. And unfortunately, like us, she had no proof. Then, she launched into a story with such vivid detail, I could see it in my mind.

THREE MONTHS EARLIER, WEDNESDAY, MAY 6, 11:27 AM

Elizabeth Scott stared out the window of her second floor, bedroom window, watching as her husband placed an oil painting at the curb. The picture had been a few hundred dollars several years ago, the work of a local, starving artist. But it wasn't the money that concerned Scott. It was her husband.

She picked up her phone and placed a call to an often-used number.

"Dr. Jon Huston, Worthington-Huston Technology," came the voice over the line.

"Hi, Jon. It's Beth. Have a minute?"

"Sure, Beth. What can I do for you?"

"It's Ned."

There was a pause. "So, he's not coming around with the counseling?"

Scott took a long breath and released it slowly. "No. If anything, he's getting worse, but I didn't call to tell you my problems. I just wanted to make sure there's been nothing new at work. Something that might have caused him to get worse."

"Something here?" asked Huston slowly. "Beth, I don't think Ned has been in the office in a month. At least, I never see him. He's not hanging around home?"

Scott sighed again. "He probably is. He's been keeping the door to his study locked. I can't tell if he's in there anymore. Look, I have to go. I need to talk to him while I can find him."

"Sorry, Beth. Let me know if there's anything I can do."

"Thanks, Jon. I will." She disconnected.

Scott left the bedroom, turning right down a short hallway. When she reached the head of the stairs to the living room, she paused. The dark, wooden handrail and carved spindles of the curving staircase was an architectural detail that had sold her on this house. Its elegance was still intact, but now it led to a room devoid of warmth and character. The picture had been the last decoration on the walls, and now, it was gone.

The smell of paint drifted up the stairs, hardly registering in Scott's mind. It had become as commonplace in their home as her perfume or the aroma of meals she cooked but they never shared. She looked down into the room. Ned was sitting on the floor, painting around the baseboard before rolling a new coat on the walls. Soon it would be the same flat, light gray as much of the rest of the house. She was losing the battle for color, and she had no idea why.

She went out to the curb, retrieved the painting, and put it in the garage. She'd move it up to the attic later, so it could take its place next to the other pictures and knickknacks she had saved from the landfill. She went back into the living room.

"Ned, honey?" she said. She might have heard a grunt in response, but doubted it. "I thought we weren't going to repaint this room."

This time she was certain that silence was the only response.

"We talked this over with Dr. Caufield. It's a common area, and we were going to leave those spaces alone. See how we felt about them later. And the picture? Can't we put it back up, at least for a while?"

Still nothing.

"Honey, don't you remember talking to Dr. Caufield about this?"

"I remember him talking. What I don't remember was him listening," replied Worthington.

"He listened," said Scott. She had expected the response, but hoped it might be different this time. "The places we share that haven't been changed yet – this room and the dining room – we were going to leave them alone. Wait a while and see if you...."

"Got better?" said Worthington coldly. "Caufield's a fool."

"I was going to say, change your mind. And Dr. Caufield isn't a fool. He's been in practice for over 20 years."

"Spewing nonsense for 20 years does not make it wisdom." Worthington laid the brush on the top of the paint can and stood. He looked closely at his wife. "You need to listen, because Caufield can't or won't. I can't work, I can't even think with the swirling chaos of this house in my head. The gray works." He sat down and resumed painting.

"But it doesn't work for me, Ned. I can't live in a house that's so...depressing."

Her husband said nothing. Scott recognized the impasse, having reached it many times before. His proclamation that gray was good enough would be his final words. This standoff had been so frequent that she and Dr. Caufield had discussed it in the last appointment – a meeting her husband had refused to attend.

"Ned, Dr. Caufield suggested a way you and I can get beyond this difference." Scott waited a beat, but he said nothing. "He believes we need motivation, more of a reason to really sit down and talk things through. It doesn't have to be at his office, but we need to talk. Don't you agree?"

Worthington moved to a new section of the baseboard, checking that the drop cloth had not pulled away from the wall in the process. Taking a brush full of paint, he continued the detailed work.

Scott sighed. "So, he thought each of us should give up something we like. He'd hold it safe until we earned it back by talking through our issues. You know how I love gardening, right?"

Silence.

"Well, I'm giving him all my gardening tools. I'll let the weeds overtake my roses, until I've gained the right to use them again. Doesn't that make sense?"

"Sense? Hardly," said Worthington, wiping a tiny drop of paint from the baseboard with a damp rag.

"Let's give it a try," said Scott. "For you, Dr. Caufield suggested you give him the big notebook that describes the Blocker. That's more symbolic than real, since you know all the information in it by heart. But that's OK with me."

Worthington froze, the brush in mid-stroke, paint starting to drip down onto the drop cloth. He turned his head so he was looking at his wife's feet. "Caufield suggested this, or did you?" He spoke quietly, his voice flat.

"What?" asked Scott. "I don't remember. Why's that...."

"Did you come up with this idea, or did he?" asked Worthington, his voice still barely above a whisper.

Scott leaned forward, straining to hear her husband's words. He looked up into her face. His eyes were empty, lifeless. She drew back, her hand coming to her throat.

"It's not a hard question," Worthington said, staring into her eyes. "It wasn't that long ago. Who suggested I give him the Blocker documents?"

Scott had seen flashes of this demeanor before, but they had never lasted. Now, however, this mask of cold inhumanity seemed permanently etched into his features.

She drew back, creating some distance between them. If she gave up on their counselor's recommendation now, she would seal the fate of her marriage. If she persisted? She wasn't sure what might happen, but she had to try one more time.

"I told Dr. Caufield the things that each of us value – my gardening, theater, volunteer work. For you, I didn't have many suggestions except work, but we can come up with something else."

Her husband stood and Scott took an involuntary step backwards. He was taller than her, but now, she felt dwarfed by his presence. His cold aggression overtook her like a gathering storm.

"Ned, please, we can find something else. Maybe your golf clubs? I know you haven't played in a while, but you love the game." Her words were coming fast, driven by a growing fear. But for all the sound she was making, she was certain her husband heard nothing. His black stare bored through her, seeing something that wasn't there, wasn't even in the room.

"You best hurry, because Caufield won't be around much longer."

Scott gasped. "Ned, stop. You're scaring me."

"It's him or me."

"What?" stammered Scott, her eyes blinking rapidly. She took another step backwards, her shoe catching on the carpet. She nearly fell. "He's not trying to harm you. He's trying to help."

"He's trying to separate me from my mind, leave my body without the world in which I live. He must die...or I will."

Worthington started toward his study.

"Ned, stop, please," pleaded Scott, tears running down her cheeks. He stopped, but didn't turn. She swallowed, hoping to steady her voice. "We can talk this out. We just need to try." She wanted to approach him, but couldn't. She raised a trembling hand to her lips, trying to hold back the sobs.

He turned around. His stare bored into her. "Don't make me think you had a part in this scheme," Worthington said coldly. "You don't want his fate." He turned and left the room.

THURSDAY, AUGUST 20, 2:44 PM

"I ran from the house and I've never been back," Scott said, as she brought her story to a close. "Of course, I called the police and Dr. Caufield, told them what Ned had said, but neither seemed to take it seriously." She laughed bitterly. "Why should they? I was describing a man possessed by a machine."

Possessed by a machine?

Her words spun in my thoughts. Why would that be? I could think of nothing in our confusing and incomplete picture of this device that would explain such a fixation.

Scott paused, rubbing a hand over her forehead. "Shortly after that day in May, I filed for divorce. I hoped the act would get Ned to meet me, hopefully to restart the dialog some place safe. But he ignored me."

Scott released a single laugh filled with disdain. "In fact, about the only people to pay attention was the press, who made Dr. Caufield and I look like criminals."

I admired Scott. Those days had been hard and to recount them for us with such candor couldn't have been easy. "It's no real consolation of course, but we'll use everything you've said to help us understand this technology."

"You're wrong," Scott said, almost before I finished speaking. "It is a comfort to me, because helping you understand the Blocker gets me one step closer to knowing what happened to Ned. Jon isn't sure he was killed, but I am." She glanced in Huston's direction.

"It's more that I don't know than I doubt it," said Huston. "Ned wasn't around here much during that time. And when he was.... Well, he kept to himself."

Scott nodded. "Anyway, after that he started trying to get his life back. He was coming into his lab here...maybe even sneaking in. I don't know. But within two months, he had requested funding for a study on training. That, of course, is when you got involved."

"Do you think he had quit using the Blocker...I mean, if he was?" asked Sue.

Scott took in a long breath, then released it slowly. "No. He was fighting it, trying to manage it...but no, I don't think he ever stopped completely. Sometimes, he'd call. And when he did, he'd sound exhausted from the battle, old and tired. I could hardly hear him, he spoke so softly. It broke my heart, but at the same time, it made it stronger. He was trying."

The Worthington she now described was the same man who had called me the night he died. Her description couldn't be a coincidence. "Did Ned warn you that you were in danger?" I asked, remembering well the phrase 'I fear for the lives of those around me.'

For a moment, there was a blank look on Scott's face, and then, realization. "He talked to you. He told you about the danger he'd created." It wasn't a question; there wasn't even a trace of uncertainty in her voice. Scott knew.

I had never mentioned the details of the call to Sue or Nicole and I hated catching them off-guard, but I had started down this path. "Yes, he did. He called when I was still in the office, the night of his death. He spoke just as you described – slowly, softly."

Scott's eyes became moist and she looked overcome with grief. I turned away, not wanting to see the pain I had caused. But in a moment, she said simply, "You need to tell this to the police."

"The police are investigating?" asked Sue, stealing the words from my lips.

"Reluctantly," Scott replied, a touch of bitterness in her tone. Then, her voice softened. "With all the strangeness in his actions, it was hard to know what to believe. And his warnings? He kept repeating them, but he never explained. I should have found out...and now, it's too late."

Her grief over these memories became too great, and she dropped her head into her hands. Her shoulders shook in time with the sound of soft sobs.

"I'm a little thirsty," Huston said quietly. "Anyone else want a bottle of water?"

Nicole and I shook our heads, but Sue said, "I would."

Huston got up and walked over toward his desk. He opened a wood panel that covered a small refrigerator. "This thing pays off when you're stuck in the office for hours on end." I had never seen or heard Scott respond, but Huston pulled out three bottles. He returned and handed one to Sue and Scott.

"I'm almost done," said Scott, as she regained her composure. She removed the cap and took a sip of water. She looked face-to-face around the circle. "I believe that A.T. killed Ned. I've gone to the police, but they say they can't do anything because we don't know who he is."

At this point, I wasn't surprised when she finally named her suspect, but frankly, I was stunned to hear the rest. "You don't know who A.T. is?" I asked, turning to Huston.

"The informed consent form that links his initials with his contact information is missing. It's not in the filing cabinet where it should be. Or anywhere else we've looked."

"But you or Laverne would have seen A.T. coming and going," said Nicole. "You'd know who he is, at least by sight."

Huston slowly shook his head. "Unfortunately, no. Much of our work is sensitive, including research on some types of neurological disorders. To maintain our patients' confidentiality, we have a separate, locked entrance to the lab in the back of the building." Huston sighed. "Ned sometimes hired part-time help, but he was running this study alone. I've been racking my brain, trying to figure out how we could identify A.T., but I've come up with nothing."

"But if the informed consent form might be in one of these boxes, wouldn't the police want to look through them?" I asked.

"Well...," Huston started, his head tilting to one side.

"Let me," said Scott. "If we find the form, they'd like to know the name, but they're not going to look. Their minds are made up. They want to close the case as a death by natural causes. And they would, except they're not sure why he died except that it was due to a lack of oxygen. It's like he was strangled, but there's no sign of a struggle. As for the form being in one of the boxes? I looked twice, but I might have missed it, so please, keep your eyes open."

"Would it be the same as the salmon-colored form I just signed?"

"Exactly the same," replied Huston.

"OK," I said. "We'll watch for it."

"Thanks," said Scott. She paused. "You should also know that what I found in those boxes – well, it isn't what I'd expect a scientist to be recording during a study. It's mostly hand-written notes about his daily activities and to-do lists."

I nodded. "Some of what we're looking for, like his observations after each session might look like that," I volunteered, partly to ease her mind and partly to convince myself this wasn't a wasted effort.

"Good," she replied. "I hope you find what you need." She stopped and wrung her hands, again searching our faces. "Beyond the consent form and your files.... Well, I was hoping you'd watch for anything that seems unusual or out of place, and let me or the police know. Would that be possible?"

What did she think was in there?

In the end, the question that flashed into my mind made no difference. Now that I had heard Scott's story, I could no more erase her concerns from my thoughts than I could swim the length of the Mississippi. We were in this together for the duration. "Yes, of course, we can do that."

Scott smiled – the smile of someone who is trying to take some small comfort from an infinitesimal gain in an otherwise losing effort. She glanced at Huston, who responded with a slight nod. "I wish you the best on finding what you need," she said as she stood to leave. "But frankly, I hope you find something to help me even more."

"We'll do our best," I said, as Scott shook each of our hands and left.

With much to do, we thanked Huston for his time and moved the boxes to the reception area. After promising Laverne I'd return for the last one, we each took one downstairs. When we stepped out the front door of the building, I said, "Nothing like a little light reading."

"And this is nothing like it," said Sue in reply.

"Sorry I didn't tell you more about the call from Worthington earlier, but it seemed irrelevant after he was found dead," I said, setting my box on the sidewalk next to theirs. "Truthfully, I was never sure it was a call for help, but I was going to meet him at a Ruger-Phillips building. One with an armed security guard."

"I would hope so," said Sue, "after you warned us over and over to be careful."

"Yeah, and that hasn't changed," I said. "You should stay vigilant." I was relieved when neither of them rolled their eyes and both simply nodded.

Sue scratched a cheek, then looked at me. "You still think Huston's just a little too helpful...like he might have something to hide?"

I turned to her and moved to within inches of her face, a snarl coming to my features. "His motives are obvious, if you weren't blind. Do I have to explain everything to you?"

Sue stepped back, her eyes blinking. "Blind?" she said with a look of concern. Then, a smile overtook her face and she shook her head. "Good one, Doc. You had me going there for a second."

"Yeah, just a case of PBS from my three-minute exposure. That's post-Blocker syndrome, in case you didn't know." I said, grinning back at her.

"And you," said Sue, looking at Nicole. "I heard that titter behind my back. He didn't fool you, did he?"

The sun was behind Nicole, but I could still see the smile on her lips, the twinkle in her hazel eyes. "Nope, not at all. The clenched fists were a good touch, but we communicate without words."

Sue shook her head again. "Doc, live in fear, because now I gotta get even." She grabbed Nicole's elbow, saying, "You're parked by me. I have something to show you."

They picked up their boxes and departed, leaving me standing alone on the sidewalk. I'd hardly heard Sue, her words finding no room among thoughts filled with Nicole's comment. Could it be that she and I were developing a rapport?

No, that wasn't possible. A mental bond isn't formed in one evening of techie talk. She just wanted to tease Sue.

Right?

THURSDAY, AUGUST 20, 8:36 PM

The Experimenter finished updating his notebook and turned his chair to face the one-way mirror. The chamber was empty, producing a pain that was physical, even if the origin was his mind. But he would endure it. He knew the price the Blocker would exact for haste, and so, Subject 4's training would wait until the upgrades from the *Advanced Design Document* were closer to completion.

Turning back to his computer, the Experimenter saw several notifications for videos waiting for his review. It had been a simple matter for him to rent a small office – little more than a storage closet – on the second floor of the building housing the WHT offices. A few days after securing it, he had the locks changed and a surveillance camera mounted above his door. No one seemed to notice that the camera focused on the stairs rather than on his nonexistent visitors. And since the camera was motion-activated, he could watch an entire day's worth of stairway activity in a matter of a few minutes. He had a similar system in the storage area, which was also misaligned. It showed the WHT share of the basement.

With Worthington gone, the research should die, and the Experimenter wondered if there was any reason to watch the comings and goings at WHT. He dismissed the notifications, then dragged the video clips to the trash. But as he dropped them, pain flared in his missing finger. He should know better.

He pulled the files back to his desktop. The clips from the basement were small and he played them first. Each consisted of a trip or two by an unknown office worker, none of whom had accessed the WHT storage area. There was nothing of interest.

Next, he opened the file covering the stairway. "Elizabeth Scott," he said to himself when her face appeared on the screen. "Just what are those two goons of hers carrying?" But he knew what it was. He'd seen these boxes in Worthington's home the night he had killed the good doctor and later, in the pictures he took there.

They were Worthington's replacement for the part of the brain that stored new situations and unfamiliar people. He too had the same...characteristic. But while Worthington dealt with this trait by generating reams of daily trivia, now stored in these boxes, the Experimenter used his notebook.

His approach was so much more elegant. Each day, he would review the last week of entries in the notebook, copy a few notes forward to the current date, and discard the rest, making it work much like memory. If something was repeated frequently enough in real life, it was remembered. If he recopied something often enough in his notebook, it too became permanent.

"No," he hissed, when more arrivals appeared onscreen. He paused the video.

Staring back at him were Sam Price, Sue Jordan, and Nicole Veles. Yes, he knew them, even though he had never met them. But like bad pennies, they kept turning up. They kept earning mentions in his notebook. They kept showing up in his videos. And now, their names and faces were seared into his memory.

"So, cutting off the head didn't kill the beast," he muttered to himself, as he leaned closer to the screen to study the images. Worthington was gone, but the study remained. Jon Huston would have had a hand in its survival, but someone else had to be breathing life into its corpse. Someone else was giving the VA hope that

Worthington's findings were not a sham. Someone else was trying to make sense of the mixed messages that surrounded the study and the technology.

That someone was Price, Jordan, and Veles. They had to be eliminated. He had an idea.

The Experimenter rose from his desk and cut through the experimental chamber on his way to the residence. He flipped on the light switch. Subject 4 sat up, glaring at him. The man had adopted noncooperation as his best weapon and had yet to eat or speak since arriving. The Experimenter wondered how long that would last, once the treatments with the Blocker started.

He removed a prepackaged sandwich and a drink from a refrigerator and tossed them into the cage. They landed next to the sandwich he had given Subject 4 nearly a day ago, when he first arrived. "Don't eat the old one," the Experimenter said. "It might make you sick."

Subject 4 said nothing.

Looking now at the cages, the Experimenter wondered why he had doubted himself. He could fit a half dozen people in the larger cage, if necessary. "Must be lonely in there," the Experimenter said. "Think I'll get you a roomie."

The Experimenter returned to his work area and examined the paused video closely. Price looked healthy, hardy. He would last a long time under the rigors of the Blocker. In fact, the more the Experimenter thought about it, the more he liked the idea. Now that the computer controlled most of the training, he could have two subjects on 12-hour shifts. Or three working eight hours at a time. Then, when one died, he wouldn't have to start over. One of the others could step in and continue the long, hazardous journey through these new mental realms.

That left the question of Jordan and Veles. Unfortunately, they would have to die from mysterious, 'natural' causes. But maybe not

Veles. She wasn't his type – he liked the dark, tall, statuesque beauties. But she was appealing, full of life, and he had his needs. She might make an interesting plaything, once relieved of some of her intellect and all her independence. And if the Blocker could recreate him, it would be a simple matter to strip her of some of her more objectionable traits.

Yes, he could have the device configured for that task in a week...two at most.

FRIDAY, AUGUST 21, 10:36 AM

I went to the window in my office, hands in my pockets looking out at a corner of the parking lot and the freeway beyond. Each Friday morning, I prepared a status report on my projects. Today, the words were coming slowly...or not at all.

So far, my report contained more holes than information. It covered our meetings with Huston and Scott. It highlighted receipt of the Blocker specifications. But there are only so many ways you can take credit for obtaining one notebook, and after I had covered all of them, our lack of progress was apparent.

For the rest of the report, I had pages for what I hoped to find in the next 20 minutes. I had a page showing the number and size of external disk drives we had found. Maybe I could even copy their directories and include that information. The listing wouldn't have any significance, but it would look good. I had a page for the number of observation reports, the number of mood surveys, and so on. I had all those blanks, just waiting for a number...any number.

Since I hadn't bothered Sue for an update since early morning and Nicole not at all today, I wandered over to Sue's desk.

"Doc," she said, when she saw me approaching. "I just ran across a statistic I know you'd love."

It sounded like a set-up, but then, I was talking to Sue. What else could it be? "Yeah, what's that?" I asked, as I sat down across the desk from her.

"I found out that 47% of males don't know how to use protection during sex. In fact, this paper said it was such a well-defined group that the researchers gave them their own name."

She paused. There was no point delaying the inevitable. "So, what did they call them?"

"Dads."

"Ouch. That's bad," I said, shaking my head.

"Thought you'd like it. What's on your mind?"

"I was wondering...make that hoping you or Nicole would have news on the missing files. Can we get her on the phone?"

Sue put her phone on speaker and dialed. After a moment I heard, "Nicole Veles, Biomedical Engineering Associates."

"Nicole, it's Sue. I'm here with Doc. He's looking for an update on the search through Worthington's notes." She turned to me. "I can summarize my progress in three words – I've got nothing. No files, no study-relevant information. Nothing."

"What's in them?" I asked.

"It's like Beth said – daily trivia and to-do lists," Sue replied. "I found receipts for lunch, for a paperback, and for a new pair of socks. I also know that somewhere in his house he did quite a bit of decorating, if you can call it that. He used two different shades of off-white and three shades of gray. Finally, I know that during one stretch, he had fish for lunch 17 straight days."

I massaged my temples with my fingertips. "I don't suppose fish craving's a left-side function."

Sue gave a short, derisive laugh. "I gave up looking for anything on the left hemisphere list a long time ago. He didn't say anything about becoming a math whiz. Or a science nerd." She paused a moment, then grinned. "Or more of one, since he was one already."

"Nicole? Better luck, I hope."

I heard a sigh over the line. "Sorry, Sam. It's the same here. It's clear he's struggling to remember day-to-day events, and names and faces seem to be the worst."

"No kidding," said Sue. "His forgetfulness is only matched by a man's the morning after."

I rolled my eyes, imagining that Nicole was doing the same in her office.

"I did notice that if he met someone often enough, after a while, he'd remember them," said Nicole.

I glanced at Sue, who raised an eyebrow.

"Do you recall an example?" I asked.

"Yeah, I just finished one. WHT hired a man to repair a wall that got damaged when some equipment was delivered. Every entry for four or five days sounded like Worthington was meeting this person for the first time. Then, about the sixth day, it was like a threshold had been hit, and Worthington recognized him when he saw him in the hallway."

"Ladies, thanks. I'll pitch in on the reading as soon as I finish my meeting with Ken."

"I'm hoping to be done by then," said Sue. "If it's not a salmon-colored page or a black, metal box, I skim the one-liners about buying paint and eating fish."

Before I could ask, Nicole volunteered, "I should be done later today too."

"Sue, Nicole, thanks. I owe you both."

"Just doing my job," said Sue.

I laughed. "I'm reasonably certain this isn't in your job description. Seriously, dinner or drinks or something. It's on me."

After getting concurrences from both women and Nicole had hung up, Sue said, "I'm sure you're looking forward to repaying Nicole more than me."

I grinned. "Maybe, but I'll enjoy whatever we do too. Hey, how about I take you and Al to that Mexican restaurant you like tomorrow night?"

"Saturday? That's prime date night. Don't you want to check with Nicole first?"

"I did. She's busy. Still at her aunt's and they have some family thing this weekend."

"Still there?" Sue said, frowning. Then, her expression morphed into a grin. "Her loss is my gain. I accept. But Al didn't read any of this. Let's leave him at home, and when we leave, I'll tell him not to wait up." Sue wiggled her eyebrows at me in an exaggerated fashion, playing the fiction for all it was worth.

I chuckled, then left to print my full-of-holes report for Ken.

* * *

"Come in, Sam. Have a seat," Ken said, when he saw me peer around the edge of his open door.

This wasn't good. I couldn't remember the last time he had used my given name.

"Is that your report?"

"Yeah, it is, but...." He didn't exactly cut me off, but the way he held out his hand made it clear he wanted it, not an excuse.

He flipped through the pages quickly – much too quickly to read them. He looked up. "I guess you've done what you can when we don't have anything. Well, when Ruger-Phillips doesn't. It looks like Biomedical Engineering Associates may be OK."

"Yeah, they have the primary document they need," I replied. "And I think we'll find our stuff soon."

"You're more optimistic than me...and that's fine. I only hope it's not for the wrong reason – like this mission that Dr. Huston and Ms. Scott have you on."

"Mission?" I asked, frowning.

"Going through the boxes of Worthington's notes looking for clues."

I knew what he meant by 'clues,' but I focused on the business reason for our actions instead. "Searching those boxes is the fastest way to get the files we need."

Ken shook his head. "I'm not second guessing you about the search. Perhaps that's the best approach, or maybe you should have let the client do his own house cleaning."

I started to object, but he raised a hand. "I happened to be walking by Sue's desk when she muttered something about Worthington finally remembering to buy a new pair of socks. Socks?"

He ran a hand through his hair, then looked at me. "She was reviewing what appeared to be a shopping list, with a pad of paper next to it with the words 'suspicious behavior' at the top. We're looking for suspicious behavior these days?"

"That was my call. I agreed to let the police know if we found anything strange or out of place when we were going through his notes."

"The police asked you to do that?"

"Well, no," I replied. "Worthington's wife asked us."

"And that's my point." Ken looked down at the top of his desk, slowly shaking his head. "You aren't to be playing detective for those people," he said as he looked up. "You're working for the VA and for me. Find the experimental data...or don't. I don't care. But don't be playing cops and robbers."

"I understand, Ken, but I don't think we've been wasting project time." I should have stopped after the first three words.

"That's garbage," said Ken. "Dr. Huston is sucking you into a drama he's got going in his labs, fueled by Ms. Scott. Don't misunderstand. I feel very sorry for her...and for him. It's tragic when anyone as young as Dr. Worthington dies. And I understand that he was pursuing a very promising technology. But you need to get out of this mad scientist, murder mystery Huston and Worthington's wife are trying to sell and back to the client's job. Is that clear?"

"Yes, it is." This time, I bit my tongue.

"OK. Now, get out of here and focus on the files we need."

* * *

"That blinking light on your phone is a frantic message from me about your meeting with Ken," said Sue. She was sitting in my office. "It says something about protecting the vulnerable parts of your anatomy. How'd it go?"

"I'm still employed...for now."

"If I hadn't had that stupid pad of paper on my desk."

"You were doing exactly what I asked. Besides, the bigger problem is finding anything we can work with. I'm guessing you aren't holding a set of disk drives behind your back."

She looked down, as her hands were resting in her lap. "Apparently not."

"So, how much do you and Nicole have left to read?" I asked.

"I have maybe four inches of folders in the last box. I'd guess Nicole has about the same. Why?"

"I stuck you and Nicole with most of the reading...and for no good reason apparently. Finishing up the last few pages seems the least I can do."

"I'd argue with you, but I'm going cross-eyed wading through that dribble. Thanks."

FRIDAY, AUGUST 21, 2:31 PM

"Twenty minutes and I'm already thinking about leaving," I grumbled aloud. Reading Worthington's notes was already getting to me. I shot a glance at my open office door. Fortunately, no one was standing there. Of course, I could show them a snippet of the minutia of Worthington's days, and they would understand.

I pulled another page from the stack that seemed to grow smaller at about the same rate as continental drift. My eyes were drawn to a paragraph about a third of the way down the page. What made it attention-grabbing was the fact that it was a full paragraph, rather than the one or two-liners that dominated his notes.

I read through it and reached for my phone, but I set it back down. I was about to do exactly what Ken had warned me not to do – get distracted by the hunt for a person who probably had done nothing more than participate in a study, gotten bored with it, and then went on with his life. And the scientist who died in his home? He probably did so in his sleep; there'd certainly been no headline-grabbing news about a murder. But getting a second opinion on this paragraph would only take a moment and I trusted Sue's judgment. I dialed her number and she offered to come by my office, saying she needed the walk.

When she arrived a few minutes later, she was talking on her phone. "Hold on Nicole." Sue put her hand over the receiver. "Just talking about the Blocker specifications document." Then, back into the phone. "I'm in Doc's office. I'll put you on speaker."

"Hi, Sam. Or should I say goodbye and let you two talk?"

"Um, no, that's OK. You can stay on the line. But Sue, would you close the door?"

I was expecting Sue to say something about how kinky it was, wanting one woman alone in my office and another on the phone, but perhaps the excitement tinged with apprehension I felt also showed on my face. She said nothing.

"I found something...well, maybe it's something in Worthington's notes. Let me read it.

"He was in the lab, doing something to one of the power supplies. But the Blocker was right there and I'm sure he'd been checking it out before I came in. I yelled at him, told him to get out. He said he'd finished anyway. How convenient. I should have called the police, but what could they do? He can't be trusted; he wants to ruin me or worse. In the end, all I could do was run Allen Trimmel out of the building myself. But if he comes back, it'll be his last mistake."

Sue dropped into the chair, staring at me. "You think Allen Trimmel is A.T.?"

"I think there's a chance," I replied. "Besides the initials, this wasn't a person he was meeting for the first time over and over, like everyone else he ran into. He knew Trimmel before this incident."

"So, this is after March, when Dr. Worthington first started having problems with faces?" came the voice from the phone.

"Yeah, it's June," I replied.

"Dr. Worthington never said he disliked A.T. when we met him," said Nicole. "And he clearly dislikes Allen Trimmel. But in June, he was having problems with his temper, so I don't think his dislike then is necessarily inconsistent with what he told us a couple of weeks ago. That is, if they're the same person."

I liked the way Nicole thought – logical, thorough. It fit my stereotype for an engineer. And frankly, I probably liked her analysis because it matched my thoughts.

"Also, the phrase about wanting to ruin him isn't exactly the same as his life being in danger," I said. "But if he thought Trimmel was going to steal the Blocker, it's close."

"I'd say so," said Sue. "Worthington said that living without it would be like living without air...if I remember Beth's words correctly."

"It's not the consent form, but I think you have plenty to take to the police," said Nicole.

I looked at Sue. Her eyebrows went up as she held a hand out in front of her, the other hand still holding her phone.

"You two have gotten awfully quiet," said Nicole after a moment.

"It's just that Ken read Doc the riot act a little while ago – told him not to get caught up in the Worthington murder mystery," explained Sue.

"He was probably more concerned about a call like this, where we end up debating the questions of means, motive, and opportunity for a couple of hours. I was pretty sure I was going to call the police before, and now, I'm certain. Thanks, ladies, for hearing me out."

"Of course," said Nicole.

"Good luck," Sue said as she turned off the speaker. She left talking to Nicole.

Since I didn't have a name or number at the police department, I dialed the WHT offices. At first, I was surprised to hear, "Jon Huston, Worthington-Huston Technologies."

"Hi, Jon. It's Doc. That's right, Laverne's on vacation, isn't she?"

"She is indeed. Doing her work is keeping me from mine, but she needed the time away from the office." His voice trailed off as he said it, but he soon recovered.

"Which reminds me, I hired some students to clean out the basement storage area, and they found a couple more boxes of Ned's notes. I understand from Sue that the others were a waste of time, and unfortunately, these are too. I've been through them. I'm really sorry about this."

"It needed to be done," I replied. "Which is why I called. Do you happen to know Allen Trimmel?"

"Is that A.T.?" he asked, his voice almost a whisper.

"I don't know. But you don't know him?"

"No, I don't recognize the name. What's the context?"

"Someone Dr. Worthington ran out of the lab in June," I replied. "I thought I'd give the name to the police, but I wasn't sure who to call."

"Yeah, Ned probably ran several people out of the lab around then," said Huston, his tone somber. "But I don't know Trimmel. The person you want at the PD is Detective Larry Ahern. Just a sec, I'll get his number."

After a moment, he read it off, I thanked him, and we said our goodbyes.

I dialed the Detective's number, but got no response. I left a message with both my office and cell phone numbers, asking him to call me.

With that done, I sunk back into my office chair, staring at the remaining pile of folders. I took about a half-inch of them and carefully bent them. There was no resistance; there was no external disk in there. I did the same to small stacks of the remaining pages, all with the same result. Everything that was left was paper. Even if every page was a printout or survey from the study, there weren't enough pages to cover the research. Even without looking, I knew we were at a dead end.

Perhaps Biomedical Engineering Associates could get a new contract to study the device using the document Nicole had. Maybe they would subcontract us. Maybe I could work for Nicole. The thought was pleasant, but unlikely.

Even though there weren't enough unread pages left to cover our requirements, I knew I'd dig through them anyway...just not today. "The hell with it," I mumbled, again surprising myself I had said it aloud. After checking that there were no witnesses, I left for the day.

SATURDAY, AUGUST 22, 5:37 PM

I pushed a finger through the slats in the Venetian blind, looking out at the street while I waited until time to meet Sue for dinner. A black SUV I hadn't seen before Thursday was sitting on the street again. Of course, black SUVs were hardly rare on my block. Two of my neighbors owned them. But this one was new and I'd never seen anyone getting into or out of it. Could this be...?

Get a grip.

A neighbor had bought a new car and nothing more. Unless I was going to plant myself by the window, I wouldn't see anyone around it until I happened on him or her loading up the kids for a soccer game, or bringing in the week's groceries, or packing for a weekend camping trip. And besides, I'm worried about someone who kills for exotic technology, not the FBI. I needed to rein in my imagination.

I glanced in the other direction. The dog walkers were out. I recognized several of them, including one attractive, young woman. That was where I should be directing my imagination. I had passed her on the sidewalk a couple of times. I knew her well enough to say, 'Hi,' well enough to know there was no ring on her hand.

True, I didn't find my dog-walking neighbor as attractive as Nicole, but I was starting to get a bad feeling about my chances with her. It was nothing specific, nothing I could name, but....

I jumped when my phone rang and nearly punched a hole through the window with my finger. "Ow." I shook it a couple of times, then picked up the receiver with my other hand.

"Hello."

"Sorry, Doc, but you're going to need to change clothes." It was Sue's voice.

"Something come up?" I asked.

"Yeah, I'm going to have to bring Al along tonight. Caught him paging through the pizza ads when I was getting ready."

Sue did help Al with his battle against the bulge, but this excuse was pure fiction. Al was coming because he was a big fan of the Mexican restaurant where we were going and because Sue wanted him by her side. After almost two years of marriage, they still enjoyed each other's company and that showed no sign of changing.

"So, sorry, Doc, but you'll need to change out of those sexy duds and put on something that won't give us away."

I chuckled. "I can manage that."

"Al will pick up his part of the tab," Sue said. "Like I said before, he didn't earn dinner by dumpster-diving through Worthington's notes."

I shook my head, grinning at the phone. "He got lunch last time, so I have tonight." That reasoning might have been fiction too. I didn't remember, but I had invited both of them anyway. "Still on for 6:00?"

"Yeah. And thanks. I guess we should be going. See you there." Sue hung up.

The restaurant was nearby, so I was walking, which meant it was time for me to leave as well. I turned off the light in the living room and started for the front door. But as I reached for the doorknob, I heard a creak in the hallway. The building was old. It didn't need a reason to make sounds, but someone on the stairs invariably made noise.

It was probably more of my imagination, but why chance it? I crept past the kitchen and living room to a closet near the bathroom. I removed my baseball bat and returned to the door. I had considered buying a gun after the scene in Worthington's office, but believed it a bit of an overreaction. Now, the option sounded much more appropriate.

I peeked into the hall. No one. The floor creaked again, somewhere behind my partially opened door. My heart started pounding in my ears. My muscles tensed. I gripped the bat with both hands and raised it to my shoulder, like I was preparing for a home-run swing. I nudged the door open with my foot.

There stood Lilly, my seventy-year-old, across-the-hall neighbor in her Cardinals jersey. Her back was to me as she stared into the apartment she shared with her husband, Jerry. I lowered the bat before she turned. That was probably fortunate; I wasn't sure I could explain to Jerry if I gave her a heart attack.

"I didn't know the Cards were calling up a secret weapon," Lilly said when she saw me.

"Evening, Lilly. You and Jerry headed for the game?"

"We are," she replied, as her husband joined her in the hall. He frowned when he saw what I was carrying.

"I'd say I think better with the bat in my hands, but since I just walked out into the hall without thinking about it, I guess that doesn't work. You two have fun at the game," I said, retreating into my apartment. I returned the bat to the closet and left for the restaurant.

* * *

Sue and Al were seated at a table when I arrived. "Did you give Trimmel's name to the police?" whispered Sue, as I slid into a chair across from them.

I glanced at Al, who was busy with the chips and salsa, then back at Sue. "I called and left a message. I didn't hear anything back...but you don't want to talk about work tonight, do you?"

"Actually, I wouldn't mind a little shop talk," said Al, taking me by surprise. "Sue hasn't been a happy camper for a while. I'm just wondering, what's your take on everything that's been happening?"

"I'm as fun as ever," Sue said, sticking out her lower lip in a pretend pout. Al reached over and placed a hand on his wife's arm. She covered his hand with her own, then smiled.

"Well, I don't know what's got Sue down." Sue's brows knitted again. "Probably nothing, because she's as fun as ever," I said, correcting myself. "But what's got me is, we have all these questions about the Blocker – did it make Worthington hostile? Or was it just stress. But we have no way to answer them. And the person, A.T., and the data that would help are also missing."

"Yeah, but you'll get there," said Al.

I took a chip and dipped it in salsa, forming the answer in my mind when Sue spoke. "That's not a given, honey. We're running out of places to look for the files and Ken is getting impatient. We could get pulled off this job anytime. As for the VA or the police getting serious about investigating? I just don't know." Sue looked at me.

"I think they will – the VA anyway, but probably not soon," I replied. "There's nothing like a smoking gun in anything we have, but there's enough that the VA will get worried. Then, they'll either cut the funding or they'll form a new team to study the technology or both. Eventually, that'll pay off."

"But if our worst-case fears are true, the delay could be hazardous to our health," said Sue.

"Yeah, just how sure are you that there's someone out there interested in knocking off neuroscientists and psychologists?" asked Al.

"And biomedical engineers," added Sue.

I cringed. The list of potential victims made the situation painful, even if the threat was questionable. "I'm not sure. We started by looking for protection from Worthington, because I thought he might lash out if he found one of us alone."

"We all felt that," said Sue.

I nodded, appreciating her show of unity. "When Worthington died, the precaution remained. But it's based on a long string of unlikely events – like someone stole the device and decided to kill Worthington to keep it. And for some reason, he or she now sees us as a threat."

Our server arrived at the table for drink orders. After Sue ordered iced tea, Al said, "Sounds like a night to drown our concerns. I'll take a margarita."

"The same for me," I said, sharing Al's feeling.

After our server left, Al said, "So, it's not that likely that there's someone out there gunning for you."

"No, probably not," I admitted, then chuckled. "But that hasn't kept me from jumping at my own shadow." I proceeded to tell them the story of my near beaning of Lily with my baseball bat, only exaggerating slightly for effect.

When I was done, the talk transitioned to more pleasant topics and dinner went quickly. As I left the restaurant, I felt better. Perhaps the act of talking through our situation had calmed me. No, it was probably the booze, and tomorrow I'd realize that this is one of those times you don't want to be on the wrong side of a one-in-a-million chance.

But tonight, everything was good.

SATURDAY, AUGUST 22, 8:47 PM

The Experimenter parked the van across the street from his destination. He smiled, still amazed by his good fortune. Knowing the place and approximate time his prey would appear were boons he'd never expected. Soon, he would have another subject for his studies.

The nearest streetlamp was about 20 feet away, but it was behind him on the same side of the street, leaving him in the shadows of the cab. He pulled a pair of binoculars from the bag on the seat next to him. He didn't expect to find any video cameras on the street; it would be unusual in this quiet, residential neighborhood, but he checked anyway.

After twenty minutes, he was convinced there were none, or at least, none that he was going to spot. He turned his attention to the building. It was an old, two-story apartment building with four units – two up and two down. In its day, it would have been considered opulent, but that day would have been around 1910. Now, it was modest living for singles or couples.

There were six steps leading up to a brick and stone portico, which was bounded by low shrubs on each side. The front door was massive, with a large, beveled glass pane. It had probably been clear originally, but because of security or privacy or both, it was now frosted. Sconces on either side of the door provided light to the returning resident. But economic concerns had outweighed security in recent years, and the illumination they provided was meager compared to the street lights. Most of the door and all the portico's floor was in shadow.

Above the door, there was a transom window with the address painted in gold numerals. The rest of the glass was clear. Still higher, there was a large, picture window, apparently on the second-floor landing. It too was clear.

Using the binoculars, the Experimenter checked the ceilings of the entry hall and the landing. He saw nothing. He started the van and backed up about three feet, allowing him to check the left most corner of each ceiling. There they were – two video cameras, one on each floor.

So far, no one had witnessed any of his abductions. Maybe his subjects had been kidnapped...or maybe they just moved away. The Experimenter liked the uncertainty he had created and decided to take his prey on the street to maintain it.

The camera on the second landing had no view of the outside. It was focused on the doors to the two residences on that level. The camera in the entry hall, however, might catch a figure coming up the sidewalk to the steps. He would need to avoid that spot. But once he or his prey reached the door, they would be hidden from the camera by the frosted glass.

He put the binoculars back in the bag and started the van, driving it around the block until he returned to the street, facing the building from about 20 yards away. He studied the ebb and flow of traffic. He observed the people strolling by on the sidewalks. He watched the windows of the nearby buildings. After an hour, he had the pulse of the neighborhood. It was drowsy. It was complacent.

Taking a pair of latex gloves from the bag, he put them on. Then, he donned a small shoulder pack that contained the Taser, the Blocker cap, and the restraints. He exited the van, crossed the street, and started slowly walking toward the building. There was no one on the sidewalks, no cars on the street, no movement at the windows. Just before he reached his destination, he slipped across the lawn.

The Experimenter pushed between the shrubs and the building, then reached up to the top of the portico's stone railing. He pulled himself a few inches off the ground. The railing was solid, stable. He lowered himself back down. The shrubs were shorter than he would have liked. He would have to lay down to be fully covered, but it was a minor sacrifice to obtain Subject 5.

He waited. He heard footsteps. As the sound got closer, he realized it was a couple. If his prey wasn't alone, he'd have to abort. But as they came abreast of his hiding position, he could see it was someone else. The couple turned into the building across the street. He gave them no more thought, because even as they entered, their hands had been all over each other. They wouldn't be looking out the window.

He settled deeper into the shadows of the shrubs and waited. Again, the sound of footsteps came to his ears. Peering carefully through the leaves, he saw his prey. He checked the street and windows. All was clear.

The man came up the sidewalk, then stumbled mounting the steps. Perhaps he had imbibed a bit too much? He stuck his hand in a pocket, fumbling for his keys.

The Experimenter raised to a crouching position, aiming the Taser between the gaps in the balusters of the railing. At this distance, he couldn't miss. He quickly scanned the area, and seeing no one, he squeezed the trigger. The barbed projectiles pierced the man's thigh, the electrical charge sending his muscles into spasms.

The man fell. But even as he started to drop, the Experimenter foresaw disaster; he was falling toward the railing. His head hit the top of the stone with a sickening crack.

The Experimenter looked on in horror, momentarily frozen in disbelief. When awareness returned, he checked his surroundings.

All was still quiet. He pulled himself up on the railing until his foot obtained purchase on the edge of the portico, then he swung himself over the railing. He dropped down to the floor. Even in the gloom from the feeble porch lights, the growing pool of blood and the impossible angle of the man's head and neck were obvious.

The Experimenter removed the man's wallet and watch, trusting the theft would help disguise his intentions. Then, he climbed over the railing and dropped to the ground. He walked quickly back to the van, started it, and drove away.

"Damn," he muttered to himself, as he rounded the corner at the end of the block. Then a smile broke out on his features and he laughed. "Probably not the way he thought the night would end, when he invited a few of his customers to the ball game. But at least he won't be machining any more out-of-spec parts."

Nils Jurgensen was dead.

MONDAY, AUGUST 24, 9:32 AM

I set the cup of coffee on my desk and sat down, dropping my head into my hands in exhaustion. The exact time my workday starts depends in part on how long of a run I take. The length of my runs, in turn, depends on how much I have on my mind. The longer the list of issues, the longer the route. Since I had spent much of the weekend building a list of problems, I really shouldn't have been in the office before noon, but my legs had given out.

I raised my head, catching the blinking light on my phone out of the corner of my eye. I replayed the message.

"Hey, Sam. Gone already, huh?" It was Nicole's voice. "I was hoping to talk, and I'm pretty sure I could stay away from means, motive, and opportunity." She laughed. I liked the sound and smiled to myself.

"Actually, my management is asking about the project," she said, her tone turning serious. My mood dimmed a bit, but at least I had a reason to call. "I know how bleak it looks, but I wanted your thoughts. Anyway, we can talk next week. Bye."

I booted my computer, found her number, and was about to dial when my phone rang. Nicole's boss must be in a hurry for information.

"I was hoping you'd call," I said, picking up the handset.

There was a delay, but someone was on the line. I could hear sounds in the background. "Well, you asked me to," came the reply in a male's voice.

"I'm sorry. I was expecting someone else. I'm Sam Price. May I help you?"

"Hi, Sam. I'm Detective Larry Ahern, St. Louis Police Department. I'm returning your call, but frankly, you were already on my list of people to contact. So, if it's all right with you, I'd like to cover my questions first."

The detective hadn't said 'his list of suspects,' only his list of people to contact, but I felt my heart rate go up.

"Sure, detective. How can I help you?"

"Is it OK if I record this conversation?"

Recording a phone call was probably standard procedure, but my heart rate increased again. I could hear the drumming in my ears. I needed to calm down or I'd be telling him about the baseball I took out of lost-and-found in third grade.

"Yeah, sure, that's fine."

In the background, I heard, "Dr. Sam Price phone interview, August 24, 9:40 AM." Then, directed to me, he said, "For the record, you had contact with Dr. Ned Worthington of WHT on the afternoon of August 10th and the morning of the 11th and a phone call that Dr. Worthington made to you on the evening of August 11th. Do you recall these events?"

After I said I did, the detective launched into a series of questions, most of which revolved around Worthington's behavior and emotional state during our encounters. Ahern appeared to be building a case that Worthington had been under tremendous stress – long hours, extreme mental demands, lack of job security, issues at home – all of which seemed indisputable. But given that Scott had said her husband died of asphyxiation, I wasn't sure why this was important.

He finished his interview with a few questions about the possibility that Worthington had used the Blocker to tinker with his own mental wiring. The detective seemed unfazed by the fact that I only had a statement from Worthington that might or might not have been a firsthand account. When he finished, he said, "I understand from your message that you have some information for me."

I was still digesting his queries, but one thing was clear – there had been no questions about threats on Worthington's life. Perhaps the detective didn't expect me to have information on that topic, since I had only known him briefly. But I did.

"Before we get to that, there was one other thing on the phone call I wanted to mention. At one point, Dr. Worthington said his life was in danger. And the lives of those around him."

"Hmm, I see," said Ahern. I expected a long delay while he pondered that fact. Instead, he almost immediately asked, "Did he say who was threatening him and his friends?"

"No. No name."

"You think it's possible he was talking about himself? That he felt out of control and might hurt himself or those near him?"

I was amazed how quickly and easily Ahern had turned that around. Worthington's statement merely reflected the stress he had been under. "Yeah, I guess he could have meant that," I admitted. I drummed two fingers on my lips, wondering if I should continue down this road.

What have I got to lose?

"I heard that Dr. Worthington died from asphyxiation. Maybe you can't tell me, but what do all the questions about stress have to do with his death?"

I could hear Ahern sigh, but at least it was not one of those dramatic exhales that say, 'Great. Another television-educated forensic scientist.'

"I can't say much because this is an open case," Ahern said. "But if the lack of air is the condition, there are many possible causes." He put emphasis on the words condition and cause, which made sense when I thought about it. I'd thought strangulation, but the cause could have been anything from drugs to drowning.

"Several causes of asphyxiation are related to stress and brain trauma. I hope that answers your question, because I can't say more."

"Sure. I understand. And thanks. Anyway, the reason I called was because I ran across a name going through some notes that Dr. Worthington wrote, mostly from March through July. The name was Allen Trimmel and the entry is from June." I read it to him.

When I finished, he said, "You're telling me this because Allen Trimmel may be A.T., the person in Dr. Worthington's research?"

"Right."

"Is Allen Trimmel mentioned elsewhere in these notes?"

"No, only the one entry as far as I know."

"You said this was June...more than five months after he left the study?" asked Ahern.

"Yes, that's right." The detective was quiet. I wondered if he was going to dismiss this information outright, so I added, "With Dr. Worthington's death being suspicious, I thought you'd be interested in talking to Trimmel. Especially if he was still hanging around the lab."

I believed that would arouse his curiosity, but he focused on something else. "Suspicious?" he said. "There's been nothing suspicious so far. No forced entry. No signs of struggle. No unexplained fingerprints. All those facts have been released to the public."

"Sorry, I haven't been following that closely. But...," I started.

"Sam, don't misunderstand. A.T. is a person of interest. We'd like to know who he is, so I'll follow up."

"Thanks. But you don't think he had anything to do with Worthington's death, do you?"

"We're still looking at a variety of possibilities," Ahern replied, using what was clearly a standard response for the public. After a moment, he said, "But I'm curious. Why do you think A.T. might be involved?"

'Because Ms. Scott said as much' didn't sound like a very convincing answer, so I gave what I suspected was her reason. "He realized how valuable the technology would be when it's perfected. It could be a theft gone wrong."

"It could be," said Ahern. "How close is this device to being done?"

"I'm not sure," I admitted.

"Any idea what it cost to get to where it is now?"

"Not really, but tens of thousands of dollars at least."

"How about over $275,000 last year alone?"

I wasn't sure how to respond, but I saw his point. Picking up that kind of development cost was not something just anyone could do.

"Look, this Blocker may be the best thing since sliced bread, but it's worthless to anyone who doesn't have the background and the money to work on it."

"But A.T. has the background."

"What?" said Ahern, his voice showing some surprise for the first time during this call.

"Both Dr. Worthington and Dr. Huston said A.T. suggested ways to change the Blocker. At least, that's what we have in our notes from the meetings with Dr. Worthington. I can send you a copy of them, if you want."

"Yes, please. I'll talk to Dr. Huston to get his statement." Ahern read off his fax number and I promised to send that page of our report.

Perhaps it was my imagination, but after I revealed this small nugget of information, he seemed to become more interested in the conversation. His voice brightened and the pace of his speech picked up. "The other thing that's new in what you've said are these notes that Worthington wrote. Where did you get those?"

"Ms. Scott gave them to us. I guess it's papers Dr. Worthington had at his home. We were looking through them to see if we could find some of the study data that's gone missing. But no luck."

"Oh, yeah, I remember that stuff now," he said, the energy in his voice now gone. "All the trivialities of his daily life, right?"

"Yes, that's them," I replied. "He seemed to be having trouble remembering things. People, in particular."

"Stress and depression are known causes of extreme forgetfulness," Ahern replied. He either knew a lot about stress or he had done his homework, but in either case, the notes also fit his theory about Worthington's death.

"He had a lot of paper, as I recall," Ahern said. "Like thousands of pages."

"Yeah, quite a bit."

There was a pause and when Ahern spoke again, there was an undertone of amusement. "It's amazing you happened to notice this one reference to Allen Trimmel in that mountain of paper."

I could have come clean, told him that we were asked to watch for it, but I suspected he knew. So, I said, "Yeah, we do a thorough job."

As we finished the call, he thanked me for being a responsible citizen and for doing my civic duty. But somehow, I knew what he was really thinking was, 'just what I need. Another dead end to chase down.'

MONDAY, AUGUST 24, 10:13 AM

The Experimenter knew he shouldn't be sitting in his work area, staring at Subject 4 through the one-way mirror. He had set up the software to control the equipment, freeing him to attend to the humdrum of his daily life. And yet, he couldn't pull himself from the drama that was playing out inside the experimental chamber.

Subject 4 had refused to eat since arriving at the residence. And after a few snarled questions to establish that he was a captive, he had refused to talk as well. His recalcitrance hadn't bothered the Experimenter; in fact, he appreciated the quiet. But now, the man was sitting motionless, receiving shock after painful shock. And since the Blocker was turned off and he had full use of both sides of his brain and full command of his body, his inaction was driven solely by defiance.

How long could the man hold out against the pain, fatigue, and starvation? He had been in the chamber nearly five hours already. Would he die before he raised a hand to push a button when it was so easy? The Experimenter slowly released a long breath, shaking his head in a combination of frustration and admiration.

Having grown concerned that the man's leg might become insensitive after so many shocks, the Experimenter had started moving the electrode each hour. He checked his notes, then the clock. It was that time again, so he placed the Blocker into a mode that would paralyze. He rose from the desk and quickly stepped into the chamber. Even with the room's ventilation system running at full power, the mixture of urine, sweat, and excrement had created an odor that brought tears to his eyes.

First, he checked the restraint around the forehead. After installing the feeding tubes, the Experimenter started leaving about an inch of slack in it so subjects could get their own food and water. The allowance, however, was unnecessary for Subject 4. Access to sustenance depended on trying, and so far, he wasn't. But his head banging between the strap and the padded headrest made the Experimenter wary. His check confirmed that the restraint was still solid.

"Not feeling the need to act yet, are we?" the Experimenter asked the paralyzed man. He released the tension on the strap that held the electrode in place and let it slide down so he could see the skin that had been under it. It was red and raw, with small blisters that glistened in the light. Not wanting the sores to rupture, he moved the electrode another inch. Then, he tugged on the binding, cinching the electrode so tight that it cut into the man's leg.

"Perhaps you think I'll relent," said the Experimenter. "And maybe I would...if I were running the equipment. But I'm not. It's all in the hands of the computer. So, the question you have to ask yourself is, what are the chances I run out of electricity?" The Experimenter shrugged, then turned and walked from the chamber.

Sitting back down in the work area, he restarted the equipment, then rolled his chair to the mirror. The light sequence played, the interval when the subject could make an entry passed without movement, and the shock was delivered. The man's mouth opened in a scream, his entire body tensing in agony. After a moment, the jolt ended, but the man's body continued to quiver, as if he was freezing in the stuffy room.

After a few moments, a new sequence of lights was presented, with the same result. And another. And another. But after the light sequence for the fifth trial, Subject 4 reached up with his right hand and quickly tapped the buttons in the correct order. An amber light showed that the feeding tubes were active, and Subject 4 leaned forward and drank greedily for the few seconds of access that were granted.

"And his resistance dies," the Experimenter muttered to himself.

He let the equipment run for another two-dozen trials, each ending with a few seconds of water or liquid nourishment. That would be sufficient to maintain the man until the next session. He shut the Blocker down.

The Experimenter glanced at the clock again, then at his notes. He looked back into the chamber, where Subject 4 waited, eyes closed in exhaustion. A glare formed on his face. "Five hours, all wasted," he yelled at the walls. "And now, I give him time to rest?" He slammed his left hand down on the desk, wincing with pain.

"I think not," he hissed to himself.

He grabbed the keyboard from the desk and restarted the equipment, then leaned back. "I must have more subjects. More grist for the mill of scientific progress."

His gaze traveled around the room, falling on the bed sitting in the corner. "And maybe a pet for myself as well."

MONDAY, AUGUST 24, 1:06 PM

I entered my office after lunch, slouched into my chair, and glanced at the light on my phone. It wasn't blinking, and in our case, no news was bad news. No one was calling about the missing files. No one was phoning with news about the mysterious A.T. I massaged my temples in a losing battle against the tension I felt.

After speaking with the detective, I had asked Sue to restart her writing assignment for the final report – turn the phantom limb material into a background section for training research. I added the caveat that the report would most likely be an epitaph for a failed project, so write accordingly. I left the same message for Nicole, after failing to reach her on the phone. She'd edit her words on the effect of the Blocker on the left hemisphere and perhaps add some initial thoughts about the electronics based on the specs.

For my part, I had to pen the words that tied it all together, making it look like we had made progress when in fact, we had nothing. I stood up from the desk and turned to the whiteboard, staring at the list of left hemisphere functions hanging there. Was there inspiration hiding in those words?

"I've got one for you."

I jumped at the sound of Sue's voice. I turned to see her standing in my doorway.

"Sorry, I didn't mean to startle you." She came in and sat down in the chair next to my desk.

"Just lost in thought." I leaned up against the whiteboard and shoved my hands into my pockets. "So, you've got one for me. Is this the one about the boyfriend you had in college who liked to talk during sex? He liked it so much that he'd even call you from the hotel?"

Sue laughed. "You still remember that? I didn't know you were so fixated on sex." For a split second, I was going to deny it, until I realized that would be playing into her hands.

"OK, I give. What have you got for me?"

I was still expecting a joke when she said, "Prosopagnosia."

I frowned, holding out my hands.

"The inability to recognize faces," Sue said.

"Oh, one of Worthington's problems." I looked at the list on the whiteboard. "Not a left hemisphere function, is it?"

Sue laughed. "You don't give up, do you? Nope, just the opposite."

"What?" I asked, startled by her words.

"Prosopagnosia?"

"No, after that. It's a right hemisphere function?" I asked.

"Yeah, seems to be. Why?"

I turned toward my window, looking out at the parking lot and the freeway beyond. "Would you call Nicole?"

"Well, I could but...," she started.

"Yeah, I know. The list of left side functions hasn't paid off." I paused, then chuckled. "And I'll probably be wrong about this too, but I'd like to run something by you two. Since you're right by the phone, can you give her a call?"

Sue shrugged, then said, "Sure." She put the phone on speaker and dialed a number. It rang several times – enough that I was about to tell her to hang up because Nicole had always answered within one or two rings. Then, Nicole's voice came across the speaker. But in place of her confident, standard, work greeting, I heard a tentative, "Hello?"

I looked at Sue. She was trying to look innocent, holding her eyes open wide, but the corners of her mouth twitched in a suppressed smile.

"Hi, Nicole. It's Sam. Sue and I are here in my office. I had something I wanted to run past the two of you, if you have the time."

"I do...but why didn't you just come by?" she asked.

"Come by?"

Nicole laughed. "Sue can explain while you walk to the conference room that's about 20 yards from your office. Bye." She hung up.

"I owe you one," I said.

"Hardly," Sue replied, smirking. "This doesn't come close to getting even for your fake episode of post Blocker syndrome." We left.

Nicole was sipping a cup of coffee with a few dozen folders of Worthington's notes scattered across the conference room tabletop when we found her. "I figured you'd want these back, so I finished the last of them here," she said. "You can probably guess, but I found nothing. Not even another reference to Allen Trimmel. Are you done?"

"I still have 20 to 30 folders to go, but they failed the bend test," I replied. "No drives in them and too few pages to have all the data from the study, but I'll check them later."

Sue and I sat down at the table across from Nicole. "As for Allen Trimmel, I gave the name to Detective Larry Ahern at the police department this morning. He said he'd look into it, but I'm not sure how hard."

"You did what you could," said Sue.

I leaned forward in my chair and rested my chin on my hands for a moment while I composed my thoughts. "What I wanted to ask about is this. When the brain adapts – when it finds a new set of neural pathways to compensate for a blocked activity – is the original function diminished? In other words, does the gain from plasticity in one area come at a cost to another?"

Knowing that Nicole was the most likely to have an answer, my gaze traveled to her face. "I believe so," she said after a moment. "If the speech function was lost due to injury, for example, and new circuits adapted to restore it, they wouldn't be doing what they did before." She paused, frowning. "But the number of neurons and interconnections is enormous. I doubt that the loss would be noticeable."

"What if you continued to deprive a function, pushing the brain to recruit more and more?"

Nicole's frown deepened. "Are you thinking the Blocker might be producing right hemisphere deficits, as well as increases in left side capacity?"

"That's exactly what I'm wondering," I replied. "I thought we could repeat the same process as before – the one we used to compile the list of left-side functions. But this time, we'll do it for the right hemisphere."

"OK," the women said in chorus.

Sue manned the computer in the conference room, while I got a few textbooks from my office. When I came back, she had retrieved the list of left hemisphere functions and had added the word 'increased' at the top. The revisions were displayed on the screen at the front of the room.

Left Hemisphere Functions - INCREASED
Processing stimuli in the right visual field
Controlling muscle responses on the right side of the body
Perceiving stimuli on the right side of the body, e.g., touch
Language (reading, speaking, writing)

Math
Science
Analytic and logical reasoning
Mental manipulation
Semantic priming
Image generation
Processing pleasurable experiences
Decision-making
Routine or well-rehearsed processes

Sue added a column for right hemisphere functions, as Nicole and I added candidates to the whiteboard. At first, the mood of the room was light, as everyone was enjoying the break from Worthington's drivel and doing something positive. But over time, our moods became darker. There was less talking and humor disappeared. When we were done, our list looked like this.

Right Hemisphere Functions - DECREASED

Processing stimuli in the left visual field
Controlling muscle responses on the left side of the body
Perceiving stimuli on the left side of the body, e.g., touch
Symbolic reasoning
Art
Spatial relationships
Recognition of objects
Timing
Empathy
Depression
Holistic reasoning/intuition
Recall of images
Recognizing faces
Mental rotation

Negative emotions
Vigilance
Self-reflection
Understanding novel situations

As I studied the list, a dark cloud of foreboding grew in my mind. After a moment, Nicole said, "Well, this explains why Worthington hated art and why he couldn't remember new people or his daily activities. But the reduction in self-regulation and the increase in pleasure?" She paused, shaking her head slowly. "That sounds like a recipe for electronic addiction. Treatments feel good. And at the same time, self-doubts and worries disappear. That would lead to craving another treatment in an endless cycle."

"It certainly fits with Beth's description of her husband as a man possessed by a machine," said Sue. Apparently, I wasn't the only one who had been struck by that phrase. "But right-side functions couldn't disappear entirely, could they?"

"I don't think so," I said. "Things that get used, like your left arm, would create demand. Those functions couldn't disappear." I paused, staring at the list, still wondering if this could be true. "But if A.T. or someone else is out there and he's using a Blocker, look at what might not get exercised. He'd have no need for sympathy. Cold logic is king and compassion is a waste of time. He wouldn't look at his motivations, because he's superior and everything feels right. There's nothing to stop a lot of those right-side functions from disappearing, and many of them are what makes us human."

"Are you saying that this person might end up with no emotional boundaries on what he'd do to keep his electronic world?" asked Nicole. "He'd be a person that's entirely...well, of half a mind?"

"Yeah, I guess I am."

MONDAY, AUGUST 24, 3:37 PM

I usually ask if anyone wants a break. Today, I hadn't. I needed it, even if Sue and Nicole didn't.

After I left the women in the conference room, I walked the halls, wondering if the Blocker really could be a path paved by electronic addiction, leading to inhumanity. I couldn't find a flaw in the reasoning that said it was possible. All we lacked was...proof. We needed the study data.

Is there a stone we've left unturned?

There must be. The data had to be somewhere. Perhaps brainstorming with Huston, maybe Scott too, would turn up some leads? It was an idea born of desperation, but it was the best I had.

When I returned to the conference room with a half-cup of coffee, I found Nicole busy on her laptop. "Ah, recording your latest insights about the Neural Activity Blocker?" I asked, smiling. "We value task focus here at Ruger-Phillips."

"No, just an email to a friend, while I had a moment." She hit send as she closed the lid.

I wondered if that filled another evening on her social calendar. But one thing was certain – there'd be no date with my name on it if I didn't stop waiting for the perfect moment.

"Would you like to come over to my place for dinner? I'm not the greatest cook, but I can hold my own grilling hamburgers. I could return the favor for the drinks the other night."

"Tonight?" She pulled out her phone. It seemed odd that she wouldn't remember what she was doing in two hours. But with as many times as I had made a lunch in the morning and then left it on my kitchen counter fifteen minutes later, I couldn't talk.

"Tonight would be fine, but how about my place, instead of yours?" she asked.

"OK," I said slowly, not sure why she wanted the change in venue. "But it'll be hard for me to cook there, unless of course you have hamburger and a grill."

"Sorry, neither. Do you like Chinese?"

"Absolutely," I replied.

"Great. There's a Chinese restaurant just down the street. I can stop there on the way home."

"I'll get the food. What do you like?"

"Their Moo Shu shrimp is good, and I'll supply the beer. The one we had before?"

"Perfect. It's a date," I said.

The last sentence came out of my mouth as Sue entered. She cleared her throat more loudly than necessary, smirking at me. I returned a grin, then glanced at Nicole. She was busy shuffling some papers on the conference table, her head down.

Did I embarrass her?

For a split second I considered saying, 'it's OK. Sue knows I like you.' Fortunately, I realized how awkward it would be if the first time I mentioned my attraction, it was in front of someone else...and that person already knew. Instead, I said, "We need to think about places where the missing data might be."

I got no farther, however, as Ken appeared at the conference room door. "Sorry for the interruption, ladies, but I need to speak with Sam. Would you mind giving us about 10 minutes?"

Sue glanced at me, then back at Ken. "Sure," she said, and she and Nicole left.

Ken closed the door, then turned and stared at me. A frown came over his face. "I thought we had an understanding."

"I'm not sure what you mean."

"I thought you were going to leave the Worthington matter to the police?" He held out his hands in a what-were-you-thinking pose, his head shaking.

"Is this about the name I gave them?"

"Have you done something else?" I cleared my throat to answer, but Ken held up a hand and shook his head again. "Never mind. Let's stick to the issues. You were away from your desk, and since it was a police matter, they tracked me down."

Ken pulled a slip of paper from his pocket and glanced at it. "It seems that the name you gave Detective Ahern, a Mr. Allen Trimmel, was a wild goose chase."

"How could he possibly know already? It's only been what – about six hours since I talked to him?"

"He asked." I jerked my head back in surprise.

"That's why you need to leave police matters to the police," said Ken. "They know what to do; you don't. He called Ms. Scott, found out that Allen Trimmel was an old friend, before she met and married the doctor. I don't even want to know how many hours your team wasted digging out that name."

I had already told Ken that our work wasn't affected – finding oddities and passing them to the police was a by-product. But Ken had rejected the argument before, so I didn't bother repeating it.

I took a deep breath, preparing for the torrent that my next comment might elicit. "We have...well, hypothesized a possible effect of the Blocker. It's troubling, what it might be able to do. I think we should tell the police."

Ken dropped his gaze to the floor, his head shaking slowly. When he looked up, he asked, "How can you possibly hypothesize an effect when you don't even know the technology works?"

"We know it works, at least when it's applied to both sides of the brain. I even tried it." Ken knew that, from my reports, but perhaps it wasn't the best time to remind him.

"Damn it, Sam. You're letting your professional standards be influenced by someone else's fantasies."

I'd never heard Ken swear before. I wasn't sure he did, until now. I took a deep breath. "Sorry, but I don't think so. Yes, we're assuming that it would block functions on one side, based on what it does on both. And yes, we're estimating the long-term effects from the differences between the hemispheres. But it's solid enough, in my opinion, that the police and the VA should know."

Ken stood motionless, staring at me for what seemed minutes. Perhaps he was checking my resolve with the silence. Perhaps he simply didn't know what to say. But finally, he said, "OK. This project is over anyway, so put it in the final report to the VA. I'll see that it also gets to the police."

"It's over?" I flinched at the directness and finality of his statement. I knew it was coming, but it still hurt. It felt like failure, even if technically we had done nothing wrong.

"Look, Doc," said Ken, his tone softening a bit. "I know you're still learning the ropes. But your job is tough enough without getting involved in the customer's politics. It's usually more in the form of them trying to befriend you or get your sympathy for some problem they've had. Obviously, what's happened at WHT wasn't a premeditated effort to compromise you – no one would go to these lengths. But the job still requires detachment."

"I understand."

"Good." Ken paused several moments looking at me. "So, is there any reason why we shouldn't shut this project down? We can always restart, if WHT finds the data."

The question was pro forma. He had already made up his mind, but I appreciated him asking. "No, I guess not. It appears the data trail has gone cold." My spirits sank even further when I said those words, but you can't keep a project going when there is nothing to go on. "We'll get to work on the final report. Everything should be ready for your review in about a week."

Ken obviously liked this plan better than any of the other schemes I had hatched over the past few days and he nodded his approval. "OK. The management review and release should take ten days to two weeks after that. As soon as the paperwork is in the cycle, we'll notify Dr. Huston and the VA of the situation, so they'll be prepared. We could have this project wrapped up in a month to six weeks."

Ken looked at his watch. "Your team should be back in a couple of minutes. I'll let you get back to work." He left without another word.

Sue and Nicole must have been standing just outside the door, because they entered as Ken left.

"We're done?" asked Sue, cutting to the heart of the matter.

"Yeah, it's over," I said. "We're shutting down due to the lack of anything to work on...the Blocker specs being the exception, of course." I paused and rubbed the back of my neck. "Would you two mind brain-storming on the final report for a half-hour or so? I need to make a couple of phone calls."

Sue frowned at me. "You're not going against Ken, are you?"

"No. Ken didn't say anything about giving the police and Huston a heads-up on our thoughts. And besides, they'll get this information later, when it's released in the final report."

"Ken didn't say anything about calling now because you didn't ask," said Sue. It wasn't really a question, so I didn't answer.

* * *

I called Jon Huston first. There was a long pause after I described our concerns. Finally, he said, "I wish Ned could hear your ideas. He was the expert, but obviously, he never expected anything like this or he would have stopped the study."

Huston sighed. "Funny, but I thought you'd find that the Blocker wasn't that effective in shutting down an entire hemisphere. There's too much communication between the sides for such drastic changes in mental abilities. But there's no doubt in my mind that Ned showed some of the symptoms you described. I'll talk to Laverne. We take some precautions anyway; some of our work is sensitive. But I'll tighten up our security. You and your team OK?"

"I think so. I was going to call the police next. Anyone else I should talk to?"

"The VA should know, but I'll take care of that." After a pause, he said, "That's everyone I can think of, but I'll give it some more thought. And, Doc?"

"Yeah?"

"If you're right, you need to be careful."

"You too, Jon."

I hung up and dialed Detective Ahern. Someone else answered his phone and took my name. After a few moments, Ahern picked up. "Afternoon, Sam. What can I do for you?"

"Afternoon to you too, detective. I'm not quite sure how to put this...but, if you're looking for someone who has used the Neural Activity Blocker extensively, we've developed some thoughts about how he might be acting."

After a pause, Ahern said, "So, this is a way we might spot A.T.? Is that what you're saying?"

"Yeah, basically."

"OK. What do we look for?"

"I can't say with certainty. We have...an educated guess about general characteristics."

The detective chuckled. "You don't like putting things in black and white, do you?" Then, seriousness returned to his voice. "Is this a guess because you still don't have the data from the study?"

"Yeah. It's still missing. This is based on theory."

I had to wait for several moments for a response, but finally, Ahern said, "OK. Let's hear it."

After I went through the two lists – capabilities the Blocker might increase and ones that might disappear – Ahern asked, "Didn't you just describe Worthington? I mean, other than the compulsion to use the Blocker over and over, that's Ned Worthington to a T."

"If he and this person both used the Blocker, then yeah, they could end up with similar traits."

"I see," he said after a moment. "OK, I'll add this to the case file."

Again, he thanked me for doing my civic duty, but again, I thought his words had little to do with his feelings. Even I had to admit that our theory about A.T. or another person yet unknown, who had killed a respected scientist to obtain an unfinished product, who had a working knowledge of electronics and software, who had money, and who had used the device to the point of blatantly disregarding the life of others sounded quite convoluted.

But then, life's not always simple.

The walk back to the conference room gave me a moment to think, and clearly, I felt a strong sense of loss. The Blocker had the potential to be world-changing. It was the kind of technology that had brought Sue and I into our field and kept us poring through textbooks and technical journals until the wee hours of the morning. It was also the kind of project Ruger-Phillips would never have assigned to an inexperienced, junior team. Unfortunately, neither Sue or I was going to reap any benefits from their mistake.

But that sense of loss was completely overwhelmed by a foreboding, somewhat for Sue and me, but mostly for Nicole. If there was a threat, Sue and I had to hold out a couple of weeks. Word would get out that we were off the project and then, we would be safe. But Nicole would have a target on her back as long as her company continued their work. She would be joined by others, of course, but her name would be the one people knew. The first on the project. My stomach was tying itself into knots.

When I arrived at the conference room, Sue and Nicole summarized their thoughts on the final report. I added a few ideas, but not many. They knew what needed to be done and even seemed more focused on work than I could manage. With that out of the way, I asked Sue, "You still keeping Al close by?"

"I am," she replied. "Although, I can hardly stand it. No woman wants to see a man feeling that secure." I frowned and Sue must have seen it, because she added. "Seriously, Doc. I'm being careful. He's been sticking around until I leave for work and I don't go home 'til I know he's there. I'm even taking different routes back and forth."

"Good," I said. "Please keep it up for a while longer." I turned to Nicole. "And I guess you're not at your aunt's any longer."

"Actually, today's my first day back in my apartment. My aunt's great, but I'm glad to be going home."

Although our surmises about the long-term effect of the Blocker were new, nothing else was. Nicole was in no more danger today than she had been yesterday, but her statement hit me hard. Compared to the last ten days when she came home to a house full of people, what she was about to do seemed very risky.

"Why don't you follow me back to your apartment after I pick up dinner?" I asked. "It just seems like a reasonable precaution, since you haven't been there for a while."

Nicole sighed, looking first at Sue, then me. Finally, she said, "Yeah, OK. Guess it couldn't hurt."

Nicole pulled into a spot a few car lengths from her front door. I stopped beside her and rolled down my window. "I'll park and be right back with the food."

When I returned, I saw her slip her phone into a pocket. She got out. "Now wouldn't be a good time for a practical joke." I looked at her blankly.

"See the man sitting up in that window?" I looked up. Sure enough, someone was looking out of a window on the third floor. "That's Mr. Fredricks. He's retired, so he can be around when I need someone to watch."

We started toward her front door and I gave Mr. Fredricks a wave. He waved back.

"This was just a demonstration," Nicole said, "so you'd stop worrying. I'll call him when I have to leave or return at odd hours, but not at times like this."

We had reached the front door, and while she entered a number on a keypad, I looked around. I saw her point. There was a couple strolling hand-in-hand on the other side of the street. A woman passed us walking her dog. A man was leaning into a parked car to kiss the woman sitting there.

"But you don't know you'll find a parking...."

Nicole turned to look at me, the door to her building open behind her. "Sam, I appreciate your concern, and I won't do anything reckless. But I won't live in fear either. OK?" Her eyes were locked on mine, unblinking.

"OK," I said slowly. She turned, we entered the building, and started up the stairs. "It's just that I feel responsible for getting you and Sue mixed up in this."

"That's nonsense...and a little degrading," she said, as she spun again to stare at me. "I'm an adult. I make my own decisions. No one is forcing me to stay on this project."

While I admired Nicole's strong, independent streak, a little less of it in this case would have been nice. But it was what made her the person she was, and no one was going to change that.

I held up my hands in surrender. "Fair enough. I'll leave it at, I'm here if you need me."

She smiled. "I know. And right now, I'm glad you are." She opened her door and reached in to switch on a light.

"I don't want to be too dramatic," I said. "But how about you stay here and I'll go in and look around?"

"How about we switch places," Nicole said. I started to object, but she explained before a word left my mouth. "I know my place. I'll know if anything has been disturbed. And I can check every spot where a person could be hiding before you'd find half of them."

I nodded slowly. "OK. Just yell if you need me."

MONDAY, AUGUST 24, 6:17 PM

The Experimenter slinked into a shadow near the fire exit door. He hadn't expected Price and Veles to be together. But after some thought, it wasn't surprising. He'd seen how Price looked at her, even from the few seconds of video from the landing of the WHT building. What he hadn't seen, however, was Veles returning the expression. But still, they might be in for the night.

He had everything he needed to capture Veles – the Taser, the Blocker cap that would stun, the restraints, even a drug he could use to sedate her. But could he collect a new toy and a new subject at the same time? Maybe. He played it out in his mind.

First, he'd go back to the entry hall and retrieve the large envelope he had seen when he followed the absent-minded, old man into the building. It would look official and Veles would open the door to sign for it. He'd pull the Taser, threaten her with it to get Price to put on the Blocker cap. Then, tasing her would leave both helpless, and he'd have them tied, gagged, and ready for transport in no time.

There was a path to success, a way to continue his pursuit of endless life. He started down the stairs, then stopped.

Yes, it could work, but it could also fail in so many ways. What if they refused to open the door? What if Price wouldn't don the cap, letting Veles suffer a moment of agony so he could fight? He could subdue one with the Taser, but the thought of physically restraining the other, even if it was Veles, was unnerving. Although she was slightly built, he was certain she'd fight like a tigress.

Better to be prepared for both.

The Experimenter considered leaving and driving by Price's apartment again. Even if he and Veles were together, the relationship was new. He'd be going home often, for clothes if nothing else. And the Experimenter knew little of his domicile beyond the few items he could see when Price left his blinds open during the day. But there was no reason to take another look at the old globe, or the antique clock, or the phrenology head that sat on his shelves, because the Experimenter's reconnaissance had already revealed the perfect time to take Price. It was during his morning runs.

He had followed Price only once, but the route that day had been perfect. It included a path around an urban park that was generally visible to nearby residences, streets, and in one section, a busy, six-lane highway. But there was also a stretch of about 20 yards that ran through a heavily wooded area. It would provide concealment for him as he laid in wait and for Price's body, once he was subdued. Now, it was just a matter of Price repeating his footsteps, and he would. Of this, the Experimenter was certain.

Deciding the drive by Price's apartment was unnecessary, the Experimenter settled deeper into the shadows to wait. Perhaps Price would leave in an hour or two. And if he did, Veles would be his.

MONDAY, AUGUST 24, 6:26 PM

"Sam," Nicole called from inside her apartment. "It's all clear."

I found her in the living room where we had talked before. Sometime during the few minutes of her search of the apartment, she had changed into sandals, cutoff jean shorts, and a dark green t-shirt. The light from a table lamp was playing across her features, accentuating the soft curves of her body. As I came closer, the room seemed to fade into the background. She looked up at me, her eyes deep pools of brown. I could feel warmth radiating from her. Fortunately, she spoke first, because I am not sure I could have formed a coherent sentence if she hadn't broken the spell.

"Sorry, but I took advantage of the fact that I live here to get comfortable," she said.

"I don't blame you. You want to eat now?"

"Maybe relax a little first?" she said.

"Sure, but if it's OK with you, how about no shop talk? I'd like a break."

"Same here," Nicole replied. She reached out and took the sack of food, lightly placing her other hand on my arm as she did. Nothing galvanized my attention like her lightest touch. "I'll put this in the kitchen. Want a beer?" she asked, as she retreated into her apartment.

"Sure."

I looked around. The room looked much the same, although the books on the table were different. This time it was *Biomedical Engineering: Bridging Medicine and Technology* and the Hemingway novel, *For Whom the Bell Tolls*. The latter I had read sometime in college; the former I never expected to crack.

"So, is Veles a French name?" I asked when she returned with our drinks.

"It's actually an Americanized version of the Czechoslovakian name, Veleslavína. My grandfather immigrated in the 1950s from what is now Slovakia and had the family name changed to reflect his new homeland. I'm third-generation. My mother's family had been in the United States longer, but had ties to France. So, my first name. What about you?"

"I have to admit complete ignorance of my family tree, other than the fact that we've been in the States for generations. I know some parts of the family have been living near Kansas City for a long time, and other parts in Kentucky. But before that? I have nothing but rumors from elderly aunts, uncles, and grandparents. Maybe someday, I'll trace down our roots, but I doubt it. Somehow, it's never been that important to me."

"I tend to feel the same, but my ties to Slovakia are a bit too obvious to miss. And really, the 'old country' has probably affected me more than I like to admit. My dad is strict and old-fashioned. He has a lot of ideas about what's proper for girls. I know it sounds trite, but he's still not sure why I didn't want to get married out of high school, have kids, and live next door."

I hesitated, rubbing my chin. I was the psychologist, but Nicole had given a lot more thought to how her environment had affected her than I.

"My dad used to give us a runt from the litters of pigs to raise. Taking care of something that's living is a lot of responsibility for a six-year-old, although I suspect he checked up on us. Anyway, it still felt like the job was ours to succeed or fail. It was the same with a lot of things growing up. My parents were interested in our lives and were supportive, but it was a 'make your own way' kind of upbringing."

Nicole smiled and nodded. "Somehow, I'm not surprised."

I wasn't certain what that meant and started to ask when she said, "Are you hungry?"

"Yeah, I am."

She led the way down a short hall to a small kitchen. The room was divided by an island with a range, microwave, cabinets, and counter space on one side. Three bar stools stood on the other. A sink below a window, dishwasher, and door to a back deck were at the far end of the room. Nicole pulled a couple of plates from a cabinet, as I unpacked the food. It wasn't long before we were seated side by side at the island, our plates filled.

I glanced sideways at her. "So, last time we established that you're the city girl and I'm the farm boy. You have brothers or sisters?"

"Three sisters, all younger," she replied. "You?"

"Two brothers. I'm in the middle."

Nicole turned toward me. "You think there's any truth about the effect of birth order on personality?"

I sat my fork down and returned her gaze. "I'm familiar with the idea, but if there's research, I've never read it. Why?"

"Well, because I tend to think I fit the description of firstborns about perfectly."

I rubbed my forehead, trying to recall what I had read. "Aren't firstborns supposed to be driven? You know, goal-oriented? Achievers?" I held out my hands. "I'd say that fits you."

"Yeah," she said, "but don't forget structured and controlling. Those are in there too, although I think it goes with the territory. Both my parents worked and I ended up watching my sisters."

"OK, are you trying to break it to me that I rolled my Moo Shu shrimp the wrong way?"

Nicole chewed on a fingernail, acting as if she was pained to tell me. "Yeah, they are a bit sloppy." After a long sigh, she said, "It's just that I like things the way I like them. But don't most people?"

"Probably so," I said, but I was thinking that 'straightforward' might be more descriptive of her than controlling. If we had a future, I would always know where I stood. While that would be difficult at times, I preferred the kind of directness and independence that she practiced over games and guessing.

I rubbed my chin, then took another sip of beer. "Yeah, I can see a lot of the first born in you, with the engineering career and all. But me? I can't see I fit a second-born at all. If I remember correctly, they're supposed to be social. I'm fairly shy."

Nicole shrugged in a way that said, 'I'll give you that.'

"And isn't pleasing people supposed to be their main goal in life?" I asked.

"That may be a bit of an exaggeration," replied Nicole, "but you like people to be happy. I've seen that in our meetings."

"I like it when it works out that way, and with you and Sue, it often does. But when I've worked something out and believe my conclusion is right, whether the message is going to make someone happy or not?" I shrugged. "It's just not that important."

Nicole grimaced in a dramatic way. "Yeah, I guess I've seen that with Ken." She paused a moment. "And the police for that matter. And you weren't exactly concerned about how Dr. Worthington felt about the files we needed either. Yeah, I guess you are pretty asocial, aren't you?" she said as a grin came to her face.

"What can I say?"

We rinsed our dishes and put the food away. Then, I followed her back to the living room.

"Tonight was fun," I said, glancing at my watch. "I'm glad we could get together, but I better call it an evening."

"I enjoyed it too." She started toward the door.

I don't know if first kisses ever go smoothly; most of mine hadn't. It also seemed like they went worse when I really liked a woman, and Nicole set new standards in that regard. But shaking hands again wasn't an option.

Nicole turned to smile at me when she reached the door.

"I can't imagine what people at work would say if I told them we talked about something as esoteric as the effects of birth order on personality." I laughed. It sounded a bit nervous even to my ears.

"You talk about your dates at work?" she asked sharply. She crossed her arms over her chest, her eyes narrowing.

"Ah...no," I stuttered.

Then I noticed that her mouth was twitching, the corners turning up in a smile. "I thought you didn't care what people think?"

"Most people, no, but I care what you think." The line wasn't clever, but in my moment of near panic, it felt like genius.

"Nice recovery." She smiled, helping my heart rate back to normal – or close to it anyway. I took a breath and stepped forward, hoping to close the gap between us for a goodnight kiss. Then...she took a small step backwards.

I wasn't sure what it meant, and I searched her face for a clue. Or maybe I knew, but wanted to find a reason to doubt my conclusion. Unfortunately, I found nothing there, because she had turned to the side and was looking at the wall behind me.

"How long will it take Ruger-Phillips to close out the project?" Nicole glanced at me, then back at the wall.

"Ah, probably around...maybe four to six weeks. Why?" I asked, thrown by the unusual turn in the conversation.

"No reason, really. Just wondering." She sighed, then said, "Well, I guess I'll talk to you tomorrow."

"OK, tomorrow," I stammered. I could hardly believe my eyes, but my arm moved forward as if it had a mind of its own and I shook her hand...again. She closed the door and I heard the lock click into place.

I started down the stairs, wondering again if I was wasting my time pursuing Nicole. But as soon as the thought entered, I knew I'd persist until I heard those fateful words, 'let's just be friends.' The only problem was, I didn't know what I should do differently to change that outcome. Did she need more space? More time? More attention? I had no idea.

But as I reached the vestibule, my thoughts transitioned from pondering my love life to apprehension. There had been a cloud hanging over me since we compiled the list of traits that the Blocker might destroy. Although I had pushed it to the recesses of my mind during dinner, it had grown darker, more ominous, more threatening in the few moments since I had left. Now, standing in the vestibule, I shivered despite the warmth. It was almost as if evil was hanging in the still air.

I turned and looked up the stairs. Maybe I should go back and check that she was all right. But that was ridiculous. I had just left her.

I cracked the front door of her building and looked out at the street. As before, the sidewalks were full of people, many walking dogs or just out for a stroll. No one seemed out of place. I stepped outside and checked the parked cars. They were the typical collection of coupes and sedans, pickups and SUVs. And none of the SUVs were the mysterious black one I had seen near my home. It all seemed calm, normal, routine. Even the street was empty, except for one white, panel van making the turn at the far end of the block.

PART 3.
CONVERGENCE

TUESDAY, AUGUST 25, 9:37 AM

I arrived at my office late, largely because I needed a six-mile run to burn off the effects of the previous day. The light on my phone was blinking. I had two messages and hit the button to play the first even before sitting down.

"Hi, Sam, it's Nicole. I wanted to say thanks again for seeing me home and for dinner. I enjoyed it." There was a long pause. "I'm sorry to have to say this, but I'll be working at my building today. Probably from now on, actually. I'll coordinate with Sue on the final report, but my management wants to...well, to get a proposal together for us to study the Blocker electronics. I wish we didn't have to go on alone, but with only the specs, there's no other choice. Anyway, let's talk later."

I dropped into my chair. Her company would be a shoo-in to win with what Nicole knew about the Blocker. I could almost see the coming press release that would put Nicole dead-center in a murderer's sights...if there was such a person.

I played the second message.

"Doc, this is Jon Huston. We found the study data." Jon was generally upbeat, but his words were bursting with energy. He paused a moment, probably pulling the handset from his mouth, because I heard a muted chuckle.

"I could take credit for diligently scouring the building for your files, and if anyone asks, that's exactly what I'm saying. But in truth, the grad students cleaning the basement found them. I checked and they seem complete. I've had everything copied, so call me and we can arrange a transfer."

He paused a moment, sighed, then continued more somberly. "I also wanted to apologize for the delay...and your wasted effort. The search you did had to be frustrating. As to why all this stuff was in the basement, I haven't a clue. Anyway, call and we'll get you everything you need. Bye."

I listened to the message twice...and then a third time, just to make sure I had heard right. Then, I called Nicole to let her know. Ken probably wouldn't have approved of calling a subcontractor before you told your own management, but I really wanted to give her the news. When she didn't answer, I left a message, breaking my own rule never to miss a chance to talk to her directly. But in this case, she and her company were wasting time on a proposal that was unnecessary.

Then, I told Ken. He responded in his normal, positive yet directive style. "That's great, Doc. Just keep out of WHT's workplace games and I know you'll turn out a great product for the VA." At least I was back to being Doc in his mind.

I walked by Sue's desk. "Oh, my god," she said as I approached. "Huston found the data."

"I'm that easy to read?" I asked, grinning at her.

"It's either that or you got lucky last night...and I've already talked to Nicole this morning."

"Yeah, it's the data," I replied, my smile dimming but not disappearing. The news was too good for that. "I'm going to call Huston, set up a time to pick up the files this afternoon. I suggested to Nicole that she come over tomorrow at 9:30. That work for you?"

"Sure," she replied.

"Great. See you tomorrow."

TUESDAY, AUGUST 25, 10:43 AM

A smile spread over the Experimenter's face, as he watched Subject 4 toiling away inside the chamber. It was much the same look a farmer might give his prize-winning hog at the state fair, because he owned the man now that his resistance was gone. And soon, he'd own his mind too.

So, with the computer-controlled equipment running smoothly, there was nothing to hold his attention inside the chamber. He turned his thoughts to Price, Jordan, and Veles – a vision that erased the smile and left his features in a glare. A solution to the problem they posed was proving illusive.

The best option for Price – catch him on one of his morning jogs – hadn't worked out yet. The Experimenter had watched the lonely stretch of trail through the park this morning, but the man had either skipped his workout or had gone elsewhere. Although he felt certain Price would reuse the route eventually, every day brought his foe closer to the truth.

Then, there was the second option – incapacitate both Price and Veles, if they returned to her apartment together. The question was, how? Two Tasers was the obvious choice, but he'd seen that approach fail already. In addition to the risk from the fall, he'd also have to monitor the second person while he restrained the first, lest he or she recover and attack him. The tactic was viable, but chancy.

Drugging them with food or drink had seemed a possibility, but assuring that both had partaken was an issue. He'd also considered using some type of sedating gas – it always worked in the movies. But calculating the correct amount when he'd have to estimate the dimensions of the apartment and transporting it to the building unseen made the alternative problematic.

The Experimenter was stymied and he could feel his enemies closing in. Worse yet, his sources of information on them were limited – what he could see on the street and his cameras at the WHT building. At least he would know if they were meeting with Huston.

He pulled up the video clips from Monday.

"What the hell?" the Experimenter asked the empty room. The files from the basement were usually small, containing one or two visits in most cases. But today, they were massive, as if the motion-activated camera was running continuously. When he looked at the first file, he realized that it had been.

Four young people – probably students – armed with a laptop, empty file folders, markers, and index cards entered the WHT storage area. In a far corner, they located two boxes of Worthington's notes, just like the ones he'd seen Scott deliver to the building a few days earlier. He shook his head, wondering how the man ever expected to find anything in this mire of paper. Two of the students left with their find, most likely to deliver them to Huston.

Then, the students started unloading the file cabinets, examining each folder, and entering information into the computer. Their task was apparent; it's relevance to him seemed dubious. The slight pang in the stump of his left, little finger, however, reminded him to keep watching. After a while, he doubled the replay speed; the pain was unchanged. Then, he increased it to four times normal, and the twinge in his hand stayed the same. Even the missing appendage must have questioned the need to obsess over their actions.

But when the time stamp on the video reached 16:52, something caught his eye. He paused the clip and moved back to the crucial moment. There it was. One of the students was holding an external disk drive. The initials A.T. were written on the side.

It was the study data.

The Experimenter pulled up the video clips from the second-floor landing and fast-forwarded to 16:52. After a few moments, he saw the same student carrying the drive upstairs. Unfortunately, the piece of computer equipment was far enough from the norm that he thought Huston needed to see it.

The Experimenter pushed back from his desk and tented his fingers in front of his face. Worthington must have put the drive and the rest of the study data in the basement. But why? Perhaps he was concerned about their security, about the insights they held? Maybe he had put them there temporarily, using the basement as a staging area before moving the precious files to his home?

"Or maybe he just ran out of room in his office with all the crap he was generating," said the Experimenter aloud, smiling at the thought.

But the humor drained from his being as quickly as it had come. Did this mean that Price, Jordan, and Veles had nothing before? That they had kept the VA interested with fantasies and promises? That they were just hoping to find the files...and now they had?

He could have had those data, if he had only known, and now, the turn of events was too cruel. He felt his instinctual rage creeping back into the corners of his mind. His vision dimmed. His heart started to pound, but he pushed his anger down.

He loathed the idea, but he would have to pause Subject 4's work. He needed time with the Blocker. He needed a better plan, because his adversaries had to be stopped. Of course, the VA would replace them, but a delay of a few months, even a few weeks would make all the difference.

Because soon, his mind would be immortal, living on in whatever body he chose.

WEDNESDAY, AUGUST 26, 6:11 AM

I stepped out of the front door of my apartment building and raised both fists over my head in a victory gesture, the exhilaration from a new beginning washing over me. Something about being on the verge of closing shop and then, getting an eleventh-hour reprieve made much of what had happened before seem surreal, almost like a dream. But I knew it wasn't, and to think that way was risky. I checked the street.

The sun wouldn't rise for another 15 minutes, but the dim rays of the morning twilight showed only vacant streets and sidewalks. Whether the parked cars were also unoccupied was more difficult to tell, but those nearby were empty. I'd just have to watch the others as I approached – something I did anyway to avoid crashing into a door thrown open in my path.

I started jogging slowly up the street when a woman I recognized – a fellow jogger with a husband and a couple of children – came out. She trotted down the steps of her building, then walked over to the ominous, black SUV I had spotted several days earlier. She started stretching, using it for balance. Then, she took a key from her pocket and opened the back.

The mystery was solved. Apparently, the vehicle didn't belong to A.T...or even the FBI.

"Morning," I said when I passed her. She was wrestling with a box, looking none too happy.

"You too," she replied. It was the longest conversation we had ever shared.

I always decide where to run after I start, and since this morning felt special, I picked one of my favorite routes. I liked it for its calm peacefulness, a textbook setting for clearing my head before a day at work. In moments, I was on 'automatic pilot,' making twists and turns I had completed dozens of times in the past and thinking about Worthington's files.

Ned had done well.

I stumbled, then almost laughed aloud when the thought struck. Not only had I showed Worthington some begrudging admiration, I had even used his first name. But I had come to believe Scott and Huston when they said he had been a decent man and a good researcher. And his organization of the data was consistent with that view. It was simple, yet thorough.

My first discovery in the files from Huston had been a short paper that described the study's methods. Random strings of digits of varying lengths had been stored as text on the computer, and then converted to voice using a text-to-speech application. This approach meant that all the numbers would be presented with the same tone and at precisely the same speed. After they were given, A.T. typed what he could recall of the sequence on a keyboard, and the accuracy and the speed of his response was recorded.

Those data were contained on a large-capacity, disk drive, one record for each trial. The written documents were neatly organized in boxes by date, with color-coded folders to indicate their type – either data from the Beck Anxiety Inventory or from the observation period.

The sound of a car horn intruded on my thoughts. Here, my route took me next to a busy highway; it was the only part of this jaunt that was less than ideal. I glanced at the scene.

Cars were bumper to bumper. The day was dawning with a steel-gray sky that promised humidity, but probably not rain. I was smiling anyway, because I was looking forward to discovering patterns in these data. I suspected that if I approached a hundred of the drivers out there on the road and told them of the simple elegance of Worthington's files and my plans for them, none would share my feelings. Most would probably run...even if they had to speed away on the shoulder.

But Sue would appreciate our opportunity and Nicole might be curious, because we'd be able to infer much about how A.T. was thinking from these few pieces of data. And that thought invigorated me.

* * *

The Experimenter slapped a mosquito on his neck, then peered through the brush to the path that ran near his hiding spot. No one was in sight. No one would have heard him.

It was his fourth day watching this stretch of the jogging path, waiting for Price to appear. He didn't mind...well, except for the bugs. But it was well worth the inconvenience if he could get rid of Price and obtain Subject 5 at the same time.

He had taken a position about midway through the secluded section of the trail, giving himself about two to three seconds before someone entering the trees would be directly in front of him and another two to three seconds before they exited on the other side. After that, the trail curved sharply and he would lose sight of his prey. But that was enough. He had even practiced the maneuver a few times. Observe Price entering. Step out just as he passes. Level the Taser. Fire. Remove the body.

It would all be over in less than fifteen seconds, but he still ran a risk. Another jogger might enter the woods just as he squeezed the trigger. If that happened, he would kill Price. He carried a six-inch boning knife, honed to razor sharpness for that exact purpose. He also had a towel and a change of clothes hidden deeper in the brush, along his planned escape route.

Today had been quiet. There were few people out jogging. Perhaps it was the gloomy, humid morning. The Experimenter raised to a crouching position. It was the best he could do to keep the circulation going in his legs. He sat back down. A couple of joggers entered the area from the east. The woman was talking about a new pair of running shoes she wanted to buy. The man looked bored. They passed by like everyone else – oblivious to his presence.

The Experimenter watched them leave to the west, his gaze lingering there for a moment in case someone entered. No one did. He looked back to the east, holding the scene for a few moments. He panned back to the west.

Someone was coming. It was Price. The Experimenter's heart sped up. His breathing deepened. His muscles quivered in anticipation.

As he watched Price approach, a tone came from his direction. A phone? Did the man really carry a phone when he jogged? The Experimenter stared in disbelief as Price stopped, pulled the device from his pocket, and started talking.

Price turned, but not to flee. He was pacing, the way people do when they're on a call. He was out of range of the Taser, but not by much. The Experimenter stood and climbed onto the path. He took a step toward Price, but the man continued to wander away. The Experimenter increased his speed, starting to close the gap.

Price stopped, then laughed at something that was said. He started to turn. The Experimenter was at the limit of the range of the Taser. If he shot now and missed, Price would be able to identify him. He might even attack.

The Experimenter turned and walked slowly away. He considered looking back, but didn't know which way Price was facing. He continued along the path. Once he cleared the trees, he stepped back into the edge of the woods. Concealment here was not as good, but it would do.

If Price emerged, should he take the shot? He studied the terrain. He could see 50 or 60 yards of the path; no one was on it. Across an open, grassy area, there was a seldom-used side street. It was empty. But even with no witnesses now, someone might appear at any moment. The risk of detection was too great.

The Experimenter waited a few minutes, then cautiously re-entered the wooded area. There was no sign of Price. He must have left from the direction he came. When the Experimenter reached the midpoint, he heard the footfall of a runner approaching from behind. He bent down, as if to tie a shoe lace. Stealing a glance, he saw a man, young, fit. He jogged past. The Experimenter stood and checked in both directions. No one. He raised the Taser and fired. The runner collapsed to the ground.

The Experimenter covered the gap between them in two strides, grabbed the man, and heaved him into the brush. He placed the cap on the runner's head, then checked his surroundings. Still clear. He moved the man deeper into the woods, then attached the gag and restraints.

He stopped, listened. There were people on the path. After a few moments, however, they passed without a pause, without a word. He moved the runner still deeper into the woods. Finding the two trees he had located before, he attached the hand restraints to one, the feet bindings to the other. He took a GPS locator from a bag he had left here and slipped it into the man's pocket. If he escaped somehow, the device's location would alert him to that fact.

The Experimenter removed the cap. Consciousness returned to the runner. He tried to shout through the gag. He strained against the bindings, then started thrashing on the ground, using the few inches of motion the restraints allowed. But on the soft earth, his movements made even less noise than the plaintive whimpers that now came from his throat.

When the runner fell still from exhaustion, the Experimenter checked the restraints and gag one last time. There seemed no chance of escape unless someone happened upon him and that was unlikely. The Experimenter stood.

"Rest easy. I'll be back for you tonight and then, we'll begin a long journey together."

A smile broke out across the Experimenter's face as he made his way back to his van. True, Price had escaped this time, but his luck couldn't last. In the end, all today meant was that Price would be Subject 6, rather than 5.

Or he'd be dead.

WEDNESDAY, AUGUST 26, 9:23 AM

Noticing that it was nearly the time for our meeting, I grabbed a box of surveys and went to the conference room. For once, I arrived before the women and took a seat. It was only moments before I heard them talking and laughing as they approached.

"Morning, Doc," Sue said as she entered.

"Hi, Sam. I hear we have some real data this time." Nicole's hazel eyes twinkled, as she pushed a strand of her light brown hair behind an ear.

"You look pretty happy about that," added Sue, grinning at me. "And it must be the data that's got you so upbeat, since we eliminated the other possibility yesterday." Nicole shot Sue a confused look as the women took seats across from me.

"Just happy to have my two favorite ladies back on this job," I said, not giving Sue a chance to continue. I already felt my face warming.

"Oh, Sam, I wanted to apologize again for interrupting your run this morning," said Nicole. "I was just so surprised when I heard your message."

"You caught Doc during a run?"

"Yeah," replied Nicole. "We were working on proposal ideas yesterday, so I didn't check my messages until this morning. Must have been around 7:00 when I called."

Sue turned to me, giving one short, mocking laugh. "After all the lectures to us, don't tell me you were out there before light?"

I opened my mouth to object, but Nicole was faster. "I know," she said, now shaking her head. "He was. He even said he was in some park. I made him promise to at least get back on busy streets."

I could see this conversation digressing into a critique-Sam session, so I held up a hand. "I admitted my mistake to Nicole and now to you, Sue. I was wrong. From now on, it's sweating on a treadmill in a well-lighted gym with two-dozen of my closest friends."

Sue didn't answer, but turned to Nicole. "I don't know how men survive without us." Then, turning back to me. "It's probably time we do some work."

I chuckled. "I think that's my line. Anyway, what I suggest for the division of labor is that Sue handles the observation reports. You can check the Beck inventory data later, but it will probably just tell us what we already know; he wasn't particularly anxious because of the study. So, if there's information about how the experience affected him, it'll have to be in those reports. And Nicole, you can continue to analyze the specs, tell us what the device was doing electronically."

Nicole nodded, as Sue said, "Sounds good to me."

"For my part, I'll work with the study data and bounce my initial findings off Sue." I looked at Nicole and bit the inside of my lip, wondering if I should ask. "Do you have any interest in this part of the project?"

Nicole didn't hesitate. "Sure. I won't have anything to add, but I'd like to listen." She glanced at Sue, then back at me and shrugged. "I'm curious how A.T. typing numbers into a computer can tell you anything about what he's thinking."

"Good for you, Nicole," Sue said, nudging her with an elbow and winking. "That way, you'll get to see Doc at his nerdy best."

I guess some people would be offended by that remark, but Sue knew me better than that. And besides, it was true.

"Yep," I said. "It'll be interesting to see what secrets we can tease out of those data. I'm going to work in my office, if anyone needs me. Sue, you can break down the written reports here or take smaller piles of them back to your desk. Your call."

"Here. My desk is too cluttered." Sue's idea of clutter was closer to most people's idea of impeccable order, mine included, but I said nothing.

"Nicole, you have the same choice. But if you take anything back to your building, you'll need to sign for it. Now that we have these files, we're responsible for managing them."

"Here's fine. There's plenty of room for both of us."

"OK, it's a plan," I said. "Let's get together at 2:00 and compare notes on progress. Anything else?"

There was. I could tell by the way Sue and Nicole looked at each other, although neither said a word for a moment. Then, Sue turned to me. "I have a name for you."

I was expecting a joke – some nickname dripping with innuendo, probably sexual. What Sue said, however, was, "Atwood."

I drew back and stared at her. "As in Dr. Sebastian Atwood?"

"Right. Or as in, A.T. Wood."

I sat staring at Sue, my mouth hanging open for what seemed a minute, but was probably less than ten seconds. Finally, I managed, "You think Atwood is A.T.?"

"We have means, motive, and opportunity." This was from Nicole, the investigative triumvirate becoming something of a punchline on our project. "He was involved, he has the knowledge, and apparently, according to the Internet, he has the money. He's done well in material research for cutting-edge, medical devices."

I shifted my gaze between the women, then blew out a long breath. "You think he wants to steal it?"

"Maybe not at first, but the Blocker is addictive," said Sue. "Worthington passes his excitement about the work to Atwood during some of their initial meetings. He volunteers for the study. Worthington wants to save money...." She held out a hand like the inevitability of the situation was laying in her palm.

"And the description of the volunteer, the male student in Worthington's paper?" I asked. "A cover for what they were doing?"

"Yeah," said Sue. "If Worthington wanted some security on his project, this misdirection would provide it. A.T. may have been hiding in plain sight from the very start."

I rubbed my forehead with a hand, looking down at the tabletop. "OK," I said when I looked up. "I'll call Detective Ahern."

"Not just yet," said Nicole. "I'm meeting with Atwood first. See what I can find out."

"No way," I said.

The emotion that flashed across Nicole's face was annoyance, if I read it correctly. I had overstepped my bounds. Before she could remind me that it was her life, I said, "What I mean is, I'm not comfortable with that. He's a potential murderer."

"It's just dinner," said Sue.

"Dinner?" I stood up, turned from them, walked the three steps to the wall, then turned back. "Is that supposed to be better?"

"You need to listen to what we have in mind," said Sue, somewhat sharply. Clearly, I was outnumbered.

I wondered if Nicole was too irritated to speak because she just looked at me, her brows knitted. I took the three steps back to my chair and sat. "OK. I'm listening."

"Nicole called Atwood to ask a few questions about the materials in the coils. He seemed anxious to meet and suggested dinner."

"Of course, he...." Both women's frowns deepened, so I closed my mouth.

"The idea that Atwood might be A.T. came up later. So, we thought she'd keep the date, because let's face it, we really have nothing on him. But Nicole knows exactly what to look for – a cold, self-centered attitude. A dislike of art. And I'll go along to make sure he behaves himself."

"I'm going...." I stopped, reconsidering my words. "I'd like to go along too."

"This is getting out of hand," said Nicole, her displeasure clear on her face. "We need a setting where he feels free to talk, not something like Worthington's office where he never said a word. Seeing the three of us staring at him from across the table?" She shook her head. "It won't work."

"How about Doc and I take a different table? Some place where we can watch the two of you from a distance. Then, you're free to use your feminine charms on him."

"Perfect," Nicole said, much too quickly for me to question the plan. "But I'm not sure you'll be able to find a table close enough."

When she said where they were meeting, I understood. The dining area was composed of rows of booths. If you were more than two away, you'd see nothing. But it was also first-come, first-served seating. "You're meeting him in that small, waiting area they have?"

"Right," said Nicole.

"OK, what if I get someone to go with me early and we stake out two booths close together?" I said. "Then, the other person can leave when you and Atwood come in. I'll sit with my back to the door, so he won't see me when you pass by. OK?"

"Al can go with you," said Sue. "He's good at holding tables. He might even be something of an expert."

Perhaps the bit of levity worked, as Nicole's frown melted a bit. "OK," she said eventually. "But it sounds like a lot of trouble for nothing. It's a public restaurant."

"It is," I agreed. "But getting there and leaving are another matter. If he's a killer, he'll know exactly where you'll be." I looked at Nicole closely, holding both hands out in front of me. "Would it be all right if Sue rode to the restaurant with you? You can walk from the parking lot by yourself, with her trailing behind."

Nicole hesitated, but Sue jumped in. "I hate to admit it, but Doc's right. You and I can leave from work together."

Nicole released a long sigh, then nodded. "OK. But after this Mata Hari act is over, we should talk. You know, not wait a day to tell you he's got a bullet with your name on it. Someone can follow me to my car after dinner, but then I'll drive in a loop and come back to the restaurant."

The plan was getting complex, but if we did it right, someone would always have Nicole in sight except when she came back. "OK," I said. "Sue will watch you from your car to the restaurant. I'll cover when you go back to your car after dinner. Just make sure no one is following when you loop back to join us."

"I will," said Nicole.

Sue looked up from her phone. "I just texted Al. He's in."

"That was fast," I said.

"He's been off work a few days. Some big remodeling project. I'm sure you'll hear all about it over dinner, because he's been driving me crazy, telling me how bored he is."

I nodded, then asked, "So, when is this dinner with Atwood?"

"Tonight," said Sue.

"Tonight?" The unease I felt when the women first announced their intentions came rushing back. But there was little I could do other than tackle the problems over which I had some control. I excused myself and went to my office to get started on the study data...if I could keep my mind on my work.

WEDNESDAY, AUGUST 26, 2:09 PM

I walked quickly down the hall toward the conference room, already ten minutes late for our meeting. As I approached, I heard Sue and Nicole talking, then a few titters.

As I came through the door, Sue said, "See, I told you Doc wouldn't forget about us." Nicole raised a hand to her lips, but the amusement in her eyes said there was a smile hidden there.

"Yeah, sorry, ladies. I got involved with the numbers and lost track of time."

"I told Nicole you'd say that. Some women lose their husbands to sports. Your wife will lose you to a spreadsheet."

"Sports are good too," I said, striking my most thoughtful pose. "I could study sports statistics all day." I received the response I expected when both groaned.

"Sorry. But seriously, when you see what I'm finding, you'll forgive me." I looked at Sue and Nicole. "Any volunteers to go first?"

"Yeah, you," said Sue. "You can't say something like that and expect us to wait."

"OK." I went to the conference room's computer, brought up the graph from the paper Worthington had given us, and projected it on the screen at the front of the room. "You probably remember this – A.T.'s memory span over the course of the study?"

It looked a bit like stair steps. Initially, A.T. had been able to remember a little over seven items, and that didn't change much in the first few weeks working with the Blocker. Then, his rate of recall shot up to around 14 or 15 items. After that, the line was flat for several more weeks, then there was a second spurt to about 21 items. A.T. had quit shortly after that last surge.

"Of course," said Sue. "Since he started around average, the question is, what did he do that allowed him to increase his recall from 7 to 14 items? And then again, from 14 to 21?"

"Exactly," I replied. "So now, time to use what we can see in A.T.'s behavior and infer what we can't see inside his head. You're familiar with silent rehearsal?" I asked, looking at Nicole.

"It's come up a few times in conversations and...." Nicole paused, looking at me closely. "Is this a trick question, because I thought it means exactly what it says. Using your inner voice to practice something so you remember it."

I laughed. "Yeah, I guess the name's not all that mysterious, is it? But what's important is that there's a characteristic pattern that goes with silent rehearsal, and it makes perfect sense when you think about it.

"So, if the first number someone is trying to remember is three, that person would say 'three' to himself. If the second number is six, he'd say 'three six'. If the third number is four, he'd say 'three six four.' And so on. By the time a list of seven or eight numbers has been presented, the person would have repeated the first few several times. So, when he's asked to recall, he would produce them very quickly and very accurately. Then, speed and accuracy go down, as he tries to remember items he's reviewed fewer times. Finally, the last item or two tend to be recalled well because they're recent.

"So, the pattern you typically get with silent rehearsal is fast and accurate, then slower with more errors, and finally, fast and accurate again. Basically, it's a V-shaped function. Make sense?"

"It does," replied Nicole. "It even seems obvious, now that you explain it."

"Good," I replied. "And here's the graph of A.T.'s accuracy when he was recalling about seven items, early in the study."

The characteristic V was apparent when the figure appeared, and both women nodded – Nicole from her new-found understanding and Sue because she would have seen dozens of figures like this one before.

"OK, good so far," I replied. "So, when A.T. reaches 14 items, his accuracy looks like this." I brought up the next chart.

Both women leaned forward, their eyes narrowing as they probed the graph for meaning.

"Oh, my god," said Sue, her hand coming to her throat. "It looks like he has two voices in his head, each doing their own silent rehearsal. He recalls the items from one producing a V-shaped line, then the numbers from the second, making a second V. We end up with this W-shaped graph." She paused. "Is that really possible?"

"It fits, but this is just the accuracy data halfway through the study. Let's see what we get later and with other measures."

※ ※ ※

Jack Gilbert slowly collapsed to the mat covering the floor, the smell of bleach and industrial cleaner on its surface bringing tears to his eyes. He hoped he was doing it right, but he'd never seen himself pass out from the knock-out drug the man gave him. He only knew he did because soon after eating or drinking, he'd wake up, lashed to a chair, ready for another round of torture.

But not this time.

This time, Jack had dumped his drink down the toilet. Of course, he couldn't be certain his tormentor, an individual who called himself the Experimenter, had put the drug there. Nor could he be sure he hadn't been seen disposing of it. And if he was, the

Experimenter would simply use the Taser. He was taking a chance, but what did he have to lose?

Under his prone body, Jack cradled a sliver of the glass and plastic material that formed his prison walls. A thin piece of it had been used to form a small shelf near the toilet. He had shattered it with his elbow and hidden a shard before the Experimenter came in to clean. Later, he had ripped up one of his shirts in what he hoped passed as a show of defiance. He had secreted a strip of it, which was wrapped around one end of the sliver to protect his hand.

Now, the time had come for him to try his homemade weapon.

Jack laid motionless, his ears straining for the sound of approaching footsteps, the soft thud of the door bolt being thrown. But there was nothing. Was his breathing right? Should he be panting? Taking in long, deep lungsful? Did this drug make people twitch? Toss and turn? Should he be rambling in his unconscious state?

Hope deserted him. How could he possibly deceive the Experimenter when he didn't know how to act? Would his captor be enraged by this deceit? Could he possibly make the pain any worse? Jack thought not, because he had been near the point of unconsciousness before. But even if the man couldn't increase the pain, he could make it go on for hours, perhaps days. He'd die, screaming in agony.

The door to the room opened. Jack wanted to jump up and beg for forgiveness. The urge was overwhelming. He couldn't win, so why not make his end as peaceful as he could?

But the feeling passed. He had to fight back, if given the chance. So, he laid motionless, trying to control his breathing, as the adrenaline in his blood had accelerated his heart to the point of bursting from his chest.

The door to his cage opened. A second wave of energy infused his body. The drumming of his heart in his ears became deafening. His hands grew sweaty around the makeshift handle to the shank. His muscles trembled in anticipation.

Jack could hear wheels on the mat, as the Experimenter pushed the chair into his cage. Then, the rustle of straps against metal came to his ears as it was laid behind him. The Experimenter was close. The sound of his breathing was just inches from Jack's ear.

"Time for a little more work, Number 4?" the man asked.

Jack spun out of his fetal position, raising into a crouch facing the Experimenter. He held the shank firmly in his right hand near his shoulder, his arm poised to strike.

The Experimenter gasped. His eyes grew wide in shock, then terror. He scrambled backwards, falling over the wheelchair. As he rose to flee, Jack drove the shank deep into the man's calf. The Experimenter fell to the floor, holding his leg and screaming in pain.

The man looked up at Jack from the floor, his body trembling. His breath came in short rasps between sobs. "No, please. Don't hurt me. I'll let you go."

Jack didn't believe it, but the words produced a moment of indecision, and he glanced away.

The Experimenter pushed himself from the floor and lunged toward the door. Jack leapt forward, driving the shank into the back of the other leg. The Experimenter collapsed. He began dragging himself forward with his arms, moaning as the pool of blood grew in his wake.

After a few feet, the Experimenter rolled over, his chest heaving in pain and exhaustion. "Every door between you and freedom is locked. You'll never get out of here alive," he hissed.

"And neither will you," said Jack, his voice calm, cold. He drove the shank into the man's stomach, blood pouring over the front of his white shirt. "You'll die here suffering. And I'll enjoy every moment of it."

Jack shot bolt upright on the floor, the dream slowly fading from his mind. It had come again. It was the fantasy that had sustained him during the first hours of torture. It was the illusion that had visited him over and over in the fitful hours of sleep in those first, few days. But it had been some time since the dream had come, and he wondered if this time would be the last.

Jack wondered that because something had started to change inside of him, inside his head. The memory of the agony remained, of course, but the sessions in the other room had become...what, satisfying? He craved them. They left him feeling calm, confident, almost invincible, even though he was shackled, left helpless in a chair.

But that was not the only thing that was changing. Like most people, he could picture things in his mind. And like most, when he thought, it was like he was talking to himself. But in the last few days, he didn't have a voice and a picture. He had two. And while these inner worlds could be and often were different, they also seemed to know about each other. If one was thinking about strangling the Experimenter and the other about the marvels of this mind-multiplying technology, the latter might suggest some questions before the former finished the deed.

Slowly, these aberrations started to feel like a metamorphosis, as if the device in the next room had awakened an ability that was his, but that had long laid dormant within him. Tasks that the Experimenter posed that were nearly impossible at first – evaluate this syllogism, rotate this 3D line drawing in your head, solve this analogy – became easy, and he was doing two of them at the same time. Or two different things. Even math, which had not come readily to Jack, now seemed simple.

And while the voices sometimes bickered, there was one thing about which they always agreed. Whatever the Experimenter was doing to him, it was making him smarter, more focused, more of a man.

Jack heard the thud of the door bolt being shoved open. The Experimenter walked into the residence, pushing the wheelchair in front of him. A man he knew only as Subject 5 sat in it, unconscious, a familiar cap on his head.

Jack stood up and walked to the edge of the cage. He looked out through the glass walls. "Do you have something for me to drink?" he asked.

The Experimenter smiled and pulled a sealed container of orange juice from his pocket. "I do. And I think you'll really enjoy this."

* * *

"That's it," I said, closing the application running on the computer. The last chart disappeared from the screen.

"Everything I've looked at so far – accuracy by position in the list, speed by position, the type of errors made, and so on – it all suggests the same thing. A.T. had two voices, two streams of consciousness in his head. They develop separately at first, then start working together. By the end of the study, he could put information into rehearsal on one side, while the other looks for a mnemonic – a trick or pattern to help him remember. And since the Blocker increases left-side functions like math ability and mental manipulation, then forming unique memory tricks on-the-fly may not be that hard for him. In the end, he's recalling some of the numbers from mnemonics he created and some from rehearsal. Well?"

Silence descended on the room. Sue sat drumming a couple fingers on her lips, her forehead wrinkled in concentration. Nicole twirled a strand of hair around her finger, her eyes off toward the corner of the room.

"Unbelievable," said Nicole, breaking the silence after several moments. "How comfortable are you with these conclusions?"

"Worthington told us from the start that there were two hemispheres at work, and that preconception might have influenced me. But there is one thing that won't change."

"The fact that his behavior is different from everyone else in the world?" asked Sue.

I nodded. "There's no mistaking that fact."

"So, no one has found anything like this before?" asked Nicole. "Maybe something from the split-brain studies?"

"Not that I know of," said Sue, turning to me.

"Me either," I said. "But there are some cases that show how the sides of the brain can work separately and then coordinate later. You remember the movie, *Rain Man*?"

"Sure, with Dustin Hoffman and Tom Cruise," said Nicole.

"Right. It's based on the savant, Kim Peek, whose name came up when I was researching hemisphere differences. Peek's hemispheres were separate and evidently, he could read two pages of a book at the same time, one with each eye. But when he recalled the story, his brain reassembled it. It's not the same, but there are parallels in the way his sides worked independently, but with something else to pull it all together."

"All I can say, Doc, is that you're forgiven for being late to this meeting," said Sue, grinning and shaking her head. "It's mind-blowing that rewiring can go to this extreme."

"It is," I replied. "I think I can use a 10-minute break, but before that, just one last thought."

"Is this the thought that spoils those 10 minutes?" asked Sue, exaggerating a frown for show.

"Hopefully not...but probably," I admitted, rubbing my chin. "Two weeks ago, I was sleeping with my Louisville slugger."

"You're talking about a baseball bat and not some hottie you picked up in Kentucky, right?" asked Sue.

I chuckled. "Right. Then, Worthington was found dead and that concern faded. A little over a week later, I got spun up again about how extensive use of the Blocker might affect people, make them driven to sustain their fantasy world. And we've done some things to protect ourselves against a possible threat.

"But up until now, all our speculation about the Blocker and its effect on people has included the phrase, 'if it works.' It may be electronically addictive, if it works. It may produce a cold, heartless drive for self-preservation, if it works. Well, in my mind, we can drop that phrase. The Blocker works."

WEDNESDAY, AUGUST 26, 2:33 PM

At last, it was time. The Experimenter had followed the guidance of the *Neural Activity Blocker Advanced Design Document* to the letter. He had 'spared no pain,' assuring that each part was built to specification, checking that each line of software code was flawless. So now, he would see if the words lived up to their promise. It was time to see if he could insert memories into another human. It was time to find where he was on the road to immortality.

After his rushed attempt to implement the Blocker's advanced features had left Subject 3 dead, the Experimenter had wondered what he should implant in the brain of his next Guinea pig. Eventually, he would embed his own thoughts, but it was too soon for that. So, after hours of deliberation in concert with his electronic ally, it came to him. And it was pure genius.

Normal communication with his subjects had always been impossible; none had taken their fate in stride. Instead, they had lied, screamed, cursed, spat, and tried to injure him. And when they realized the benefits of the Blocker and became willing participants, the Experimenter still couldn't trust them. Subject 4 appeared to have turned that corner, but soon, if not already, he would be hatching plans to steal the technology so he could have it for his own.

So, without anyone to trust, how was the Experimenter to know if the latest enhancements worked? How would he know when a memory of a warm summer's evening had been successfully implanted? Or when the sensation of plunging into an icy lake had been formed? He wouldn't.

But when the Experimenter saw the answer, it was obvious. He would leave Subject 4 with the experiences of a young child. A child with a benevolent, but strict master. With nothing to guide him but the memories of the Experimenter sustaining his worthless life for years, Number 4 would divulge every thought, undertake every task, make every sacrifice. He would be, in short, the perfect subject. But what made his idea even better was that his discoveries would serve double duty. The same blueprint would work perfectly when he captured Veles.

The first step was to erase the person's memory. All the stored fragments of past sights, smells, and sounds spread among the various visual, olfactory, and auditory areas of the brain – the grist from which the hippocampus rebuilds a memory – must be removed. It was the equivalent of a factory-reset. He would remove the old, leaving a blank slate on which he would write the sights, sounds, and smells of his life...or those from a fiction he wished to create.

The Blocker was configured for the reset. The Experimenter took one last look into the experimental chamber. Subject 4 was ready. He entered a command on the keyboard, then rolled his chair close to the one-way mirror.

The device was now driving signals deep into the brain, the likes of which no one had ever experienced. The man's features remained steady. He sat still, looking forward, as if waiting for the next task to begin. Did he know his past was fading? Did he see the memories disappear? Did he feel the loss? Or once they were gone, was it like they had never happened?

Two hours passed, and although the Experimenter wasn't sure how long the process should take, the time seemed adequate. He returned to his desk, shut down the Blocker, and released a long breath.

"Time to meet a man with no past," he said to himself. He rose from his chair, entered the chamber, and approached. "Number 4?" he said.

The man's eyes opened, but he said nothing.

The Experimenter crouched down and raised his voice. "Number 4? Can you hear me?"

The man's eyes went wide, as he stared at the Experimenter's lips. Then, his mouth began opening and closing rhythmically, like a fish in water. Drool started running down his cheek. Then, from his lips came a gurgling grunt.

The Experimenter dropped his head, then looked back up at Subject 4. "You're not a man with no past. You're a fully grown newborn."

Subject 4 became more excited as the Experimenter spoke. His eyes darted back and forth across the Experimenter's face. His mouth worked faster, as the grunts and gurgles came in a rush.

The Experimenter stood from his crouch and retraced his steps back to the work area. From a desk drawer, he pulled the misaligned Blocker cap, the one capable of killing. He was getting more use from his chance discovery than he had ever anticipated. He returned to the chamber, removed the laboratory equipment, placed the cap on Subject 4's head, and turned it on.

The Experimenter closed the door to the chamber as he left. He didn't need to watch; he'd seen life slip away under the effects of the cap before.

He sat at his desk and leaned back, rubbing his chin as he studied the gray walls. He was confident in his ultimate success. After all, he only sought to duplicate a natural phenomenon. He wanted to use his electronics to create the equivalent of retrograde amnesia – the loss of one's past, while general knowledge such as the ability to speak remained intact. But he also knew that the theories that linked brain locations to so-called episodic memory were incomplete. In this attempt, he had selected the most likely regions. Obviously, they were wrong.

He removed his notebook from a desk drawer and reviewed the areas he had targeted. Then, he calculated the number of tests he would need to cover all the combinations of the most likely regions. The number, 28, was larger than he had expected and much greater than he had hoped.

In nearly two months of experimentation, he had caught five men. At that rate, it would take him nearly a year to study even the most likely groupings. But what if the answer lay outside that set? Was he headed for a quagmire of promise never realized? Would he be chasing an unobtainable goal like a thirsty man pursuing a mirage in the desert?

The number, 28, grew in his mind. It crowded the light of success, the hope of immortality. The room dimmed. He turned, expecting to find the numerals looming over him, but there was nothing save the growing darkness.

But then he realized, anyone with a memory would work for this part of his research. Men. Women. Children. The face of Jordan popped into his mind, pushing back against the shadow of his rage. She wouldn't have to be wasted. He knew what needed to be done, and the darkness receded. "Tonight, I hunt. And I shall not come back empty-handed."

"Who's next?" I asked, as I entered the conference room. Sue was looking over Nicole's shoulder, as they studied something on a laptop.

"I've always lived by the adage, ladies first," said Sue as she slid into a chair. "And that would be you, Nicole." She nudged her coworker with an elbow and received a roll of the eyes in reply. "But in this case, I can finish my report in two minutes and give Nicole the rest of the meeting."

I raised my eyebrows. "Two minutes?"

"Yeah, I know," she replied. "Now that we know the Blocker works, the big question is, what does it do besides allowing A.T. to remember the phone numbers of three women at a time, rather than just one."

"And you're not finding anything in the observations?" I asked, trying to hide the concern I felt. If the Blocker had corrosive effects on the mind, that conclusion wouldn't come from the test data. It would come from the observations after each session, if it came from the study at all.

"I'll have something soon, but nothing firm yet," replied Sue. "What I'm working with are the answers to four standard questions and an open-ended description of A.T.'s behavior for the 30 minutes after each session. After that, he went home. The four standard questions were...." She scanned a page of notes. "Memory for location, recall of the day's date, eye-hand coordination, and navigation. The last question involved either walking to or giving directions to a well-known, nearby spot.

"I expected that my graphs on these questions would look the same as Worthington's, and they did. A.T. always knew where he was and the date. He made a few, small mistakes on navigation, but they were simple errors, like giving the wrong street name. And eye-hand coordination showed a typical learning curve."

"Learning curve?" said Nicole. "That's a large improvement at first, but then leveling off?"

"Right."

"So, no disorientation...at least on these tasks," I said.

"That's the way I'm reading it," said Sue, "which leaves the notes from the waiting period. I've looked at about 20% of them, picking some from early in the experiment, some near the midpoint, and some from the end. Of course, I'll cover it all before I'm done, but already I can tell that after about two or three weeks, he stopped doing anything and just sat there."

I looked at Sue closely. "He sat motionless for 30 minutes?"

"Yep."

I opened my mouth, but Sue held up a hand. "Before you ask me a bunch of questions, I'll answer them all. I don't know what it means. At least not yet. But I have some ideas and I'd like until tomorrow afternoon to look at them. I'd also like to have Nicole help, because she can come at this from a fresh perspective."

It was unfair that this pivotal issue had fallen to Sue, but I could think of no one more qualified. What I could do with numbers – find systematic patterns in what appeared a chaotic mess – Sue did with open-ended text. She also knew psychology nearly as well as I, although that wouldn't help. Our answers lay outside known theories and research, and that's where Nicole would come in. I'd seen a bit of her creative side in her choices of books and her art. As a team, they'd do great.

"OK." I settled back into my chair and released a sigh. "I'll put my curiosity on hold until tomorrow. Let me know if I can help." I tilted my head toward Nicole. "Looks like the floor is all yours."

Nicole glanced at her laptop. "The specifications we received from Dr. Huston have three sections. The first is a 12-page overview of the device. It's like a brochure you'd give a perspective customer...which is how I think Worthington used it. It's more advertising than technical. The second part gets into more detail, and that's where I've spent most of my time. There's a lot of information in it, but I think there's only one topic we need to discuss."

"The coils or the software?" I said, guessing it had to be one of these two innovations.

"Yeah, you're going to tell us all about his solid core design using specially manufactured, ferromagnetically active materials and a modified, H-coil geometry, right?" asked Sue, struggling to keep a straight face as she read the words off a piece of paper near her elbow. She turned to me. "This is what we talk about, when you're not around."

"Well, no," said Nicole, straight-faced, as if she hadn't noticed Sue's tone. "The coils and the software are amazing. But no." She paused a moment, looking at her laptop.

"The way Dr. Worthington designed the coils, any one by itself can't produce a response in the brain. But by having the signals from two or more of them converge inside the skull, the threshold can be reached. The software controls which coils fire and so, how deep inside the brain the reaction occurs. It also controls timing, so that a wave pattern can be produced. Voila, you have a Blocker that creates a wave that overwrites other activity."

At first, Nicole's lack of response to Sue had thrown me...until I realized that she wouldn't see this as an area for humor. Nicole was imparting facts, and she didn't want any misunderstanding even in jest. And as her description unfolded, it was easy to read her passion for these technical details. Even with a technology she was learning, her speech was more rapid, her gestures more animated.

"The way you describe the Blocker's operation – signals converging inside the skull to set up a wave of brain activity. It sounds precise, but I'm guessing it's not, since Worthington had to aim his device at half the brain."

"Yeah, pinpointing the reaction is not as simple as it sounds," replied Nicole. "The path of magnetism is difficult to predict due to the irregular shape of the brain and the fact that magnetism isn't conducted uniformly. Individuals differ as well. When Dr. Worthington said that he didn't have the precision to treat pain in a specific limb, what he meant was he lacked a way to develop a map for a person."

She looked around the room, then chuckled and shook her head. "But I guess I got a little off-topic. What I wanted to talk about from Section 2 is the user interface. I think I solved the mystery of what A.T. meant about adjusting the Blocker."

"User interface?" I said, leaning forward in my chair. "There is one?"

"Of sorts," said Nicole. "It only controls one thing – the wavelength of the blocking signal. The user can change it from the computer."

I laughed at myself. "One of the few things Detective Ahern found useful in everything I told him was that A.T. must have had some technical background, if he had ideas about adjusting the Blocker. Looks like that's out the window. What did he have to know? How to use a pull-down menu?"

"No, type in a number," said Nicole, exaggerating a grimace. "It accepts anything between 0.5 and 45. That would be Hertz, or cycles per second."

"OK. I'll give Ahern a call," I said, still shaking my head. Then, realizing I might be emphasizing the bad news too much, I added, "Nice catch, Nicole. Definitely something we and the police need to know. Thanks."

Nicole nodded, a slight smile coming to her face.

"So, a half to 45 Hertz," said Sue. "That's anywhere from being in a coma to higher level thought. Anywhere from darkness to a rush of disjointed images and ideas. I'm betting he wanted the rush."

"I was thinking he might go for the lower frequencies," said Nicole.

"Eww," said Sue. "And plunge half his brain into a coma? Why would you think that?"

Nicole turned toward me. "I understand the words, Sam, when you talk about how split-brain patients can have two, separate experiences. But thinking about what that's like? It's hard for me." She paused, shook her head. "No, more like impossible, but it seems like the separate realities would be confusing, disorienting." She turned back to Sue. "Setting the Blocker to the lowest frequencies would eliminate that tension. It may explain why A.T. argued for his changes vigorously, as Dr. Huston put it."

"I hadn't thought of it that way," said Sue. "But it makes sense. And it's probably good that Worthington didn't allow the adjustment, or A.T. would have been living entirely in the right side of his head during the sessions. All of the effects of the technology, good and bad, would get magnified, maybe by a lot."

"Yeah," said Nicole slowly. "My thoughts too. That's everything I wanted to discuss on Section 2. Questions?"

"You may want to come up with some," said Sue, turning to me. "Even trivial ones, because you're not going to like what she has to say about Section 3."

"I think that's a bit of an exaggeration," said Nicole, but her words lacked conviction.

I looked at them, hoping to find some clue about what was to come. I found none.

"I'm good on Section 2, but let's take 10 before we get to the maybe bad, maybe not-so-bad news."

∗ ∗ ∗

It was quiet in the conference room when I returned with my typical afternoon, half-cup of coffee. I set the cup down and wandered over to the other side of the table. Nicole's notebook was open, jottings on the discussion covering one page. On the facing side, there was a sketch of the podium and edge of the conference table.

"It's not very good," came Nicole's voice from the doorway.

"I disagree. Just pen and ink – no color – but that's a lot of detail." I looked at her, my eyebrows raising. "Now I'm wondering if your hemispheres work independently – one side keeping up with our talk and the other drawing?"

Nicole came over to her chair, brushing me as she passed. My arm tingled from her touch. She turned and looked at me, her eyes twinkling pools, more green than brown.

"I think my engineering background conflicts with my art. I try to make everything perfect, so I'm slow. I've been working at getting faster. That's about ten minutes, before Sue came back after lunch."

"Wow. Now I'm really impressed," I said.

Sue entered the room, so I retreated to the other side of the table and we all took a seat. Nicole opened her notebook to a new page and cleared her throat. "Well, here goes," she said, making me wonder if Sue had exaggerated at all. "Section 3 of the specifications deal with producing specific thoughts and perceptions inside the brain.

Even taking the thoughts of one person and putting them in someone else."

I physically recoiled at her statement, rocking back so hard in my chair that it nearly tipped over.

This is disastrous.

Someone without emotional constraints on his behavior would be dangerous enough. But someone without those restrictions and the capability to impose their thoughts on others would be a monster. He would be capable of anything in the pursuit of his own vision. As was often the case with me, questions piled up in my mind, each seeking priority to be voiced. But before the process had gone far, Nicole continued her summary.

"However," she said, drawing the word out, "I believe that even though this topic is in a specifications document, it's more conceptual than real."

"I like the phrase you used earlier today," said Sue. "It's speculation, not specification."

"OK," I replied, "but we need to be certain of that...or as close to certainty as we can be."

"I agree," replied Nicole. "The reason I think this section's about the future is because it's like a literature review – the kind you might find at the start of a research paper. Researchers at the University of Washington used an EEG to read brain waves from one person. This signal was then sent via the Internet to a second person wearing TMS coils. The idea was that the first person would think about moving his finger and the second person would complete the action. And it worked."

"OK," I said slowly, "but that's a fairly simple response – move a finger. If you put the coils in the right place, wouldn't it just about guarantee you'd get a twitch?"

"In large part, yes. But the unknown is what happens when you drop Dr. Worthington's TMS capability into this setup. It would do more than stimulate a motor neuron. At least, it would as soon as the aiming issues are resolved. But how much more?" She left the question hanging, raising her open hands in front of her. "And he only hints at the advances that would be required to do more than a simple muscle response."

"He hints at it?" I said.

"Yeah," she replied, slowly shaking her head. "It's complex – over my head. I need to study it another day or two before I even have the right questions to ask around work. I'll have something more concrete for you next week."

"OK, thanks."

I was beginning to relax, but a look at Nicole told me she wasn't. She tapped her mouth with a closed fist, her gaze dropping to the table before returning to us. "There's one other unknown in all of this. Dr. Worthington writes as if there is a companion document – the *Neural Activity Blocker Advanced Design Document*. And his writing implies it exists. The problem is...no one can find it."

I squeezed my eyes closed for a moment. "Have you checked all the files on the server?"

Nicole started to answer when Sue said, "She did, and I double checked. I also double checked the documents in every box you brought back from WHT. The document's not there."

I nodded to acknowledge Sue's words, but thought her message was probably something else – like don't ask such obvious questions. I had to agree, but then, I wasn't thinking. I was reacting.

"After we checked the files on the drive, I started wondering if our copy might be flawed for some reason," said Nicole. "So, I called Dr. Huston and asked him to email me a copy of the directory on his. I verified every file name and size on our drive against his original. They match. And finally, Laverne's back from her vacation, so Dr. Huston had her go through both the upstairs and basement files again. No luck."

"So, we can't expect them to pull another miraculous discovery out of their hat," I said with a bit more derision than I intended.

"No, another seems unlikely. By the way, he did apologize again for misplacing the files."

I held out my hands. "Sorry, my comment was petty. He's said the same to me." I sighed. "Did Jon happen to talk to Beth about this missing document?"

"I called her," said Nicole. "She says she's removed every scrap of her husband's papers from their home and gave it all to Dr. Huston. That's what we have, except for the two other boxes that the students found in the basement. But there's nothing in them. Both Dr. Huston and Laverne went through them again."

"Nicole, thanks. If you and Sue have missed anything, I don't know what it is. And thanks for calling Beth. That couldn't have been easy."

Nicole smiled, but a sadness showed in her eyes. "You're welcome."

I sighed again. "I guess this document is either permanently missing...or maybe it never existed. Worthington might have referenced a separate paper, intending to write it later."

"Dr. Huston mentioned the same possibility," said Nicole. "That's all I have right now on the electronics. Other questions?"

"None from me," said Sue.

"Same here," I replied.

I glanced at my watch, only now noticing a tension in my neck that must have been there all afternoon. My stomach started to churn. In less than an hour and a half, Nicole would be having dinner with a man who might be a murderer.

"Doc?" I turned to Sue. "Al's on his way to the restaurant. Should be there in about 20 minutes."

"Yeah, I should get going too. Do we need to go through everything again – who's where and when?"

"No," they both said without hesitation.

I hoped they were as confident as they sounded, because my inner voice kept trying to convince me of one thing.

It'll be OK.

WEDNESDAY, AUGUST 26, 6:03 PM

"Is there something wrong with the toasted ravioli?"

I looked down at a half-dozen of the St. Louis favorites, the plate going cold, then up at my server, Sandy. "No, they're fine. I'm just not as hungry as I expected." Truthfully, I could hardly eat at all.

I glanced around the restaurant, knowing what I would see. The place had been empty when Al and I arrived, but by now, many of the booths were taken. Sandy couldn't be happy about the tips she was losing by me sitting here alone.

"Hey, I'm sorry it's taken so long for my friends to show up, but they should be here any minute. You have some type of Mexican or southwest salad, don't you?"

She frowned. "The buffalo chicken salad?"

I hadn't looked at the menu closely, but figured everyone had something like that. I was wrong. "Chicken Caesar salad?"

"Anything to drink?"

"I'll stick with the water."

"Very good," said Sandy, although I suspect she meant the opposite.

Al was sitting across and down the aisle from me. The angle was perfect. I could see about half of the bench seat. I glanced over. As I watched, Al's eyes widened. Atwood must be coming. I tensed, looking down at the table top. If he happened to look into my booth, I didn't want him to see my face.

Someone tapped my shoulder and I jumped, hitting my knee on the bottom of the table. "Easy, Doc. It's just me," came Sue's voice.

Not by choice, I slid over on the bench. I wanted to be able to see Nicole during her meeting with Atwood, but Sue's description would have to do.

"Nicole's in the waiting area and I saw Atwood coming down the sidewalk," said Sue, as she sat beside me. "Oops, Al just got up. They must be coming."

I looked down again, seeing Sue's bowed head beside me, then motion in the aisle. A moment later, there was more movement and Al slipped into the seat across from us, having crossed over to a parallel row of booths and circled around.

Sue was stealing a peek down the aisle, frowning. "What's going on?" I asked.

"I'm not sure," she replied. "They're just standing there, talking. They better...oh, crap." Sue lunged toward me, pinning me against the back wall of the booth.

"Nicole gave Atwood the seat facing us," Sue said in a hurried, hushed whisper. She took a cautious peek around the edge of the booth, then pushed harder into my side. "Sorry, Doc, but if I move over at all, he's gonna see me."

Al was chuckling quietly. "You two wanna get a room?" He had brought his empty beer glass and appetizer with him when he deserted his booth and he popped the last onion ring in his mouth.

"Al," said Sue softly. "I'm going to hide my face and switch places with you."

But before she could get up, Sandy returned with my salad. She looked at Al, glanced down the aisle to where he had been, and shrugged. When her eyes came back to the table, she studied Sue and I, then placed the salad on the table.

"Your chicken Caesar salad," Sandy said, pushing the plate until it touched the back wall of the booth where I was pinned.

Funny.

"Can I take your orders?" she asked, looking at Sue.

"Just an iced tea for me."

I expected a glare from Sandy, but to her credit, she just made a note. "And you, sir?"

"Half–pound burger, medium rare. Sweet potato fries, large order. And another beer." He held up the now empty glass.

"Very good," she said, and I think she meant it this time.

After she left, Sue and Al switch places, Sue shielding her face during the maneuver. At least now, I could move my arm if I decided to try the salad.

"What are they doing?" I asked Al.

"Just talking. Oh, she must have said something funny. Atwood's laughing. He's pointing at something on the wall. He's laughing again. Now, he's...."

"Al," said Sue.

"Yeah?"

"We probably don't need the play by play. Just let us know if he lunges over the table and starts to strangle her."

"Sure, hon."

I had to agree with Sue; the running commentary wasn't helping. I was glad Nicole was safe, but...what? I hoped Atwood would be boring? Sue pulled out her phone, apparently convinced she had nothing to do but kill time until Nicole returned with her report. I turned to Al, hoping to distract myself.

"So, your wife says you're off work this week. How's it feel to be a man of leisure?"

"It was just these last three days. It's back to the salt mines tomorrow. But you know, I'm sort of looking forward to going back. It's been a little boring."

Sandy returned with our drinks and he took a sip of beer before he continued. "Sue says I won't retire well, because I've been a bit antsy. But this break was out-of-the-blue. In retirement, I'll have it all planned out. A little of this, a little of that, and the days will fly."

"So, what are all of these hobbies you'll discover when you hit 65?"

He stopped with his beer halfway to his lips. "65? Who said anything about 65? I'm retiring when I'm 55, maybe even 50."

I noticed he had changed the subject, but before I could point that out, he leaned toward me and whispered, "Don't tell anyone you heard it from me, but I think Huntington Taylor is planning a major expansion. Like more than double."

I wasn't sure why Huntington Taylor taking on new clients, or taking more of the savings of the ones he had, would be confidential, but perhaps it was. More likely, Al wanted to make it sound important. "So, what makes you think Taylor & Associates is expanding?"

"Well, first, there's this massive remodeling effort. He said the improvements were to congratulate everyone on such outstanding performance. You know, better digs because the company's doing so well."

"That well, huh?"

"Oh, yeah. Big time. That was the first clue. And then there's the whole security upgrade," said Al.

"Security?" I chuckled. "You mean you're going to get someone at the reception desk who doesn't do her nails all the time?"

Al was about to answer when Sandy came back with his food. He gave me one of those 'lock my lips' gestures as he nodded his head in her direction. I almost laughed aloud.

When she left, he said. "Yeah, we're not sealed up like you guys, but that's about to change. Before they kicked us loose on this break, a bunch of painters were in, trying some samples on the dining room walls. It's gotta be paint that forms some type of electronic shield, because there was no way these ugly shades of off-white could be considered an improvement."

From some of the government work that Ruger-Phillips did, I knew that computer facilities were sometimes shielded, so that emissions from the electronics couldn't be intercepted outside the building. But barriers that were painted on? I wasn't certain about that.

"I thought all your computers were in the basement," I said. "What're you protecting in the dining hall – the secret sauce on the hamburgers?"

"Yeah, that stumped us too, for a while. But about the only place Taylor goes other than the basement computer complex is the dining area. If he takes any type of device with him when he eats – a phone, a tablet – and it's linked to the systems downstairs, the signal might be intercepted."

I had noticed Al said that the paint choice had stumped "us," and I pictured two or three bored analysts sitting around, generating plots worthy of a James Bond movie. Of course, as someone recently accused of sending the police on a 'wild goose chase' by my management, I was no one to criticize anyone's overactive imagination.

"Might be running the numbers on his phone," I admitted, but I was thinking it had been a while since Al had updated me on what was happening at Nicole's table.

"Could be," said Al. "Or just generating the numbers in his head and using the phone to send them downstairs. Guy's a math whiz...which is a good thing." Al grinned and shook his head. "Cause he can't remember people worth a lick."

"What's Atwood doing?" I asked.

Al glanced over to their table. "Eating."

I laughed at myself, wondering if I really expected an answer like, 'He's dragging her out by the hair. How did I miss that?'

So, I turned the conversation to sports, and by 'sports,' I mean baseball. At this time of year, anyone in St. Louis would. Excitement was building, as the Cardinals were only three back in the wild card race with 31 games to go. And with a game at 8:30 tonight, that fact seemed to be weighing on Al's mind. He kept checking his watch.

"Hon," he said. When Sue looked up from her phone, he leaned across the table. "Would it be OK if I go home and watch the game?"

Seeing the exasperation growing on her face, I said, "I'd be glad to give you a ride home. Al's not going to be interested in what Nicole has to say anyway."

Sue sighed. "OK, but why don't you leave the same time as Nicole and follow her in your car? If no one is tailing her, you can go home when she turns back."

"Sure, hon." He sat up straighter, looking down the aisle. "Perfect timing. Looks like they're leaving. And Doc, don't forget what I said earlier. Huntington Taylor's your guy."

I nodded, then ducked my head as two pairs of legs passed by our booth. Al and I stood and headed for the door.

When we exited, I saw Atwood and Nicole walking down the sidewalk to our left, about 20 yards away. "There they are."

Al had been looking the opposite direction, but swung around at my words, a groan escaping his lips. "That's great. I'm parked the other way."

I should have asked where everyone was parked. Strike one.

"No worries," I said. "I'll follow them while you go get your car. When Nicole pulls out, I'll call you and you can drop in behind."

"OK," Al replied. "What's she drive?"

Strike two.

"A silver, two-door. Maybe a Toyota or Honda? But I have no clue about the license plate."

"OK," he said again, as he headed out at a trot.

I turned back to the left and spotted Atwood and Nicole. They were crossing the street, nearly 30 yards away. I dialed Al as I started out at a jog.

"Hey, Doc," he said when he picked up. He sounded a bit winded.

"I think Nicole's headed to that lot on the south side of the street. You know which one I mean?"

"Yeah, sure," he replied. "I'm almost to my car. I'll be coming back down the street, heading west. She'll turn that way, right? I mean, I can't very well do a U-turn."

Damn.

Was that strike three? It was likely that she would head west – it was the quickest way out of this commercial area, but we hadn't discussed that detail.

"Probably. I'll let you know."

I left my answer at that, because the rest of my thoughts involved him using a traffic circle and me jogging down the street as Nicole made her way through the string of traffic lights to the east. That option wasn't complete folly, but close.

I trotted across the intersection against the light, two cars honking at me in the process. I had closed the gap to about 20 yards again, but they were about to take a side street to the lot. I'd lose sight of them, if only for a few moments. I sped up.

When I rounded the edge of the building, Nicole was standing beside her car in the dim light of dusk, a few other cars circling the lot behind her. The street lights were just coming on and I noticed she had parked under one. Smart. I stumbled to a stop, nearly tripping over something in the twilight. I looked around, but didn't see Atwood. I stepped back into the shadows.

I dialed Al again. "She's getting into her car," I said before he answered but after I heard the panting on the other end.

"Me too," he managed to say.

Al must have put his phone on speaker, as the sound of jingling keys and a slamming door reached my ears. A moment later, his car started.

"She's pulling onto the side street and up to the intersection," I said. "Light's red. Her turn signal's on and good news. She'll be heading west."

I was hoping the light would be long; they usually were. But for once, it wasn't.

"She's turning onto the street." There was no response. "Al, did you hear me? She's headed west."

"Yeah, I see her. Several cars up."

It sounded like he was shouting, but I understood the reaction. My heart was also pounding, partly with the exertion, but mostly with concern that Al would miss her. But then, this was only a precaution we had added at the last minute and I told myself to relax. No one had followed them to the lot. I just wished I knew where Atwood had gone.

"OK, I'm hanging up and heading back to the restaurant. Thanks, buddy. I owe you one."

"No problem," I heard as I broke the connection.

I turned around and started walking slowly back to the restaurant. It would be awhile before Nicole would return.

* * *

When I saw Sue sitting in the booth at the restaurant, all the nagging concerns that had stubbornly refused to leave my thoughts during the walk back came rushing to the fore. Her face was ashen. She was blinking rapidly. She had her phone pressed to an ear, her other hand trembling slightly as it covered her mouth.

"What is it?" I asked.

Sue dropped the phone from her cheek and squeezed her eyes closed for a moment. "Nicole. She didn't turn around." The words caught in her throat. "She kept going west, then turned north on I-170." Then into the phone, she said, "Doc just came in."

It felt as if someone had punched me in the stomach, all breath leaving my body in a rush. I fell into the booth. I looked down, studying the dirty plates and half-eaten food, afraid of the condemnation I would see in Sue's eyes. I should have stopped them and I hadn't. I forced my head up. "I'm calling Detective Ahern."

"Can he do anything? Even if he's there at this hour?"

"He damn well better," I said too loudly for the small area. A few diners turned our way.

"Sorry," I said to Sue. I had mastered the volume, but I could feel the blood rushing to my face, my heart racing in my chest. "Can you ask Al if he can pull alongside them, see who's in the car with her?"

I'd get a reaction from the police if I knew it was an abduction. Otherwise, I had little to tell them except that Nicole had stood us up for an after-dinner chat.

Sue raised her phone and made the request. Then, I waited. It seemed like several minutes, but it was probably less than one when she blurted into the phone, "What?"

I held out both hands, my eyes pleading for an update.

Sue raised a finger in the just-a-moment sign, then said into the phone, "Go home." My heart stopped. After another short pause, I heard, "No, just go home. We're calling the police." And she hung up.

My eyes narrowed as I studied her face, waiting for the worst.

"Al was almost even with her when she got off at Page. He couldn't get over in time to follow. If he could have...."

Sue didn't finish as her gaze dropped to the tabletop. After a moment, she looked up, her eyes moist. Then, without a word, she jumped up and ran passed me down the aisle. I wondered if she was seeking the sanctuary of the lady's room, but when I turned, she was...hugging Nicole.

A moment later, the women came down the aisle talking excitedly. Sue sounded almost giddy when she said, "Al must have been following the wrong car."

I rose from the seat, and although I wanted to hug Nicole too, I settled for taking one of her hands in mine. "It's great to have you back from the land of the missing."

As we sat back down, Sue said, "I'm gonna kill Al when I get home."

"Don't," I said. "It's my fault. I didn't ask where Nicole parked. I didn't know what kind of car she drives. Or the license plate number."

"That's crazy," said Sue. "Where we parked wasn't an issue until I asked Al to follow. I should have told him."

Nicole looked sideways at Sue, then at me. "And you're both missing the fact that it was probably a good thing Al didn't follow me. I pulled onto a side street about four blocks from here and had my phone ready. If some car had pulled off and stopped nearby...well, we'd be explaining ourselves to the police about now. We just need to plan better next time."

"Or not have a next time," I said.

"I'll second that," said Sue. "I've texted Al to let him know everything's all right, so now, can we get the scoop on Atwood? I want to get home, because all this drama has me exhausted. And half sick to my stomach."

"Me too, so I'll make this short," said Nicole. But before she could continue, Sandy approached.

"Anything else?"

"No, I think we're wrapping up," I said. "Just the check, please." She must have been expecting that response, or hoping for it, as she placed it on the table and left.

"Unless we have it all wrong," said Nicole, "Atwood's not A.T. He isn't self-centered. In fact, he's very nice. He kept apologizing for Dr. Worthington. And like everyone, he wonders if Worthington used the Blocker on himself, but he doesn't have any proof. He's not an art collector, but on the other hand, he's not uneasy with it."

Nicole paused a moment as if recalling something, then smirked. "And although I'm sure he's good at math – someone in his line of work would almost have to be – he's no whiz."

"What does that mean?" asked Sue, raising an eyebrow.

"Well, it was a working meeting and our company's policy says I should offer to pay. Dr. Atwood refused, but when it came time to split the check and figure the tip, he took forever. And then he got it wrong."

Probably flustered. I know the feeling.

"Guess we have our answer about A.T. Wood," declared Sue.

"Seems that way," I agreed. "I'm done for the evening, if you ladies are?" Both concurred, then excused themselves to use the restroom before we left. I pulled some bills from my pocket to pay for our dinner. I was about to place them on the table when I saw our server headed my direction.

"Sandy." She stopped and I handed her the check and the money. "Sorry about tying up your table...no, make that tables for so long."

She smiled. It seemed genuine. "No worries. Nothing could bother me at the moment."

"Win the lottery?" I asked, looking up and returning her grin.

"Not quite, but some guy dropped a fifty on the table for an appetizer."

"Sounds like a nice guy," I said. I stood to head for the front door where I was meeting Sue and Nicole.

"Maybe," replied Sandy. "But actually, he looked like he'd seen a ghost."

SAME DAY, SAME TIME

The Experimenter turned around on the barstool for what must have been the twentieth time since arriving and stared at the door to the dining room. Price and another man had entered about an hour ago and were still seated inside.

The evening had started with great promise when the Experimenter spotted Price leaving Ruger-Phillips and followed him to the restaurant. A few minutes later, the second man had appeared. He and Price had spoken briefly before going into the back room.

The second man had seemed familiar – enough that the Experimenter had kept his face turned away or hidden behind a menu. But he couldn't place him. And when the Experimenter went to the restroom, so he could risk a peek into the dining area, he found the two men sitting in different booths. It must have been a chance meeting.

"Freshen that tea for you?" asked the bartender from behind the Experimenter.

But as he turned to answer, the Experimenter saw Veles enter the front door. His spirits soared. He'd finally decided to purchase a second Taser, settling his internal debate on how to catch both at once. If one got injured, so be it, but he couldn't delay any more. And now, it looked like waiting would be unnecessary.

Deciding he'd be less conspicuous if he was eating, the Experimenter said, "I'm done." He placed a ten-dollar bill on the bar. "Keep the change." Even if he couldn't find a booth close enough to see Price and Veles, he could at least watch the door and leave when they did. But as he turned, he saw Veles go into the waiting area. Odd. Didn't she know Price was already inside?

The Experimenter stopped halfway between the bar and the entry to the dining room, not sure what to do. He rubbed his chin, his gaze shifting between the alternatives.

Jordan entered the front door. The Experimenter didn't believe that any of the Ruger-Phillips people knew him, but as a precaution, he hid part of his face behind a hand that idly massaged his forehead. He expected a reunion between the women, but as he watched, Jordan walked past the waiting area, only glancing at her friend.

"What the hell?" the Experimenter muttered under his breath, a frown growing on his face. What should he do? Finally, the weight of two prizes in the dining room vs. one in the waiting area tipped the scales. He headed to the back.

The Experimenter turned down the aisle where he had seen Price earlier. A furtive glance told him that Price was still there, but now Jordan was sitting next to him. He passed by, then turned slowly, shielding his face as he had before.

Two other people were approaching and he looked up to their faces. One was Veles. But when he recognized the second, he froze in shock and horror. Coming down the aisle toward him was the only living person who might be able to connect him to the Neural Activity Blocker research. It was Dr. Sebastian Atwood.

Almost a year ago now, during the early stages of the study, there had been a problem with the Blocker. Worthington had called in Atwood to consult, and while the two men worked, the Experimenter had watched them from behind the one-way mirror. He had never spoken to Atwood, had never been introduced. But when the men took a break or when Atwood returned to his lab, he and the Experimenter shared the space of Worthington's office, if only for a few moments.

The Experimenter wouldn't have known Atwood's name or what he did, if he hadn't asked. But later, when he needed a cover to approach a small, engineering company with some exotic metal and a very, exacting order, that knowledge had come in handy. Now he wondered if that ploy, which had seemed a masterstroke at the time, would be his downfall.

Seeing that the booth beside him was empty, the Experimenter hurriedly slid in. His eyes scanned the table, seeing only seasonings and relishes where he hoped to find a menu. He pulled his phone from his shoulder bag, careful not to expose the Tasers and restraints. Then, he looked down, studying the blank screen intently.

Veles and Atwood passed him, and after a moment of talk, they sat in the booth behind and across the aisle from him. The Experimenter bent down as if to tie his shoe, seeing the cuff of Atwood's pants below their table. Atwood was facing in his direction.

The Experimenter sat up and looked down the aisle. Coming toward him was the 'familiar' man. He ducked his head again, rubbing his forehead with his fingertips. He no longer had to feign the action; his head was starting to throb. The man stopped and sat in the booth with Price and Jordan.

Both the man who seemed familiar and Atwood were facing toward the door. If the Experimenter simply stood and walked out, they would only see his back and he could shield his face from Jordan and Price one more time. He slid to the edge of the bench, but just as he was starting to rise, Jordan stood. She and the man traded places, so that he was now facing in his direction.

The Experimenter slid deeper into the booth. He was trapped, Atwood facing him from one side, the man from another. He could try hiding his face again, but all the furtive glances and half-hidden peeks were adding up. Soon, his strange behavior would draw attention.

He slipped farther into the booth, his shoulder pressing against the back wall. His mind was screaming at him, 'run.' Yet, if he sat quietly, they would leave. He grabbed one of his legs, squeezing hard as if trying to force this logic on the limb. He started breathing rapidly. The walls were closing in. In his mind, he could see Atwood and the man coming, their stares hard and icy.

"Are you all right?" asked a young woman standing near his table.

He blinked. The words from his surroundings returned some semblance of order to his thoughts. "An appetizer," he said barely above a whisper.

"OK, which one?"

"Any of them." He saw his phone was still in his other hand. "Then, I have to make a...a text. Please leave me alone."

"Of course." She left.

Noticing the pain in his leg, the Experimenter looked down. His knuckles had turned white as he crushed muscle against bone. His fingers were cramped, but slowly, they relaxed their grip. Blood returned. He straightened his leg. It hurt, but it moved.

His waitress came back, so he returned his attention to the phone. She placed a plate of nachos on the table and left without a word. He leaned back, his heart rate and breathing coming closer to normal. He was still surrounded, but he was undetected. He relaxed further, realizing he was in an unprecedented situation to learn more about his enemies. Price, Veles, and Jordan were all within earshot.

He concentrated on Veles and Atwood first. They were speaking quietly, and unfortunately, few others were doing the same. But occasionally, words would reach his ears. He caught 'blocker' and 'coils' and several technical terms. But he also heard 'Worthington' and 'deranged,' and he became angered.

He forced his attention in the direction of Price and Jordan. Jordan was quiet and Price had little to say, but the familiar-looking man was hardly taking a breath. Unfortunately, the talk revolved around baseball. The Experimenter was wasting his time. He had just decided to turn his attention back to Veles and Atwood when they stood to leave. The conversation between Price, Jordan, and the man changed. They too were preparing to go.

But just before they stood, the familiar man said something that reached the Experimenter's ears clearly and distinctly. And it shattered his calm. The darkness came again, stronger this time, more determined. Again, his mind screamed 'run,' and nothing would stop his flight response this time. He pulled a bill from his wallet, threw it on the table, and waited for Price and the other man to clear the entrance. Then, he fled. He burst through the restaurant door, nearly knocking a woman to the sidewalk.

"Hey, watch where you're going," yelled her companion.

The Experimenter spun away without a word and raced down the sidewalk, his eyes darting right and left. He reached an intersection with a small, side street. In the harsh rays from the alley's floodlights, he could see a trash dumpster. He ran there, bent behind it, and vomited.

After a moment, he stood, trying to find enough saliva to spit the last of the acrid bile from his mouth. It was no use. He wiped his mouth on a sleeve.

"How the hell do they know that?" he snarled under his breath. His eyes continued to probe the darkness, watching for movement, watching for danger, watching for Price, Jordan, or Veles. They were now undoubtedly the mortal enemies he had feared, because in the final words from the familiar man he had heard his name – Huntington Taylor.

THURSDAY, AUGUST 27, 12:53 PM

Arriving at the conference room, I found Sue's and Nicole's notes spread across the table, but no women. They were probably at lunch.

I seated myself, thinking that we had covered the ground between skeptical curiosity and growing confidence in a very short period. We had only started looking at the study data less than 30 hours earlier, and already we were certain the Blocker worked and even how it increased short-term memory.

But those thoughts were made ominous by the nature of what we suspected but couldn't prove – that this technology was also an addictive corrosive to the mind. Unfortunately, no one shared our concerns. Our most recent finding, that anyone could adjust the Blocker from the user interface, was only relevant to who might be using it. And yet when I reported it to Ken and Detective Ahern, their meager interest seemed to wane further.

And the VA? I felt certain we had accumulated enough troubling data that they would investigate, if Huston asked for additional funding. But if he didn't, they would have no reason to look. And even if he did, it would be weeks before the VA fielded a team to do the necessary research and months before that team had findings.

Can we wait that long?

I heard the voices of Sue and Nicole shortly before they entered the room. Sue's notebook was lying next to my elbow. She grabbed it, walked around the table, and sat down next to Nicole.

"I was afraid I wouldn't be able to resist putting my hand on your knee if I sat there," Sue said, straight-faced. "Either that, or Nicole and I planned this meeting something like a tag-team and I wanted to face the audience."

A single laugh escaped my lips. "I'm buying the second."

"So, we've completed our review of the observational data," said Sue. "And unless we intend to submit a report that says the only behavior after the first few weeks of training was to sit and stare, we'll need to make some inferences about what was happening inside A.T.'s head."

"You've finished the reports?" I asked. "Yesterday, you were at 20%?"

"It was a joint effort in what was nearly an all-nighter," said Sue.

I sat up, my forehead wrinkling as I looked at her. "Seriously? You came back here after what happened last night?"

"OK, not really. But I did switch to Al's regular starting time. You know, when normal people are sleeping. And because I mentioned the plan to Nicole, she joined me here at 6:00. Hey, we know it could be important if there's anything in these reports."

I nodded. "That's above and beyond, but thanks, because I agree."

"Sure, boss. Anyway, in his notes after each session, Worthington recorded the time A.T. spent standing, sitting, or pacing. During the first two weeks, he spent an average of 6.3 minutes standing, 14.8 minutes sitting, and 8.9 minutes pacing."

"OK," I said after a moment considering the numbers. "Perhaps a bit nervous, but that doesn't seem unusual."

"Same thoughts here," said Sue. "But after those first two weeks, things changed dramatically, like I mentioned yesterday. Pacing disappeared completely and standing was down to 0.3 minutes. I was telling Nicole earlier, 'became a sitting statue' was about the only behavior."

"Whoa," I said, staring at Sue. "That's what...18 seconds of standing and the rest of the 30 minutes is sitting. That hardly seems possible. Any chance Worthington was, well, mistaken?"

"It's possible," said Sue, as she held out a hand. "But I didn't notice any change in his notes. His handwriting is the same. The level of detail is the same. Every report is thorough and they're all signed."

"OK," I said slowly. "Did A.T. have a cell phone with him?"

"He had a phone, but he had to remove all personal items before each session – watch, cell phone, any papers he might have on him. And he didn't get them back until he went home."

"That limits the options," I said. "But still, sitting motionless for that long? Strange."

"True," replied Sue. "Nicole and I generated a few ideas why he might act that way – angry with Worthington, sleep deprived, and so on. But we only found evidence for one of them."

Sue paused, apparently for the drama. I could only respond with a 'haven't got a clue' shrug. Then, Nicole said, "We think A.T. may have developed some type of extreme introversion and it's connected to numbers."

Even though it was the engineer who made this assertion and not the psychologist, I was sure Nicole meant introversion in the formal, psychological sense – the tendency to be predominately interested in one's own internal, mental life.

"Introversion?" I said, tapping my fist against my lips. "How in the world...? Just what did you find that led you to that conclusion?"

"It was Nicole who noticed that many of the written notes described where A.T. was looking." Sue glanced at a sheet of paper. "In fact, 63% of the time, we could tell either what A.T. was staring at or the direction he was looking." Sue raised a hand to her partner.

"So, I called Dr. Huston and asked if I could see the room where A.T. would have been sitting. He had no problem with that, but when

I explained what we wanted, he said looking at the room wouldn't help."

"Let me guess," I said. "It wouldn't help because Worthington pitched everything in there when he went through his Spartan-decor phase."

"Correct," said Nicole. "Dr. Huston said that everything was different, floor to ceiling. So, I asked if he could describe it. He sent an email a couple of hours later saying that he and Laverne had gotten together and listed everything they could remember."

As any PhD does, I had read widely in my field. For my doctoral preliminary exams alone, I had studied professional journals and texts for 10 to 12 hours a day for half a year. But nowhere, in all those hours in the library or my office or at home did I recall a single study in which the researchers had tried to reconstruct what a participant might be thinking based on the decorations in the waiting area. The women got an "A" for ingenuity in my book.

"He answered all your questions with a straight face?" I joked.

Nicole place a finger on her lips and looked up at the ceiling, exaggerating a thoughtful pose. "He said something about me hanging around with psychologists so much I was starting to sound comfortable inferring something I couldn't see or directly measure."

"Yeah, we've about ruined you for engineering," said Sue, grinning.

Nicole pulled a piece of 11 by 17 paper from her notebook, but didn't immediately show it to me. "Their email described a small room – about eight by ten – with beige walls, hardwood floor, and an area rug with a geometric pattern of ovals and arches in browns, blues, and black. There was a table, with a laminate top made to look like pale, brown granite and two chairs, each with brown, padded seats, backrests, and armrests. There was a clock and a calendar on the walls. There were also two pictures. We'd originally thought there was only one, because the pictures were seldom mentioned in the reports. There was a magazine rack, although he never read anything from it after the first three weeks. The last objects were a potted plant in one corner and a small trash can in another."

Nicole turned the paper toward me. It showed a sketch of the room she had just described. It was not the floor plan I could have made with a ruler or using a computer program, but a pencil sketch from what would have been A.T.'s perspective when seated at the table. It was detailed. Finally, I asked, "Twenty minutes?"

Nicole smiled in a way that took over her entire face. "Actually, it's second generation. They marked up the first, but yeah, about 20."

"Is that a picture of the St. Louis skyline on the one wall?"

"We think it was the John Pils' print, *Reflections of St. Louis*, but Dr. Huston wasn't sure. The other picture was an Ansel Adams photograph from Yosemite National Park."

"OK, I'm impressed. But I guess the question is, what did we learn from all this?"

"Which is my cue," said Sue, pulling a printout from her notebook. "If we take the logs where either the direction or the object of A.T.'s gaze is known, after the first three weeks he spent 35.4% of the time looking at the calendar and 52.2% looking at the clock. And Doc, before you spend too much time on the mental math, those numbers leave 12.4% of the time looking at everything else."

I was too surprised to speak, my eyes wandering around the room as if in search of an explanation. "Did he have access to pencils or pens?" I asked.

Nicole cleared her throat and I got the message. Looking at her sketch more closely, I saw a cup holding a collection of pens and pencils on the top of the magazine rack. "He never even doodled in the margins of a magazine or found a crossword puzzle?"

"Not after the first few days," said Sue. "There was a pad of paper in the magazine rack, and about the second or third day, he used it to make a 'to do' list. But Worthington made a copy. Said he needed it as part of his observations, so A.T. may have stayed away from the paper on purpose."

"And the connection you made to numbers?" I said. "That's because he was looking at the clock and the calendar?"

"Right," said Nicole. "Of course, the magazines would have numbers in them too, but only if you look through pages with pictures and bright graphics to find them."

"The other thing that suggests A.T. was mesmerized by numbers was the fact that most of his time staring at the calendar was during the first few days of a month. After that, he had learned all its secrets." Sue put air quotes around the last word. "The rest of the month, he studied the digital clock. Its display includes the date and room temperature as well as time, so it's constantly changing."

"And finally, none of the missing 12.4 plus percent of A.T.'s time was spent on the pictures, the plant, the magazines, or the trash can," said Nicole. "He didn't even look at the floor, which had some geometric patterns. From what we can tell, he was staring at a blank wall."

I sat for a moment and slowly shook my head, unsure if I was more amazed at how the women had attacked this task or what their findings said about the Blocker. I finally decided. "When you said you thought introversion might be why A.T. was acting like a statue, I thought you'd never be able to prove that. But what you did is brilliant."

"Thanks," said Sue, as the women nodded to each other. "There's just one more thing we were going to do, and since it's not finished, you can help."

"OK, sure. What did you have in mind?"

"It seems likely that Worthington used the Blocker at some point," said Nicole. "For one thing, there are several obvious similarities between his behavior and A.T.'s, like their disinterest in art. So, we thought we'd compile a list of both of their behaviors, see where we have matches and where we don't."

"Sort of the full behavioral profile, assuming Worthington dabbled with the technology?" I said. Sue and Nicole nodded. "I like it. Let's just keep the source of the information clear, so when we forward it to management, the VA, or the police, they can weigh the evidence however they see fit."

"Sounds like a plan," said Sue.

I glanced at my watch. "You two have already been here more than a full day...and again, thanks for doing that. I have status meetings with Ken tomorrow morning, so can we get together tomorrow at 1:00 for this composite?"

Sue and Nicole agreed and left the room, reliving a bit of the previous night's misadventure. I was still pondering their suggestion for tomorrow. I had an impression about the composite of Worthington's and A.T.'s oddities and it was troubling. But it paled compared to our speculation about the empathy-killing effects of the Blocker. Building the profile promised a break from the worst-case scenarios that had dominated my thoughts and I welcomed it.

After all, worst cases never come true.

THURSDAY, AUGUST 27, 1:17 PM

Taylor paced his office, raging at the walls as his fists clenched and unclenched. It did nothing to ease his fury. He was being driven from his mental life, deprived of his progress toward immortality by a couple of wet-behind-the-ears psychologists and an engineer.

He dropped into the chair behind his desk, exhausted from his rant. "Why can't I shed this useless emotional baggage?" he muttered aloud. "I am the personification of calm, hard logic, and yet today, I can hardly think from the pounding in my ears."

Taylor leaned back, eyes staring forward as he gripped the armrests of his chair. "But my mental world is like the air I breathe. Without it, I die." He paused and gritted his teeth. "And we know, that will never happen."

He stood and walked to the one-way mirror, staring at the empty chamber. "It's time to go, isn't it?" He released a long sigh and turned back to look at his desk. "I knew it was coming, but so quickly?" He shook his head, then returned to his seat. "Time for the diversion."

To complete his exit, Taylor needed a few days of confusion before the authorities focused on him. He felt he had the means to get two, perhaps more. By the time law enforcement figured out what was happening, he would be a new person in a different country. Only his agenda would remain unchanged.

He pressed a button on his desk phone. "Yes, Mr. Taylor?" came the voice from the speaker.

"Please schedule a flight to San Antonio for Saturday morning at 5:30 with a return on Monday at the same hour."

"Yes, sir. Any other arrangements?"

"No. I have them covered. Also, please inform my direct reports that I'll be out of the office all weekend."

"Yes, sir."

Taylor released the button, and as was his custom, he checked that the transmit light was out. Today, that seemed insufficient. He unplugged the phone.

"Not that I'll need that return flight," he said smiling. His eyes went to the dozen charged battery packs laying on the desktop. "Those will give me several hours of my true life. More than enough to make it to my new home, as long as I ration myself."

Taylor rose again and paced around the room. His new lab was already built and fully stocked, save the subjects he would procure once he arrived. He had no concerns on that front. And the trickle of money he had diverted to run his studies and set up his new operation had become a deluge in the last few hours. Thousands of dollars were now pouring into his foreign accounts. He couldn't hide this theft for long, but that too would be unnecessary soon.

"I'll have enough money for years...although fleecing a new populace won't be a problem. Humans are so flawed, I'm surprised they accomplish anything."

He stopped pacing and glanced back at his desk. "But those damn researchers. They're responsible for this. A few weeks, a couple of months, and I would have been invincible. But no, they couldn't leave things alone. And for that, they must die. But how?"

Taylor started pacing again, trying to escape the walls that were closing in. But after only a few steps, he stopped and spun back to his desk. "You're right."

He hurried to his chair and grabbed his keyboard. After a few minutes work, he leaned back and reviewed the words that appeared on his computer screen.

My dear Dr. Price,
You will soon die, not at my hands, but because of me. And when your final hours come, it won't be a trained killer, a stranger at your door or on the street. It will be someone you thought of as a friend, perhaps even a lover. Don't try to hide...or do. It makes no difference, because I am going to field an army of people, all with the burning, insatiable need to find, befriend, and then kill you.
You may think this cruel, but it's nothing more than what you wished for me. Good luck with what's left of your life.

Taylor leaned back, smiling at his handiwork. "Now, schedule delivery for next Monday, with separate, personalized copies for Jordan and Veles. And Huston too. He could have stopped them but didn't."

Taylor rose from his chair and started to leave the lab. There was much to do before starting his new life and beginning the next phase of his research. As he reached the door, he turned back to stare at his desk. On its top rested a phrenology head, just like the one he had seen in Price's apartment. And on top of the head rested the Blocker cap, now set for a single purpose – to satisfy his every mental need.

"You're right, my friend," he said to the porcelain figure. "Why have the power to create a mind and not use it?"

FRIDAY, AUGUST 28, 1:04 PM

I wouldn't give up trying to get to know Nicole better, but that didn't mean I had solved the age-old question of how does one work with an alluring member of the opposite sex? Letting my feelings color our professional interactions would never do – for either of us. Perhaps even the closeness I felt and showed to Sue was too much. I wasn't certain. I'd just have to keep my eyes open, see if I could solve some small part of the puzzle that was Nicole.

But for my Friday morning meeting with Ken, I had pushed that issue to the back of my mind. At least, I told myself I had shelved it, although I had to return to my office twice during our meeting to retrieve papers I had forgotten. And now, I was late for the 1:00 meeting with my team.

When I arrived, the room was empty, but it was clear the women had been there. Their handiwork showed on a chart that was projected on the front screen. It contained a table with two columns labeled 'Exhibited by A.T.' and 'Exhibited by Worthington.' In the table's cells, they had entered observations about each man.

Some of the entries were exact matches, such as 'shows a disinterest in art.' Others were close to the same but not quite, like Worthington's redecorating in gray compared to A.T. staring at a beige wall over more colorful alternatives. And there were definite lacks of a match as well. A.T. had an extraordinary memory for numbers, but no one recalled Worthington coming in one day and spouting off the first 50 digits of pi. Clearly, the women had put a lot of thought into this table.

"I was impressed with the detective work you did."

It was Nicole's voice and I turned to see her entering the room. At first, I thought she was talking about Ken's warning, the phrase 'detective work' misleading me. But after a moment, I realized what she meant.

"Thanks."

"I've never taken any classes in cognitive psychology," she said, "so I didn't know what to expect. But to see what you found out about A.T.'s thinking from things like how quickly he answered or the errors he made...." She slowly shook her head. "It's impressive."

I was, of course, flattered, but figured I should set the record straight. I wouldn't want her to be reading a cognitive psych paper next week, only to find I was taking credit for someone else's work. "Truthfully, I'm just using methods other people have found."

"Of course," she said, smiling. "I didn't really think you came up with those tests any more than the detective who uses fingerprints or DNA. But to know what to look for? And what it means when you find it? That's what impressed me. I could have looked at those data for a month and never noticed what you found in a day."

"Well, thanks again. But I think what you and Sue did is a lot more remarkable. Figuring out what A.T. was thinking by what he did in a waiting room? That's not in any books."

She nodded, her smile growing.

"OK, keep your hands to yourself," said Sue, speaking somewhat loudly and bursting into the room.

"Did you even look to see who was in here before you said that?" I asked, chuckling.

"No, it's a universal request. I embarrass quite easily." Sue didn't wait for a response, probably because our double takes were sufficient. "So, what did you think of our table?"

"I just got started, but it looks great," I said.

Sue sat down at the keyboard and over the next several minutes, we went through the table, cell by cell. It was as good as I had originally thought. But what I'd hoped for but didn't experience was any type of insight about what it meant to be Worthington or A.T. The content was all familiar ground.

When we finished, Sue pushed the keyboard away and leaned back in her chair. "Lady and gentleman, I give you the long-time, Blocker user. A math whiz who'll meet you in his gray rooms, but won't remember you tomorrow."

I sat bolt upright, staring at her. "What did you say?"

"I said, a math...."

I waved her off. "No, sorry, I heard it. It's just the phrase you used," I mumbled, mostly to myself.

I leaned forward, putting my elbows on the table and resting my head in my hands. An association that had been on the edge of my consciousness for days had formed. But it was an association so unlikely, so fraught with complexities that I was momentarily stunned. As I had been so badly mistaken about Allen Trimmel and we had all been wrong about Atwood, I felt I should check out a few facts before saying anything more.

"Is there something wrong?" asked Nicole.

"No, not really. Would it be OK if we take a 15-minute break so I can check on something?"

"Fifteen minutes of work followed by a fifteen-minute break works for me," said Sue.

"Is Al still at work?"

"Al? As in my husband?"

"Yeah."

Sue checked her watch. "Should be. It isn't even 2:00, so he should be around for another 30 to 45 minutes."

"Thanks," I said, as I ran out of the conference room without another word.

* * *

The low murmur of conversation disappeared when I came back. Sue and Nicole looked up, still in the same seats as if they had been waiting the entire time.

"Sorry to leave so abruptly," I said, taking my seat. "Something popped into my head, and I had to check out a few things."

"We knew that much," said Sue. "But the rest is a total blank. What popped into your head that would have anything to do with Al? This project or a wild stock tip?"

"The project." I leaned forward in the chair and took a deep breath. "I'm still thinking this has to be a coincidence, but Sue's description of the habitual Blocker user? Well, it sounded eerily like something Al said to me."

Sue shifted in her chair, glancing sideways at Nicole, then back at me. She knitted her brows. "What did he say?"

"In effect, he described Huntington Taylor using almost the same words as you. A math whiz, surrounded by gray walls, couldn't remember people. It seems like it has to be a coincidence, but...that's an unusual trio."

"You think Huntington Taylor is A.T.?" Sue asked, her eyes wide in a stare.

I let out a long breath. "Yeah, I know. Someone who's well on his way to being one of the richest men in St. Louis, maybe the nation? Not exactly the kind of guy you'd expect to steal half-finished science projects from a commercial lab. Unless...," I said, drawing out the word, "he got hooked on it during a study when he was finishing up school."

"And you called Al about his education?" asked Sue.

"No. I got that from an online search. He graduated in December with a master's degree in business, so he could have been in a study last fall. Shortly after school, he joined a three-partner, investment company. One partner retired. The second spun off a separate insurance company, and he bought out the third after three months on the job – perhaps enough time to use the Blocker to amass the money."

"So, Al gave you the company gossip?"

"Exactly," I replied. "Although I knew most of it already. Stuff like, everyone thinks Taylor is a math genius. Or the way he had the one place he goes in the building – the dining room – painted gray."

Nicole bit her lower lip, then said. "But wouldn't math aptitude go with being the head of a hedge fund?" she asked. "That leaves poor decorating taste, which isn't a crime." She glanced at Sue, but Sue was resting her forehead in a hand, looking down at the tabletop.

"That's good," I said. "Let's debunk this here and now, rather than in front of Ken. Or Detective Ahern...which reminds me of something he said. He said they weren't considering theft of the device seriously, because it would take too much specialized knowledge and too much money to develop it. But both could come from using the Blocker."

"But the name's not right," said Nicole.

"Actually, it is," I said. "His name is A. Huntington Taylor, although you don't hear the first initial very often."

Nicole's frown deepened. "Could a public figure like Huntington Taylor have the kind of personality we think the Blocker produces?"

"Maybe," I replied. "I'd say he has a cold indifference to others, but you'd just tell me he's in a competitive, cutthroat business."

Nicole's frown was momentarily replaced by a tilt of the head and a smile. "Yeah, I probably would."

"He's also known to be reclusive, which could fit," I continued. "In fact, I couldn't even find a photo of him online that was taken in the last year. Al says he lives in the basement of the Taylor & Associates building and rarely comes up, except for the most important clients or the occasional lunch."

I glanced at Sue, wondering if the mention of her husband would break into her thoughts, but she continued to stare at the table. "His life style could cover up a lot of Blocker-induced memory problems...or it could just be his personality."

Nicole rubbed her forehead, then looked up at me. "Do you remember when Worthington said he knew there were no side effects of the Blocker because A.T. had gone on to bigger and better things? I think those were his exact words. There are few things in St. Louis bigger or better than Taylor & Associates."

"I remember," I said nodding.

"What else did Al have to say?"

"That's about it, really. So, like the names we had before, Trimmel and Atwood, there's nothing conclusive that links Taylor to this research. But unlike them, the police are going to need something a lot more solid before they even consider investigating. I'll mention the name to Detective Ahern. But since my reputation is already shot, I don't expect anything."

Finally, Sue broke from her ponderings and looked up at us. "Then, we need to give the police something more concrete."

Nicole and I both turned to her. "You know something else about Taylor?" I asked.

"I'm not going to be able to give you details, but Al has mentioned a few things about Taylor being forgetful. I mean, forgetting things that a CEO shouldn't. Like one time, he announced a policy change three times, and each time he talked about it like it was news."

"But...," Nicole started.

Sue held up a hand. "I know. Just more circumstantial evidence. The overworked executive is a bit forgetful. We have an awful lot of coincidences already, but if we need more, let's get them."

"OK," I said slowly. "But how do we do that?"

"We'll ask him."

An involuntary laugh escaped my lips. "Sorry," I said. "I didn't mean to sound rude, but I can't imagine he'd be interested in talking to me. Last time I checked, I'm several million dollars light in my savings account."

"I didn't mean we'd open an account," said Sue. "You'd probably end up talking to Al about that anyway. What I'm suggesting is a chance meeting and an off-hand remark. If we said the right thing, we might learn quite a bit about what's going on."

"OK, but one thing at a time. Just when and where might I accidentally bump into Mr. A. Huntington Taylor? I haven't seen him at the Bread Co after my morning jogs."

Sue leaned back in her chair, smiling at me. "Try Saturday morning, 5:30 AM at the Spirit of St. Louis Airport."

"How do you know that?" I asked.

"Al mentioned it last night. Taylor has a weekend trip, and he leases a jet that flies out of Spirit of St. Louis Airport. But you won't be bumping into Taylor." She paused long enough to let the bewilderment grow on my face. "We'll be bumping into him."

"Whoa. Wait a second. Why should both of us go? It might end in some type of confrontation."

"I wasn't thinking we'd resort to a fistfight," Sue said chuckling. "We both go because we get more information that way. I met Taylor for the first time a few weeks ago. Although it wouldn't be conclusive – like everything else we have – it would be another piece of evidence if he doesn't remember me."

"I don't know about this," I said, looking to Nicole for support. She tilted her head in a shrug.

"This isn't going to become a confrontation," said Sue. "We'll be in a public setting in broad daylight...or early morning light anyway."

I took a deep breath, looking back and forth between the women. Sue was determined. Even if I said no, she'd probably go by herself. And Nicole was siding with Sue. "OK. Maybe," I finally conceded. "But if we do this, let's keep the plan simple."

"You mean not like the multi-step, constantly evolving scheme that worked so well with Atwood?" said Sue, faking a look of shock.

"Yeah, not like that one," I replied. "We need a comment that sounds innocent, but that forces him to reveal something about what he knows...if he knows anything."

Everyone was quiet for several minutes. Finally, Sue spoke. "How about something like, 'Do you know Dr. Ned Worthington?' If he says no, you could apologize and say you thought you'd seen them together somewhere. If he says yes, you could ask if he'd heard about Worthington's death."

"Not bad," Nicole said after a moment of thought. "If he's trying to hide an association with Dr. Worthington, either way he goes, we might get a reaction."

I wasn't as sure, and it must have shown on my face as Nicole asked, "Concerns?"

"I like the first possibility, where he denies knowing Worthington. Saying I'd seen them together will put some pressure on him. But if he answers yes, all I'm doing is mentioning something anyone would know from the newspapers."

"Then, let's keep it direct," said Sue. "If he says yes, you ask if he knows Worthington from one of his studies. Now, he either lies or as much as admits he's A.T."

I released a long breath. "OK," I said finally. "Of course, he's probably a world-class poker player, and we'll get nothing but a blank stare."

"In which case, we'll go with my backup plan," said Sue.

She almost had me, but after a moment, I asked, "You mean, the one where you ask if the buzz from the Blocker is better than sex?"

"That would be the one," Sue said, as Nicole tried but failed to suppress her titter. "So, shall we meet at the airport at 5:20? We'll need this accidental meeting to occur somewhere before he gets through security."

"I guess so," I said. "There's nothing like a chance remark to get the bad guy to spill his guts."

"And this is nothing like one," replied Sue, right on cue.

Trouble was, she was right about that.

SATURDAY, AUGUST 29, 5:14 AM

I checked my watch. Still six minutes until Sue should arrive. I wasn't sure my car would last that long, idling at the Spirit of St. Louis airport, air conditioner on maximum, but failing to keep pace with the morning's heat and humidity. Both were in the 80s. And sunrise was still 40 minutes away.

After Sue, Nicole, and I had hatched our scheme, I had gone by Ken's office. I wanted to schedule a meeting with him. I'd probably have little new after our 'chance encounter' with Taylor. Maybe a flicker of recognition when I mentioned Worthington. Maybe he'd fail to recognize Sue. But even if I had nothing from the airport rendezvous, I wanted to meet. I wanted to make sure our message about the Blocker's possible effects was getting through to management and eventually, the VA. I had promised the women it was, but the tendency of every subordinate to paint a picture that was a bit rosier than reality made the chain of command more of a roadblock than a conduit. The VA needed to know our thoughts.

Ken hadn't been in, so I had our admin put me on his calendar for 10:00 on Monday. Scheduling that meeting helped quiet the alarm in my head...but it didn't stop it.

As Friday evening wore on, I had tried to distract myself. It should have been easy, as the baseball Cardinals had pulled within one game of the wild card lead. The city was on the verge of pandemonium, but my unease wouldn't be quieted, wouldn't be buried. So, I had phoned the police department to request a face-to-face meeting with

Detective Ahern. The calls between us had done little to convince him, so I figured a look of sincerity on my face, coupled with a touch of concern in my voice might help.

The phone message I left for him was a bit cryptic – I wanted to talk about someone new in the Worthington case, 'a prominent member of the community,' but I couldn't bring myself to mention Taylor's name. Was I that unsure? I didn't think so, but I sat down and recorded each of the 'coincidences' that tied Taylor to the research anyway. It was talking points, for whenever Ahern wanted to meet.

After that, I played through the coming meeting with Taylor in my mind. Generally, my mental theater centers on positive outcomes. My boss concedes my superior performance and gives me an enormous raise. I run a half-marathon, besting my personal record by 15 minutes. I lean in to kiss Nicole and she kisses me back. Well, that was my brain's video until recently. Now, it's more like we shake hands, over and over.

But what bothered me about my thoughts on meeting Taylor was that none of them ended with him confessing. Or even tripping himself up with a contradiction. It looked so easy in the movies, but when you are being truthful with yourself the night before, you know that's a fantasy. Most of my mental simulations ended with him ignoring us. Why wouldn't he?

I jumped at the sound of tapping at my window. It was Sue.

"Wake up, Doc. If I can drag myself out of bed the one morning Al is in the mood, you can pry your eyes open." I chuckled, enjoying the quip more than it warranted. The familiarity of her banter was a welcome break from my thoughts.

"Morning, Sue," I said, shutting off the car. "Ready?"

"Always," she replied, and we headed off at a fast walk, neither of us wanting to stand around in the heat or hurry so much as to raise more of a sweat.

A blast of cool air greeted us as we entered a large waiting area. Two food stalls flanked the door, each most likely serving day-old doughnuts and coffee to match. Directly ahead, a dozen or so early morning travelers dozed in chairs scattered around the space. Departure gates were distributed along the remaining three walls. In front of one was a sign bearing the Taylor & Associates name and logo. We had arrived and there was little to do but wait.

Sue pulled a phone from her bag. "I'm going to sit over there," she said, tilting her head toward some chairs near the gate with Taylor's name. "I'm going to text Al, but I'll keep an eye out too."

"Al gets up at this hour, even on the weekends?" I asked, somewhat surprised.

"Yeah. He's even playing workaholic this morning, now that his forced vacation is over. I dropped him by the office and I'll collect him when we're done." Sue left for the chairs.

I glanced around, looking for a vantage point. There were four, flat-panel televisions distributed around the room, all showing the news, all leading with the same story – the weather. No one was watching. We already knew the plot. It was miserable and going to get worse.

After four laps of the room, seeing the same wad of gum on the floor, the same guy snoring in a corner, the same selection of high calorie, low nutrition snacks in the vending machine, I positioned myself in a row of seats across from Sue. Taylor's departure gate was to my right and her left. We couldn't miss him.

I pulled out my phone. It was 5:47. Taylor was late. I opened a solitaire app. I liked it because with the liberal use of undo and replay, I could win most of the time. Besides, a typical game would chew up six to ten minutes, and I had little else to do.

I played two. It was 6:00, and Taylor hadn't appeared. I played three more. It was nearly 6:30 and I looked over at Sue. She frowned. Then pointed at her phone, shrugged, and shoved it back into her bag. I thought about going over, but she pulled out a magazine and started reading. When I finished three more games and the time reached 6:52, I stood to join Sue so we could discuss options.

But at that moment, in walked Taylor. Even with the dated picture I had studied and the strange looking sunglasses he wore, I was certain it was him.

Immediately, I noticed one difference between reality and all the times I had played this scenario in my head. In the real world, he wasn't alone. I should have guessed that someone with his wealth would be driven to the airport and escorted to the safety of his waiting plane. Other than those two duties, the man with him would also have the responsibility of keeping people like me away. Our plan for a chance encounter was on the brink of failing even before it began.

As they walked closer, I noticed a briefcase in Taylor's hand. It was around six inches thick and clad in metal. A chain ran from the handle up under the sleeve of Taylor's jacket, almost certainly to a handcuff. The chauffeur/bodyguard walked on the other side and slightly behind, pulling a small, roller bag. He looked tired and hot. His clothes were rumpled. Either driving a limo was harder work than I thought, or he had been doing something else. Maybe fixing a tire?

I stood. The bodyguard must have been well trained, because his eyes immediately swung in my direction. If I had any doubts about his purpose, they vanished the moment he locked eyes on me. I took a step to intersect Taylor. The bodyguard sped up to come between his client and me.

My world narrowed to three people – Taylor, the bodyguard, and me. Taylor strode calmly toward the gate, head high. He looked the important, wealthy businessman he was. I could see the bodyguard clench his jaw, his eyes narrowing as he studied my movement. I could feel the floor push back against the soles of my shoes, as I took another step to intercept them. It would take a lot to widen my field of attention...but something did.

The background noise in the room had increased, and it was continuing to climb. I looked around. I couldn't make out any words, but people were gathering around the televisions, pointing. The din increased again.

"Larry, you gotta see this," one man called across the room.

"Linda," shouted a woman, waving at another to join her.

Someone turned up the sound on a television. The first words to reach my ears were, "...a massive explosion at the Huntington Taylor Building in Earth City."

On the screen was a live shot, showing flames and rubble. The building was only one story when standing, but looking through the smoke, there was nothing taller than a foot or two. If this was where the building had been, it was gone. The camera panned to part of a wall that had separated the building from an outside dining area. There was some writing on it in a language I didn't recognize. The media were already using the words 'terrorist attack'.

The bodyguard had stopped and was gaping at the television, like everyone else in the waiting area. Taylor, however, continued his stroll to the gate, not even turning to look. The possibility that he was simply lost in thought and oblivious to his surroundings was shattered when he turned to the bodyguard and barked, "Move you fool. You've made us late enough already."

"But...," started the guard.

"I'll deal with that later. Now move," Taylor yelled. His eyes shifted to my face. "Price," he hissed.

I stopped dead in my tracks, my eyes wide in astonishment. I was certain we had never met, but he knew me. How was that possible?

Taylor started walking again and his associate fell in behind, rousting me from my shock. I took a step forward.

"Sir, you need to stay back," warned the guard, as he held out a hand.

"You need to ask Mr. Taylor how he can put a meeting before the destruction of his business," I said, holding my ground.

The bodyguard hesitated in a moment of indecision. Then, as if remembering who signed his check, he said, "No, sir, you need to move along."

Taylor had continued to walk and now was only a few paces from the agent standing at the gate. To ask him now if he knew Worthington was ridiculous. I doubted that he would even acknowledge such a feeble question amid this apparent emergency. I needed to be off-script, so I shouted the first thing that came to mind. "Is the Neural Activity Blocker worth all this cost in human life?"

The question implied more than I knew from the facts, but it also embodied much of what I feared. Taylor turned to me with a look of contempt and said, "You have no idea the value of that device, not just for me, but for all mankind."

The full implications of that simple statement hit me like a train. The case chained to his wrist held a Blocker. He had killed Worthington to secure it, and he was willing to shed more lives to keep it. Now, he was within seconds of stepping through the departure gate and disappearing, perhaps forever.

My eyes scanned the area frantically for law enforcement. I was under no delusion that they would believe the bizarre story I had to tell, but surely, his identity along with the ongoing news story about the explosion at his office building would be enough to have him detained until the facts could be determined. But I saw no one.

Taylor had reached the gate. The bodyguard was trailing behind, glancing over his shoulder at me. I brought up the rear. I must have come too close, as the guard stopped and reversed direction. "Sir, this is your last warning. Please stand back or I'll have no choice but to call security."

"Yes, please do," I said. Raising my voice, I yelled, "Call security, because that man is Huntington Taylor. He shouldn't be getting on a plane."

I pointed at him, but no one looked. Everyone's attention was still focused on the drama playing out on the screens scattered around the room, all with their volumes now set to the maximum. My shout of his name merely joined the same words echoing around the building from the blaring televisions.

Over the guard's shoulder, I could see that Taylor had reached the gate agent. I tried yelling to the man, but in vain. A combination of the din from the crowd, the blast of the televisions, and the bulk of the guard standing between us conspired against me. The agent appeared to be questioning Taylor, perhaps asking if he realized what was going on at his office. At one point, he gestured toward a television, but Taylor merely waved a hand.

As the gate agent returned Taylor's papers with a shake of his head, he turned his attention to me and scowled. He evidently decided I was the greater threat and he started toward me. The bodyguard realized he was relieved of his duty and turned to leave. Taylor stepped toward the door. He was about 10 yards from escape; I felt miles from success.

My only hope was to outmaneuver the gate agent. Then, if I could create enough commotion attacking Taylor's companion, maybe someone would pry their eyes from the televisions and call for help.

As I was preparing to lunge forward, I heard the voice of a woman scream, "You bastard." It was Sue.

In the bedlam of the attack on Taylor's business and my failed attempts to stop him, I had forgotten about her. She had approached the gate from the opposite side and now stood about five feet from Taylor, tears streaming down her cheeks.

"My husband...he used to work for you," she sobbed. "Until you killed him."

With those words, I knew what had happened. She had been texting Al at work, but his responses had stopped mysteriously. Now she knew why.

The bodyguard started toward Sue, as Taylor turned to her. A look of contempt covered his face. I looked back at Sue, hearing Taylor snarl, "Save me this maudlin display of...."

Time slowed. In the seconds it took Taylor to say those six words, Sue reached in her purse, pulled out the gun that Al had given her, and leveled it at him. She blinked. The pain in her eyes seemed to recede, replaced by a look of hatred.

"No," I yelled.

Sue's eyes flicked to my face, but only for an instant. She turned back to Taylor and fired four shots into his body. At least one hit his forehead, as a pinpoint of red soon blossomed into a stream of blood that ran down his nose and across his lips. Taylor slowly collapsed to the floor.

Sue sunk to the ground, placing the gun in front of her. I rushed to her side, putting my arms around her. Her body shook and I could feel the dampness of her tears on my shoulder.

I glanced up. Our scene had finally escalated to the point where it competed with the news, and three airport security guards now ringed us. Each had his hand on his holster, but none had drawn their firearms. Apparently, no one felt the need to point their gun at the woman who now sat on the floor sobbing uncontrollably.

THURSDAY, DECEMBER 17, 9:22 AM

I stood at my office window, hands in my pockets, looking out at the slow-moving traffic on a cold, gray December morning. It had been over three months since the blast at the Huntington Taylor Building and the shooting at the airport. Time seemed to have stopped for me after those events.

Immediately after the shooting, Airport Security had called the St. Louis police. But because of the possible tie to terrorism, the police called the Federal Bureau of Investigation. Soon, FBI agents were on scene, supported by the local police and personnel from the Department of Homeland Security and the Federal Air Marshall's service. They all wanted to talk to Sue. And to me.

They set up interview rooms – or maybe Airport Security already had them – equipped with audio and video recording equipment. Over the next six hours, I met with an endless string of faces and names, all with the same questions. They never batted an eye when I implicated Taylor in the theft of the Blocker technology. A business man stealing industrial secrets? It was an all-too-common story. Besides, the case chained to his arm contained one.

Skepticism grew when I suggested he might have killed Dr. Worthington to secure his ill-gotten prize. One of St. Louis most prominent business executives was a murderer? That was harder for them to believe.

But communications broke down completely when they got to the question, 'why did you suspect Taylor of these crimes?' 'Brain rewiring run amok' was not an explanation they could accept.

A little after noon, they let me go, with the instruction not to leave the area – no surprise there. They took Sue into custody. I found that infuriating and told them so. She had just lost her husband and if we were right, he had been killed by a man who was nothing short of pure evil. 'If we were right,' however, was the key phrase, and no one was buying that we were.

On Sunday afternoon, I was asked to meet authorities at the downtown office of the FBI. If anything, they seemed even more certain that the explosion at Earth City was a work of terrorism and that Sue had mistakenly killed an innocent man; all their questions dealt with why we suspected Taylor. And each time I mentioned that we were 'hypothesizing' or 'generalizing' from published research, everyone in the room started writing.

When I left, I tried to visit Sue. But on advice of counsel, she was only meeting with him or family until the picture became clearer. And her family was still in Oregon. Logically, I understood, but I felt bad that she was going through this alone.

The tide of suspicion started shifting on Monday...at the exact moment Taylor's emails were delivered to four different inboxes around St. Louis. Unfortunately, before I realized what it was, I read it. Even though Taylor was dead, I shivered as if his hand was reaching out from the grave.

By the time I reported the message, the authorities already knew of the emails to Huston and Nicole...and perhaps Sue too, although they wouldn't confirm it. I was asked to surrender my laptop, the original email, and all the documentation we had on the Blocker. After verifying policy with Ken and our Law Department, I went back downtown with everything they had requested. The agents promised to return my laptop as soon as the examination was complete. They made no similar promise, however, about the reports we had on the Blocker.

If the emails produced a seed of doubt in the minds of the investigators, the events at the explosion site were the sun, rain, and soil that nourished them to fruition. First, there were the bodies.

It was the evening news on Monday that reported the recovery of the bodies of three security personnel, one maintenance person, and one Taylor & Associates employee. Even without names, I knew the last to be mentioned was Al. I couldn't seem to swallow the lump in my throat.

Through blurry eyes, I nearly missed the commentary that followed and soon it was fueling a media frenzy. Two other bodies had been pulled from the rubble and these couldn't be connected to Taylor's business. Even more ominously, the reporter described charred remnants of medical equipment and an enclosure described as a 'prison'. Even forewarned about what the Blocker might do, I was haunted by the pictures these words created in my mind.

Tuesday's and Wednesday's news involved more recycling of the same facts. Only the speculation changed, becoming more gruesome and bizarre by the hour. It also seemed to be getting more accurate, if my team and I were right.

On Thursday, the two John Does were identified as a missing businessman from Seattle and a young, postal worker who had disappeared during his morning jog. I had mostly come to grips with the revelations of these first days, but when I heard where the jogger had been taken, a new wave of unease overtook me. I began wondering if Taylor could have set his threat in motion. Logically, it seemed improbable, but I was still jumping at every shadow and flinching at every sound. And sleep came slowly, if at all.

With the accumulating evidence of Taylor's cold-blooded inhumanity, Sue was released on Friday on her own recognizance. I called as soon as I heard, learning that her family had been with her most of the week. For that, I was grateful. I offered to come by, but she declined. She also wouldn't hear a word of sympathy for her loss, although we talked for over an hour about...well, nothing really. The weather, the coming fall, people at work, Nicole. Sue wasn't herself, but even over the phone, I could tell she was fighting back.

After that, the flow of public information dried up. For about a week, reporters spent their waking hours locating experts to bolster one or another of the competing theories about Taylor's mental state. Then, two weeks after the blast, the FBI rocked a city that was just starting to relax by releasing a major announcement. Graves containing at least four bodies and several documents had been found below the basement floor of the Taylor & Associates building. The body count was growing.

Somewhat in the shadow of that story, the FBI also released a statement saying that the symbols that were painted on the half-standing wall, which had led many to suspect terrorism, turned out to be nothing; they were not even in any language. At first, I wondered why anyone trying to create a diversion would have been so careless. After all, it would be a simple matter to find an appropriate saying on the Internet. But after the authorities had spent two weeks trying to decode the gibberish, I understood.

Partly because of business and partly because misery loves company, I also kept in contact with Jon Huston at WHT. His misery was different from mine, as mine came from the death of a friend and the destruction of the life of another. But Huston's loss of years of intense, scientific focus and endless hours of sacrifice was also a bitter pill. It was clear, he'd never see the Blocker again.

Huston also tried to shoulder the blame for the blow to neuroscience. It was, after all, his lab that had let the technology get out of control. But the public and the profession blamed Worthington, as the authorities held that he had conspired with

Taylor. His death was a falling out among thieves. Only a few – my team, Huston, and Scott – believed otherwise.

Again, the news outlets went quiet, this time for almost a month.

When the word came, I had missed it, but Huston sent me an email with a link. I nearly fell out of my chair when I read the story on the other end. After 'extensive testing,' the FBI declared that the Neural Activity Blocker was a hoax. It had no real effect on thought or brain waves, and only delivered general stimulation much the same as a couple of cups of coffee.

I called Huston, planning on telling him that if we bottled this electronic brew, I was certain we could take over the coffee-drinking world. But when we were connected, he said, "I take it that you haven't been visited yet?"

"Visited? What do you mean?"

"Well," he said slowly, "someone will be dropping by your office soon. When they do, you'll understand why I can't talk. In fact, I have to go now, because my company's still here."

It was a strange and somewhat unsettling conversation, but I didn't have to wait long for an explanation. Within the hour, Ken, a representative from our Law Department, and an FBI agent showed up at my door. The agent asked me to sign a document saying I would never disclose any information about the electronics or software used in the Neural Activity Blocker. It was a strange request, following on the heels of an announcement that the Blocker was a hoax. But a look at the three faces across the desk from me told me that pointing out that contradiction was a waste of my time. I signed.

If the document was an attempt to keep the technology out of public view, which was the only rational explanation I could see, it had no chance of success. Several other labs were not far behind Worthington and quarantining his hardware and the related research was not going to change that. And if mind-to-mind interfaces were the next wave in social media, as many have speculated, today's computer cameras would soon be supplemented by tomorrow's TMS coils. Who would want to talk or trade video, if you could share thoughts? Who, that is, other than perhaps Sue, Nicole, and I?

The following Monday, Ken told me the FBI had requested more of my time and I was to meet them on Tuesday, back downtown. He had no other details, except that Nicole, Huston, and Sue had also been summoned. They were rounding up all the usual suspects.

The mystery of these meetings was also short-lived, however. Within the first five minutes, it was clear they were concerned about the third section of the device specifications, which dealt with the capability to upload and overlay a person's memories with new ones. Their questions focused on who had read Section 3 and how thoroughly. They already had my status report from that week, so I verified its contents. It identified Nicole as the only reviewer, but also stated that she had just started to study its contents.

I wondered if Nicole had found time to return to Section 3 and study it detail with everything else that happened in those final days. But I knew I'd never ask. The promise to never discuss the technology was one I intended to keep.

Shortly after that meeting, Sue was acquitted in the shooting death of Taylor. I never heard the official reason, but I suspected the city, the nation, and perhaps the world would have revolted had she been brought up on charges related to killing a demented, mass murderer in the moments after her husband's death. Personally, I thought she should have been given a medal, but no one asked me.

Sue quit Ruger-Phillips and moved back home to Oregon. I never saw her after that fateful day at the airport, although we talked on the phone often. I only hoped she would find peace and happiness back with her family, because she deserved it.

I turned from my office window and dropped into my chair, my head sinking into my hands. The hour of the last meeting on the

Neural Activity Blocker was nearly upon me. In moments, Nicole would arrive, we'd sign the forms, and that would be it.

* * *

"Hi, Sam." Nicole's voice was soft and I felt a chill run down my back despite the fact I was expecting her. I raised my head. She was standing in the doorway. Here was a person who embodied everything I sought in a woman – direct, smart, incredibly cute...and probably out of my reach.

Nicole and I had talked several times in the last three months. At first, we spoke about the investigation. Later, it was just about how things were going because...that's what friends do. I was nearly certain that was exactly how she saw us – friends. I had asked her out a couple of times and she had politely declined. I had tried to steer the conversation that direction a few others, and she had been called from the phone unexpectedly. If friendship was the extent of our future, I would feel the loss but I had tried.

"Hi, Nicole. It's good to see you. Even better that we can finally close out this VA project. I don't know about you, but I'm anxious for my career to move forward."

She smiled, a trace of sadness in her face. "Yeah, I'll be happy when it's over too, and I didn't go through anything as tough as you."

I nodded, not wanting to retread painful ground once again. "We have a few forms to sign and Ken's expecting us. Shall we?" I asked, gesturing toward the door where she stood.

"Sure," she replied. She turned and we walked over to Ken's office, neither of us saying a word.

The sign-off was quick and painless. Ken did 'the manager thing,' telling Nicole how good it was to work with her and Biomedical

Engineering Associates and that he hoped we would have other opportunities in the future. I voiced my agreement.

We left Ken's office and I walked Nicole to the front of our building. In the reception area, I shook her hand, incrementing my mental counter on handshakes. "Nicole, it was great working with you. But hopefully next time, it'll be a little more routine."

"Yes," she said. "A little more normalcy would be nice."

I expected her to leave, but she didn't. She glanced over my shoulder at the receptionist sitting there, a slight frown forming on her face. "Can we talk a second?"

"Of course." Like most of our reception areas, there was a small meeting area in this one – just two partitions in a corner surrounding a table and two chairs. I led Nicole in, sat at one chair, and waved to the second.

Nicole remained standing, then took a breath, long enough and deep enough that it couldn't be missed. "Thanks, but I can only stay a minute. My management has my plate full."

"Soon, I hope mine will be too." I stood up, since she wasn't going to sit.

She took another breath, looked down at her shoes, then back up at me. "The project is over now, right? I mean, totally and officially?"

I shrugged. "Signed, sealed, and soon to be delivered. But yeah, your company's part is officially complete."

"Then, I wanted to give you this," she said. She reached out and handed me her business card.

"Thanks," I said, staring at it. "But I have one already. Maybe a couple of them."

She reached over and took my hand in hers. The sensation was nothing like a handshake; my whole arm seemed to warm at her touch. She turned my hand over. Written on the back was a phone number. "You might want to try this. After working hours."

I stood staring at her, my mind racing through the possible meanings, but always ending up at the same place.

Finally, I said, "I will. Tonight. For sure."

She smiled, the first real smile since she had arrived. Then, she turned and left without another word.

On the way back to my office, I wondered why she had waited until now to say something. And then when she did, why it was so cryptic? My thoughts came in jumbles about actions and appearances, about being the first to say 'I like you,' about what it means to have old-fashioned views on relationships. But I had covered only a few yards of my trip when I decided, I'd probably never understand, but I understood enough.

The door is still open.

I glanced at the clock when I entered my office. It was only 10:36, almost eight hours until I could call her. The time couldn't go fast enough.

I decided to fill it by repacking and returning the last of Worthington's notes. Even the authorities had recognized them for what they were – landfill – and had left them in our care. So, I started throwing them into a box, literally. Among the ones in my office were the few remaining folders that passed the bend test – they didn't contain a disk drive – but they had never been read.

I opened one folder idly, finding a few comments about the state of his shoes – he needed a new pair – and about getting his lawn mowed. I turned the page. More of the same. I flipped to one more, thinking this would be the last when I found a neatly typed sheet. It was the start of an experimental report.

R.J. was a 23-year-old paid volunteer who completed 87 hours of training with the Neural Activity Blocker....

Worthington had used the technology on another individual, and he or she was still out there.

ACKNOWLEDGMENTS

An abbreviated, initial version of this story was published in 2015 under the title of *Half A Mind*. Several of the ideas for this remake came from reviews of that book and so, I'd like to recognize everyone who read and provided comments. Your thoughts were helpful. Thank you.

I'd like to thank Ms. Janet Harrison for reading an earlier version of this manuscript and providing helpful suggestions. My thanks also go out to Dr. Liz Gehr for helping me watch my technical Ps and Qs. Any inaccuracies are mine; hopefully, they're all intentional to build the fiction.

Special thanks also go to Ms. Emma Jaye, accomplished author and skilled content editor for many helpful remarks. Finally, thanks go to my talented daughter, Courtney Perrin, for the design and creation of the cover art.

I hope you enjoyed *Of Half A Mind*. Thank you for reading it. Authors thrive on feedback, so please consider leaving a review on Goodreads or the website of your favorite bookseller. And if I ever pen a second remake, you will find yourself thanked in its acknowledgments.

ABOUT THE AUTHOR

Bruce Perrin has been writing for more than 20 years, although you will find most of that work in professional technical journals or conference proceedings. But after completing a doctorate in Industrial Psychology and a career in psychological R&D, he is now applying his background and fascination with technology and the human mind to writing novels.

Besides writing, Bruce likes to tinker with home automation and is an avid hiker, logging nearly 2,500 miles each year in the first five years of Fitbit ownership. When he is not on the trails, he lives with his wife in St. Louis, MO.

Please join him at www.brucemperrin.blogspot.com for a closer look at his writing life, book reviews, and progress on his upcoming novels.